Praise for *A Cleft in the World*

"*A Cleft in the World* serves up southern charm with a quirky main character, combining page-turning intrigue in a small college town with a long-lost love story. The result is a novel that keeps you guessing but has you cheering for a win."

—Kathryn Dodson, author of *Tequila Midnight*
and president of the Good Book Collective

"A heartwarming, hopeful story with glorious prose and inspiring characters."

—Dara Levan, author of *It Could Be Worse*
and host of the *Every Soul Has a Story* podcast

"*A Cleft in the World* showcases a woman's journey to push past her fears and become the person she's always wanted to be. Wafler creates a visual world that is beautifully written with well-developed characters. This story will leave you smiling and missing the characters long after you close the book."

—Leslie A. Rasmussen,
author of *After Happily Ever After*

T0007712

A
CLEFT
IN THE
WORLD

A CLEFT IN THE WORLD

A Novel

ELIZABETH SUMNER WAFLER

SHE WRITES PRESS

Published 2023

Printed in the United States of America

Print ISBN: 978-1-64742-452-7
E-ISBN: 978-1-64742-453-4
Library of Congress Control Number: 2022922361

For information, address:
She Writes Press
1569 Solano Ave #546
Berkeley, CA 94707

Interior design by Katherine Lloyd, The DESK

She Writes Press is a division of SparkPoint Studio, LLC.

This book is lovingly dedicated
to the memory of my father,
Dr. Len Sumner, extraordinary educator
and the planet's best punster.

How easy it would be to live one's life
out in some cleft in the world.
—Willa Cather

CHAPTER ONE

2018

Twenty-four winters have barged in and lingered since I arrived at Willa Cather College. As an eager young French teacher, I'd found the pastoral Virginia campus a ripe peach, its cleft well defined. With my propensity toward seclusion, I had been the perfect candidate to slip into the rosy niche. I hadn't given a thought to how long it might hold me. When I'd dropped my bags on the steps of the beautiful old town house the college provided, it had been too late anyway. I was home.

This morning, I shiver at the thought of padding the eight steps from my bed to adjust the capricious old radiator and decide I'm too cozy to get up yet. One would think that with my tenure, the school would improve my heating system.

My cell beetles across the bedside table. Snaking an arm from beneath layers of down, I fumble for it.

"Happy forty-fifth, Georgie," Lacey says, before adding, "you old thing."

I grin. "If I let you live after that remark, you'll be the same age next month." While my best friend sings me a froggy new

1

riff on the old birthday song, I snare my robe from a bedpost and quickstep to turn the radiator valve wide. "Thanks, lovie. What are you doing up at this hour?"

"I just got in from a hard night turning tricks."

I hoot, conjuring her wicked grin. "Lacey!" A principal in a Manhattan firm, Lacey sleeps late and rarely arrives in her office before nine. I love her because she is the one friend who remembers when we were twelve and figured out that Nancy Drew didn't have time for boys because she had business to attend to.

"What's on tap for your big day?" she asks.

Snuggling into the upholstered chair by the window, I tuck my socked feet beneath me. "Oh, you know, a long lunch with Kevin Costner."

"Seriously, babe, you need a man."

I wait while the radiator hits high gear with three clanks and a hiss. "Lace, I live at a women's college. And the male faculty is either too young or drawn to other compass points."

"So you've said."

The room warms, and my cat, Voltaire, pokes his dark head from beneath the comforter. I poke my lips out to him in an air kiss as Lacey goes on about how she'd found me the perfect birthday card but hadn't mailed it. The mid-January sunrise pinks my lace curtains. Shifting to draw back a panel, I look down on the still-ghosted quadrangle. In seconds, the blush of the sky is shot through with orange and yellow above the sunup violet of the Blue Ridge. As a tall figure appears and starts across the quad, I remember the news. "Actually, we have a new guy coming on staff today, a Mr. Potter or Porter or something. My students are buzzing about new eye candy. They're hoping he's young and a cross between Mr. Darcy and Harry Styles. I'm just hoping the dining hall has grilled cheese and tomato soup for lunch."

"Ha! Well, keep me posted. I love you, Georgie. Happy birthday."

I end the call, my mind ticking ahead to the day's classes, and pad to the kitchen to make coffee. Voltaire yowls at my heels for his little red bowl to be filled.

By the time I've had a scalding shower, dried my hair, and pulled on a tunic and leggings, I have a missed call from Ron. I'll ping my brother back between classes. Why hasn't Mom called? Doing up the clasp on my watch and checking the time, I find that I'm running out of it. I make sure the radiator valve is closed and that the coffee pot hasn't managed to turn itself back on, then hurry out the door and down the steps to the old brick walk.

"Bonjour, Madame Bricker," two students call in tandem from the depths of their hooded coats.

"Bonjour, mesdemoiselles!"

Sometimes, it's still surreal being surrounded by girls. That I was raised a faculty member's daughter on the campus of an all-boys' prep school is a paradox that's a big hit during ice-breaker games. But I never clear the smiles from people's faces by describing the rest of the story. How I left that campus a scraped-out shell, tormented by memories of murder. Fear in my blood, as though I swallowed it down every morning with my vitamins.

Crossing the quad, I pull my coat closer, inadvertently drop a glove, and stoop to retrieve it. Laurel Cross strides from behind a copse of hollies, her long brown legs bare. It's a plume of cig- arette smoke that rises above her dark head rather than steam. "Bonjour, Madame!" she cries, her hand to her heart before sprinting like a gazelle in the direction of the library. Shaking my head, I brush debris from my glove. They all experiment. And Laurel's my girl, the one who, as a freshman, twined her- self around my teacher's heart. She's sure-footed, captain of the lacrosse team; she'll figure it out. If only I'd been as strong and confident when I was her age. I decide to let the smoking go.

Mounting the steps to my office in ivy-robed Collins Hall, I hope my secretary has arrived early. Motherly Mrs. King is eighty and still keeps my academic life humming on its axis. That reminds me I haven't heard from my mother. She can't have forgotten my birthday! Since we lost my English-teacher father when I was fourteen, mom's been a rock. The thought of her as forgetful makes me want to sit down and howl.

I open the door to my orderly oasis. Though the administration has issued directives about conserving heat, Mrs. King cheats and keeps our section of the building toasty. Apples and butter meet my nose and make my mouth water. A lattice-topped French tart sits on a paper napkin on my desk. Poked in the top, a perky pink candle waits to be lit and extinguished on a wish. Mrs. King makes me *sourire jusqu'aux oreilles*: smile up to the ears.

Down the hall, her voice flutes and falls with Lina DiMora's, my friend and Willa Cather's Italian teacher. Versed in conversational French, Mrs. King is now poking a toe into Italian. I grin again and pour a cup of coffee. I have plenty of time to call my mother.

Julianne Bricker understands me all too well. Years after my erudite father died, mom fell for a sinewy carpenter, Barrett, a clear blue lake in which no one could ever drown. And though she never judges me, she can't resist tossing a well-intentioned suggestion regarding my love life from time to time.

She picks up on the fifth ring, wishes me a happy birthday, and relays the latest Folly Beach, South Carolina, gossip before nudging me, "It's never too late to find love, darling,"

"You're right, mom." Slipping on my readers, I boot up my laptop and glance at the clock. I don't tell her about the mysterious new staff member coming on today. That would send her into rhapsodies of speculation. "What have you been up to this morning?" I download templates in preparation for the day, the start of winter quarter. "I mean, yours is usually the first call I get on my birthday."

"The cold makes it harder to drag my bones out of bed, that's all. I was about to call." The cold. I punch up the weather app on my phone. Folly Beach's sixty degrees is my twenty-eight. It hurts my heart to think of my lithe mother growing brittle.

But the tart under my nose puts my stomach in full-on competition with my heart. "Well, get your rest; I need to get to work. Mrs. King made me a French apple tart for my birthday." As if summoned, my secretary pops her head around my door. I grin and gesture for her to come in.

"How thoughtful. Tell her I appreciate her taking care of my girl."

"I will. I love you, Mom."

"I love you, darling. Have a happy day."

Behind my secretary, the foreign language department dances in to sing "Happy Birthday," but in a cacophony of discrete languages—like a celebration in the Tower of Babel. Laughing, Mrs. King distributes paper napkins and tarts to everyone.

As Lina lights the candle on my treat, the hotshot young Mandarin instructor wipes crumbs from his beard and says, "Don't forget the faculty meeting starts early today, at four."

Closing my eyes, I make a wish—may this year bring me something extraordinary—and blow.

ॐ

My junior class hands me a birthday poster, their handwriting full of swoops and swirls, the words in French. "Merci, mes filles!" In my Southern way, I have called them girls, though they are women. My chest warms as I recall how much they have learned. Laurel Cross, an only slightly embarrassed quality to her smile from our early morning encounter on the quadrangle, asks me how old I am.

"Lau-rel!" Malika and Morgan say in tandem.

"*Quarante-cinq*," I respond and watch their eyes, assessing who knows the number right away and who is figuring it out.

"My auntie's forty-five, and you look way younger than her," Malika says.

"And you're so pretty with your long brown hair," Collins says.

Laurel plants her hands on her sturdy hips. "Forty-five is the new thirty-five." The rest chime in, affirming this wisdom that must have come from *Glamour* magazine.

I decide to mess with them. "Well, if that's true, then twenty . . . must be the new, uh, ten."

This cracks them up, and a chorus of "no ways" rings out.

I survey these free-range creatures—their youthful complexions, the gleam of their smiles—and enjoy their exuberance. I seat them according to a chart I've made for the winter term.

As the girls settle in, my heart fills with a sense of new beginnings: an unsullied term, a new year of life. I send up a silent prayer of thanks for the best work in the world and start the syllabi around by passing the stack to Laurel. I glance at the portrait of Willa Cather above my SMART board. Old Willa herself would agree that Laurel epitomizes the spirit of women's education. Though she lost both parents in an automobile accident when she was only six years old, a Baltimore aunt took her in and raised her to be strong and fiercely independent. Laurel's animated brows are full of hopes and dreams. She's eager to learn, unafraid to speak her mind, and always, always questioning. Will she be the one to lead the senior class next year, to maintain our legacy, to lead the next generation of game changers?

⚬╪⚬

After a lunch of not only tomato soup but also a magnifique pimento cheese sandwich—a minor miracle with the budget cuts—I return to my office and call my brother, who picks up on the first ring. "Happy birthday, Sis." Eight years my junior, former squirt Ron Bricker seems as tall as the houses he builds in the Carolinas. Thankfully, *he* was young enough when our father died that he doesn't bear the pain of scars that won't heal.

After catching me up on his wife and daughter, Ron listens to my concerns about Mom. I extract a promise from him that he'll make the trip to check on her soon. But I hear his sigh before adding, "You know you can count on me," and ending the call.

"*Chou de dieu!*" I say to my coffee mug—God's cabbage—the go-to expression I use in lieu of cursing, and I toss my cell atop my leather binder. My brother has long understood that for me, making a trip to South Carolina would be like making a trip to a far-flung planet.

I haven't left Foxfield in more years than I'll admit. Family and friends come to me for visits. Ron is the one who checks on mom. The reminder that I burden him in this way makes my breath hitch. But the primary care physician with whom I long-ago established care here in Foxfield said that as long as staying close to home didn't affect my quality of life, it was okay.

And it has been okay. My life is fine. I've been as content as anyone I've ever known. I'm warm and fed when millions of people are not. I have an amazing job at a top women's college, one that empowers young women to grow as independent thinkers and leaders. Though the irony of someone in my anxiety-worn shoes helping to cobble bold women is not lost on me, it's this campus, founded in 1869 on one of the most beautiful spots on earth, that's kept me safe.

I am loved, physically healthy, and stimulated—at least intellectually—and as fluent in French as someone who's never been to France could be.

Meanwhile, I spend Sunday nights with a gorgeous man, James Malcolm Alexander MacKenzie Fraser. So what if he's an eighteenth-century Scotsman and confined to my TV, and the fur in my four-poster bed is not his but that of a green-eyed black tom with a sweet white spot on his throat?

And so, I count my blessings and my years.

The radiator hisses *forty-five*.

Above all, be the heroine of your own life,
not the victim.
—Nora Ephron

CHAPTER
TWO

The reading room of the Charlotte Cabot Library has been set up for the faculty meeting, not with the usual round tables but in regimented rows of chairs. Exchanging puzzled glances, Lina and I slip into two seats toward the back. Behind a podium, Dr. Susan Joshi, Willa Cather's president, slips off her jacket and hangs it on the back of a chair. Sweat stains make crescents at the armholes of her shift. As she calls the meeting to order, Lina leans in and whispers to me, "Why's the board here?"

"I have no idea." Our board of trustees comprises half of the front row. We knew Susan would be introducing the new finance guy but assumed that would be part of the normal agenda.

"Susan's too young to be flashing, isn't she?"

"Years too young."

The math instructor to Lina's left, who is also my grumpy next-door neighbor, leans forward in his seat. He flips us a look: shush.

No agendas. No diet sodas and pretzels. I shift to see who else is seated in the front row. The chief financial officer, Sawyer Hays, and a tall guy with longish gray hair. Must be the finance geek. Too old to be Mr. Darcy *or* Harry Styles. The girls will be bummed.

Stepping forward, the board chairman, Beau Duffy, pulls a slight smile, accepts the clip-on mic from Susan, and attaches it to his navy-and-red striped tie. He clears his throat.

Lina pokes my thigh.

A local pediatrician and the kind of guy who would come over and roust a mouse from your house, Beau surveys us a moment. The room has the preternatural hush of a moon. My deodorant is breaking down, my armpits growing slick.

"I'm not going to dance around this," the chairman begins, the microphone fuzzing his words for a moment. "In the last two years, Willa Cather's endowment—that which keeps us in the black—has dropped sixteen million dollars." Alarm pricks at my skin like an incipient rash.

The chairman motions to the CFO, Sawyer Hays—who resembles a formal Pierce Brosnan—holding a stack of papers to his chest. An agenda? Sawyer's face and hands are deeply tanned, as though he's spent a month on his sailboat, *The Willa*. Considering the state of our endowment, he hasn't been commanding our helm.

The chairman speaks again. "Coming to you are the exact figures." All heads turn to follow the passing of the stack. The only sounds are the rustle of paper, the creak of metal chair. "As most of our endowment is restricted—it must be used to fund scholarships or faculty salaries and the like—we have been forced to draw from the unrestricted portion for operating expenses."

I look at Lina as she passes the stack to me, her hand the chill of granite. She murmurs her Italian version of *what the hell*, "*Che cavolo?*"

Beau's ruddy complexion deepens. "Ladies and gentlemen, we are twelve million dollars in debt." Fear clamps sharp little teeth around my core.

The math instructor fumbles the stack. Pages drift and slide on the marble floor. No one moves to help. A voice rises from near the front, and then a surf of questions breaks.

"Why are we just hearing about this?"

"Two years?"

"What does this mean for salaries?"

Beau raises his hands like a bank teller in a holdup. "Please. Let me finish."

A gust of wind carrying breath mints and alarm brushes the back of my hair, as people behind us bend and shuffle to grab up the scattered pages.

"The board has voted to create a new position—a one-year interim position—of vice president of finance and administration. Truman, will you stand?" Truman. That's a name I haven't heard in a while. The man stands and turns to face the faculty. My chest tightens the way it had when my car narrowly missed getting T-boned on Fourth Street. "Truman Parker comes to us from Emory University and Columbia Business School. He . . ." The chairman's voice echoes in the suddenly airless, book-lined room, bounces off the ceiling.

"The Ivy League to the rescue?" I think I hear Lina whisper over the blood pounding in my ears.

Truman Parker smiles and buttons his navy suit coat, his blue eyes giving off sparks in the dim old room. Something breaks loose near my heart. The rest of the board chair's introduction is lost on me. I don't remember losing my first tooth, the Christmas I first understood that Santa wasn't real, or what I wore for a Halloween costume in fifth grade. But I'll never forget the first time I saw the fourteen-year-old strawberry blond, the first boy to capture my heart.

Truman nods at the group in a reassuring way. A shaft of sun from the tall windows silvers his hair. "Thank you," he says to Beau in a voice from my dusky dreams. He moves to the podium. Images of The Browning School for Boys in Laurel

Ridge, Virginia—where Truman Parker was sent from Atlanta to live as a boarding student—pass before my eyes. The tunnel where we first kissed. Hampton Circle overlooking the Laurel River. The baseball fields and pine woods.

The equipment shed.

No.

"Excuse me," I say, rising, my heart throbbing in my throat. I stumble down the row. And flee.

⟡

Footsteps reverberate along the rough moss-stained planks of the dock. Lina's black boots appear at my side. "I thought I might find you here," she says, her words made round and echoey by the sheltering upper deck. When I don't respond, she lowers herself to sit beside me. Cold humiliation emanates from my pores, and I shiver. She drapes her woolly coat around my shoulders. Though I begin to relax beneath its warmth, my words won't come. "Georgie, all of us were blindsided by the budget news . . . but you looked positively spooked." I feel her eyes trace my profile, but she waits. A small flock of black-and-tan geese land near the center of the lake, sending up a mighty arc of water. The lake is brown from recent rains, the grasses and skaggy trees at the edge steeped in muck.

"Truman Parker was my first love." My words, tinny and fragile, hang in the air.

Lina's lips part. She exhales a huff of amazement.

"Yeah, I know. But it's not Truman himself that spooked me. It's the memories that seeing him again dredged up." I fall silent, gathering my thoughts. Darkness crowds closer, deepening the green of the firs and pines. "Remember I told you my father died when I was a teenager? And my mother and brother and I had to move away from The Browning School?"

"I do."

Tears gather in my eyes. I give a great sniff.

"There's a tissue in my pocket," she says kindly.

I dig for it and come up with a hair clip and a sharp square of foil. I stare at a condom on my palm and flip Lina a look.

"I found that in the hall this morning," she says. "Is it yours?"

I chuff a laugh and lick tears from my top lip. Lina, like Lacey, can make me laugh just when I need it.

Lina takes the items. "Try the other pocket."

I fish the tissue out and blow my nose, honking along with the geese.

Lina drops her head to my shoulder. "So, what about Truman?"

A trio of girls galumphs down the boathouse steps, sees us, and silently about-faces. I sit, shredding the mascara-blackened tissue, and wait until their voices reprise as they regain the gravel drive. It will be all over campus tomorrow that Madame Bricker was boo-hooing at the boathouse. Before today, I would have fretted over that for days; now it has the significance of a hangnail.

Truman. "He was with me when my father died." I trace a row of rusted nailheads on the deck with a finger and unbiddenly begin connecting the dots between the images that had bloomed before me in the library. My panic rises. I open my mouth and gulp the night air. "I can't, Lina. It's just . . . I can't go there."

"It's all right, cara. I had no idea you had suffered so."

"That was the plan. I became . . . gifted at keeping it six feet under. Or so I thought."

"Hush now," Lina says. She rubs circles on my back until my breathing slows. The wind rises. We sit huddled on the dock for what seems like a very long time. At last, I get to my feet and shuck out of Lina's coat. "Thank you, my friend."

I give my lakeside retreat a last look. Muddy water licks and laps at the dock. I miss the summer blue of the water, the kin-dergarten-colored canoes tethered to the dock. But soon rowdy, yellow forsythias will gild the campus, and daffodils will send their tender shoots from the brown grass. Lina and I begin the short hike back to the parking lot, my knees feeling as though they need oiling. The last of the sunlight profiles the landmarks I love: the dome and spire of the chapel, the sleek triangles and swoops of the modern library. "What happened after I left the meeting? Truman is going to do what exactly?" Though I've tasted his name ten times since this afternoon, it's still like Bengali.

"Basically, he's going to come up with a strategic plan to grow the endowment. He's done consulting work for other ail-ing schools."

"Hmm." My mind ticks again to this grown-up Truman, and I imagine him communing with a laptop and a gin and tonic on a private jet.

Lina goes on. "Did you know his mother went to Willa Cather?"

My stomach twists. "You're kidding!" The patrician Eleanor Parker. How had I not known?

"She's the one who asked him to take the consulting posi-tion. Obviously, they're advocates of single-sex education and don't want to see a women's college close."

My tired mind slams an iron gate down over that portal. "We are not going to close!"

Lina frowns at me. "I certainly hope not, Georgie. Look," she says, taking my elbow, "Truman is a visionary. He's propos-ing restructuring departments into three 'centers.'"

"Centers? What happens to foreign languages?"

Stopping under a streetlamp, Lina pulls a folded handout from her pocket, whisks her readers from their nest in her dark hair, and reads it aloud. "Engineering, Science, and Technology;

Human and Environmental Sustainability; and Creativity, Design, and the Language Arts."

"The language arts, thanks be to God!"

"I know. And he seems confident about restoring the endowment. People seemed to relax after he spoke. Oh, and he wants to meet with each department next week to discuss ideas about bolstering programs."

My thoughts leap and tangle. Meet with Truman Parker. I might as well meet with the prime minister of France. Will I be as big a surprise to him as he was to me? He couldn't have known I was at Willa Cather. Or could he? Has he even thought of me in all these years? Where will he live? Surely, not on campus.

"You'll have to face him, Georgie," Lina says.

I let a breath go. "I know."

"Listen, Carmen's making pasta." Lina and her husband live in a pretty, old Georgian in Foxfield where he is editor of *The Foxfield Journal*. "Come home with me."

"I'm not hungry. But, thanks. Give Carmen my love."

"You sure you're okay? Will you sleep?"

I'm exhausted, but this could be one of those nights when sleep won't be mine. "I'll be fine. Enjoy your dinner."

"*Buona notte*, my friend," Lina calls, heading for her Subaru.

I watch her go. The news of the debacle will be the biggest thing to hit Foxfield since the union army stormed Virginia. Lina will be lucky if Carmen doesn't eat his dinner standing up and bolt back to the paper.

Minutes later, I mount the steps to my town house. Voltaire's face appears in the lowest square of window beside the door and makes me smile. "Ba-by! I'm sorry I'm so late," I tell him, twisting the anachronistic lock.

I change into pajamas and pour a glass of wine. I slip a Carole King album onto my old turntable and sit in the chair by the window. Voltaire curls like a skein of wool in my lap. The first fat snowflakes twist down. I try calling Lacey in New York but reach her voicemail.

They say be careful what you wish for.

This morning I'd wished for something extraordinary.

I'd won the Academy Award for best drama, when I would have settled for a free box of popcorn.

My gaze travels my living room. I've loved living here—the character of the fireplace and sweetly carved mantle, the bookcases and Federal-style crown molding at the ceiling. But a flicker of annoyance sweeps me as a new water stain catches my eye. How many times have I emailed maintenance? Should I have realized the staff had whittled months ago? The house isn't getting the attention it once did. I can't have it falling down around my ears. Or Willa Cather College, my *raison d'*être, my reason for living.

Truman Parker out of the blue.

So he's a visionary with a school-saving strategy behind those peacock's-neck blue eyes. But I won't sit around twiddling my thumbs waiting for someone else to save the college.

Maybe Truman Parker isn't the only one who can hatch a plan.

We will never lose the land.
—Willa Cather

CHAPTER THREE

Carmen DiMora got his scoop. For a solid week, the *Journal* has served up one heaping dish after another. Today, the cherry on top is a quote from a tenured but loose-tongued professor: "The board has a great deal of explaining to do. Believe me, they will answer for this." Stamping my snow-dusted boots on the mat outside Antonia's Café, I ask myself for the dozenth time how the CFO and chairman have allowed us to get into such a predicament—Willa Cather on the skids!

I purchase a large latte and take a seat at my favorite high table next to an outlet where I can plug in my phone. I pull the *Journal* from my bag and study the headshot below a caption, "Parker Named Interim Vice Pres of Finance," though I could no more forget the face than the lines of my own palm.

My phone chimes: Lacey. Following up on a conversation we began last night. The background blat of taxi horns tells me she is walking to work.

"How are you this morning?" she asks.

I rub my eyes, taking care not to smear the mascara I'd applied with a weary hand. "I'm okay. I just sat down with a coffee." I blow across the surface of my cup and take a sip.

"Whatever you do," Lacey says, "don't over-caffeinate."

"Only till I get through the meeting today. Truman's picture is on the front page of the *Journal*."

"Is he attractive?"

"Yes, he's attractive, Lacey," I whisper into the phone. I cast a furtive glance at the door. "That's not the issue. Keep your eye on the ball! My life as I know it is about to capsize. I had four minutes of sleep last night and the department meeting is in half an hour. I have to sit across a table from this human lightning bolt from my past and figure out how to save the college." My cup trembles on its path to my mouth and sends coffee to splash the lapel of my this-means-business suit. I scrabble for paper napkins.

"I'm sorry. I don't mean to trivialize what's happening to you. But maybe the situation isn't as dire as you think. Institutions face financial difficulties all the time."

"You're right, I know you're right."

"See what happens in the meeting and what Mr. Parker has to say. Truman Parker . . . those blue eyes and freckles." She sighs longingly.

"Lacey."

"Sorry. It's just . . . who'd ever believe we'd be talking about him again after all these years? It's an insane plot twist."

"Yeah, it is."

"It's going to be okay, G. Are you wearing your bracelet?"

Several years ago, she had sent me a silver cuff for Christmas. Now, I center it on my wrist and buff the engraving, *Breathe*, with my sleeve. "I am." I inhale and exhale for my friend.

"Good girl. Call me later."

I thank Lacey, gather my things, and then visit the restroom, where even the tiny hexagonal tiles in the floor form letter *T*s before my eyes. *Breathe*.

Picking my way across the quad toward my meeting in Collins Hall, the wind-chime laughter of students rings above the voice of the wind and gives me a moment's respite. But as a freshman in a striped wool cap tries to scoop up enough slush to make a snowball, I'm pierced by poignancy at their vulnerability, their breezy confidence, their blind faith in the paths they have chosen.

What bliss it is to not yet know something terrible.

With clarity, I recall a years-ago classroom memory. I'd been sitting in my director's chair before a lively group of juniors when a blanched Mrs. King had tapped on the door and wordlessly gestured for me to turn on the dust-fuzzed, wall-mounted television. My students and I had been laughing about a scene in Flaubert's *Madame Bovary* at the moment a bomb had ripped through the Alfred P. Murrah Federal Building in Oklahoma City, killing 168 people and injuring almost seven hundred.

Next week, our president, Susan Joshi, will meet with the students.

Next week, she will rock their worlds.

I wish I could make the world stand still for them.

At the edge of the quad, a maintenance man in paint-spackled coveralls balances on the top rung of a ladder. He's putting up another marketing banner, one of a new series featuring a student's photo and slogan. As the man pivots away from the banner, Laurel Cross's image smiles across the quad, the words *Find Your Fierce* emblazoned in blue letters below her crossed brown arms. Dread makes its bed in my belly.

Oh, Laurel. I wish I could protect you from what you don't yet know.

Find your fierce. The slogan's brilliant. I slip my phone from my pocket and take a picture of the banner. We're all going to need to be fierce. I'll have to dig deep for mine. How long has it been since I was ferocious? Since I was even passionate about anything other than my small contribution to education?

Outside the Collier conference room, I stop at the water-bottle-filling fountain and top up my bottle. Anxiety displaces the dread in my belly. I have to handle this like a professional, regardless of who's sitting at the conference table. I am responsible for the French department. I am the French department. Capturing a breath, I hold it and round the corner.

The room is so brightly lit one could perform a liver transplant. Wearing her gray suit and pink blouse, Lina is seated at the single round table that commands the room. She's flanked by the Mandarin and Spanish instructors. She tips me a supportive wink: all will be well. Pasting on a smile, I take a seat next to the man-bunned teacher of Classics, who leaves off fingering a pimple on his chin and shoots me a cool, "Ça va?"

"Ça va bien," I say with the last shred of sangfroid I have left.

Truman and Susan walk in together. As if spurred, my heart picks up to a gallop. I concentrate on Susan. She's smiling, though the smudges beneath her eyes speak of restless nights. My heart goes out to her. She begins introducing the members of the foreign-language team to Truman. Still on his feet, he first shakes the hand of the Spanish instructor. I await his attention, feeling as though I'm trying to breathe through a cocktail straw. Those shoulders! I can't trust myself to look at his face. Instead, I study the cut of his gray suit, his blue silk tie. Blue, the color that inspires confidence, that's associated with naval and pilot uniforms. Truman Parker won't let this ship go down.

The others make polite chitchat. But I'm dumbstruck in this man's presence. In my late teens, I'd imagined too many ways of our meeting again, yet none like this. Truman is his father's clone, elegant and charismatic. And like Conrad Parker—I'm amazed I've remembered his name—Truman appears successful, but the creases around his eyes and mouth show he hasn't become so for free. I wonder if he is happy in his life.

When it's my turn to be introduced, he takes my hand.

Voltage leaps up my arm as a tickle of *isn't this something* flits across his face.

"Georgie. Nice to see you," he says warmly, and he gives my hand an extra pump before releasing it. "I've meant to stop by and say hello, but . . ." He gestures at the others, the real order of business. My team looks at me as though they have never seen me before.

"Yes. It's . . . nice to see you too," I manage.

He nods distractedly, tweaks the knot in his tie, and finally takes a seat next to Susan. The electric line that our contact activated snaps as if under the weight of ice.

Susan gets down to business. "I know you've been working on your ideas for promoting your sections," she says, "and I thank you."

I take a sip from my water bottle and catch Truman eyeing me. Before his gaze skips away, I choke, sputtering and coughing. Lina shoots me an are-you-quite-all-right look over the top of her readers.

A blush creeps up my neck. "Excuse me," I mutter. Truman seems to take no notice. Muffling a last cough in my sleeve, I turn my attention to the Classics teacher, whom Susan has asked to make the first presentation.

Man-bun's idea for a fundraising event, in which teams would compete in ancient Olympic Games, isn't bad and is met with guarded enthusiasm. Lina and I had half expected a proposal for weekly toga parties.

When it's my turn, I open my leather binder and slide out the twenty-four-page proposal that has consumed me the past three days. What if the others think it's ill conceived? What if Truman thinks I'm incompetent? Skimming the bullet-pointed first page, I finger my bracelet beneath the table and follow its instruction.

"Willa Cather needs a study abroad program," I say to the

sweating water pitcher at the table's center. "It is one of the only private colleges of its caliber that doesn't yet offer the opportunity. We could launch the initiative with a French experience, and then—"

Uncharacteristically, Susan raises a finger. "I agree wholeheartedly, Georgie, but with our budget in the red, I fail to see how we could undertake a program of that complexity."

Man-bun leans back and crosses his arms.

I take a sneak peek at Truman, and my stomach takes a nosedive. An elbow on the table, his eyes closed, he rubs his forehead, back and forth, back and forth.

Susan looks at me intently.

I had anticipated this reaction and had done my research. *Find your fierce.*

In turn, I touch the other instructors with my eyes. "I have an old and dear friend in Paris, Genevieve Beaulieu, who serves on the board of a women's college, Ecole Viardot." At my elbow, Man-bun elaborately checks the time on his phone. I want to flick the punk on his ear. Instead, I turn a serene smile on Susan. "Madame Beaulieu is the woman who inspired me to become a French teacher. She was my first teacher." Both Lina and Susan smile. Truman leaves off rubbing the bridge of his nose, blinks, and looks at me. One corner of his lips curls up.

He remembers.

I let out a shaky, silent breath. "I have talked with Madame Beaulieu—whom I trust with my soul." I lock eyes with Susan. "I have made her aware of our situation. Ecole Viardot has also been investigating an exchange program. They are interested in a swap with a select group of juniors—students who could generate their own funding . . . until our situation improves." Truman rubs his forehead again.

"How would they do that, exactly?" Susan asks.

I consult my notes. "Genevieve and I discussed three options that have been successful at other private colleges. The first is for students to apply for grants, both government and private." Truman writes furiously on a lined tablet. "The second involves student initiative . . . and timing. Students who have jobs generally receive tax refunds in the spring. If we designate spring semester for the exchange, they would have an influx of cash halfway through the semester. And then, there's crowdfunding. Students set up websites detailing their goals, their hopes and dreams, and ask subscribers for donations. Apparently, it's a common practice now. And while the program wouldn't generate immediate revenue, it would make our program more enticing for students . . . raising enrollment." The others look at Susan—whose smile tells me she is impressed.

"That's exciting, Georgie," someone says.

"Great idea."

"It could totally work."

Man-bun pokes out his lips and nods in agreement.

Awash in affirmation, I conclude my presentation, and then it's Lina's turn. As she and the others pitch their ideas, I will myself not to look at Truman, but my eyes stray to him as though tethered by a retractable leash. His light-brown freckles are darker, but, like constellations, their patterns are the same. The current leaps. His silver hair looks distinguished and handsome, and my fingers itch to smooth it. In the bat of an eye, I am a teenager again and making out with him in my family's den, just before we were busted.

Stop it, tout de suite, Georgie Girl!

The nickname Truman gave me back then bushwhacks me. I gape at him as though he has said it aloud, my professional bravado faltering. I close my eyes and grip the leather arms of my chair, scrambling to recapture my composure.

Susan puts down her pen and knits her fingers on the table. She leans forward and then surveys us all in turn. "Thank you all for your hard work. As we know, when programs are cut, the arts are usually first to be pruned. Confidentially—and this is not to leave this room—Truman is already taking a hard look at the visual arts." Truman draws his bottom lip between his teeth and nods, his eyes aggrieved. "Languages could be next." My ears ring. This cannot be happening. "This is our reality," Susan goes on, spreading her hands on the table. "The sections with the lowest enrollment for fall will be the ones we have to consider cutting . . . at least for a year."

I peer down at my notes, tears stinging my lids. If I can't make a case for the study abroad initiative and energize the French section I've built over twenty-five years, we could very well lose it. I'd be out of a job. Where in the would I go?

As the meeting concludes, I pass a copy of my proposal to Susan, ashamed of how my hand shakes, and then gather my things. I have a block of time to call Genevieve in Paris before the big one o'clock meeting with the students. She will boost my spirits. Madame will restore my confidence, just as she did the year I competed for the French award in her eighth-grade class. Though I'm single, she is the reason I go by Madame instead of Mademoiselle.

Susan assures us our ideas will be considered carefully. She asks us to be patient. She adjourns the meeting, and the team files out. I lag behind, hoping to speak to Truman. But he stands at the window, his back to the room, as silent as an oyster.

The enormity of his task wafts to me.

I slip from the room, wondering if the boy who once fortified me is the man who will dismantle my career.

༺⚘༻

A rising sense of unease fills the auditorium and my chest. My heart squeezes with empathy for the girls. It's February 1, and since I've been aware of our financial straits for a week, I'd thought I'd be ready for this. Now, I wish I had a paper bag to breathe in.

Seemingly undaunted, Susan sits on the edge of the stage, her legs crossed, as if some women's fiction author has come to give a book talk. She often sits like this when addressing the girls. It allows her to connect with them, shows her sincerity and authenticity. She's delivered the news that the school is "struggling financially, and that there may be some rather-significant changes in programs." While she untangles loops in the microphone cord before handing it to Truman, the young women of Willa Cather turn to each other, their faces baffled. My student Malika and her roommate, seated next to Lina and me, narrow their eyes at us as though we're conspirators in some tasteless April Fools' prank.

A fusillade of whispered chatter breaks the stunned silence.

"Dude!"

"What is she saying?"

"What the f-?"

"Tell us this is a joke."

Truman takes the mic and casts a winsome smile over the assembly. "Ladies," he says, the familiar timbre of his voice sending a reflexive tremor through my core. I press my tongue against the roof of my mouth the way I do to keep from sneezing. "It's an honor to be here on this beautiful, historic campus that you love. And amid such a wealth of talented students." Wealth. Will they see Truman as some rich dude with a fancy-labeled snake oil to sell?

Malika flexes and squeezes her hands in her lap, her knuckles pale. Laurel Cross, whom I hadn't noticed in the row in front of us, slowly turns and gives me a suspicious frown before pretending to scratch her chin on the shoulder of her sweater.

A pang of regret presses between my eyes. I hadn't prepared my students for the news. And I know all too well what it's like to be blindsided. I felt the same way staring at the blast email message from Susan this morning: "Be prepared to meet, at least briefly, with your advisees after the meeting. Simply reiterate what Truman and I tell them. Thank you for your hard work this week and your faith in Willa Cather. Gratefully, Susan."

What is unspoken is that if chaos erupts among the students, they could panic and start transferring out. This cannot happen. Our students are our most valuable currency, the rosy fruit of our labors. Without adequate enrollment, the school will self-destruct.

And so will I.

⚭

When I arrive at my office in Collins, a quartet of students is waiting, sitting against the wall on the blue carpet outside my door. Madison's eyes look as though she has been swimming in an over-chlorinated pool, Laurel looks defiant, and the others look like emojis with question marks for eyes.

"Aww, lovies," I say, their distress tripping my heart. "Let me just run to the restroom. Go ahead inside."

Sitting in a stall and hoping no one else has to go, I summon the courage to set aside my own cache of fears while quieting theirs. After the meeting, Lina had asked her advisees to bundle up and meet her at the boathouse. A new text from her says that social media has exploded with the news of our debt. My lips give a wry twist. "What took it so long?" I say aloud. I take a long time washing my hands, thankful I'm not on Facebook or Twitter to witness the fracas.

I would love to take my advisees to some retreat center. But the farthest my anxiety would allow me to go would be the Sleeping Beauty Motel in Foxfield. I dry my hands on a brown paper towel and wish for the hand lotion beside my kitchen sink.

I stop cold when the answer hits me.

There is something I can do.

I have my own retreat, my personal space and sanctuary: my home.

This, I will open to them, though it's unconventional.

When I return to my office, five more students are waiting for me, two sitting and warming their backs against the radiator, all of them grim-faced.

"Ladies," I say to them with the warmest smile I can muster. "Get your pajamas and meet me at my house at six. It's time for a sleepover."

Women are never stronger than when they
arm themselves with their weaknesses.
—Madame Marie du Deffand

CHAPTER
FOUR

Settling into the driver's seat of my Mercedes-Benz Coupe is like slipping into a fine wineskin, its leather rich and earthy and slightly sweet. But as every bag has its bottom, the coupe has a confine: if cars could dream, I'm sure mine would long to hit the open road, exercise and clean its pistons, blow out carbon. But *hélas*, alas, it's limited to driving through campus and the two miles into the quaint streets of Foxfield, where I wave to locals: the mail carrier; a realtor, with whom I had a couple of underwhelming dates last year; my hairdresser; the dry cleaner; and the owner of The Bus Stop boutique.

I'm considered a good customer here in town, though it's the UPS and FedEx drivers, who make deliveries to my home, who know my birthday, my cat's name, and what flowers I grow in my garden.

Why I spent my money on such a fancy car is a mystery to those who know me best, especially when they were spending money to clothe and educate their children, or to travel. But I love the security of a well-made luxury car, the solid schwoop-suck of the door as it closes.

I corner into Carter's Market and park the coupe in a

coveted end spot. Here I'll load up on tonight's sleepover sundries, sustenance for the girls and me as we process the events of the last days.

Robert the cart gatherer calls to me as I get out of the car. "Hi, Madame." He tugs a cart loose from the metal-and-plastic train he has made. "Want one of these?"

Even in town, I'm known as Madame. "Sure. Bonjour, Robert," tickling him by pronouncing his name with a French accent, Ro-bear. "I bet you're ready for some sunshine, huh?"

"Yes, ma'am."

Inside, the market is warm, and I have the narrow aisles to myself. It's Thursday— my free afternoon—and most people shop on Fridays. Two of my advisees can't make it to the sleepover. Tucking my purse into the child seat of the cart, I stop to take out my phone and set myself a reminder to catch up with them tomorrow. Thursday's a big date night for girls who go out with guys from George Wythe College in Mountainsburg. Go *out* is probably not the term for it anymore. Maybe it's still *hook up*? I'll ask Lacey; she'll know.

As I fill the cart with bottles of water, I ruefully remember how long it's been since I've hooked up. Like a carnival car on rails, my mind swerves to Truman Parker. Is he married? The *Journal* piece hadn't said anything about a family. Adding orange juice and milk to the cart, I recall his long hands on the conference table. His neatly trimmed nails. The handsome watch on his freckled wrist. The way his pen flew over the yellow tablet. Was he wearing a wedding ring? How could I fail to notice?

"Damn it, Georgie," I say aloud *en français*, "it's not your business if he's married or not. You're not hooking up with Truman Parker!"

I whip my head around, searching the aisle for French-fluent interlopers and remind myself to keep my thoughts of Truman to myself. I stand glaring at the top-shelf bottles of Pinot Grigio, grab two of them by their necks, and shove them into the cart. For after the sleepover. I loop the aisles, crowding the cart with boxes of cereal and bananas, chips and salsa, and a package of salmon treats for Voltaire. My sweet boy.

A boy. That's it! I only knew Truman as a boy. It's normal to be curious about him. To see how my first love turned out— what he's like as a man. Anybody would be. After I've talked with him a time or two, I'll be satisfied. And that will be that.

Giving myself a mental high-five on being able to self-analyze, I head to the bakery section. I exchange greetings with Big Tully, who's been piping icing since the George H. W. Bush administration. She inclines her head toward the top-shelf tray of her bestselling double-chocolate cupcake, the Loverboy. "A lover today?" she asks with a sly grin and plants her hands on the hips of her butter-stained apron.

Ten girls are coming to the sleepover. I consider the questions I will have to answer about what's happening at the college. "At least six of the Loverboys. I'll need a couple dozen cupcakes in all."

Big Tully cuts her eyes at me. "Two dozen? Honey, you want to sit and talk about it?"

I laugh and twist off the cap of a water bottle. "I'm hosting a slumber party for my advisees."

"Ah," she says, pulling on plastic gloves, her eyes lighting with the prospect of some juicy morsel of college gossip. News of the debacle has probably trickled into every crevice in town.

I peer into the glass case. "So let's do six of the Loverboys, six of the Frankly Scarletts . . . let's see . . . six of the Strawberry Fields Forever, and . . . six Plain Janes."

Big Tully begins filling a white box. "Things as bad as they say over there?"

I gulp the water. "Oh, no. It's all good. We just need to tighten our belts a little."

"I figured those kids would be leaving skid marks getting out of there."

"Nope!" I say, giving her a thirty-two-toothed smile. I think of Laurel and tap on the case with the sparkly cupcakes. "Can I substitute six Unicorns for the Plain Janes?"

Big Tully deflates. In a rare silence, she fills three boxes and ties them together with white string.

I move through the checkout line, past the national tabloids, where I half expect to see news of Willa Cather shouting from their covers. I inch past the candy, wondering how it would look for a middle-aged professor to suck on a ring pop.

Back in the parking lot, I load the groceries in the trunk and then leave the car and tread along a historic cobblestone sidewalk to Huck's Humble Pie down the block. The bell on the door alerts Huck, nicknamed for his Mississippi accent and snub-nosed, ragtag appearance, to my entrance.

"Four large pizzas, comin' right atcha, Madame," he says. I thank him and wait, listening to Steely Dan's "Reelin' in the Years" from big black speakers while a teller from the bank pays her check. I scan Huck's colorful collection of Humble Pie and other '70s album covers on the wall. The cover of Cat Stevens's *Teaser and the Firecat* catches my eye as it never did before and dredges up yet another Browning memory. The Kane family, for whom I'd babysat, had that album. It was Blue's favorite. Odd, sweet little Blue Kane. His quicksilver sister, Clover, who'd gone missing. The search for her in the storm. At once, I'm gasping for breath, a sense of dread rolling over me. Another attack. I flail a blind hand out to clutch the edge of the counter, my purse thudding to the floor. Metal tubes of lipstick leap and skip across the tile. The bank teller—Alex, I think—takes a step back in alarm but then stoops to gather my things. Can the others smell the fear slicking my body?

Before I can speak, Huck's around the counter. He's at my

side, concern riding his features. He's taking my arm. "Are you
. . . do you have an inhaler or somethin'?"

I would rather conduct lightning than draw attention to my
condition. "No. I left it at home," I lie, sucking air like I've run
a hundred-yard dash. Silently, I curse a society where asthma is
more acceptable than anxiety. Huck sits me down at a table like
an unwieldy package. Steely Dan throbs on with *Reeling in the
Years*. Arms crossed over my midsection, I bend and lower my
forehead toward my knees.

At last, the slow tide of my breath returns. An inhaler.
Maybe I could buy an inhaler at the pharmacy to keep in my
pocket. As a prop in case this happens again.

Other customers begin trickling in. I get to my feet and collect my pizza boxes from the counter. I lay a fifty and a ten on
Huck's counter, tossing a, "Keep the change, Huck, and thanks
so much," over my shoulder.

In the parking lot again, a gauzy darkness gathering, I sit in
the safety of my coupe, my hands on the wheel, my breath fog-
ging the windows. Since Truman Parker came to town, memories
I've avoided have swirled and concentrated—settling themselves
apart from the rest—like unwanted soil in a gold panner's sluice.

I can't let what happened in the pizza place happen again.
I could be seen as unstable, unprofessional. I could lose my job.
Shoving the key into the ignition, I power the engine. With
memories from that teenage year ricocheting through my head,
I will have to be more guarded.

I will avoid Truman Parker the way I would tequila shots.
Either could make me lose my head.

ᚱᚢ

It's a quarter to six by the time the coupe's headlights sweep
over my house. Laurel and another junior, Sutton, are sad-look-
ing lumps on my front steps. Whether from apprehension or

hunger, my gut twists, and at once, the aroma of hot cheese and bread in the boxes on the passenger seat makes my mouth water. There's no time now to straighten up the house or feed Voltaire before his space is invaded, but at least Laurel and Sutton can help me unload the car.

I step out on wobbly legs and greet the students with a smile. "Bonsoir, mesdemoiselles."

The girls stand and collect their duffle bags. "Hi," they say in tandem, their enthusiasm for French greetings apparently leeched out of them.

"Give me a hand with some groceries, *s'il vous plaît*," I ask brightly. "I bought pizza and cupcakes," I sing out, trying to bring a smile to their faces, "beaucoup cupcakes."

"That's the best thing I've heard all day," Sutton says, flashing me a small white grin. Sutton's from Atlanta and the personification of a Georgia peach, fair and round.

Truman's from Atlanta. God help me.

"Me too," Laurel says, reaching for a box.

Three more students plod into the spill of light on the driveway: Penn, Emily, and Victoria.

"Welcome to my home," I say to them *en français*. They offer me sober greetings but all pitch in, carrying bags and boxes to my side door. Flipping up the overhead light switch with my elbow, I catch a glimpse of the back quarter of my cat streaking toward the stairs. It's past his dinnertime, but he can wait.

Victoria's eyes light. "Was that a kitty?"

"Yep, that's Voltaire, and he's probably under my bed by now," I say, arranging water bottles on a counter. "He's not used to company."

"Oh, poor baby," Laurel says.

The girls quietly help unload the grocery bags. In class, I'm forever squelching their banter, but now I long to hear it.

A knock on the front door brings the remaining five in

from the cold: Alexis, Malika, Hollins, Madison, and Kennedy.

"Thank you so much for inviting us," Alexis says, and the others chime in.

"Your house is really pretty," Penn says. "Can we look around?"

I smile. "*Bien sûr*. Turn the lamps on in the living room, will you? We'll eat in there, on paper plates, if that's okay."

"Sounds great," Madison says. "The pizza smells good."

Laurel does a little quickstep and hovers over my shoulder. "Did you get veggie?"

I grin and switch the oven on to warm. "I did, especially for you and Alexis. And one Everything, one plain cheese, and one pepperoni."

Laurel gives me a hug around the shoulders. The almond soap she uses wreathes my head, reminding me how badly I'd like to shower.

"Cupcakes!" Madison and Kennedy say in tandem, spying the butter-spotted boxes and then pretending to sprout fangs and claws and pounce on them.

"Dude, I could eat five after today," Sutton says.

I pull a chip-and-dip platter down from a high cabinet and run the dust out of it with a dish cloth. "Will you put out the chips and salsa?" I ask her. "I'd love to grab a quick shower and change. And someone put the pizza boxes in the oven? Help yourselves to water, and there are Diet Cokes in the fridge."

"We will," Kennedy says, taking the platter.

Someone calls out from the living room. "Ooh, vintage albums . . . cool. Can we put one on?"

I smile, happy my girls are feeling good for the moment. I only hope it lasts once we get down to why they're really here.

❧

Upstairs in the shower, the hot water pelts my back. I'm calmer and more centered. I pluck my lavender soap from the wire

34

basket and rehearse what I plan to say to the girls after dinner. I replay Susan's email directive from this morning: "Just reiterate what Truman and I have said."

At once, his man-image materializes out of the steam. His eyes rival the Aegean Sea. One corner of his mouth curls the way it had in the conference room, when I'd mentioned Madame Beaulieu. Soaping myself, I wonder what he thinks of my round-as-a-handful-of-bubbles body. I toss the soap back in the basket. Vous imbécile! *He hasn't noticed your body!*

Twisting the tap to cool, I plunge my head under the spray and then furiously shampoo my hair. The man is likely married with grown children. He hasn't come here to think of me; he's come to help save the college. And he'll be working across campus in the admin building. It's not like I'll be sharing an office with him.

I squeeze the water from my hair. Of all the gin joints in all the towns in all the world, Truman Parker walks into mine.

I step out onto the mat and reach for a towel. Led Zeppelin pounds away downstairs. Remembering the fastidious math professor next door, I allow myself a small grin and hope the noise is pissing him off. The girls' laughter floats up the stairs. I vow to focus on them for the rest of the night. I'll light the birch logs I keep laid in my small fireplace. We'll be cozy while we eat. And talk.

I dress in lounging pajamas and then coax Voltaire from beneath my bed skirt. "Okay, sweet man, time to confront your fears. Tonight, you're a therapy cat. The girls are going to love you."

☙❧

Sutton is the first to spy Voltaire in my arms. "Aww, he's precious!"

Before the cat can let out his don't-mess-with-me yowl, he is surrounded.

"Just give him a minute to get used to you." I let the cat down. The girls step back, and Voltaire stalks like the prince he is into the living room, his nose lifting at the mingled aromas of food and unfamiliar females. "Let's turn the music down a little too."

I fill Voltaire's bowl while the girls serve themselves from the boxes on the counter, licking the grease from their fingers. I follow suit, and, navigating the pile of Vera Bradley bags in the hallway, we congregate in the living room.

The late-January wind howls at the windows as if it wants to come in. I sit next to Alexis on the hearth and take a few sustaining bites of pizza. I love the way Huck lines his pans with cornmeal. "How about a fire?" I say, brushing crumbs from my chest.

"Ooh, that would be nice," several of the girls say.

I reach for the box of long matches from between my pair of French lamps on the mantle and light the kindling. "For those of you who didn't bring sleeping bags, I can bring blankets down to make pallets, and we can sleep here. How would that be?"

"Really cozy," Emily says from her spot on my tufted Louis XVI–style sofa between Penn and Malika. The others make coos of assent around mouthfuls of pizza.

Instead of flat-ironing it as she usually does, Laurel has left her curly hair loose, and it's hanging in her eyes. I long to brush it aside. Once, when she was a freshman and standing at my desk, I'd handed her a bobby pin from my top drawer. "I'd really like to see your eyes when we talk," I'd said.

She'd turned the pin over in her hands and drawn her bottom lip between her teeth. "I'm good," she'd said. Over time, I'd realized that when she's vulnerable, she curtains the windows to her soul. Well acquainted with coping mechanisms myself, I observe the rest of Laurel's broad features, the tightness of her mouth, and hope the night will be good for her.

"You're so sweet to do this for us, Madame," Malika says.

"Uh-huh," the rest agree.

My heart warms. "It's my pleasure," I respond to them in French.

After a third slice of veggie, I feel ready for the night to come. The girls thank me for dinner, agreeing to save the cupcakes for later. In turn, they pad into the kitchen to throw their paper goods away, refill their drink cups, and visit the powder room.

Madison and Emily flip through my album collection. Emily plucks out a Fleetwood Mac album and makes a big show of revealing its cover. "Let's play this!"

I grin. "I'm impressed you know who that is."

Penn's eyes light. "OMG . . . my grandparents used to dance to that." My level of cool takes a header. I turn, huffing a little laugh at the fire, and give the logs another poke.

The students unroll their sleeping bags—jockeying for position close to the fireplace—and take turns courting Voltaire.

Laurel is first to broach the conversation. She is sitting on the floor, leaning back against Emily's legs. The bummer rolls over us again, floating in the air, prodding for purchase. "Madame Bricker, with the school in debt, what's going to happen to our programs?" She looks forlornly around at her friends. "I mean, most of us are either majoring or minoring in French."

Kennedy, who is cradling Voltaire, chimes in. "Yeah, like, I'm minoring in French but majoring in design. Are they going to cut the design program?"

Sutton worries her sleeping bag zipper back and forth. "I heard they might cut arts programs, and I'm an art history major."

"I have not heard that that is going to happen," I say evenly. The fire pops and cackles.

My students' fear is palpable.

Victoria's forehead is practically corrugated. "Like what programs could get cut? I'm a music major."

Firelight plays off my silver cuff. I breathe for Lacey. Sleet ticks at the window and keeps time with the clock on a side table. I place two more logs on the fire and remember a nugget of wisdom I picked up somewhere along the way: "Don't tell a child more than she wants to know. She will usually be satisfied." I am the mature adult here, the teacher, the authority figure. But these are not children; these are young women.

I want to tell the truth. But I have received a directive from the president. If I confirm my students' fears, telling them the administration is already looking for programs to cut, I could lose my job. And with social media, nothing the girls know would stay secret for long.

I turn to the fire and prod the logs with the poker. The secrets I kept as a teen flicker and threaten to flare along with the writhing orange-and-purple embers. Laurel interrupts my thoughts, and I start, dropping the poker. Voltaire pokes his head up from his nest in her sleeping bag. "How is the finance guy's plan going to help?"

I set the poker back in its stand with a trembling hand and consider this. It's speech time. "Mr. Parker has a lifetime of experience in business and consulting. He's a visionary." It's surreal discussing Truman with these girls who are only half a dozen years older than I was when we were together. "Remember that he wants to help us restructure departments into centers? Redefining programs will help strengthen them. As Dr. Joshi said, foreign language will be classified under Creativity, Design, and the Arts. Students who want to study more than one thing under the umbrella will have the opportunity to do so. That will make a WCC education more appealing and increase enrollment."

Hollins, the math major, cuts to the chase. "So, if enrollment increases, the school makes money."

"Right."

Malika frowns. "But why did they have to bring in an outsider? Don't they have to pay him, like, a salary?"

Hollins turns to her. "Well, yeah. But a what . . . probably, five-figure salary . . . is a drop in the ocean compared to heavy debt. Whatever that amount is. Mr. Parker didn't exactly tell us."

My heart sinks for Truman; he's been branded an intruder. I remember his posture as he stood at the conference room window. For the first time since he came to Willa Cather, my heart feels soft rather than cleaved in two. I add another log to the fire, composing an answer. None of this is Truman's fault. He has been hired to do a difficult job, to help save the college. I have to stop thinking of him as the enemy, just because I have a self-control problem.

Suddenly, it's important to me that the girls see Truman as genuine and human, a man who cares about people and respects women, a man who himself benefitted from single-sex education. If they were to rally against him and his plans, they could unwittingly seal their doom by revolting against their "savior."

The Truman I loved was a fine young man, honorable and good to his marrow. I am banking on that still being true.

"Let's get the cupcakes," I say with a smile. "I have a story to tell you."

You can't be that kid standing
at the top of the waterslide, overthinking it.
You have to go down the chute.
—Tina Fey

CHAPTER
FIVE

"Truman Parker was my first love." Three mouths drop open. Four leave off licking icing to gape at me. Alexis sprays cake crumbs.

"You're kidding!" and "No way!" she and Kennedy cry at the same time.

I grin like the Cheshire cat and then stretch my arms above my head and yawn elaborately. "I think I'll turn in now. I'm really tired." I move as if to rise.

Laurel and Victoria pounce on my feet. "Tell us!" Laurel cries.

"C'mon, your secret's safe with us," Hollins says.

Laurel flips her hair from her eyes and nods around at the others. "*Mais oui.* What happens at Madame's stays at Madame's."

Yes, *this* secret's safe. I smile and then narrow my eyes at them. "Well, I'm counting on you to keep it behind the teeth, as the French say."

"Bien sûr," several of the girls declare.

I push a throw pillow behind my back and sit cross-legged. At once, I feel like Scheherazade in the story "One Thousand

and One Nights," preparing to spin a tale for the king and thus save my life. Will sharing my story about Truman build their trust in him and help save the French department and my career?

"I was fourteen."

Cell phones fall to sleeping bags.

"Dude, so young," Malika and Penn say at the same time and then smirk at each other.

"Shush, let Madame tell it," Victoria says with hearts for eyes.

"He was the cutest boy I had ever *seen*—we didn't say *hot* back then—and his eyes were flame blue. Remember that I grew up at a boys' school?"

The girls nod. "Yeah, that had to have been bizarre," Emily says, reaching for another cupcake.

I gaze into the fire for a moment, allowing pictures of the aristocracy of Browning—the ivy-robed Tudor buildings and the old clock tower—to move like a panoramic photo in my head. I survey my audience.

"I didn't know anything different. I'd grown up with hordes of teenage boys who were like big brothers. But that year my best friend and I were the same age as the sophomores. And nothing was ever the same. Truman was assigned to sit at my family's table in the dining hall, along with four other students. But I only had eyes for Truman." I recall his adult eyes for the tenth time that day. Though lined and slightly hooded, their blue is undimmed. "When he looked at me, heaven blew in." I grin as more images rise. "I know it sounds corny, but he smelled like fresh leaves. And he had a habit of saluting people."

Laurel laughs. "Saluting?"

I cut my eyes at her. "Yes. And I found it entirely endearing," I said prissily. "He told me he was a legacy, that his father had attended Browning when it was still a military school.

There was something about him that made me feel sassy, and I guess womanly for the first time. I nicknamed him Legacy." Though the other special name I'd called him had just poked its head around the corner of my mind, I decide to keep that one to myself.

Penn tilts her head coyly. "What did he call you?"

"Georgie Girl."

The girls wriggle with pleasure and say, "Georgie Girl!" and "That's super cute!"

Penn begins telling us the pet names her first boyfriend gave her. I take a minute to open a fresh bottle of water, deciding how much more I will tell them. While the others hoot Penn down, I take several sips, assessing my level of discomfort. How close might I be to prying the scabs off my old wounds? But I feel calm. I feel good. These memories feel safe.

I give them more. "His hair was longish, like it is now, but strawberry blond, like Madison's."

Eyes turn to Madison, whose cheekbones rise with a plush smile.

"Did you kiss him?" Penn asks.

Victoria wads up a napkin and chucks it at Penn. "Let Madame tell it!"

Awash with a silvery string of memories, I busy myself by adding another log to the fire. Truman striding across Hampton Circle, tanned and taller from the summer we'd spent apart. He and I standing below the river bluff among the buttonbushes, close to the silty bank. He'd taken my face in his hands and asked me if I still loved him. I'd answered yes, and my tears had spotted and darkened his T-shirt. "Oh, yes," I say to the girls, "I did a lot of kissing that summer."

The girls melt into their sleeping bags, puddles of delight.

"Madame," Malika says with a mental exclamation point, "This is a whole new side of you."

Laurel gives me a saucy smirk. "So, old Truman was a good kisser, huh?"

Old Truman—ha! I tuck my robe around me, tightening its sash. Enjoying myself, I cast fresh bait. "Bien sûr." I let a couple of beats pass. "He was in the gifted class for it."

The girls hoot and roll around on their blankets, Laurel pedaling her feet in the air.

This. This is what I wanted for my students tonight. They are teenagers again themselves, without a care for their futures. Laughing with them, I breathe a sigh of relief.

Penn bites a cupcake, leaving green icing to ring her lips, and gives her head a wistful shake. "You and Truman were OTP, one true pair."

The coals are incandescent now, tumbling through the grate in a bed of roiling heat. "We were," I say, edging away from the fireplace. "He was the finest of boys. He wanted to be an English teacher. *Like my father,* I don't say and mentally elbow that memory away. He wrote me a valentine poem. The notebook sheet—folded, you know, into one of those paper footballs—lay in the bottom of my jewelry box until I went to college." My mind turns back to the kissing. "I can still hear him saying, once—when we had almost gotten carried away—how if our love was going to last forever, we were going to have to take care of it and do what's right."

A sigh escapes Penn. "L'amour vrai."

"Yes. I believe it was true love."

"But surely you had others," Sutton says levelly. All eyes are on my face.

"Never one like . . . that." We are quiet for a space of time. "See, that's the problem," I finally say, and I realize I'm only just figuring it out. "It's awful to fall for a wonderful boy when you're fourteen, because he becomes the gold standard no one else ever measures up to."

"So what happened?" Laurel insists. Voltaire slinks under her hand, and she strokes him absently.

"Well, my family moved away. We wrote letters. That's what we did back then, before cell phones and texting. It was harder to stay in contact. We said we'd visit . . ." My voice trails away, and as if in vignette, I see my ponytailed self in the back bedroom of my stern grandmother's house, which smelled of cough drops and mothballed fur coats, burying myself in books—the romantic mishaps of the Bennet sisters—as the letters began to peter away.

Surprising tears sting my nose. Willing them away, I pluck a Unicorn from the last box. "But I never saw Truman again. Until last week, when he showed up here."

The girls are like pop-up figures in a picture book.

"That's terrible!"

"What?"

"That's all wrong."

They wait.

Then Hollins squints at me. "And he didn't become an English teacher."

"Not that I'm aware of," I say.

Malika prods Hollins with a socked foot. "Hollins! That's not relevant here." She asks me, "Is he *single?*"

I can't help but laugh. "I've no idea." *Yeah, like you haven't given it a thought.*

Laurel's face is baffled. "Does he know you're single?"

Does he, Georgie? Has he asked anyone about you? "I don't know what he knows."

"But you have to go out with him, see if there's still something there!"

"Whoa," I say, tossing the cupcake paper into the fire. "We're not going there. I'm not interested in romance." *You lie like the rug you're sitting on, Georgie Girl.*

44

Laurel persists like a petulant toddler. "But why not?"

"Because, Truman has a big job to do here, and so do I. I am working on a project for the French department," I wiggle my brows, "top secret for now, but something sure to stoke the program."

Sutton regards the others. "Well, you have to promise us you'll keep an open mind about love."

I smile but feel a slight pang at their relatively inexperienced perspective of love. "I promise."

The girls look pensive then and on the slippery slope toward troubled.

Victoria studies me like a documentarian. "So, you think Truman can get us out of debt?"

It's strange hearing the girls saying his name. But at least I know I've humanized him.

"I do. He and Dr. Joshi are on this, along with the board. I feel very encouraged, and so should you. We need to focus on doing our work and letting them do theirs." Light flashes from my phone: a missed call from Lacey, and I remember a photograph I took the other day. I collect my phone and scroll quickly through my camera roll. "You know the new banner outside the dining hall?" I look at Laurel and roll my hands in a ta-da motion. "Our celebrity Laurel's banner? Find your fierce?" Laurel grins, her brown face darkening. "That is what we are going to do. And right now, I'm going to haul my fierce fanny upstairs to brush my teeth."

I rise, to appreciative laughter. The girls begin talking among themselves and checking their phones. "Dude, I forgot my tampons," Hollins says, "does anyone have one?"

"I do," Malika says, groping for her striped duffle.

I mount the stairs, my mind ticking back the months. It's been three months since I had a period. I feel like a dried-up spinster. Though I barely have enough energy left to put another coherent thought together, I brush and floss, wash my face, and slather on moisturizer. Passing my bed, I take a longing look at my pillow-top mattress. But the sleepover was my idea, and I won't bail on the girls. It won't kill me to spend a single night on the floor.

As I take the stairs down again with a stack of blankets, I find that after all the recollecting I've done about Truman this evening, I'm almost looking forward to seeing him again. I really want to find out who he is after all these years. Maybe I can be a friend to him in this place where he's a foreigner. He'll need the support of a devoted faculty. And dried-up spinster or no, devoted to Willa Cather, I am.

After we're settled in for the night in my darkened living room, I lie cocooned among the girls as though in the cabin of a snug, well-decorated craft in a winter sea. I think of sleepovers with Lacey, when we were still full of hopes and dreams unsullied by decades of grim reality. I need to call her back. Tomorrow.

Late, late, the girls' phones flare like lightning bugs—probably good night texts with their significant others—and keep me awake. I wonder where Truman is laying his silvery head, where he's living, to whom he says good night. I give my pillow a punch, turning it to the cool side, and pull my blanket over my head. Finally, I drift to sleet at the window like rice flung at a wedding, the scratch and sift of kitty litter in the laundry room, and soft snoring from Penn's sleeping bag.

⎆⎆⎆

Friday morning, I set out for my office in Collier. The sun, so long shrouded by clouds, seems freshly created, and I raise my face to it. Lina and I haven't had a chance to catch up, so we settle down for a cup of coffee in the workroom. I tell her about the sleepover and the personal information I divulged to the girls, telling her I hope I didn't overshare. But Lina reminds me of the trust I've built with my advisees and of how much they value me. My heart warms, but at the same time a flicker of doubt traces the back of my neck.

Mrs. King, who's been late or absent from work approximately three times since the invention of fire, rolls in from a dental appointment. "I'm so sorry I'm tardy," she exclaims, glancing at the clock and shrugging from her scarf and nubby orange wool coat. Devotion. If we are all as devoted as Mrs. King, we will succeed. My spirits ease.

"You are fine," Lina and I smile and say in tandem.

"Sit and have a cup," Lina says to her, "it's Friday."

I push myself to my feet. "You two enjoy. I'm secluding myself in my office until one fifteen." I give Mrs. King's arm a squeeze. "If anyone calls for me, say I'm not available." I can't see anyone until I've gotten my ducks in a row. Truman comes to my mind again. My next hair appointment can't come too soon.

The old paneled door closed, I unload my bag and dive first into a stack of papers to grade, on which I am uncharacteristically behind. Eventually, the name Laurel Cross floats to the top of the stack. I turn the pages, disbelieving. She has marked four multiple-choice questions incorrectly and left three items unmarked entirely. I've never had the heart to actually include the letter F along with the numerical grade on a test paper. A D, yes, but not an F. The students are all too aware of the grading scale. With a blue pen, I write "64%" on the header of Laurel's test.

When I've evaluated two sections of papers and recorded the grades in a database, I slide them into my satchel for class. I attend to the files I've created for the study abroad initiative, and my thoughts volley from the task to Laurel. I wonder if there is more going on with her than her concern for the college finances.

When Mrs. King's noon microwaved soup drifts through the crack under my door, I'm reminded to call Madame Beaulieu and, ruefully, of all the sugar I consumed last night. At 6:00 a.m. in Paris, Genevieve is up and lingering over her *petit déjeuner*, her breakfast.

I plug my phone in and navigate to her number on my favorites page. Pressing her contact photo, I marvel at the exponential leaps in technology since the eighties. Lacey and I, weaving pot holders on red plastic looms, would never have dreamed of walking around with phones no bigger than decks of playing cards. If we'd had this instant communication then, would Truman and I have—

"Bonjour? Georgette?"

"*Ah, oui, madame, bonjour. Je suis desolate.* I was adrift in thought."

"Of course, you were. You have a great deal on your mind."

I flop back in my chair. "I do." Though I've called Genevieve to discuss our project, I start by telling her about the sleepover. "And it's just . . . you know, the girls are looking to me for reassurance, and I'm not all that confident myself."

"All will be well, Georgette. Now," she says, brightly *en français*, "I have good news. Five alumnae of Ecole Viardot have agreed to serve as sponsors for your students. They will help orient them to the city, to the culture, inviting them into their homes for meals, taking them shopping, and the like."

My spirits soar. "That is fabulous! And so quickly! How on earth did you—"

At two sharp raps on my door, I sit bolt upright. It's not Mrs. King's soft knock-knock-knock.

"I'll call you back, Genevieve," I chirp into the phone, and I scramble to pull my skirt toward my knees and straighten my jacket. "Yes? Come in, please."

Susan Joshi, an official smile above a pink bouclé ensemble, pauses in the doorway. "Madame Bricker, may we speak with you a moment?" *We?* "Our new finance VP and I have a proposition for you."

My heart bumps around in my chest.

Susan and Truman step into my office. I get to my feet. "Of course. Please come in."

"Hello, Georgie," Truman says pleasantly, his eyes registering on mine. A sheepish Mrs. King appears and grimaces at me from behind them. "Would you care for something to drink, Diet Cokes? Coffee?"

Both Susan and Truman decline, and I indicate the pair of chairs opposite my desk. "Please have a seat."

Susan begins. I cross my legs and swivel my chair thirty degrees in her direction. The unmistakable leafy tang meets my nose. My heart leaps.

And though I gaze intently at Susan, I'm distracted by a fine peripheral slice of broad shoulder, green silk pocket square, and freckled hand on chair arm. Ringless. Is that his right hand or his left? Mentally flipping Truman's image to my side of the desk, I get that it's his left. But some men don't wear wedding rings these days . . .

"With your tenure," Susan is saying, "I thought you'd be the ideal faculty liaison."

I stop the slow swinging of my foot beneath the desk. "Liaison for . . ."

"For Truman's committee," Susan says, eyeing me curiously. "You'd meet with the committee in his office a couple of times a week and then communicate with the faculty.

Truman's committee? I'd imagined communicating with him as a colleague and friend at a comfortable remove, like a satellite with its command center. With blue-eyed temptation personified across a conference table, how am I to stick to the business of saving the school? I'll lose my job and the only home that has ever made me feel safe. Simultaneously, our cell phones sound with an emergency-response alarm. Susan and Truman scan their screens and then dismiss them. I study mine. An Amber Alert. A missing girl. Last seen with a man in a brown pickup where Route 30 intersects Cloverhill Road. *Clover.* I close my eyes. *Clover was still missing. I had to find my father, tell him—*

"Georgie?" Truman is speaking as though from the far end of a Swiss rail tunnel. With clammy hands, I drop my phone and clutch the arms of my chair, pursing my lips against nausea, and seek the position of my wastebasket. I cannot throw up in front of the college president and Truman Parker. My trembling legs ache to lunge to the window and fling it wide.

"Georgie? What can we do?" Susan is asking. Truman stands and extends his hands as though to catch a ball.

And then Mrs. King is there. She takes one look at my face and hurries around the desk. Taking my arm, she guides me toward the door.

When she has shepherded me to the padded bench in the ladies' room, I am cognizant of nothing but the tide of precious breath. Mrs. King returns with a kitchen towel, dampens it at the sink, and then holds it against my cheeks, my forehead. "A panic attack, honey?"

My secretary's loving voice, like my mother's, never fails to bring whatever emotion I'm suppressing to the surface. Tears well in my eyes at the thought of my mother getting wind of the college news and worrying about me. I take a mile-deep breath. "Yes," I confess, a heap of misery, "after so many years! I had one in Huck's yesterday, picking up the pizzas." I close my eyes on that image, and Mrs. King presses a tissue into my hand. "And now it's happened in front of administrators." I spin around to gape at my secretary. "Oh, no! Are they still here?"

"No, they left when I told them you had a touch of flu."

"I'm so ashamed," I wail. How will I face Truman again?

"They were just concerned about your health. Dr. Joshi said to tell you she'd get back with you. And besides, you know there's no shame in this."

Other than family and Lacey, only Mrs. King knows my anxiety issues. She has weathered near-panic episodes with me twice before: the first time, when my mother was in the hospital and I couldn't go to her, and the other—before webinars—when the president asked me to speak at a conference in Chicago. Mrs. King was there with paper lunch sacks for me to breathe in, herbal teas to sip, and inventive excuses to dole out. She would never betray my confidence.

The bench groans as my secretary lowers herself to sit. We fall into a companionable silence. If only my grandmother had been as sweet and understanding as she. When my mother and brother and I had moved into her home, she'd insisted we sweep what happened to my father under the rug and never speak of it. But I always felt I teetered around the edges of a sinkhole.

It was not until I enrolled as a first-year student at the University of Virginia that I suffered my initial panic attack. That one sent me—certain I was dying—lurching into the emergency clinic, my palms leaving marks on the sliding glass doors. The attending physician diagnosed first-time-away-from-home anxiety. At his mention of home, memories of my father's death had slipped specter-like through the transom of my mind. Ushering them out again, I lost my opportunity to insist that homesickness wasn't my problem. The doctor clicked his Bic, closed my file, and sent me back to the dorms with a vial of mild tranquilizers. A week later and blessedly distracted by rigorous coursework, I'd flushed them down a toilet. But my unexamined anxiety and remote nature remained.

Now, I purse my lips and blow out a great gust of stale breath. "I guess I need help."

"Let me make you an appointment with a psychiatrist." I've never talked about my problem with a professional. Maybe a shrink is what I need. "There are all sorts of medicines for anxiety," Mrs. King goes on. "I see ads for them every night. While I'm watching my John-and-Marlena show, you know, my *Days of Our Lives* recording."

In spite of my chagrin, I chuckle and then blow my nose with a honk. I lay my head on my secretary's shoulder. "I thank God for you, Mrs. King."

"I thank God for you, too, Madame," she says, rubbing small circles on my back.

"Go ahead and make the appointment. I have too much to do for this shit."

If it's a good idea, go ahead and do it.
It's much easier to apologize than it is
to get permission.
—Grace Hopper

CHAPTER
SIX

The following Monday morning in the dining hall, the history department secretaries gather at a table to celebrate a birthday. They pass around cards opened by a gal with a polka-dot gift sack and giggle at the punchlines. Though my mind has been a perpetual storm since Truman Parker hit town, *vie continue*—life goes on—at Willa Cather College. Along with the thawing hem of the lake, the emotional weather has grown milder. Only occasional flurries of nervous talk dampen our cleft in the world.

I sit alone at my favorite high-top, glancing over the rim of my cup—past the birthday party—to the entrance again. Lina has overslept. Neither Susan nor Truman have made an appearance. My colleague and friend Truman, who was concerned for my health, and who hasn't given another thought to the scene I made in my office. I hope.

The secretaries cheer over a birthday card with Michelle Obama's picture on the front. One eye on the door, I check my class notes—my least favorite freshman class is this morning—and twine a stray curl at the nape of my neck around my finger.

At my hair appointment, my hairdresser Rhonda had sighed and run her fingers through my hair a final time. "You should wear your hair down more. This chestnut shade is luscious."

I'd shrugged. "I don't know . . . the French twist is just me. You know, I'm Madame."

"You're also a beautiful woman."

I'd smiled and thanked her reflection in the mirror, and I'd felt beautiful. And at bedtime that night, with my hair tumbling around my shoulders, I'd dropped my cotton nightgown over my curves, desire ringing in my core as it hadn't in a long time. I wanted a man to tell me I am beautiful.

Now, my phone shimmies against the table. Lacey's texted me a good morning cartoon, a fat orange cat lying on a kitchen counter and sipping a martini.

I respond with a "Too funny," and before pressing send, I add a "Because I know you are dying to know, no, I haven't seen Truman again."

The phone still in my hand, my email alert buzzes: Truman Parker. My cup clanks into the groove in its saucer. I click on the subject line: Meeting Today?

Hello, Georgie,

I hope you're feeling much better. If you're in the office today, would you buzz by? I have some info re: your study abroad initiative.

"Buzz by." Like, "Pass the salt, would you?"

Lina's headed my way, balancing dishes on a cafeteria tray. She tosses a fluting Italian birthday greeting to the celebrating secretary as I read Truman's email twice more. He signs it "Best": a notch above "Sincerely" and two above "Cordially." Reaching my table, Lina removes a fruit plate and cup and saucer from the tray. "Sorry I'm late, Georgie."

"You're fine," I say, drily, "I've only been waiting an hour."

"You have not; I know better."

I smile, despite my case of the jits. "Guess who I just got an email from," I say, brandishing my phone screen.

Lina reads it, her lips forming his words, and then says, "Okay, rock and roll. Go see him at noon and get it over with."

A refrain of my tiff with Lacey circles back to mind. I'm not spineless. I'm Madame Bricker. My classes this morning conclude at a quarter to twelve.

I pluck the reddest, plumpest strawberry from her plate. "You're right," I say, standing. "I've got this."

◦◦◦

My last morning class: freshmen, who today look anything but. They're slouched in their seats and stifling yawns: too much weekend.

But I'm still riding a conviction high. "Pop quiz time: five questions."

Amid muffled groans and one unprecedented eye roll (that I elect not to confront unless it is repeated), I smile pleasantly and direct them to turn to page forty.

After class, I jot a note to Laurel Cross on a premade slip, asking her to come and see me.

At 11:51, I'm striding across campus in my coat and cheery raspberry scarf. Passing the Find Your Fierce banner, I give it a brisk salute.

I halt in my tracks, looking at my hand as if it has just appeared at the end of my wrist.

Where did that come from?

But I know perfectly well. Truman Parker. Like kudzu, he's invaded the painstakingly ordered landscape of my life. I tug the brass handle of the admin building door. Our board chairman Beau Duffy is on his way out. He stops and thanks me for my study abroad idea. Just the bolstering I need: word of my work has reached the board.

I take a left at the first hall. Despite my coat and scarf, I feel naked. My eyes fly to my torso. I stop outside Susan's door. What have I forgotten? My binder! I sailed out of my office without a compass: my notes or anything to write on. But I'd sure made time to put on fresh lipstick.

A sheet of paper on the door of the next office with a computer-printed TRUMAN PARKER catches my eye. Someone has tacked it to the conference room door as a temporary nameplate. Slinking toward it, I tap my knuckles against the textured privacy glass.

I'm composing a professional smile, while behind the glass, a shape grows tall. Truman opens the door. He is alone in the windowless space and gives me a transient smile. "Hello. How are you feeling?"

Meeting his dazzling eyes, I'm reminded how hideous I must have looked in the throes of the panic attack when he'd last seen me, and hope he's taken a mental leapfrog over the image. I remove my abruptly blazing coat and scarf. "Hello. Much better, thank you. How are you?"

"Good, good," he says heartily. But it's noon, and his face is as worn as if he's spent the morning pushing and shoving on a trading floor. He nudges the door as if to close it but leaves it ajar, buttons his jacket with his ringless left hand, and pulls out a chair from a place next to the head of the long table. "Please, have a seat."

"Thank you," I say, inhaling a whisper of what must be grassy vetiver shaving cream and sink into the leather chair as he seats himself at the head of the table. Though his laptop is front and center, the mounds of old folders on the table beyond it resemble the Blue Ridge.

After grappling with it all morning, I've decided I won't be the first to mention our past, so I'm dying to hear his first words. Lowering his chin at me, the ghost of his old grin plays across his mouth. But as high heels begin clipping along the hall, his eyes zip to the slice of open door—where Susan passes by—and he presses his lips together. He turns his attention to a copy of the report I'd given Susan and slips a pair of brown plastic glasses from his breast pocket, puts them on. The breath escapes me like the air from a leftover party balloon. "Your proposal was very well written. I'm anxious to hear what you've done since the meeting," he says, his voice too loud.

A dart pierces my heart. So, I guess we won't be friends. We'll just be colleagues who once pledged undying love to each other beside a river. I paste on a professional smile. "I appreciate that. I've been talking with Genevieve Beaulieu in Paris about a reciprocal system for our students."

A hint of a smile animates his face again at the mention of Genevieve's name. But his phone burrs. He picks it up, and the smile vanishes as quickly as a bird from a branch. "Let me take this. One second," he says, raising an index finger. He holds the phone to his cheek and utters a brusque, "Yes?"

Truman responds to the caller as though his every word has to pay a toll before it passes his lips. I pass the time by breathing through my nose and admiring the relative tautness of his chin and neck. His freckled face is clean-shaven. He had just started getting his whiskers the last time I saw him. Short red-gold and silver hairs sprinkle his earlobe and the back of his neck above his stiff white color. I'm mentally replacing his gray hair with a pelt of his former strawberry blond when he says a terse goodbye into the cell and drops it to his leather binder. Before the screen on his phone goes to black, I catch sight of the name Anne. Who is Anne? I start as he says, "Sorry about that." He looks at me again, but his eyes are as impenetrable as hieroglyphs. "Please. Tell me about the reciprocal program."

I tell him the news and say how pleased I am that the Ecole Viardot alumnae have nurturing spirits. While in Paris, these young women will be four thousand miles from home. I, of all people, know how much feeling safe and comfortable means.

Truman's lips curl. My stomach flips: here we go! But at a lift of conversation in the hall, he blinks, looks away, and reaches for a folder. "Here's what I wanted to discuss with you. As I'm sure you're aware, the organization and oversight of study abroad programs aren't without risks. We have to be pro-active. The health and security of students—on both ends of the program—is a concern, not only in the study abroad office, or at this point," he tilts his head to me, "in your office. A high percentage of claims are made to the governing body, United Organizers, each year by plaintiffs involved in their programs." He picks up his paper cup and sips at coffee I'm sure has grown cold. He nudges a page in front of me, and we look at it together. His breath stirs the tendrils of hair in front of my ears. With the tip of his pen, he indicates a graph. "Most claims or reports," he goes on, "are made concerning sexual misconduct, injury, or illness, with sexual misconduct responsible for over half." *Sexual. Can we say the word a couple more times?*

Though I'd been vaguely aware of concerns of this nature, Truman has obviously done his homework. And, as advertised, he's a big-picture guy. At once, I feel like I've stuck my neck out without considering all the technicalities. I clench my hands in my lap. But Truman doesn't seem to be judging my perfor-mance, only presenting the facts. As he continues, I draw my bottom lip between my teeth. Why did Susan choose him? Of all the consultants in the country?

"We need to go ahead and draw up a set of guidelines for the program, as well as appoint other administrators."

Other administrators. The scope and scale of the project looms over me again like a storm cloud. We can't afford to hire anyone else, and I don't have time to administer something of this magnitude by myself.

My stomach growls, and I press a forearm to it.

He laughs softly. "You know what? It is lunchtime." My empty stomach fusses. *He'll ask me to lunch!* But taking up his phone, he thumbs across the screen, pulling up a calendar. "What's your class load . . . uh, Tuesday the twentieth? Do you have time that afternoon to start a draft?"

I curse myself again for showing up as unprepared as a star-ry-eyed freshman and try and make a mental picture of my calendar. "I believe I can do it at one thirty."

Truman pokes at his phone. "Got it."

The chairman's face appears around the door. Drumming on the frame with his fingers, he looks at Truman. "You ready for our meeting with the finance committee?"

Truman looks at me. "Thank you for your time, Georgie. I really appreciate it."

I push back from the table. A month ago, I would have sooner believed I'd be recruited as a starting pitcher for the Yankees as meet with Truman Parker. Now, I've been alone in a room with the boy whose lips I'd once tried to suck off his face, and we hadn't exchanged a single personal word.

Awash in disappointment, I stand, reach for my coat, and put my answer on autopilot. "You're welcome, and thank you." I regard the chairman as his gaze moves between Truman and me. It's February, yet his blue Oxford collar is stained with sweat. *What's up with him?* I extend my palm, indicating Truman and his folder mountains. "The study abroad program initiative is in good hands."

⚬⥿⚬

I make my way to the foyer, where one of the few remaining custodians is dusting the gilt-framed alumnae portraits. At once, a brainstorm sets my anxiety over Truman's aloofness to a low simmer. The alumnae are our most generous benefactors, women who have gone on to estimable careers in business, the arts, the law. The alumnae value their WCC educations as unique and highly personalized.

The alumnae are the answer. *Why hasn't our board tapped into this? Are they that laissez-faire?* My thoughts backstep to the turbulent January faculty meeting and Sawyer Hays's deeply tanned face. I haven't seen him on campus since then. Shouldn't our CFO be working 24-7 with the chairman and Susan to get us out of this mess?

I quicken my step.

Back in my office, I flip through former student files. Though the younger faculty don't bother keeping hard copies of documents these days—Man-Bun's office down the hall is a Spartan's quarters—it's comforting for me to do some things the old-school way. Following Madame Beaulieu's example from French class, I present a French award each year to the most diligent freshman. I flip through the Ps, and there she is, my first winner: Elizabeth Pattison, class of 1998.

I open the file folder. Elizabeth's freshman photo—her smile achingly young and earnest—is clipped to pages of our correspondence. Elizabeth Pattison Lofton has design studios in Richmond, Atlanta, and Dallas. Just last month, her new line of Le Fleur tableware was featured in both *Southern Living* and *Vanity Fair*.

I take the folder to my desk and open the paper-wrapped sandwich I'd picked up at Antonia's. Like a perky terrier who's sniffed out a treat, Mrs. King appears in my doorway. "Ooh, the Bikini Panini? Where's mine?"

I use my napkin. "You know I'd have brought you one."

"Just kidding. I brought leftovers today." She walks to the window and pokes a finger into the soil of my rabbit's foot fern. "Don't let this dry out again."

"Yes, ma'am," I say around a bite of sandwich.

Mrs. King dips her chin at me. "I called the new psychia-trist's office." My stomach lurches at the word "psychiatrist." "Her name is Dr. Chu. She moved into the same office building as Chairman Duffy's pediatric practice. His nurse told me. The doctor can see you March 1." A piece of avocado drops onto my blouse. Letting a rare curse fly, I retrieve the green blob and futilely dab at the oily spot it's made with my napkin. But the opening in the doctor's schedule is a sign: this is supposed to happen.

Before answering her, I twist the cap off my water and take a long swig. "Okay . . . thank you so much." I make note of the appointment on my calendar. "Oh, do you remember Elizabeth Pattison?"

"I do. I talked to her last week."

I gape at her. "You did?"

"She called me for my Hummingbird Cake recipe.

I laugh. "Mrs. King, you are a bird on this earth."

She grins and rises, then looks at me over her glasses. "What are you up to?"

"I've had an inspiration. I'm thinking of soliciting help from the alums. I thought I'd call my French award winners first."

"Great idea, chickie. I'll buzz you with Elizabeth's number."

"Merci."

Mrs. King moves off to search her big honking Rolodex. Returning to my computer, I create a file: Rescuing Willa Cather. My choice of verb takes me by surprise. Is "rescuing" too strong, an extreme notion at this point? After all, it's been weeks since we've heard bad news. I pull more files from the cabinet and compose a list of five former students.

I lean back in my chair and gaze out the window at the foot-hills—as sharp-edged and brilliant today as though cut from blue felt—and consider my course of action. I buzz my secretary. "Hey. Did you say anything to Elizabeth Pattison about our debt?"

"Nope. I thought it best that I not. And she didn't mention it."

"Good job. Thanks." I press end, wondering who has heard our news aside from the locals.

Should I get Susan's approval about approaching the gals on my list? Chill creeps my spine at the thought of what keeping secrets cost me in the past. I reach for my sweater. *Should I run it by Truman?* My mind returns to our meeting, his patent fatigue, his professional reserve.

I flick the concern aside. The other's efforts could fail. *What if this is mine alone to do?* My daily rationalization swoops in right on time: if the alumnae are already aware of the debt, my outreach will be a nonissue.

I'm doing this. Checking the time, I leap to my feet and begin packing my things.

With the tête-à-tête with Laurel Cross on my mind, I turn out the lights and pour the last of the bottle of water into the fern.

Courage doesn't always roar; sometimes it's the
quiet voice at the end of the day whispering,
"I will try again tomorrow."
—Mary Anne Radmacher

CHAPTER
SEVEN

"Madame Bricker!" Elizabeth Pattison returns my call with a birdsong of French: "*Quel plaisir de recevoir de vos nouvelles.* How lovely to hear from you."

Slipping the copy of *Southern Living* magazine from beneath a stack of folders, I turn to the piece on Elizabeth's tablescapes. I laud her success before gently probing, like a dentist with her pick. As I'd suspected, news of our debt has reached her by way of the Atlanta alums, who meet for cocktails each month. When she's caught me up on news of family and former classmates, Elizabeth pauses and then lets go a breath I'd swear stirs the papers on my desk. "Madame. I'm so distressed. How can I help?"

I open with the inchoate study abroad program. In a heartbeat, Elizabeth agrees to be my alumnae point person. Then she adds, "You know . . ." and I can picture her knit brows. "Our twentieth reunion is coming up; Sloane Smith is spearheading it. I'll reach out to her. Instead of donating benches or something to the campus, maybe our class could fund your program." My breath leaves me. Through grateful tears, I strew thanks like a handful of luxe bath salts into the phone. Elizabeth assures me she'll keep me posted.

Ending the call, I let out a whoop that makes Mrs. King buzz me on the intercom.

"I hope that was a happy outburst."

"It was! Get in here. Elizabeth may have just saved our derriere." I briefly fill my secretary in and then sit back, as she scurries to answer her phone. If this works out, the French program would rocket to new heights. Images of glossy and vibrant brochures dance through my head, until they're tripped up by fear. *What if I had to make a trip to Paris myself? My old doubts resurface: What kind of a French teacher can't get on an airplane and take a selfie with the Eiffel Tower? And what if I've jumped the gun? The program hasn't been officially approved. I could get a knuckle-rapping from the administration. Should I have consulted the alumnae association first?* And then another rationalization arrives, a super-juicy one: *I haven't divulged state secrets, only told a former student an idea.*

Elizabeth is such an accomplished person. And so are a large population of other alums. We should take advantages of opportunities to bring noteworthy alums to visit and interact with our students. Maybe Elizabeth would even like to come and speak to our business majors about her success as an entrepreneur. I make a mental note to mention my idea to Susan.

I turn my attention from alumnae affairs to assess student work, but Truman's blue eyes keep peeking into my mind. The week has blown by like scenery through a car window. Though I've not seen him since our meeting, every redhead on campus has captured my eye and brought to mind his teenaged self. I've imagined him bent over his work in the stuffy conference room, rubbing his weary forehead. Bringing my phone to life, I note the time: five minutes before I meet with Laurel, forty-five before I'm due at Truman's.

UGG boots shuffle along the hall: Laurel's early. I take off my glasses and clean them on the hem of my skirt. But it isn't Laurel. It's Madison and Hollins. They pause in the doorway, their countenances rabbity. Hollins breaks an insufferable silence. "May we see you, Madame?"

"Bien sûr," I say. But my eyes are riveted by yellow slips of paper in their hands.

The girls take seats across from my desk, and Hollins comes out with it. "We hate to have to tell you this, Madame," she says, exchanging a pained look with her roommate, "but we're applying for transfers." She lowers her eyes. "My parents are freaking out."

But Madison's dark eyes implore mine. "Mine are too. They feel like the school might not make it, and I'd end up without a college for senior year."

A clew of inchworms wriggles through my midsection. "Where?" I ask, as if it matters.

"Martha Jefferson College," Hollins says, and Madison nods.

The inchworms stretch and crawl, stretch and crawl. If enrollment plummets, WCC is sunk. Despite my big talk and bravado at the slumber party, it's come to this. "I understand. I do. I'm glad you came to me first."

The girls hand me the slips I'll sign as their advisor. While I take my time attending to them, a tide of soothing thoughts sweeps in: *A few students transferring won't result in the closing of the school. We'll be fine. Our faculty is strong; not a single link weakens the chain. And with the program bolstering, we'll have this thing licked before May.*

My anxiety demon pokes me in the chest: *But what if we don't?*

In the doorway, Laurel's smile catches my eye, but her smile falters as she takes in the other girls, my face. Inclining the slips to Madison and Hollins, I channel my mother's wisdom. "Be prayerful about this."

The girls thank me and, following my gaze to Laurel, turn to spot her and exchange greetings. The three of us rise. My hands make fists on the edge of my desk. "Laurel and I have a meeting now."

"Oh, of course. We should have made an appointment," Madison says. The girls offer up closed-lipped smiles, but their eyes sweep Laurel as they leave the room. When I close the door behind them, a draft brings a whiff of cigarette smoke from Laurel's hair to my nose and a blip of disappointment to my heart.

I move around the desk and collapse into my chair.

"I'm sorry to be late, Madame," Laurel says in melodic French. But her twisting hands belie her tone. "You want to see me about the test?"

Where do I start? Leisurely turning the failed test in my wooden inbox faceup, I lay it before her and let her squirm for a full minute.

Until irritation plucks a hair from my head. "What the hell are you doing smoking?"

She flinches as though I've set off a cherry bomb. "I—I don't know." Then rebellion—a quality I admire in her—flares in her eyes. "It relaxes me. I have a lot on my mind."

That's utter bullshit, I want to say, but I harness my tongue. "You know that nicotine's a stimulant and just death to your lungs."

Laurel examines her fingers. Her nails are chewed, sad little stubs of aqua. The worms form a tight knot. I lean over them, toward Laurel, and make my voice soft. "Honey, you're an athlete. Why would you smoke? What's this about?"

Pinpoints of light appear on her lashes. Wordlessly, she shakes her head. I reach across the desk for her hand, and she takes it with a barely suppressed sob. Tears roll her cheeks. "It's just . . . everything. I'm one raw nerve."

I hold her hand between my palms. "The budget issue has everyone on edge." The skittish quality of the look she gives me tells me there's more to her misery than what's happening with the school. I lift a tissue box from my credenza and incline a white plume. As she takes one and then another, my mind races: *Is it family? A lover? A breakup? Lord, she can't be pregnant. Not my Laurel.* Jerking down a roller shade on that thought, I wait.

Laurel takes a great sniff and scrubs at her eyes with tissue. "A lot of girls are talking about transferring." She cocks her head toward the door. "Is that what Madison and Hollins were doing here?"

I heave an inward sigh. "I can't give out information about other students. But Laurel, I understand that tensions are high, and though I believe such actions are premature, everyone has to do what she thinks is best." I wait again, willing her to confide in me, but her face clicks shut.

I can't force her to tell me. "You've never failed a test before. I'm going to allow you to retake it."

Laurel straightens her spine. "Oui. Merci, Madame."

"Monday. After class." I make note of the retake on my calendar. Laurel forms a ball of the shredded tissue and then aims it for my wastebasket. I follow the clean shot in and smile. "Two points. Two more if you come back and want to talk."

When Laurel has taken off for the library, I take my time gathering my things, making sure I'm prepared to meet with Truman. But my thoughts ricochet to my students. I have to keep my finger on the pulse of morale. I collect my purse, wondering how many others are thinking of transferring.

I take the stairs down and out of the building. "So much for keeping doubt and fear at bay this morning, Georgie Girl," I chide myself aloud. Truman's nickname for me has dropped from my brain to my tongue of its own volition. But it tastes sweet. I want to run to him, to make him the way he was when we he was a boy. I want him to hold me against his chest and comfort me, to tell me it's all going to be okay.

Susan is sitting next to Truman in the conference room. "We're talking about a loss of another sixty—" she says before biting off the end of her sentence as they catch sight of me. We exchange hellos. Truman, his tie askew, moves as if to rise, but I wave him down and pull out my own chair. Another loss? How much debt has the school accrued since the first report? As Susan gathers her things and she and Truman agree to catch up later, I unpack my bag, wondering if it would be out of line to ask. But the image of being handed my derriere by the president is a restraining hand on my shoulder.

As Susan leaves, she turns back for a moment. "By the way, Truman, congratulations on the house."

My heart jolts, my eyes darting to Truman's. "The house?" I can't help myself.

"I bought an old Victorian downtown."

Truman bought a house? The charming blue one on Randolph Street?

"The old Ballentine place," Susan says, her eyes casting me a Heaven-help-him look.

He shrugs. "I figured I'd do some work on it and then flip it, but," he waves a hand over the foothills of folders that have only grown steeper, "the tyranny of the urgent."

As Susan leaves, I open my laptop and compose a pleasant smile. I screw up my courage. "That's my favorite house."

"Is it?" he says, and his eyes scan my face. "It's beautiful on the outside, but the rooms are like rabbit warrens." His blue eyes deepen. "It needs light, new life."

My heart canters. "And you know how to give it that?" My foot begins a slow swing beneath the conference table.

"I'd like to give it a shot." He gives his head a little shake and clears his throat. Abruptly he snares his readers from the table to peer at his computer. The moment lost, I press a palm to my thigh to stop the swinging. Truman gives the keyboard a few brisk taps. His tone is officious: "Ready to start the draft?"

My heart slows to a walk. "Yes. Of course," I say to a file folder on my desktop.

"Want to create a Google doc and then share it with me?"

I navigate to Google, my heart sinking. Apparently, he'll to stick to business again. "Yes."

Two hours later, the first draft of the study abroad program is complete. I take my dozenth peripheral peek at Truman. He rubs his forehead. His freckled jaw is clenched, and his shoulders are inches lower, as though yoked to a plow. But through his jaded professional veneer, I glimpse the boy I first loved.

I touch his sleeve gently. "Want to table this for now?"

Truman sighs and straightens. He gives me a smile. "Yeah, let's do that. Thank you, Georgie." He consults his watch, and his red-gray brows rise. "We still need to write up your liaison report for the faculty meeting." In my preoccupation with his discomfort, I'd forgotten about the progress report I'd agreed to share at faculty meetings.

I smile. "Oh, we can do that quick."

He punches at his keyboard and turns the laptop around, so I can share his view of the screen.

Scanning the list, I marvel at what he's accomplished with other committees. I create a new document. "Do you mind reading the list to me?"

"Sure."

Whenever he pronounces hard consonants, his breath wafts to me. It's grown stale, but it humanizes him again. I dip a hand into my tote for the extra bottle of water I've tucked away. "Want a water?"

Truman rewards me with a grin and a "thanks." I swish my own mouth with a sip from my bottle. He gulps water and stretches his neck side to side. My fingers long to knead it. Instead I glue my fingers to the home keys.

We're finishing up when brisk raps on the door freeze us. Truman leans back and exhales as though he's spent twenty-four hours filibustering.

Susan, wearing a raincoat, opens the door. "Knock-knock." Is it raining outside this room that knows no day or night? She gives us a steely grimace. "Our Classics prof has just given his notice." Man-bun! The little pisher has jumped camp. There was a weak link in our chain! "He's concerned about our situation and has taken a position with UVA." She looks at me. "Georgie, I'm sending an email about a midmorning department meeting tomorrow; we need to circle the wagons."

I nod, my lips forming a hard line. First students and now faculty! Man-bun. Defecting to my alma mater. What if more faculty bail? Would admin be able to replace them? What happens to Foreign Language?

I type the last items on the list while Truman quizzes Susan about a science department report. Truman and I pack our things and walk out with the president and into a chilly drizzle.

I make straight for Antonia's to meet Lina. We're alone in the café, except for my neighbor, the grumpy math teacher, whose back forms a comma over a stack of tests. The tatt-sleeved sophomore behind the counter gazes at her cell phone, sighing and grinning the way one does when in the throes of a new relationship.

I spear a cherry tomato. "The man is an enigma, Lina! He hasn't said a word about our intimate yearlong relationship. It's maddening. And I have to see him all the time."

Her lips twist. "Well, why don't *you* broach the subject?" Grumpy shuffles his papers, rapping the edge of the stack on the table. *Whap! Whap!* Lina casts a frown his way.

"Well, he's like . . . my superior right now; I don't want to look unprofessional. Maybe that's all it is with him; he's trying to be professional." I sit back with a huff, pick up my iced tea, and survey the quad through the plate glass window. Truman strides the walk toward the parking lot. "*Et voilà*," I say with a flip of my hand.

Lina follows my gaze and grins. She leans back and studies me. "So what do you want to happen?"

"I don't know." The two of us watch as Truman grows small and winks from sight. He must be headed home to that lovely house. "Lina! He bought the old Ballentine place. I can't believe I forgot to tell you."

"You're kidding! Why would he buy a house? He's only here for a year."

I give her a wide-eyed shrug. "We did have this odd little exchange today . . . I found myself like super . . . pashed on him for a minute those damned eyes of his—while he was telling me about the house. He said it needed light, needed opening up. It was like he talking about me. I thought we were flirting . . . but then he just shut it down."

"I'm sorry, *cara*. I know that stung."

I chew a layered bite of kale, bacon, and cucumber and watch the sophomore behind the counter take a pouty selfie. "Don't you think it's just weird that he hasn't mentioned the past?"

"I don't know the man. But, yes, it's strange."

I nod like a bobblehead. "Right?" I stab at my salad. "And though Susan has no idea about our history, it's uncanny that we're on this *intime* committee of two." I position my knife and fork across my salad bowl. "I don't know if I can handle it."

"You can handle it. You're a pro. Besides, once the study abroad program is mapped out and approved, the meetings are over, aren't they?"

I sigh, the image of the calendar, the year, stretching before me. "I suppose. But I'm still faculty liaison to his committee."

"Maybe those things can be handled by email."

"Maybe they can." I survey the quad again. "And it's only a year, right?"

"Right." Lina reaches for her raincoat. "I must flee. I am woefully behind on grading."

I push myself to my feet with a groan. "Me too."

The rain has stopped. But as I plod home, my tote grows heavier with each step: two sections of essays and three of tests. I've never been this behind on grading. I can't allow this . . . attraction to Truman, this jonesing for him to distract me from my work.

More than ever, I must be Madame.

The venerable Madame. Unsinkable, like Molly Brown. If she survived the *Titanic*, I can survive a cruise with Truman Parker.

⊙⊕⊙

Propped in bed, the essays graded, I thumb the TV remote. No new *Outlander* episodes until November. The Droughtlander has me bummed. No Jamie to ogle. No escapist adventure. Tired of scrolling, I settle on *Something's Gotta Give* and drop the remote. I've seen the movie enough times that I can mark tests while keeping one eye on it. Diane Keaton's character finding true love, at her age. My traitorous thoughts sliding to Truman, I picture him in paint-streaked shorts and a T-shirt, sweaty and swinging a sledgehammer at the cramped walls of the Victorian. But my mind rebels at the image; he's much too stuffy. From a wealthy and powerful family, he probably has no shortage of perpetual debutantes with their eyes on him. I push my glasses up my nose. Why would he be interested in a bespectacled forty-five-year-old with crow's feet? I shake my head.

We're colleagues; he's made that clear.

Wondering if Susan's sent an email about the morning meeting, I grope the covers for my cell. "Where's my phone?" I ask Voltaire. Lifting his head, the cat stretches and relocates to the foot of the bed, uncovering the cell. "What a clever boy."

Two emails in my inbox: Susan Joshi: "Dept. Meeting"; and Truman Parker: "Dinner Friday."

My heart boomerangs inside my chest. Dinner with Truman?

I open Susan's email first. The meeting's at nine thirty. Check. In no mood to read the rest: Man-bun's fine year of service to the school. The enfant terrible. I close the message. I milk the thrill of opening Truman's note and lay my phone on the bedside table, as though it's a Fabergé egg. I pad to the kitchen, pour a tall glass of wine, and snare a round of wax-wrapped cheese from the fridge.

Returning to the bed, I punch up my pillows, settle in, and say to Voltaire, "*Allons-y.* Let's go." With a flourish, I poke open Truman's note.

Georgie,

Thinking of you and wanted to thank you for your time this afternoon. I'm encouraged with our progress. If you're free, I'd like to take you to dinner Friday night.

Truman

My chest rushes with exhilaration. Thinking of you! But is it a date? Or does he want to celebrate our progress?

I read the note through three more times and draw a different conclusion each time.

Finally, I compose a reply, following his pattern.

Truman,

Thank you for thinking of me and for your kindness. I'm also encouraged by our progress. I'm free Friday night and would enjoy having dinner with you.

Signing it with a simple *Georgie,* I push send and hold my breath, hoping he will ping me back. I drink my wine and watch Diane Keaton and Jack Nicholson in the kitchen in their pajamas. I look down at my ink-stained cotton nightgown. What does Truman sleep in? The phone chimes, sending my heart back to the racetrack.

I hear The Red Fox Inn has the best food in town. If it's a place you enjoy, I'll make a reservation. Pick you up at 7:00. I'm looking forward to it. T.

He's done his homework. Does picking me up mean it's a date? Imagining the two of us toasting our success by candle-light, I reply.

Seven is good. I'm looking forward to it too. Thank you. G.

When I've turned out the light and slipped into the embrace of my comforter, I drift.

But an hour later, I'm staring at a new crack in the ceiling and engaged in a full-on mental debate over Truman Parker's intentions.

And my own.

There is communion of more than our bodies
when bread is broken and wine drunk.
—M. F. K. Fisher

CHAPTER
EIGHT

F riday night finally arrives. Truman fills my little porch.
"Hello, Georgie," he says. His eyes flit over my emerald silk
tunic and pants. "You look very pretty."

My words sail out high-pitched and foreign. "Thank you,
won't you come in?"

He smiles as he crosses the threshold. My eyes skim his navy
blazer and the French blue shirt that's no competition for his
eyes. My nose scores another grassy trace of vetiver. "Would you
like a glass of wine?"

"Please. Red?"

"I have a nice cabernet franc."

"Perfect." He slides his hands into the pockets of his khaki
slacks and follows me into the living room. I busy myself at the
sideboard, opening the bottle and wrestling a package of cocktail napkins open, while Truman surveys the space. "What a
beautiful home," he says. He studies the Herend porcelain collection on my mantle and picks up a bunny, turning it over
in his hands. I wish I had an intriguing story to tell of how I'd
picked up this-or-that piece in Paris or Hungary or Florence.

The truth—all of them were gifts from friends—is lovely, but doesn't make for jaw-dropping conversation.

But Truman Parker's presence in my home is exotic, like a gloved Louis XIV turning up to appraise the French-reproduction furniture I bought in Foxfield or inherited from my grandmother. Though I tremble inside, my grip is steady as I hand him his glass and napkin. "Please. Sit."

We make ourselves comfortable, and then Truman raises his glass. "To your hard work."

Though the sentiment falls short of the one I'd had in mind, I smile and incline my glass. "And yours. Cheers."

He takes a sip and sets his glass down on a lacquered table. "So, you've lived here twenty-five years?"

"I have. The years have zoomed by," I say, making an airplane out of my hand and sending it off.

Voltaire slinks down the hall, his nose and tail a-twitch. "Here's Voltaire coming to check you out."

Truman follows my gaze and smiles. "Voltaire? Pretty cat." "You like cats?"

"I do, I guess. My mother wouldn't allow pets in the house when Trask and I were growing up. But my sons had a dog." He humphs a little laugh. "A golden retriever. Chewbarka. Helluva dog."

I grin at the name, but my heart skips a beat at the abrupt information drop. He has sons. He did marry. Had his brother Trask—once a Vietnam soldier—survived the war? And his mother, the ever-elegant Eleanor. Is she the same snooty socialite I met once?

Voltaire arches his back under Truman's hand. I sip my wine, watching him rub the cat along his length. "He likes you."

Truman grins. His teeth are white and straight, though one top incisor has canted slightly. The imperfection adds to his authenticity. I'm emboldened. "So, you have sons?"

He looks into his glass. "Twins. Juniors this year at George Wythe College in Mountainsburg."

"Ah, they're nearby." Twin boys. I picture them as catalog models, tall, blue-eyed like their father, and athletic. "My advisees date boys from GW; I wonder if they know them."

"They very well may." Truman consults his watch. "We'd better get going. I made the reservation for eight."

"Let me just grab a wrap." I fetch my pashmina from where I draped it over the banister, my thoughts spiraling. *Are the boys what brought Truman back to Virginia? Is he close to them? What about their mother? Who is she? Would she approve of him taking a woman to dinner, even if it's a non-date?*

Moments later, we step from the front door. I wish Truman could see the pink dianthus and cascading jasmine that will explode in a couple of months, smell their heavenly fragrance. At once, I'm reminded of the honeysuckle vines at The Browning School, of home.

My breath hitches. What's made me think of Browning as home?

This is my home. As if there could ever be another. As if I could leave here.

He pauses beside my white coupe, his eyes glinting. "That's one sweet ride. Is it new?"

"Nope. It's a 2008."

"Really?"

The bump-a-thump of Bob Marley heralds a little blue car cruising along my street. The driver's brown face turns toward me. Laurel! She smiles and raises a hand. But as her eyes flick to Truman, the hand falls. Her eyes flash. She slaps the visor down and speeds away. "It's in perfect condition," he goes on, oblivious. "How many miles you have on it?"

As we move toward his silver Range Rover in the street,

I'm puzzling out Laurel's behavior and answer before thinking, "Um, ten thousand, I think."

His brows rise two inches. "Ten thousand miles in ten years?"

"I . . . I don't drive much. You know, I live where I work," I say neutrally. I'm not ready for him to know how close to home I stay.

Truman opens the passenger door of the Rover for me, his brow furrowed. "Amazing."

We pull from the curb. He slips a pair of black-framed glasses from his breast pocket and slides them on. We make our way through campus and into town. "It's weird riding with you," I shyly say, as an old Joni Mitchell song comes on the radio. "The last time we saw each other, we didn't have our licenses."

"Wow, you're right." At a traffic light, he turns his smile on me. I'm losing myself in how sexy he looks in the glasses when a van behind us lays on its horn. Both of us jump a foot. Truman shoots a pissed look into the rearview mirror and guns it beneath the green light. Two blocks later, he blindsides me. "So. You got your undergrad degree and master's at UVA, and you taught in Charlottesville before taking the position with Willa Cather. And you never married." I turn to gape at his smug smile. He shrugs a shoulder. "I asked about you the first day."

I feel like I've been assessed by an employer on a résumé I haven't submitted. He can't be bothered to walk down memory lane with me, yet he had time to piece together my bio? My temper rises like heartburn as Truman corners the car into the gravel drive of The Red Fox. "You did, did you?"

"I did."

The Rover crunches toward a valet slumped on a stool. Catching sight of it, the young man hops to his feet and opens my door. I step down, toss the pashmina over a high shoulder, and head for the door. Truman catches up with me on the brick walk. He whisks off his glasses and offers me a sheepish look. "Forgive me for that? I guess my flirting is a little rusty."

I stare at him. "You were flirting," I say flatly. "And this a date." Another couple approaches the entrance, and we step to the side.

Truman exhales. "I thought so." He works his shoulders in his coat. "I mean, I wanted it to be a date."

I wait until the door closes behind the couple. "Then why have you been so damned formal and remote all this time, all those hours in the conference room?"

He looks at his polished loafers and raises his eyes to mine. "I was trying to be professional. Susan was right next door. She and the board have placed a great deal of trust in me. You're her star professor. They didn't hire me to . . ." He shakes his head. "Listen, I'm sorry. I'm working my ass off."

"Well, so am I," I say hotly.

He raises his hands and lightly takes my upper arms. His touch sends my heart swooping. "Georgie, it's more than that. I was afraid I'd make a fool out of myself, if you weren't . . . interested in me." He drops his hands. "You were formal too. Does the guy still have to make the first move?"

Mollified, I purse my lips. And then a grin has its way with them. "Why don't we start over?"

He returns the grin and peers ostentatiously at his watch. "Let's start now."

Though it's too cool to dine outside on the flagstone terrace, the hostess—whose day job is shampoo tech at my beauty salon—seats us by a window overlooking the sprawling grounds, where a thousand twinkle lights nestle in the trees. The hostess hands us our menus and checks Truman out. He studies the wine list as though he'll be quizzed on it later. I sip my water, wondering how long it will take for news of Madame Bricker's dinner with the financial consultant to make it to the salon and therefore the town. Would Susan and the board frown on our seeing each other? A wisp of fear whooshes into my chest. Is it possible that we could lose our jobs?

Astrud Gilberto's "Fly Me to Brazil" drifts from the overhead speakers as Truman orders the wine. He turns his smile on me, and I exhale the fear about our jobs in a great tide; my fear won't ruin a lovely evening. He surveys the room: candlelight flickering on exposed brick, the ceiling beamed with reclaimed barnwood, slate floors and fresh flowers. "Really nice," he says, and he opens his menu. "I love French food. What's your favorite here?"

"Well, the Madeira-glazed scallops are superb," I say, secure on familiar turf and pointing at the second entrée. "And the lobster risotto is to die for." What I'm dying for is for him to tell me about his marriage.

When the wine arrives and we've placed our orders, he asks, "What's your favorite spot in Paris, Madame Bricker?"

Distress travels my limbs. My Breathe bracelet clanks against my knife. I push the cuff up my arm, my thoughts leaping. He was surprised by the low mileage on my car. But he doesn't know I don't leave town. Or the full extent of my anxiety. Everyone assumes my knowledge of Paris stems from firsthand experience. Only my family and closest friends know the truth. I can't recall anyone ever challenging my finely wrought, book-taught facade.

Closing my eyes, I swallow back dread. At the touch of his hand on mine, they snap wide. His expression is tender and at once as familiar as the topography of my own face. "What is it?" he asks.

A waiter arrives to refill our water glasses. Ignoring him, Truman gives my hand a little squeeze. My eyes dart to the blazing-red exit sign. "Look at me, Georgie."

I do and pitch my voice low. "Truman, I've never been to

Paris. I don't fly. I don't . . . travel. I haven't left Foxfield in years."

There, I've said it. My pulse pounds as I wait for his reaction.

His lips part. He probes my eyes. I start counting to ten in French and reach six. "But what about your family?" he says.

"They come to see me. Lacey too. I've suffered anxiety my whole adult life."

He runs his thumb across the peaks of my knuckles, east to west. He looks at me, his eyes giving off not pity or judgment, only concern. "I'm sorry. I didn't know."

"An amuse-bouche/mouth pleaser from the chef," our waiter announces, and he flourishes two tiny plates. Truman lets go of my hand and resituates his wine glass. My napkin falls to the floor. Torn between relief and regret at sharing my most personal truth with him, I want to tunnel up his sleeve, inch my way to his chest, hide myself inside his shirt.

The waiter arranges the plates in front of us as though designing a set and retrieves my napkin. "I'll bring you another," he says, sweeping the linen behind his back as if it's stained with something repulsive.

Truman gives me a small smile as the waiter returns and ceremoniously whisks a fresh napkin across my lap. "Where's your brother now?" he asks, blessedly changing the subject and returning my heart rate to a near-normal rhythm.

I take a sip of wine. "Ron's an architect, a home builder in Charleston."

His eyes lighten. "Really. Ron. Funny how when you haven't seen someone in years, they stay the same in your memory. I picture him as a four-year-old."

"I know what you mean."

Picking up our forks, we sample the chef's creation of foie gras, figs, and apricot and pronounce it delicious.

"And your mom?" Revived by the first bites of food, I tell

Truman about my mother going back to college when we moved back to South Carolina, how she worked as a librarian at Ron's elementary school to support us and later remarried. "Hey, good for her. I loved your mom."

My chest rushes with warmth. I've told him the truth about my life, and neither of us sprinted for the door. Has intuition kept him from mentioning what happened to my father and possibly upsetting me? Does he still think about that terrible night? "Tell me about your family," I say lightly.

He stiffens. "My parents are alive and well in Atlanta."

O-kay. Let's move on. "What about Trask?" I ask. "You'd just gotten the word he was coming home from Vietnam."

"He did." Truman looks into the middle distance for a moment before meeting my eyes. "When he came back to the states, he was hospitalized for a long time. I expected to talk to him. Man, I couldn't wait to hear about his experiences, you know? But he didn't speak for weeks. Literally. I kept thinking he'd talk to me even if to no one else. He'd just sit there, sometimes with these soundless tears rolling down his face. He was my big tough brother, a war hero, and all he could do was cry."

A gob of grief has formed in my throat. "Oh, Truman."

"But he came around eventually." He looks at me levelly. "Therapy is a good thing. People get better."

I squirm as the waiter delivers our entrées and gratefully tuck into my risotto. Truman talks about Trask's battle with PTSD and his work with the Veterans Administration. I sip my wine. A Carly Simon song soars. Whether from the confession, the food, the wine, or the music, I relax. Truman wipes his lips with his napkin, sits back, and studies me. "You became a French teacher, like you planned. I remember how you loved Madame Beaulieu. It's cool that you're still friends."

"I know! I love her. It's been a wonderful relationship. But what about you? How did you end up in finance? You wanted to be an English teacher."

He seems to withdraw to the back of his mind for a minute, his eyes tracing the lines of his placemat. He rests his elbows on the table and makes a steeple against his lips with his index fingers. "Georgie . . . It's not easy for me to share my feelings, to talk intimately."

My stomach flutters at the word "intimate." "I'm sorry."

"No. Don't be. I married badly. It burned my heart at the stake." He butters a piece of bread but holds it aloft without taking a bite.

I'm stunned by the way he's plunged ahead. "Who?" I sound like a distressed owl. "I mean, who did you marry?"

Truman looks at his bread as though it's grown moldy and lays it back on his plate. "Anne Emerson Callicot, the daughter of my father's business partner." *Anne. The name on his phone.* "I was about to graduate from Emory and had told my parents I'd applied for grad school to earn my MFA in teaching. By then, it had become clear to my father that his firstborn, Trask, wasn't stable enough to join the firm, so he had set his sights on me. I was lying on the sofa in my apartment one afternoon, nursing a beer, watching a Braves' game. He called me from his Buckhead skyscraper." Truman stares through the expanse of windows, the reflection from the glittering trees providing the only light to his eyes. "I could just see him behind his desk at Callicot Parker Capital, thumbing the wheel of his silver lighter. Anticipating lighting a celebratory cigar." He takes a couple of sips of his wine. "He said, 'Your mother and I are sending you on a grand tour this summer.' The pompous-ass words! 'Your itinerary is all set. You'll visit the haunts of your literary heroes, write in that journal of yours in Parisienne cafés. End up on the beach at Cannes. You're of age now, my boy; you can order drinks with umbrellas right from your chaise.'" Truman lowers his voice.

"'Sow your wild oats,' he said, 'and when you return, you'll pro-pose to Anne Emerson. And I'll pay for grad school.' The strings attached to the offer felt as thick as tug-of-war rope. I could feel my palms blistering along with my pride."

"But why marry Anne Emerson?" I ask.

"Charlie had no sons. And Anne Emerson had no head for finance. But she wanted me. Turns out Charlie had some-thing on my father. I never found out what it was, but it was big enough that my father was willing to sacrifice my future."

I sip my wine, conjuring a scrawny blonde, my risotto for-gotten. I didn't know if I hated the woman for what she did to Truman or loved her for divorcing him.

He is silent for a long time. "She only liked me because she thought I was a comer. We had a couple of dates the summer before. I hadn't even kissed her. She cared nothing about my poetry, my desire to teach. She and my mother became thick as thieves."

The waiter arrives to clear the dishes and offers dessert and coffee. Truman's brows ask me if I want them. Scooting back from where I found myself at the edge of my chair, I murmur a "no, thank you" to the waiter.

A new crinkle has formed between Truman's eyes, and it doesn't go away. "At Colombia, I discovered I had a knack for finance. I joined Callicot Parker, drank the Kool-Aid. I went through the motions of being Anne Emerson's husband, but I wasn't into her social scene. She wanted to go to every party, out to dinner every night. And though the firm thrived, by the time I was twenty-nine, I was burned out—on my career and the marriage. Eventually, she got pregnant. We had the twins, and so I stayed. When the boys were in high school, a buddy from Columbia asked me to do some consulting work." He shrugs. "I figured it was a way I could be involved in education. But I was away from home for weeks at a time." He pauses, his throat working with emotion. "My boys resented me for that. I haven't seen them since I've been in Virginia; they've had some excuse or another for not being available . . ." His eyes shine with unshed tears. "I want to get to know them as they are now—as men."

Words escape me. His boys. They are why he's here, not because his mother is an alumna. I peer around the restaurant, aware again that others are present, that others exist. Can they see the waves of pain coming off him?

The candle between us is a lake of cooling wax, the flame long extinguished.

Truman meets my eyes. His exhalation is as weighty as though it contains his soul. "I can't believe I told you all that. I haven't talked this much in . . . years. And never about my boys. It's you, Georgie. You're the same genuine and loving girl."

My heart gives a swoop of joy. I recall the exact words he said all those years ago—I can see the page where I wrote them in my diary: *You're the best girl I ever met.*

I reach for his hand, tears stinging my nose. The nickname I'd reserved for him when we'd been alone escapes my heart, springs to my tongue. "True."

He sniffs and twines his fingers in mine. "What a pair we are. Neither of us faired the way we thought we would."

I laugh softly. "We are. OTP—as my students say—one true pair."

The waiter parts us, presenting the leather binder that holds the check. Truman clears his throat, produces a credit card, and slaps it atop the binder. "At least you have a wonderful career. And mark my words: Willa Cather's going to survive this setback."

For the first time, I believe that the college will and that I will too. I sit back, sated, not just from the food but from the honesty, the intimacy. "Thank you for dinner."

"My pleasure," he says, pouring the last of the wine into our glasses. My pulse picks up as Sade's "The Sweetest Taboo" settles around us. Truman sits back with his glass and surveys me. "Your eyes are as green as ever."

A slow smile travels my lips. I put my palm to the back of my neck, gather my hair in one hand, and pull it over one shoulder. "I didn't know you'd noticed."

He gives me a lazy grin. "Oh, I noticed."

Just like that, I've bought a ticket for a hair-tossing, foot-swinging, flirt festival. My ankle grazes his calf. I look at his mouth. I pick up my wine and take a sip, my lids at half-mast.

My lips part as he leans forward and reaches for my hand. "It feels so good to be with you," he says. "I didn't realize how lonely I've been. Would you like to go somewhere for coffee? Talk some more?"

Coffee and talk? I swallow the purr that has formed in my throat. "I'd love to."

Outside, the night sky is all wind and air and space. I draw my pashmina close as we take to the brick walk. Blinking owlishly, the valet hops from his stool. He gives us a snappy salute. I laugh as he trots off to get the Rover and say to Truman, "I found myself saluting the other day without even thinking about it." When he doesn't respond, I try again, "My first boyfriend used to do it. He was super cute." I poke him with my elbow, expecting a grin.

But his features sag. "Anne Emerson broke me of that. On our wedding night, she told me she found the gesture an 'unseemly and inelegant habit.'"

In his expression, I see his entire adult life. "I'm sorry. That's pretty harsh."

"Yep," he says shortly, and he palms the valet a five. We slide into the Rover.

When we reach the main road again, I offer him my hand. He takes it without comment.

He drives several blocks before stopping at a crossroads.

He turns to me. "Where are we headed, Georgie?"

I meet his heated gaze. A firestorm of want blazes and crackles through me. "How about showing me your new house?"

The heart of another is a dark forest always,
no matter how close it has been to one's own.
—Willa Cather

CHAPTER
NINE

A bove the flat-topped mansard roof of Truman's newly acquired Victorian, the clouds part; the moon sails high and white. In the gravel drive, I lean against the Rover, surveying the bays, the elaborate gables and gingerbread trim, the deeply shadowed picketed porch. "I've always thought this was the prettiest house in town."

Overhead, the maple tosses its head. Truman retrieves a fallen branch from the small front yard and hurls it toward the trash bins at the back of the drive. "Have you been inside?"

"Never."

"Just wait," he says with a chuckle and then leans companionably against his car. "The last owner spent all his bread on the exterior."

"Oh, no." My hand misses the warmth of his palm, the way he'd held it on the ride over. As though reading my thoughts, he waggles his fingers for mine. "Prepare yourself. If it's what's on the inside that counts, you may think I left my mind at the realtor's office."

Hand in hand, we mount the front steps. Anticipation thumps behind my breastbone. *Now, stop it tout de suite. He's going to show you the house. You'll have coffee. You'll talk. That's all. Then why did you shave your legs this afternoon?*

I smile witlessly as Truman unlocks the door, flings it wide.

My first impression of the front room—though he has flipped on a light switch—is that of a cavern, the hanging wires, junction boxes, and plaster scraps stalactites. "Did I miss the part where they handed out the hard hats?"

Truman laughs. "I think you're safe. This room's the worst." He moves to adjust a radiator similar to mine. But the parallel I'd drawn of both of us living in older homes ends at the heating system. Unlike this neglected pile, my town house—only slightly younger—bears the patina of TLC. Truman looks happily about. "I can't wait to get to the heart of this place."

I consider the dust furring every surface. "Like archaeologically?"

He laughs again. "C'mon through to the kitchen."

I follow him, skirting sawhorses and toolboxes. "My mother always said the kitchen is the heart of the home." As the radiator clanks and pumps steam like a fire-breathing beast, I tug the pashmina from my shoulders. "You know, where you cook together and bake cookies, gather for meals." I've revealed another parallel between our homes: their solitary circumstances. Neither kitchen would bring to mind a Rockwellian scene. The side-twist of Truman's mouth as he regards his small farmhouse table tells me he's thinking the same. At least the previous owner revived this room with tile, sleek stainless appliances, and upscale pendant lights. Is Truman this tidy? Or did he plan to bring me here before I suggested it? The thought that he had brings me a little quiver of thrill. "Well, it's really nice," I say, laying my wrap over a chair.

Truman shrugs from his blazer and drops it over the pashmina. "How 'bout some music? He thumbs a Bose Bluetooth atop the fridge.

"Sure, I like the old stuff."

He grins. "Is there anything after 1983 worth hearing?"

"I know! The music was so . . . organic and great then."

"Right? All the rock and roll and R & B?" He swipes at his phone. "Do you like the Eagles?"

I stare at him wide-eyed. "The Eagles are my favorite." How does he know these things? Are we that much in sync? "It was so sad when Glenn Frey died."

He shakes his head. "Big loss." The first notes of "Hotel California" spill from the Bose. He looks at me again. "Ready for a tour?"

Several dim narrow rooms hold sheet-shrouded furniture. "The previous owner left a lot of old furniture," he says. "Maybe you can help me decide what's worth keeping."

"I'd be happy to help you curate a collection."

Upstairs, he only gestures in the direction of the largest room, where moonlight peers through deep gabled windows. "That's where I'm sleeping."

I allow myself a peek at a sleigh bed piled with down before turning back. "Cozy." And oh-so inviting.

Back downstairs, Truman opens a cabinet. "Want some decaf?"

The Eagles' "Wasted Time" skirls over the room. "Actually, I'm not in the mood for coffee." *What are you in the mood for, Georgie?*

He grins. "Neither am I. How about a pinot gris? We can sit in here," he says, showing me into a small room off the kitchen—maybe a former maid's quarters—where great stacks of books rise like Stonehenge around the only piece of furniture, a sofa draped by a drop cloth. A TV sits like an after-thought on a moving box in one corner.

Truman whisks the cloth from the sofa. I give a little involuntary cry at the swooping curves of the Queen Anne piece.

"How beautiful." The upholstery is a vibrant blue velvet and appears recently recovered.

"Thanks. That's actually mine. My grandmother's." He sets two glasses of wine on a small field bar and takes a seat at one end of the sofa.

I sit at the other end. Where do we begin? We sip our wine.

He crosses an ankle over a knee. "What about Lacey. Have you kept in touch with her?"

He's amazed when I tell him that Lacey and I are still close. The fun memories bubble to the surface as though they've been held under for too long. We drink and laugh and keep it light, starting a great many sentences with "Do you remember . . .?" I watch Truman's face as he talks, loving his handsome maturity, even as the lines around his eyes have smoothed since dinner. When the playlist ends, we are quiet for a time, the only sound the *ticktock* of the kitchen clock. I survey the towers of books on the floor. "Are you going to build shelves for all of these books?"

He laughs and turns to consider them. "I need to. There are a lot more in my room. Maybe I'll make the front room into a library."

"That's a great idea. Good light there." I smile and incline my arm in a sweeping gesture. "I can see the fireplace working, a gleaming mantlepiece, Victorian andirons, and a pair of deep leather wing chairs." A *pair* of chairs. My cheeks heat as though we're sitting before that blazing hearth. But he smiles.

I take a deep breath. "Well, I guess we should think about getting me home."

He reaches for my hand, laces his fingers with mine. "Don't go, Georgie Girl."

The old endearment plays like heat lightning inside the cloud that's taken over my brain. Does he want me to stay the night? Does he want to make love? Do I? My voice comes out quavery. "Okay, I'll stay awhile. But I'd like to freshen up. Should I use the bath down here?"

He smiles. "Enter at your own risk. Oh, actually, the water's turned off to that one. Use mine. Go through my room."

Upstairs, I feel my way through his dark bedroom and slip into the bathroom. I sit right down on the toilet without thinking about it, the way one does with family. Swishing mouthwash, I regard the light brigade of grooming products atop a small chest: a hairdryer and brush, a razor and shaving cream—vetiver scented, I knew it!—an Ultrasonic toothbrush and crumpled tube of paste squeezed in the middle. At the clean but rust-ringed old porcelain sink, I wash my hands and regard my reflection in the mirror. Though my lipstick has been eaten away, my cheeks and lips are rosy. A froth of desire fills my chest.

I open the door and an Al Green song floats up. I follow it down. Truman's on the sofa, a fresh glass of wine raised to his lips. His eyes light over the rim when he catches sight of me. Swallowing, he sets the glass on the table. "Want another glass?"

I dip my chin and smile. "Bien sûr."

He fills my glass and then sits back, rolls his sleeves up his forearms. The hair there is still reddish, his arms more heavily freckled. I realize I've never seen his chest—we'd not dated in the summer—and my cheeks send up another flare.

Truman's mouth arranges itself into a diffident smile. "There's something I want to tell you . . . I haven't told you my boys' names."

Oh, God, I've been so self-centered and swamped with lust, I haven't thought to ask. "Oh! Please do." I straighten my spine and cross my legs.

"Though my . . . Anne Emerson didn't concede me many points, she agreed that if the babies were boys, I would name them." He gives a wry twist of his mouth. "She was sure they'd be girls. But the boys arrived. I named the first one for my brother."

"Trask? Oh, that's so neat."

"And the second . . . after your father."

My heart gives a fishlike flop. My father? "Asher?"

"Yes." He reaches for my trembling hand. "Asher Truman Parker," he says simply, and a glint of tears brightens his eyes. "Your father meant a great deal to me, as an English teacher and advisor, and of course as your father. I wanted to honor his memory."

I am undone. "Oh, True, I . . ." I scrub my face into the tufted back of the sofa. "I thought I would do the same . . . if I ever had children. This means the world to me. I . . . want to meet him, your son. Both of your sons." I gaze toward the front room to the door that leads to the porch to the street and to the road that leads to Mountainsburg. Could I go as far as Mountainsburg with Truman to meet his sons, my father's namesake? Fear runs a quick tongue up my spine.

But Truman gives my hand a little pump of approbation. "I hoped you'd be pleased. I wish I had let you . . . and your mom know a long time ago, but I . . ." He kneads my palm with his thumb. "Will you tell her for me?"

I close my eyes for a long moment, savoring his sweetness. I swallow. "Of course, I will." We smile into each other's eyes as Jefferson Starship's "Miracles" begins. "I'm loving this old music."

"Me too." Truman's eyes travel the length of my hair the way they had in the restaurant. "I'm glad you still wear your hair long. The last time I saw you, I think it had a ribbon in it. You were the prettiest girl I'd ever seen."

A surge of joy sweeps me. I slip off my shoes and tuck my feet beneath me. "Why did we stop writing to each other?"

He gives his broad shoulders a little bounce. "I don't know . . . I guess we just got caught up in being teenagers. I was always busy with sports and school. I was just a dumb kid. I couldn't see the future. Think of us being together again."

"Why did you leave Browning for the high school in Atlanta?" I want to hear that it's because I was no longer there.

"Trask came home," he says simply. "I wanted to be close to him." He takes a sip of wine. "Besides, when you left—you and your mom and Ronnie—Browning no longer felt like home."

"Oh, True."

He smiles again, the corners of his eyes crinkly. "You know you're the only girl that ever called me that?"

"Really?" I say with a satisfied grin. "I don't know who loved you more, my little brother or me. He thought you scattered the stars in the sky. Remember what he called you?"

He lays his head back and studies the ceiling. "God . . . yes, actually! True-man." He huffs a laugh. "No one ever called me that either. What a funny kid."

"But Ronnie was right. You were already a man."

Stretching his arm out to rest along the carved back of the sofa, he looks into my eyes again. "Ah, Georgie, you did love me, didn't you?"

I bite the edge of my thumb. *Maybe I never stopped.*

"You grew up so beautiful, it hurts just to look at you."

"Truman . . . I'm forty-five years old."

"So what? I'm right behind you."

We laugh together. But after a moment, he studies me again, his blue eyes heating and sizzling. "Don't you know how elegant and bright and fine you are?"

My heart breaks loose from its home and inches its way to my throat. I touch its hollow. "Knowing how special you thought I was got me through some tough times later, True."

"I'm glad."

Somehow, we've met in the middle of the sofa. He slips his hand into my hair. "Remember the first time I kissed you?"

"Of course, I do." I challenge him with a saucy smirk. "Where were we?"

"In the tunnel—the old clock tower," he says, triumphant. "I thought I was James Bond."

I grin. "I remember touching your chicken pox scar," I say, raising a tender finger to the barely perceptible dent above his upper lip.

He runs a thumb across my left eyebrow, where my own scar has all but faded. "And I yours." Swoony with incredulity and pleasure, I nudge my face under his wrist. "I even remember what I said."

My eyes at half-mast, I trace the contours of his lips. "What did you say?"

"Kiss me, Georgie Girl." And as though that kiss were only hours before, he takes my face in his hands. He kisses me once, twice, a third time.

I twine my arms around his neck and kiss him like it's National Kissing Day.

Sometime later, Marvin Gaye growls his best song "Let's Get It On." We're breathing as though engaged in manual labor. Truman pulls away and makes the T for time-out signal with his hands. "This may be a good time to admit that I haven't had sex in . . . a while."

I still. "Neither have I."

"It's been . . . like a year for me."

"For me too."

He pulls a pained face. "Actually, I haven't had sex . . . in almost two years."

"Neither have I."

We fall back against the sofa, laughing. His eyes sweep my breasts.

"What about now?" I murmur against his mouth.

His answering breath is a torch in my ear, "Georgie, Georgie."

His hands are everywhere.

Our clothes fall away, and our bodies blend like threads in a tapestry. Despite the imperfect time-worn warps and wefts, we're a magnificent work of art.

The fact that I was a girl never damaged my
ambitions to be a pope or an emperor.
—Willa Cather

CHAPTER
TEN

I wake in stages, remembering that I'm in Truman Parker's bed.
With a rush of deliciousness, I recall the night. His body is
warm, though it no longer wraps me like a vine. Is he awake?
Lying very still, I roll my head on the pillow —that smells of us—
to take a peek. He's sleeping, his arms crossed behind his head as
though sunning himself. Above the crisp fold of sheet, the skin
of his chest is fair and peppered with freckles. The reddish hair
curls softly there and in darker tufts in the pale of his underarms.
I think of the places his mouth had been last night and flash hot
and cold.

In the bathroom at 2:00 a.m., I'd texted Lacey: *I've just made*
love with Truman Parker. When I'd hit send—making damn sure
I was sending it to the right person—the purport of the night
had come crashing in: What does this mean? Are we in a relationship, as people say? Those notions had spiraled into fretting
about what he thought of my mature body, my considerable
flesh. I'd lain awake for an hour, watching his whiskers grow.
Does Truman like me for the me I am now or for his former
Georgie Girl?

Last night, we'd laughed about feeling as though we'd won

the lottery. But in the light of day, I realize my world—already swerving on its base with my job in jeopardy—is in danger of becoming untethered. This town is too small; if Truman and I are in a relationship, others will know in the time it takes to lace a shoe. What if it's just a fling? In its aftermath, working together would be awkward and miserable and could thwart our efforts to save the school. While Truman softly snores, I upbraid myself up for allowing my lust to do all the thinking last night.

I need coffee to clear the cobwebs. Voltaire. My cat hadn't even entered my mind last night! I have to go check on him. But first, I'll take a shower and make coffee for True and me. True and me. I slip from between his sheets and pad to the bathroom, the grin stretching my lips again.

Ten minutes later, I cross the room where he is still zonked out, lying on his side, the sheet pulled to his nose. I close the door softly and trail down to the kitchen, squeezing at my wet hair with a towel. Pouring water into the coffee maker, my gaze wanders to the sofa in the little den. I flush at the thought of the intimate talk, the fabulous kissing. And then, *chou de dieu!* The coffee maker chuckles.

Idly, I pick through a bowl on the counter filled with receipts, a postcard from Spain from someone named Mike, a tangle of rubber bands, a premium-quality lavender envelope addressed to Truman in a woman's fine script. My eyes flit to the doorway, the ceiling. The coffee pot fills, the robust aroma wreathing my head. I rise on tiptoe to reach for mugs in a cabinet. No footsteps above. Beneath the envelope is a single sheet of fine lavender stationary. It practically unfolds itself. I fill a mug with coffee and blow across its surface, ears pricking for signs of life upstairs. Skipping the body of the short note, I hone in on the closing: *Mother.* Not *Love, Mother.* Just *Mother.* What a cold, cold woman. I cock my head: no creak of stair.

Dear Truman,

Anne Emerson has let me know that your court date is next month. I urge you once more to reconsider. Though your sons are men, they will be affected by the divorce. They will wonder if their parents' love was real or a lie.

I drop the note as though it's burned my fingers and watch it drift to the floor. The *click-clunk* twist of Truman's old brass bedroom knob brings footfalls down the stairs. He appears in the doorway in boxer shorts and an Emory T-shirt, looking sleepy and tousled. And damnably adorable. "Good morning," he says. His eyes travel my body. "So that's where my robe went."

He takes in my face before his eyes fall to the note on the floor, then dart to mine. He bends to pick it up, his jaw muscles working. "Reading my mail, Georgie?"

I stare at him, my heart thudding in my throat. "I thought you were divorced."

"I am," he says after a moment. "I mean, for all intents and purposes; we've been legally separated two years."

I recoil, sloshing coffee, slam my cup on the counter, and push roughly past him. "I *trusted* you," I spit.

Upstairs in the bedroom, he catches me by the shoulders and spins me around. "Wait. Let me explain."

Raised by a Shakespeare-obsessed English-teacher father, I can spot a soliloquy coming a mile away. "Save it." I snatch up my clothes where they lay like crumpled hopes on the scratched hardwood floor. Trembling all over, I hurry into the bathroom and shut the sight of his stricken face away. I throw his robe into the wet tub and pull on last night's tunic. *Oh, dear God, what have I done?* I spent years determined to shut out the past. By some miracle I meet Truman again. I let him in, bare my soul to him. And look what happened! I poke my legs into my pants, staggering and wishing for an escape portal.

Truman knocks softly at the door. I place my palm against the three-inch thickness separating us—that may as well be three miles—grief constricting my throat. "Please, Georgie, just come out and listen a minute." I open the door and stand before him. Despair rises from the man. "Have coffee with me." This is Truman, the boy and the man. I've never heard a false note in his voice. And I don't hear one now. "I don't want to lose you."

"Then don't." *Don't betray my trust again.*

In the kitchen, we sit at the farm table, hot mugs before us. I won't meet his eyes. I won't let him see the fear inside me, the pummeling regret. They hiss and sneer at my recklessness. We've had one date, one night together. Though it feels authentic, we've made no promises. I don't want to lose him either, but I won't be some for-old-time's-sake fling for a married man. The fine lavender stationary lays atop a bowl of bruised fruit on the table. His parents blackmailed him before. How much power do they still yield over their son's life? I spread my hands on the table. "Truman, I was lonely before you came back into my life, but I was okay." *Well, not exactly okay, but your unexamined heart was pure bliss.* "With what's happening at the college, I don't need the distraction of a family drama." Neither does he. He has to focus on this job. "Look, maybe we should take a step back. The most important thing now is saving the school."

As the words float toward Truman, I want to snatch them back. *Is that the most important thing, Georgie?* But what if we build a relationship and then lose the school? If Willa Cather folds, neither of us stays in Foxfield. Oh, Lord, to leave this place! I see myself clutching the front campus gate like some mad protestor, a police officer bodily wrenching me from it.

Truman sags in his chair. "Yes, of course it's important. But after . . . last night," he says, indicating our state of familiarity— he in his boxers, my braless nipples poking from my top—"Don't we owe ourselves the chance to find out if this is real?"

My gaze snags on the Victorian sofa across the room in the little den. At the sight of my bra on the floor by the coffee table, my eyeballs practically tumble from their sockets. Leaping from my chair, I dash across the room and scoop up the lingerie.

"Oh, Georgie . . . it's okay," Truman says gently.

Is he accustomed to women's underwear underfoot?

I look at him again and my mortification ebbs. Of course, he's not.

But shaking my head, I stuff my underwear into my bag. "I can't do this right now." I stand, my sinuses aching as though I'm taking a cold.

He sits at his table for one, his face like that of a bayonetted soldier. "Georgie, I can't lose you twice."

I pull out my phone and thumb to the Uber app that Lina insisted I practice using but never have. "Then don't," I say again.

❦

Voltaire is displeased. After adding fresh kibble to his bowl and sending Lina a text cancelling our pedicure plans, I crawl into bed, sending a tote full of student papers tumbling to the floor. I dial Lacey's number and pour my heart out along with a spate of fresh tears.

"Babe," she says, when I am done, "get some sleep." Voltaire, who's been giving me his most malevolent slit-eyed stare from the corner, springs onto the bed and curls into my side.

I pluck the last tissue from the box. Blow my nose. "You're right."

"Call me later. I love you. The papers can wait. And turn off your phone."

"Love you too," I murmur, before following Lacey's direction and plunging into an emotion-induced coma.

Four hours later, my achy bladder wakes me. And though

I'd figured I'd not be hungry again until sometime around the Fourth of July, I find myself in the kitchen pillaging the refrigerator. I make myself a huge sandwich and sit at the table to eat it on the solitary yellow placemat. Will I eat here like Miss Lonelyhearts in *Rear Window* for the rest of my life? I picture Truman at his table. Has he called? I turn on my phone. Two seconds later, my ringtone—Neil Young's "Harvest Moon"—startles me.

I take a deep breath. "Hello?"

"Georgie."

Determined to think rationally, I draw myself to a board meeting posture. "Hello, Truman."

"Are you all right?"

I carry my plate to the dishwasher. "Yes. I've been napping," I say crisply.

"Would you take a walk with me?"

I gaze out the window at my greening garden. It's a lovely afternoon for a walk. But I sigh. "I don't know that we should be we seen on campus together."

"You know we must have been seen at The Red Fox."

"I know. But then I didn't know it was a real date or what . . . was to come."

"How about the city park then?"

Sprawling, tree-filled Riverside Park where the young townie families recreate and not many WCC people hang out. "Okay."

Twenty minutes and a quick pep talk by phone with Lina later, I draw the coupe alongside Truman's Rover. He climbs out of the vehicle wearing a windbreaker, the T-shirt he'd put on that morning, a pair of faded Levi's, and worn running shoes. Is he a runner? I know so little about him. I've struggled into the last pair of jeans that fit me and a long cotton sweater.

Tacitly, we stroll along the grass toward the river. At the water's edge, the cattails are shooting up among the reeds and tender wild violets. There, a green metal bench faces the water, and we take a seat. He stretches his long legs out, crossing them at the ankles. The violets remind me of the lavender stationary in his kitchen and how it got us to this place.

"Why don't you ever talk about your mother?" I say, breaking the silence. "I heard she's a graduate of Willa Cather, but you've never told me that."

"I try not to think of my mother." He looks out at the water. "About the note you saw: remember what it said?"

I could no more forget it than an aching tooth. "I believe so."

"About whether or not my marriage was a lie? She knew that it was from the start. Since I filed for divorce, just being away from Anne Emerson was foremost in my mind. The boys had been gone for three years. I threw myself into my work. Anne Emerson and her attorney contested—though God knows the woman hates me—but then she took off on one girlfriends' trip after another, dragging out communications and missing court dates. Then the opportunity at Willa Cather came up. Until now," he says, "I haven't had a reason to get back into the slugfest."

I watch the river, absorbed for a moment in the dancing spots of brilliance where sunlight shines. I think of the other river—the Laurel—the one that changed and charted the course of our lives. *Has my subconscious just connected the river with my favorite student's name? Laurel's trauma—my father's . . . No.* I dig my nails into my palms. *I'll not allow myself to dwell there.* I turn to Truman and paste on a smile. "And now?"

His gaze locks on mine. "Things are different now. It's you, Georgie. I want to get to know you again."

"I want to get to know you too. That's, well . . . why I was snooping through your things this morning." Tears threaten again. "But Willa Cather is my life."

He searches my eyes. "Your whole life?"

"I know that seems . . . pitiable."

"I don't pity you. But you deserve to live a life without fear. I wish you'd . . . seek professional counseling. It helped heal Trask."

The week-at-a-glance March calendar on my office desk appears before me, the appointment with Dr. Chu on the first. "I'm actually seeing someone soon." Whether from shame or the sun, my cheeks smart. "Can we find some shade?"

We climb a mossy rise to where giant shade trees meet and combine. We sit on the ground, this time facing each other. Keeping my eyes down, I trail my fingers across fresh moss. I pry up a pretty little hillock of it and hold it on the island of a palm on which the nail marks are fading. Truman trails a finger over the moss and then captures my gaze. "Will you forgive me, Georgie? For not telling you the whole truth?" I see nothing in his eyes but contrition and raw hope. I so want to trust him. But our morning confrontation is like a skinned knee, still stinging when I flex and turn it over in my mind. He has a wife in Atlanta, whether or not they are separated. And then there are his boys. And there's no telling how far his mother might go to disrupt the divorce. Would I be a fool to risk ending up in the middle of it all? Yet, it's Truman. We've met again for a reason. I hold the moss as though it's the heart I've protected for so long. "How about we just sit with things awhile?"

"Will you go out with me again?"

I smile to myself. "Probably."

At the twang of tennis rackets, we momentarily shift our eyes in the direction of the public courts. "But I don't want to have to skulk around to see you," he says.

Another smile tugs at my lips. "Skulk?"

He pulls a daffodil from a clump. "You know what I mean. Maybe we should let Susan know we're . . . dating." He toys with the yellow flower. Would Susan understand? We have two married couples on staff at the college, and as far as I know there isn't a moratorium on faculty relationships. He slides the bloom behind my ear, his finger down my lobe. Woozy again at his touch, I murmur, "I'll make an appointment to talk with Susan."

His grin is the only affirmation I need.

⚬⳾⚬

I step briskly into my sunny classroom on Monday morning, but my feet falter at the sight of Madison's dark head, Hollins's anemic-looking heart-shaped face. Their impending transfers swoop on me with talons. Touching my Breathe bracelet, I inhale the familiar scent of bound books, close-packed sweetly scented girls, sun-heated windowsills and blinds. I open my plan book and remember that we're beginning a unit on French art, a favorite. Putting on a cheerful smile, I greet the class *en français* and then note Laurel's empty seat with a prickle of annoyance. I power up the SMART board. "Where's Laurel?" I ask the girls.

Penn, hunched into herself and reading, looks up and around, her topknot bobbing. "She was in her room studying when I left to get coffee."

I sigh inwardly. "Well, hopefully she'll be here in a minute. Okay," I say, taking a seat in my tall director's chair. I aim a remote at the board and open an art file. The image of my favorite painting brings dovelike coos from the girls. "Voilà. Renoir's *Luncheon of the Boating Party*. Tell me three things about the light in this masterpiece."

Laurel enters the classroom ten minutes after class is over, as though strolling the French riviera. Dropping her books on a desk, she shoots me a bored glance. "Bonjour."

"Are you all right? Why were you not in class?"

"I was studying for the test."

"Laurel, you can't skip class to study for a test."

She lifts a defiant chin. "What difference does it make?"

I channel my mother's patience and reserve and after a moment indicate a framed quote from Willa Cather on the wall. "Will you read me that quote, please?"

She barely glances at the wall before reciting it in a sing-songy voice. "The fact that I was a girl never damaged my ambition to be a pope or an emperor."

Even strong girls like Laurel have down days. And I have to help her push past this. I hand her a new copy of the test. "We're facing a setback, Laurel," I say, my tone authoritative, "but we're not giving up on our goals."

She bends over her work with a sigh but then seems to breeze through it. After she leaves, I spot-check her answers and breathe a sigh of relief: 90 percent.

I'm preparing for my next class, a group of seniors, when Susan appears in my doorway. A classroom visit from the president is as unexpected as champagne and caviar in the dining hall. "Hello, Georgie. May I see you for a minute?"

I rise, a cautious smile lifting my cheekbones. "Of course, come in." She nods and waves me back down in my desk chair. She climbs into the director's chair. I'm not sure why she's here, but she's saved me a call and visit to her office.

Crossing her legs, she peers into my face. "Are you and Truman Parker romantically involved?" My head snaps back as though trapped in the gale of a wind tunnel. "You know how word travels in Foxfield."

A blush rises from my throat to my hairline. "We have had a date. But you have my word that it won't affect my work."

She gives me a slight nod. "And what about his?"

My eyes dart to the clock on the wall. My class arrives in twenty minutes. "I need to tell you something." I get up and close the door on a clamor in the hallway. The memory of the slumber party waves a red flag. Had one of the girls started the news around? Was it the hostess at The Red Fox, or could it have been someone curious about the new owner of the Ballentine place? I feel like drawing the dusty blinds.

I perch on the desk closest to the director's chair and implore my boss with my eyes, wishing I'd had time to write up some talking points. For eight minutes—in which the palms of my hands leave prints on my skirt—I recap the relationship, picturing the information in bullet points in my mind so I can recall it later. Susan studies me like a judge presiding over a particularly perplexing case. I want to weep when, at last, a sliver of understanding appears in her eyes. She gives me a smile. "Georgie, in all the years I've known you, I've not seen you take a false step or make an error in judgment. You're an exemplary professor and, frankly, our most devoted. I trust that you and Truman won't allow your . . . relationship to affect your work."

"Thank you. You have my word."

Susan holds my eyes again. "New information is coming down the pike. Take good care." Unease gnaws at my midsection as Susan hops down from the chair. Halfway to the door, she turns and smiles. "By the way, the women of the class of '98 have made a gift to the school, marking their twentieth reunion. I'm not going to ask how this came about, but they have donated thirty-five thousand dollars toward your study abroad program. Congratulations, Madame Bricker. Your initiative is approved."

As the president softly closes the door, I clutch the nearest desk, blinded by tears of gratitude. Who do I share the news with first? Genevieve? Lina? Truman? Truman. Striding to my desk, I snare my phone and take a selfie, flashing an exuberant grin and a "V for Victory" sign. I'm about to caption the photo, but I pause, my finger in mid-punch.

Two victories have been won. Which is the one my heart wants to trumpet?

There are some things you learn best in calm,
and some in storm.
—Willa Cather

CHAPTER
ELEVEN

I indulge myself three snooze alarms before swinging my legs off the bed. "I need coffee right meow," I say to Voltaire and drop a kiss between his silky ears. "I have to go to the headpeeper." I start the coffee and head for the shower, belting out "In My Own Little Corner" from Rodgers and Hammerstein's *Cinderella*.

I'd consulted Lina last night. "Do I really need to keep the appointment when things are going so well?"

A silence had spun out before she'd answered. "Go and hear what she has to say; if you don't want to go back after that, don't."

I arrive at Dr. Chu's medical building with five minutes to spare and grab a lucky end spot. I open a text from Truman, the second of the morning: *Have dinner w/me after the faculty meeting, sweetheart?*

Sweetheart. I lean my head back against the headrest, awash in pleasure; after a week, the man's attention still dazzles me. We're meeting in the conference room at four o'clock to go over information Madame Beaulieu has sent about curriculum integration for the study abroad program. Grinning, I type a quick *Yes!* and then glance to my right and to my left before brazenly adding, *And dessert later?*

Once inside, I step from the sanitized, chrome tang of the building's lobby and onto a plush Persian rug in the psychiatrist's waiting room, where a diffuser sends up a soothing cloud of lemon balm. Two other patients sit in ikat upholstered chairs across the room from the reception window. I covertly eye them while the receptionist concludes a phone conversation: an older woman with Willie Nelson braids, mumbling to herself, "Shit and Shinola, shit and Shinola"; and a clean-cut young man in a suit and tie, clutching a battered copy of *Harold and the Purple Crayon*. I give the receptionist my name and a grimace and take a seat right next to the window and the door to the inner sanctum, as far away from the others as possible. These people seem certifiable. *Chou de dieu*, am I in the same category? I bury my nose into the first magazine I see, a glossy copy of *Men's Health*. An article title: "Dating Two Women: How It Works" makes me shut the publication and turn it upside down on the table.

A mechanism clicks on the door. I jump as though I've been goosed. *They lock you in?* "Ms. Bricker," the receptionist says, "you may go in."

I take a last peek at the others. Maybe they're waiting for one of the other doctors. "Thank you."

Dr. Chu is everything and nothing I'd expected. Asian and fine-boned, her eyes snap with intelligence, but she beckons to me from a door off the hall as though inviting a playmate into a clubhouse. "Ms. Bricker? Come in! I'm Celeste Chu." I take a seat on a purple velvet slipper chair and cross my legs. She opens a small refrigerator and extracts a bottle of water. She waggles it at me: want one?

"No, thank you." She opens her bottle and takes a few sips before picking up a file from her desk. I take a peek at her bookshelves: succulents in tiny clay pots; a collection of silver thimbles (*Thimbles?*); a pair of celadon foo dogs bracketing psychology books; a book displayed on a wooden easel, *An Unquiet*

Mind (*Book of the month for shrinks?*). The bottommost shelf is filled with volumes on meditation, yoga, running, and self-care. She lands on a desk chair opposite me, slips off her yellow pointy-toed pumps with twin *oofs*, and props her bare feet on the coffee table. A tinge of eucalyptus meets my nose. "Runner's feet," she says ruefully before quietly studying the file. I force a small smile to show that I'm hip enough not to be offended by her unconventional ways but then find myself skimming the framed diplomas on the wall to make sure she's legit. I flinch when she asks, "What's so great about fear?"

"Pardon me?"

She smiles. "On the forms you completed, you used the word 'fear' eleven times."

"I did?"

"You did."

"I guess maybe my fears keep me safe?"

"Is that a question?"

"I . . . well, I don't know."

"Will you be more specific about your fears for me?"

I take a deep breath. "Right now, I'm afraid I left the iron on and the house will burn down. I'm afraid Voltaire will be traumatized because I'm bringing a man into our home. I'm afraid of losing my job and my life. I'm afraid of being afraid all the time."

Dr. Chu peels an elastic band from her golden wrist and twists her long hair into a high ponytail. "What does 'safe' mean to you?"

"That nothing . . . terrible is happening to me."

A single wrinkle appears between her large dark eyes. She peers at the file again. "I believe it's loss that you are afraid of," she says slowly. "Have you experienced great loss?"

My heart drums in my chest. I gape at her. "My . . . my father. He died when I was a teenager."

She waits, her eyes soft.

"But I don't talk about that." If I talk about that, I'll have to think about my part in that. I will my shoulders down from where they've bunched around my ears. I purse my lips.

"We don't have to talk about that now," she gently says. I let go a grateful breath. The doctor takes another look at the file. "You rated your level of happiness as a five out of ten."

Truman's image glows before me. "That was a couple of weeks ago. It's about a nine now."

She smiles again. "Well *that's* good. What's the relationship between safety and happiness?"

"I guess when you feel safe, you feel happy."

"Why do you feel safe and happy now?"

"Well," I say, looking pointedly at the folder in her lap, "you saw on the form that I've been worried about my job, but an initiative that could help save it was just approved. And then there's a man—a man from my past, actually—who's come back into my life."

"Well, that's wonderful," she says warmly. "But before today, you've felt happy about half the time?"

"I guess so."

"And this has been going on how long?"

"Most of my adult life."

She blinks and gives her head a little shake. "I wouldn't settle for that."

I look at her: a physician, smart and beautiful with a platinum engagement ring and wedding band on her finger. The happiness I'm feeling is temporal. If I lose my job, I'll be back to a five on her happiness scale and on the slippery slope toward a one. I draw a ragged breath. "I'm tired of settling for it."

Her face is as gentle and kind as my mother's. "I know you are," she says. My eyes well with tears. Holding them wide, I reach for a tissue to save my mascara. Dr. Chu makes a note in her file and then adds, "You've said that you feel you function pretty well in your everyday life?"

"I work so very hard to keep everything under control, to keep people from learning my secret fears."

"But it's an impossible task isn't it?" I nod miserably. "So you're a woman showing one face to the world and living a different life within."

I sniff. "Pretty much."

"Do you have some good friends?"

She must think I'm completely pathetic. "Oh, I do," I say, thinking first of Lacey. "I've been best friends with a woman— Lacey—since we were toddlers."

"Great. That's a pretty name, Lacey." She makes a note on her pad. "How often do you see her?"

My heart skitters. "About once a year. She comes to see me." As she makes another note, I rush to add, "But we talk almost every day.

"And would you like to see her more often?"

"Yes."

"What about your family? Do they come to see you too?"

Guilt touches down on my shoulders, flutters its great wings. "Yes."

"Would you like for that to change? Would you like to feel free to go wherever you want?"

"More than anything," I say.

She smiles again. "And you've let this man into your life. May I ask his name?"

I don't guess it will hurt to tell her his name; after all, what one says to a psychiatrist is confidential. "Truman. He was my first love."

Dr. Chu plants a hand on her sternum and pokes out her bottom lip. "Aww." She scribbles another note. And then holds my eyes. "Does Truman know your fears?"

112

"He does."

Her eyes light. "And how did he react?"

"He was understanding." I fold the Kleenex into a tiny package. I don't tell her that Truman didn't fan all his cards out for me, that he was untruthful about his divorce. *But did you think about it, Georgie? You could have asked if he was divorced. Did you tread light out of fear and choose to assume? Is it just as much your fault as it was his?*

Dr. Chu studies me with the fixed gaze of someone looking through a telescope. "What would happen if you had to leave Foxfield tomorrow?"

My lower belly sharply cramps. "What do you mean?"

"That was figurative. I mean if you had to leave immediately."

My belly tightens. "I'm afraid I—would die."

"Ms. Bricker, we're going to get you feeling better, less fearful. I want you to feel comfortable and most of all hopeful, regardless of what's going on in your life. I'd like to start you on a medication. It's actually an antidepressant, but it can help with anxiety and panic. Is that okay with you?"

I crawl up, sputtering, onto the life raft this kind young woman has tossed me. "Yes."

She taps her laptop keys again. "I'm sending in an electronic prescription for you. To the pharmacy on Main?"

"Yes, that's the one."

"It takes a little bit for this med to get into your system," she says. "So I'd like to see you again in two weeks."

We rise, and I feel like throwing my arms around her. "Thank you," I simply say.

"My pleasure," she says with a namaste-like bow. "It is an honor to know you."

The waiting room is as empty as my cache of fear feels right now. I stop at the reception desk and make the appointment. In my coupe again, I feel hopeful, as smoothed as the leather seats. As I drive to the pharmacy, I call Mrs. King, imagining her solid presence at her desk, gratitude for her friendship filling my chest. "Thank you so much, Helen," I say, using her first name, as I do about as often as I clean my oven. "Dr. Chu was brilliant."

"I'm so glad, honey!"

"I'll be there for my nine-fifteen class."

Three bars of "In My Own Little Corner" later, I'm breezing through the automatic doors of the pharmacy and I run into and exchange greetings with the tiny woman who alters my clothes at the dry cleaner's. In line is a librarian from the college, her arms full of paper towel rolls, talking with the Foxfield postmaster pushing a cartload of boxed wine. Suddenly, I feel as sheepish as if Dr. Chu had penned the prescription across my forehead. Head down, I follow a blue arrow on the floor to the prescription window that reads DROP OFF in foot-tall letters. I speak to the pharmacy tech—who's refilled my allergy medication and the occasional antibiotic—to make sure they have received the e-prescription, and I mumble a thank-you. While I wait, I snare a blue plastic basket—wiping the handles with a germy wipe—and then wander the aisles filling it with shampoo I don't need, hair clips I won't wear, and gum I won't chew.

In the magazine-and-card aisle, I navigate around a young woman sitting on the floor and absorbed in a tabloid. The headline on its cover makes my foot scuff against the blue carpeting and almost sends me sprawling: another celebrity suffering from depression has committed suicide. The overhead speaker crackles, and the tech booms out, "Prescription ready for *Bricker*."

It dawns on me how celebrities and others are beginning to talk openly about mental health issues. So many people have them. I square my shoulders and refuse to feel embarrassed about it any longer. I march straight to the counter and pay for my antidepressant, my shame shriveling with each step.

Back at the office, I hug Mrs. King until she giggles and gasps, then head into my office to catch up on the day's correspondence. I skip lunch but take my first dose of medicine with a protein bar. When my afternoon classes are done, I brush my teeth and freshen up in the ladies' room in preparation for my meeting with Truman.

In the administration building, I spot him in the hall outside the conference room talking with Jillian, the director of admissions. My heart leaps with gladness at the sight of him. Truman turns, catching sight of me, and does a double take, his eyes lighting. Joining them, I stand and make polite chitchat and simply breathe his presence. This man knows my fears, and still he looks at me as though I am sunrise. "The study abroad meeting's been delayed," he says, just as the door to Susan's office opens, and the Mandarin instructor steps out, his face darkened.

He passes us as if we're potted ficus trees. Susan looks around the door, her face drawn. "Next," she says with a mirthless chuckle and motions to Jillian. Her eyes skim Truman and me, and she briefly apologizes for the meeting delay. Truman lifts his brows in a wonder-what-that-was-about expression at the same time I shrug. Then he glances up and down the hall before placing a hand on the small of my back and shepherding me into the conference room. Closing the door, he takes me in his arms behind the privacy glass. "You're the best thing I've seen all day."

I lock my hands behind his neck and smile up into his handsome face. I raise my mouth to his. At a knock on the door, we pull apart. I smooth my hair and draw a finger over my lips as Truman tweaks his tie and opens the door.

Thirty-something springs have passed since I've laid eyes on the woman in the hall. Eleanor Parker is as splendidly elegant as she was the day we met, her gleaming platinum hair in a classic chignon, her face meticulously smoothed, tucked and taut. A moment of ringing shock passes before Truman says, "Mother? What are you doing here?"

"Hello, Son," she says in the cultured patois of the gentrified Old South.

Truman strings the words together as though they are one long word. "Is father all right?"

"Oh, yes, he's perfectly fine."

Truman exhales and then looks down at me. "Mother," he says, his cheekbones reddening, "This is Georgie Bricker . . . head of the French department."

Mrs. Parker looks at me as though I've just materialized. The corners of her lips rise a centimeter. "How do you do?"

My name didn't ring a bell with her. Of course, it wouldn't. "How nice to meet you, Mrs. Parker."

She murmurs a barely audible *mmm* before her gaze returns to her son. She peers around him and into the conference room. "May I sit down? I've had a long trip." Batting her eyes, she pushes her cheek to him.

"I'm sorry; of course," he says, brushing her cheek with his lips and moving to seat her at the table. "Would you like some coffee or water?"

"A cup of coffee, please. Black. Thank you, Son."

"Excuse me," I say to Truman. "Maybe we should reschedule for tomorrow."

He shoots me a grateful look. "Yes, thanks." As his mother digs to retrieve something from her handbag, Truman raises his index and pinky fingers to his cheek: I'll call you.

I nod my understanding. "It was a pleasure to meet you, Mrs. Parker," I say, and I step into the hall but leave my heart in the conference room with Truman. I would give a back molar to know why she has come.

I step from the building that had been chilled by Eleanor's

presence and back into the unusually warm March afternoon. Students cross the quad in waves, at once buoying my spirits. Smiling, I shake my head. How do they not run into lampposts, always peering down at their phones? As they eddy around the benches and tables, I wonder how many of them are determined to stay the course and how many may be thinking of transferring. I drift toward an empty bench in the shade of a river birch. How long will it be until Truman appears? Given the contentious color of their relationship, I'm betting the conversation between him and his mother won't take long. I wave to a couple of sophomores and decide to stay for a while, to take advantage of the nice afternoon. I pull out my phone and check my email. The receipt from the visit with Dr. Chu has made its way into my inbox. I let out a huff at the hit my credit card has taken and am grateful for good insurance. Without my job, I'd have no health care benefits, no medicine. I jerk my mind abruptly away from that thought before the jaws of my anxiety can latch onto it.

The slanting sun sifts through the budding leaves of the birch, dappling my lap and knees. I lay my head back on the bench, imagining the new medication skirling through my veins, balancing the chemicals, quieting my worries. My stomach grumbles. I look up at the administration building where Truman meets with his mother and assume our dinner date is off. Eleanor Parker at Willa Cather.

When I was fourteen, I thought she looked like Kim Novak, the beautiful and mysterious Madeleine in the movie *Vertigo*, which I'd seen on TV. She and Mr. Parker had come from Atlanta to attend the underclassmen awards day at Browning. Truman was awarded the freshman English award and was stunned when the English teacher, Miss Foxie Frame—our neighbor and friend—had called him to the stage a second time to present him a prize for poetry. At the reception afterward, I longed to run to Truman, to give him a hug. But the sight of Mrs. Parker in a severely tailored suit at his side stilled my feet. With her carefully sculptured hair and tasteful gold jewelry, the woman looked as though she'd been dipped in shellac. Truman had proudly introduced me to his parents as "Georgie Bricker, my girl."

Mr. Parker's eyes were amused as he took my hand. "How do you do, Miss, ah, Bricker, is it?" The handsome planes of Truman's young face, his blue eyes, and the shape of his mouth and nose were mere counterfeits of Conrad Parker's splendid features. He looked like a cross between Paul Newman and the prince in *Cinderella*. I'm sure I gawked at him.

But my enchantment with Eleanor Parker had fizzled like a dud firecracker when her moonstone eyes moved from Truman's face to mine and skimmed the Easter dress my mother had made for me, the white sandals my father had polished for me that morning. Beneath the weight of her gaze, I'd felt like Elly May Clampett in *The Beverly Hillbillies*, the sash of navy ribbon at the waist of my dress like a length of frayed rope. "Well. I'm happy to meet Truman's . . . little friend."

I had put out my hand as I'd been taught. "I'm pleased to meet you, Mrs. Parker."

She'd raised her painted-on eyebrows and taken my fingers as though they might be creeping with lice. Just then, my parents had strolled over to congratulate Truman. I'd watched Mrs. Parker survey my mother—her three-year-old spring dress, her plain gold wedding band, her softly waving dark hair, her slender ankles in the special shoes she wore because one leg was shorter than the other. I'd watched Mrs. Parker look back at Truman's happy face. She'd placed a manicured hand on his arm, the diamond in her wedding set the size of a Fordhook butter bean. "Will you bring me a cup of punch, please?"

The laughter of young women returns me to the present. I wonder why Eleanor has the ability to make me feel inferior every time I meet her. I'm a grown woman, an accomplished professional. Why do I allow her to make me feel otherwise? The sun sinks toward the chapel and for a moment seems to impale itself on the steeple. A little shiver runs through me. Noting the time on my phone, I wonder if Truman and his mother are still in the conference room.

Lina exits the library. I wave an arm overhead. "Lina," I call, capturing her attention.

"I was about to call you," she says, shifting a stack of books from one arm to the other. "Want to grab a coffee?"

I stand and give the admin building one last glance. "Sure, but the doctor says I should switch to decaf."

Her face lights along with the automatic lampposts on the quad. "Tell me."

⚜

I'm halfway through my cup of decaf, and I've told Lina all about Dr. Chu. "I'm so happy you like her," she says, "I have a girl crush on her already."

I smile, but my thoughts flip to the conference room and Eleanor Parker. I find myself telling Lina about meeting her that first time at Browning. "When she turned away from me at the reception, I'd thought I'd seen the last of her. You know how it is when you're a teenager: you're so wrapped up in your boyfriend, you think only obliquely about his parents. And the Parkers lived in the faraway land of Atlanta. They had nothing to do with me and my small world."

She nods. "I get that. Still, it looks like she's back in his life, or trying to be."

I look at my phone. The lack of response from Truman seems to underscore Lina's words.

"I need to vamoose," she says, pushing her paper napkin into her empty cup. "I have a boatload of papers to grade."

"Me too. At least if my date's cancelled, I should get them done tonight."

Lina and I head our separate ways. I plod across the darkened campus, but I stop at the lamppost in front of the chapel and take another peek at my phone. A new email has landed in my inbox: Susan Joshi to "All Faculty and Staff." Crossly, I poke open the note that's not from Truman. The note reads,

I apologize for the late notice but would like to invite you to join the chairman and me for breakfast in the faculty dining room tomorrow morning at nine to meet a visiting alumna from the class of 1949, Truman's mother, Eleanor Randall Parker.

My hypocenter quakes, anxiety spreading in waves along my limbs. I fumble the cell and helplessly watch it topple to the old brick. Thanking God I'd bought a bumper case for it, I pick it up and rub the scratched corner against my pants leg.

My thoughts race. I strike a trot for home as though I can outpace them. Alumnae often come to campus for special celebrations. But it seems that Eleanor has ingratiated herself with Susan in a singular sort of way. And something Truman mentioned last week flickers to mind: Eleanor as thick as thieves with Anne Emerson Callicot—the young debutante with the propensity to wound a fine young man like Truman. I can't help feeling that Eleanor's here to meddle in Truman's divorce. Has she come here on Anne Emerson's behalf?

In my living room, I kick off my shoes and pour myself a glass of wine. I pad to the kitchen, annoyance displacing fear and filling my chest. I reach around my back to unhook my bra without taking off my shirt, the way Lacey's sister Karen taught us when we were thirteen, and hurl it onto the stairs. I take the time to hand-wash Voltaire's little bowls—a mundane task that calms me. I feed him and then make myself a plate of cheese and crackers and carry it to the living room. As soon as I've eased my behind into a wing chair and taken a deep breath, my phone rings.

"Truman, how are you?"

His gentle voice curls into my ear. "Sweetheart, I'm sorry about our date. I'm exhausted. I can't believe my mother just showed up like that. She's checked into the campus guesthouse. God, my spine feels like it's been compressed."

I want to know why his mother has come. I want to know long she is staying. But I want him more. "Come over. Let me rub your shoulders."

I'm not afraid of storms;
I'm learning to sail my own ship.
—Louisa May Alcott

CHAPTER
TWELVE

Mini muffins and Styrofoam cups? In the faculty dining room, Susan, the queen of elegant events, is clearly staggering beneath the weight of her crown. Both caterers in Foxfield are at her beck and call. Historically—even with short notice—she would have arranged for a spread. I sit at a table between Lina and Truman and note, with a pang, the lavender smudges beneath our president's eyes, the way the back of her hair is parted and flat as though she's just risen from her bed.

When Eleanor Parker had appeared at the breakfast in her honor, she'd given me a cool but cordial greeting before taking a seat at our table on her son's other side. I can't help but take an occasional peep around Truman at her, who, in contrast to Susan, looks as if she's spent a week at a five-star spa with Ponce de León.

I watch Susan as she bends down next to the chairman's seat at the head table, exchanges words with him. She nods once, straightens herself, and makes her way to the podium. She addresses the packed house, "Good morning, Willa Cather."

"Good morning," we respond, the faithful chorus. Taking a mental roll call, I see not one missing member of the faculty or staff. All faces are rapt, except for my secretary's and my math-teaching next-door neighbor's. Mrs. King's examining the contents of a mini muffin basket with a frown, and he's busy checking out Truman and me. *Yes, that's whose car spent the night in my driveway, Snoop Dogg.*

"I appreciate everyone coming on such short notice," Susan says, then pauses to clear her throat. "I wasn't sure how long Eleanor would be here and didn't want you to miss the opportunity of meeting a special alumna, who has devoted her life to bolstering charitable organizations." So. They are honoring her because she's a noteworthy alum. I scribble a note to Lina: *Hope they're in the mood for a frosty treat.* She delivers a soft elbow to my ribs.

Susan's secretary tiptoes up behind her and places a Styrofoam cup on the podium. The president acknowledges her with a nod and takes a sip so small, I know it must be coffee instead of water. "Before I tell you more about Eleanor," she says to us, "I have a few . . . announcements." She takes another short sip. "First, I want to thank Dr. Emily Chambers, our dean of studies, who has done an outstanding job coordinating curriculum. Dr. Chambers has taken a position with James Madison for the fall term." Oh, no, oh, no. Susan looks toward our table and, I could swear, at Lina and me. Is someone else from our department leaving? "Second, Dr. Noah Tian, who piloted the Mandarin program at Willa Cather, and who's been an excellent teacher, is leaving us at the end of the term to pilot a similar program at Emory and Henry." Battered and stunned, I slump against the back of my chair. What Susan doesn't say is who will cover the summer Mandarin classes and of course whether they will fill his position. Leaning over a legal pad and sending an intimate whiff of his deodorant to my nose, Truman rubs at his forehead. He makes a quick column of dots and then scratches Susan's info next to them.

I startle when Lina touches my hand. She has scribbled across my notepad the words, *Another of us down*, and she now punctuates them by adding *WTH?* with more slashes of her pen.

I regard the pale oval of her face, take the pen, and write: *We can't maintain a foreign language department with a skeletal staff. Especially when the arts are in danger of being one of the first forests to fell.* She nods and leans her head against mine for a moment.

Susan takes a longer sip from her cup and then regards us again. I plead with her silently, *Stop now. Isn't this enough already?* But she continues, her voice like that of someone being strangled by degrees: "And David Collins. Head of. Our fine engineering department. Is moving on. To another opportunity." She sways slightly but then raises her chin. "Emily, Noah, David, will you stand so we can thank you for your service to Willa Cather?"

Truman's pen skitters across his pad. Light applause begins. An automaton, I raise my hands, but they seem to dangle from my wrists. Murmurs of dismay, small snatches of talk swirl up and under the applause and linger after it is done. Across the table from Lina, the development director, who must be too wrecked to modulate her voice, turns to her assistant. "Oh dear God. If we can't replace David and engineering goes under, we lose a five-million-dollar gift." A few heads in her vicinity turn and stare at her with the eyes of prey animals.

The engineering department is a big draw for our students. A great many girls come to WCC rather than a coed school to study engineering because they won't be the only woman in a class of men. The department and its endowment are crucial to our success. I stare at the back of David's head, wondering how he could leave us at such a time. Bailing on us while we are limping along must mean he's had some world-class offer, or simply that he is getting out while the getting's good. Have we come to that? An every-person-for-herself mentality?

I look at the dean of studies. Her top knot is steady, her hands relaxed and folded on her table. She's young and can afford an early-career hiccup on her résumé. I glance beyond Lina at the Mandarin-piloting hotshot whose arms are crossed over his scrawny chest. *Don't let the door hit you on the derriere on your way out.*

Susan taps on the mic. I spread the fingers of one hand over my chest as if to ward off another blow. "While David will be sorely missed, I want to reassure you that our chairman Beau and I will be conducting a nationwide search for a new engineering department head." A gust of Lina's coffee breath brushes my shoulder.

Shaking his head, Truman finally looks at me. Smoothly lowering his hand beneath the tablecloth, he places it over mine. The blue of his eyes, the warmth of his touch is all it takes to transport me. A magical moment from the previous night replays like a movie reel: the two of us lying face-to-face in my bed. In a soft pool of lamplight. Making love, all the while staring into each other's eyes.

Someone in the back has a coughing fit and the mind-movie pauses. But Truman's secret touch has given me strength. I turn a grateful gaze on him. But at the spectacle that is Eleanor on his other side, my heart gives a great, clumsy lurch. Leaning forward, one emaciated elbow on the table, she peers around Truman and looks pointedly to below the tablecloth where our hands are joined. Her eyes rise to my face. She arches a brow.

The mind-movie snaps and flaps wildly around its reel.

I have to learn how to keep my composure in front of this woman. Though my lips tremble, I force them to give Eleanor a cool smile before returning my gaze to Susan. My feet itch to take wing as they did in the January meeting, when I'd panicked and run from the library.

Oblivious to the interplay between his mother and me,

Truman rearranges his hand—where it's grown sweaty—around mine. Susan makes a few remarks about the class of 1949. She talks about how frightening and freeing at the same time it must have been for a woman in 1945, heading off to college with the close of the Second World War. Empress Eleanor nods and smiles as though she is a glowing amalgam of Mother Teresa and Gloria Steinem, before rising to join Susan at the podium.

I'm eyeing the red exit sign above the nearest door when Truman gives my hand another squeeze.

I close my eyes, a sudden calm sinking in and coating my insides like Pepto-Bismol. I'm making room in my life for an amazing man. His shoulders are broad and strong enough to bear the weight of my fears when I need it.

I have the support of friends. I seek Mrs. King's face across the room. Gazing fixedly at me, she smiles and gives me a slow wink.

I'm through running.

❧

Frowning at my laptop screen, I put on my glasses and adjust the brightness. Why is it so damned dark in here? Untangling my feet, I get up from my office desk to look out the window. Though it's midafternoon, the sky has darkened to the gray of tarnish, and dusty rag-like clouds obscure the mountains. I stretch my arms and my back and flip on the overhead light. The voice of the wind keens through a slice of open window. I push it closed just as rain begins to thrash the panes. The quad below is depleted of life, but light glows in a hundred windows and brings cheer to my heart; there are others working hard to save this place I love.

I'd spent an hour googling Eleanor Randall Parker and hopping down every rabbit trail. A six-time president of the Atlanta Junior League, Mrs. Parker's a member of what is apparently the swankest country club in Atlanta, the Piedmont Driving Club, where she made her society debut in 1946. I'd started tallying the number of charity balls and events she's chaired through the years on my notepad but tossed my pencil aside at twenty-two. Who would believe her bio?

Typically, I only log on to the college website to post French-class information or to update my professor page, but this afternoon, I've been drawn to it. I navigate to the annual campaign page. Is there an archival list of those who've given money to the school?

Mrs. King peeks through the cracked door and nudges it open with a foot. She waggles a can of Diet Coke at me and grins. "Caffeine free."

I push my glasses up to ride my head and pinch the bridge of my nose. "Yes, please, and thanks."

Mrs. King inclines a can of her own. "Cheers. Thought you could use one. You've been cooped up in here for hours."

I pop the top on the cold can and take a long sip. "Something is nagging at me. I may stay late and do a little sleuthing," I say, indicating my laptop. Truman had called earlier to let me know he had a late meeting with Susan, Beau, and Sawyer Hays, the CFO.

"You'll figure it out, chickie," my secretary says.

At the window, plucking dead leaves from a plant, she mumbles something about hoping the power doesn't go out. I smile abstractly. Mrs. King is the kind of woman who gets a big charge out of watching The Weather Channel. With my secretary in the room, my solitude is animated but not broken. I work better because I know her sensitive hands are busy.

I swig my Diet Coke, my eyes on the computer. "Uh-huh . . ."

When I look up again, Mrs. King is softly closing the door behind her.

I smile, remembering the last time she called me "chickie,"

the day she'd given me Elizabeth Pattison's phone number. Elizabeth and her classmates' devotion to the school that launched them into the world as strong and confident women made them eager to help.

Wiping the condensation from my can of soda, I have an epiphany: our efforts to recover the debt should be centered around alums who are passionate about the school, not high-society matrons like Truman's mother. Though she is an alumna, what has she really done for the school?

Truman had been angry when he called earlier. "Beau asked my mother to come to the meeting. Why the hell would he include her? It's embarrassing. I feel like a little kid whose mother has shown up in the cafeteria to cut up his meat."

I'd giggled. "I'm sorry to laugh, but that was too rich."

He'd sighed. "So far, my mother hasn't mentioned the divorce, though that has to be why she's come. Maybe she's planning to drive over and see the boys while she's here. Despite her many flaws, she loves her grandchildren." I try and imagine the brittle socialite cuddling Truman's blond blue-eyed cherubs, but the pixels scramble. "Maybe she's planning to donate some obscene amount of money to help bail us out."

"Maybe," I'd mused, "I mean, big money would help stem the flow, but long-term, I can't help feeling there's a better way." I'd treaded carefully; this was Truman's mother we were discussing. "That women who are . . . more personally invested in the college can do something to help insure that our legacy continues for the next generations. Has your mother donated a lot of money to the school in the past?"

"I have no idea what she gives," Truman had said. "It's the attention she gets from the charity galas that she loves. The foyer of my parents' penthouse is practically papered in framed covers of *The Atlantan* and *Town & Country* magazines she's been featured in. I'm not kidding." When Truman had ended the call, I didn't know if I felt more disdain or pity for his mother.

The rain streams down the windowpanes. I click on the development-office page and watch a slick, looping slideshow at the top: photos of the beautiful library and reading room where students built an arched entrance out of colorful old books; the up-to-date cafeteria with six specialized food bars, including baked potato, vegetarian and vegan, Italian, and Thai; the lacrosse field where the girls play on top-grade Astro-turf (an astonishing gift from a student's father five years ago); and a shot of the front gates with a thousand daffodils in bloom. There are equally vibrant pages on the site for admissions, student life, and athletics.

But the alumnae page has all the pizazz of a tax return. Who's responsible for maintaining it? The development office? The alumnae liaison? Does such a position exist? I should know that. Hunching over the laptop, I realize I've been scrubbing my hand over my mouth and chin. If I keep it up, my chin will break out. I bounce my fists on my desk. It's a no-brainer to keep graduates involved with the WCC community by enticing them with photos and information about their classmates. I dash off a quick reminder to contact someone about the alumnae page.

I return to the annual campaign page, where there is a list of donors since the year 2000. Though I search this, as well as archives that go back as far as 1955, I find no mention of Eleanor Randall Parker. Many donations were made anonymously, but the notion of Eleanor doing that makes me yip a laugh. Randomly picking back through the lists, I notice a sprinkling of gifts made "by the estate of so-and-so." Wealthy people must include charities in their estates all the time. I sit back in my chair. Ordinary people could do it, too, in modest amounts. Our faculty numbers one hundred twenty. Wrinkling my nose, I subtract the four known defectors and amend that number to one hundred sixteen.

Maybe I have another proposal to run by Susan. Why couldn't the administration ask the faculty to consider including the college in their estate plans? And why stop with faculty? Why not suggest it to alumnae as well? Lightning illuminates the window, and a "one thousand one, one thousand two" count later, thunder booms and my desk lamp dims. Unplugging the power cord from my laptop, I glance at the little battery symbol at the top of the screen: 75 percent. The lamp I leave alone. Power interruptions are common in this old building, and my pretty lamp hangs in there until the power comes back to full strength.

"Another brownout!" Mrs. King calls excitedly to someone in the hall.

I stare at my lamp and dust the base with a finger. Maybe what Willa Cather's experiencing is a sort of brownout, just an interruption of the power structure. Losing faculty who either don't have the guts to stay or who want to graze a greener pasture could be a good thing. Maybe the college will be revitalized when the power comes back. A tide of elation washes over me.

I add the estate planning idea to my to-do list, feeling more optimistic than I have in weeks. Is Dr. Chu's medicine kicking in, or am I growing stronger? I smile. Hopefully, both are true. My stomach growls loud enough to drown out the rain, and I remember I haven't eaten anything but a banana since the mini muffins at the breakfast.

My thoughts return to Eleanor. If Truman's mother isn't a major benefactor for the school, why do Beau and Sawyer hold her in such esteem? What makes her a big enough deal that she would be included in a confidential meeting? What power does she yield?

I take the last sips from the can of soda, and my empty stomach rebels by sending up a burp that makes me glance at my door to make sure it's closed. I check my phone for a text from Truman. Will he be finished with his meeting in time for a late dinner?

Mrs. King knocks again.

"Come."

Tying a plastic rain bonnet over her beauty-parlor-set hair, she says, "There's a break in the rain. I'm going to head out. Need anything?"

"I'm good, honey. You know what? I think I'll go on home too."

"See you tomorrow, chickie."

Outside, the rain has stopped, leaving everything earthy and green. A wild profusion of crocuses and daffodils greet me. Water still rushes across the lowest ground, sings through the metal culverts, flows from the gutter pipes, making small lakes around the buildings. I turn toward faculty row. Laurel trots down the steps of the history building. She catches sight of me and yanks her hoodie over her black curls. The memory of her cruising my street in her little car and snapping the visor down at the sight of Truman rouses itself.

"Bonjour, Laurel," I say brightly when she reaches the brick walk.

"Bonjour, Madame."

I study my student, the one who's been my secret favorite since she sat down in the front row of my classroom as a freshman and tossed her professor a grin and a breezy, unprecedented "Ça va?" I feel keenly the loss of her playful ebullience, the affectionate nature of our relationship.

"Guess they cancelled lacrosse practice this afternoon?"

"Yes, but . . . actually, I'm, um, thinking of quitting lacrosse."

A feel a curl of fear. "No! You're the captain of the team." Without Laurel, the team will crumble. And the National Collegiate Athletic Association rules that if a college doesn't participate in scheduled games, it can lose its eligibility, another blow for the college. "And your scholarship, Laurel. Wouldn't you lose it? Why on earth would you risk that?"

She toes at a puddle with a hot-orange sneaker. "Because," she finally says in the voice of a second grader. I study her face for a telltale sign, but it's like trying to see the bottom of a kettle through its spout.

Malika calls to her from the quad, waves to us both, "C'mon, Laurel!"

Laurel returns the wave. "I have to go, Madame."

At five feet eight inches, she towers over me. But I'm not only her teacher but also her advisor. I draw myself up to my full five foot three inches. "Darling, will you come and talk with me about this before making such a big decision?"

A long buzzing moment passes. "I might. Merci, Madame. Au revoir."

"Au revoir," I say as she breaks into a sprint and sloshes through the grass to the quad.

By the time I reach my town house—fretting about Laurel more with each step—I'm starving my brains out. I've still had no word from Truman, so I toss a quick scoop of kibble into Voltaire's bowl and rummage the refrigerator for salad makings. I quickly stem spinach, slice heirloom tomatoes and Persian cucumbers, and combine them with handful of shredded turkey in the first bowl I put my hand on: a medium-sized mixing bowl. I add a big splash of champagne vinaigrette to the top and carry the bowl out onto my back stoop. I survey my sweet little backyard.

Nearly two decades ago, I'd poured over garden catalogs and chosen flowers and foliage that seemed captured from the pages of the Tasha Tudor illustrations that enchanted me as a child. Now, in the summertime, it's an oasis brimming with life and color, charming me every time I come out. This year I will plant no fickle annuals, only more perennials, beauty that will renew itself along with the college as the years pass.

My phone shimmies against my thigh. I pluck it from the pocket of my linen pants, hoping it's Truman. Or Laurel.

Though I'd expected weariness, there's a bright edge to Truman's voice. "Hi, sweetheart. Have you eaten?"

"I'm just having a salad," I say, poking at the last cucumber slices in my bowl.

"Want to go stargazing, Georgie Girl?"

"Stargazing?" I look up, and a little trill escapes me. Though the sun made a brief appearance before promptly setting a scant hour ago, the evening star glows steady. A fairy-tale first-quarter moon casts a sugary light across the sky. "It's beautiful," I breathe.

"Let's go down to the boathouse and sit on the dock. I hear it's nice there."

A runner of fear trickles through my chest at the memory of the last time I'd been to the boathouse—with Lina—the night the terrible memories first resurfaced. An image comes. My father's face, pallid beneath his dripping slicker, when . . . I press my hand to my chest, willing the gut-twisting picture away. Looking back at the sky, I say into my phone, "I'd love to go stargazing."

"Wonderful. Pick you up in ten. And bring a blanket."

When we've reached the weathered old dock extending from the boathouse, Truman drapes the blanket around his shoulders and leans back against one of the thick posts used for tying up canoes. I settle back against him in the cozy tent made by his bent legs. We tuck the blanket around us, and he holds me against him. His chin, roughened by end-of-the-day beard, brushes the top of my head. "It's good and dark out here."

Is he glad it's dark so we can see the stars more clearly or because we're hidden away from prying eyes though it's a weeknight when students are studying? Though we've done nothing to disabuse anyone of the fact that we've become a couple, we're still professionals. The private quality of our romance makes it all the more thrilling.

In the Range Rover, I'd noticed that the lines around Truman's mouth had grown deeper since I'd seen him six hours before.

"Tough meeting?" I'd lightly prodded.

He'd searched my eyes and sighed. "I'm telling you in the strictest confidence, but you'll be getting an email about it in the morning anyway: Beau suggested eliminating 5 percent of the faculty from the philosophy and history departments."

"Oh dear Lord." Though a bland weariness had settled over me, I'd breathed a sharp sigh of relief that the foreign language department had been spared for the present. But I'd felt a great tug of dismay for the effected faculty, friends who I knew were tenured. I wanted to ask Truman about his mother's involvement in the meeting or if she had mentioned me. I'd wanted to tell him about Laurel. But when we'd reached the lake, he'd asked if we could declare a moratorium on college news for the night. "I just want to be with you," he'd said, driving all thoughts of trouble from my mind.

I lean my head back against his shoulder and gaze into the sky again. Suddenly, I feel the way I used to feel when playing tea party at the bottom of the pool at Browning with Lacey. Just before I ran out of air, my lungs about to burst, I'd look up toward the surface of the water to a summer day full of promise and adventure.

A constellation materializes as though someone has flung a handful of bright pebbles into the heavens. "What's that one; do you know?" Truman asks, pointing west.

"I've no idea. The only one I can ever make out is the big dipper. The registration line for astronomy at UVA was too long."

He chuckles, his chest rumbly, and I feel the way fussy babies must when held against a man's chest, smoothed and cosseted.

I wonder what Truman was like with his boys when they were little. Among the other five million things we've yet to learn about each other, we haven't talked much about the boys. But first, since he can't see my face, I ask him something that's been lurking about the angles of my mind, something long overdue.

"Truman, we, neither of us, have mentioned birth control."

An owl hoots in the woods. Truman stills against me. "Yeah? I mean, right. We haven't."

I take a breath. "We talked about how we were both, you know . . . clean, but did you assume, because of my age, that I was done with menopause?"

"I guess I did," he says, and then adds in a rush, "aren't you?"

"I haven't had a period in three months, so I believe I am."

He exhales and holds me tighter. "Good."

Melding into his body again, I survey the sky and then jump. "I think I just saw a shooting star!"

"Where?"

I snake my arm from under the blanket and point. "There, above the evening star."

"Missed it," he says, and he is quiet again for a space of time. Then, he bursts forth with a recitation, a poem about the star.

"True," I say, "That was . . . beautiful. Is it Longfellow?"

I feel him give a little shrug. "Yeah."

"I used to love that about you, how you liked poetry. Do you still?"

"I do."

The poem he'd written me in his round boyish print drifts into my mind. "Do you remember writing me a Valentine's Day poem?"

He laughs. "Sort of. What a putz I was!"

I turn and seek his face in the darkness. "You were not a putz! It was good. And you were romantic and adorable."

He dips his chin. "Am I still adorable?"

"More."

His voice cracks a little. "You're beautiful, Georgie. Your smile . . . warms me to my backbone." He pauses, kisses my forehead, my lids, my cheeks before working his way to my lips. A billion shimmering stars seem to rush through my veins. He puts me away from him again. His throat works. "I love you."

Awash in the most undiluted happiness I've ever known, I whisper, "Oh, True. I love you too."

People live through such pain only once.
Pain comes again, but it finds a tougher surface.
—Willa Cather

CHAPTER
THIRTEEN

I wake in joy, though the other side of Truman's bed is empty, rumpled and cool.

After we made love last night and I lay with my head on the sweetmeat of his chest, he said he might go running this morning. Now, rising to my elbows, I look under the chair where his yawny-mouthed Sauconys live in a drift of dust bunnies, but they're gone. I grin, remembering how he'd popped his belly—grateful he hadn't popped mine—and said he needed to get back in shape. Long after he'd fallen sleep, I'd studied his face—the little horizontal forks at the corners of his eyes, his freckled cheeks, the slight down-turned curve of his lips—and listened to the *fwoo-fwoo-fwoo-fwoooo* pattern of his slumber. I'd thought of how he'd shared a bed with the woman who had borne his children and felt a hitch of grief that I'd never share that part of him. I wondered how he'd looked in his twenties, in the prime of his thirties, and when his hair had grayed. How beautiful he and his wife must have appeared on the surface, like the exterior of this built-to-impress Victorian. Its gracefully turned wood, carefully contrasting colors, and elaborate trim, belying its interior, dark from neglect and decay. I remember

Eleanor, here in Foxfield, and wonder if I'll have to face her again today. Hadn't she known her son's marriage was a misery to him? Had Eleanor assumed he'd fallen in love with Anne Emerson after the deal was sealed or by the time the children had come?

My eyes had traced the furrows of his face again. While his suffering had shaved off a small slice of my heart, it hadn't reached the part that's relieved the woman didn't make him happy. I want to be the one to make him happy. I want to complete him. But am I sure I have what it takes after all the years I've spent alone? It's not like I have the blueprint for a perfect union of souls rolled up in a kitchen drawer. My longest relationship—with a guy I met in my third year of college—lasted just two years.

But this is Truman. My first love. Does finding each other again mean we're meant to be? Our circumstances—his pending divorce and the contretemps of Willa Cather—have given our relationship the tenuous quality of a wartime romance, one of thrill and risk but also sacrifice.

I stretch across the bed to retrieve my phone, where it lays in a swatch of morning sun atop the moving box that serves as Truman's bedside table. It's as though there are secret chambers I've just discovered. Nothing about his setup speaks of permanence. Will that change now that we're in love? Will he stay in Foxfield? Every time he holds me, another part of my heart opens.

I check the time: nine minutes until my morning alarm goes off. I drop the phone to the mattress and stretch myself the way Voltaire does when waking from a nap. My old friend guilt traces my heart. I'd left my cat overnight again. Though I'd added an extra scoop of food to his bowl and topped off his water before leaving for the lake, I still have to remind myself that animals don't perceive elapsed time the way humans do.

Truman should be back soon. I need to get up and shower. But I can't resist rolling to my side, lying a cheek against his cool pillow, inhaling his scent. "Truman Parker loves me," I whisper into the down. The stacks of books next to the blue Chinese jar lamp (Had Anne Emerson chosen that?) on the moving box catches my eye. I love that Truman's a sophisticated man who appreciates nice things and reads instead of watching endless games of football. With an inner tickle, I recall the way he looks in his tortoiseshell reading glasses, the way he runs his knuckles across the hollow of his throat when absorbed in a passage. I survey the books he's curated for his bedroom: a fat yellow-edged copy of *A Tale of Two Cities*, it's paper cover mussed with coffee rings; the slimmer volume of *The Great Gatsby* in a glossy black cover; a black leather-bound Bible; a hardcover copy of *Key Management Models* bracketed between *A Farewell to Arms* and a club-sandwich-thick *Poetry of Dylan Thomas*; and at the bottom, a derelict copy of *The Adventures of Huckleberry Finn*. I run my finger along that spine, grinning at the thought of this one being with him since his Browning days.

Smoothing my hand along the sheet where Truman has lain, I whisper in French, "Hands joined and face to face, let's stay just so." It's from the poem "Le Pont Mirabeau," which I'll be introducing to my freshmen today. The passion the man has roused in me will add nuance, freshness to the poem I've taught a dozen times. It's Friday, and the weekend stretches before me like a mile of sunflower fields. Truman's asked me to spend it at his house. He's told his mother about us, and I can just imagine how that conversation must have gone. *"But she's lea-ving to-day, ay,"* I sing out and kick off the covers. She's driving her rental car to Mountainsburg to have lunch with her grandsons, before taking an evening flight from Dulles to Atlanta. Encouraged by a phone conversation with Trask and Asher, Truman wants to drive to Mountainsburg to see them on Sunday. "Go with me, Georgie," he'd urged.

I'd hung my head, suffused with shame. "I . . . I can't."

A shadow had crossed his face, but he'd lightly said, "It's okay, baby, another time."

If only I could have brought the sun back into his eyes. At that moment, I'd hated my anxiety swiftly and savagely. It would be so great to be spontaneous, even adventurous. Will Truman get tired of a woman who can't even do a simple thing like ride over to the next town?

I tell that worry to haul ass, rise, and pad to the bathroom. Tomorrow he wants to buy wood for bookshelves and a litter box and bowls for Voltaire. The first purchase speaks of permanence, the other more of convenience, but both make me happy. Lathering my hair with Truman's shampoo, I wonder if I should bring a bag of toiletries to leave here. What would he think if I commandeered the empty drawer in the bathroom chest for my own?

☙❧

Two weeks later, neither True nor I have heard a peep from Eleanor. Laurel has not been back to my office to talk. In class, she's detached, and a graph of her grades would resemble a length of rickrack. I hope to talk to her at the once-a-month lunch I have with my advisees today. The area of the cafeteria where we pick up our food always makes me wish for a pair of mittens. "Bonjour, Madame," Hollins greets me, shivering herself and hugging a trapezoid meal tray to her chest. Dressed in their "I'm going to the gym right after class, I swear" outfits, Penn and Malika inch along the line.

"Bonjour, mesdemoiselles," I say to them. Apparently in high spirits, Penn gives me a hug. She says Instagram has declared it National Chocolate Day and they're following suit, pulling out the dark chocolate they hoard for emergencies like exams, breakups, or PMS. The one grumpy cafeteria woman bumps through the swinging door from the kitchen with a tray, bringing a whoosh of baking chocolate in her wake. Penn's nostrils flare. "Ooh, petit lava cakes!"

Malika and I funnel into the baked-potato-bar line. "I enjoyed your paper on Renoir," I tell her, "the way you juxtaposed his reported misogynistic attitudes with his portraits of women."

Her full-moon face beams. "Thanks. I worked really hard on that."

I spoon chopped tomato, black olives, shredded cheddar, and salsa onto my potato. "And congratulations on your first lacrosse goal."

"Thanks," she says, smothering her potato in chili and queso.

I finish off my potato with a sprinkle of green onions and then—in the spirit of National Chocolate Day—snare two lava cakes on little Styrofoam plates. "You're off to a really good start this season," I say to Malika, handing one of the plates to her and hoping that if Laurel has quit the lacrosse team, Malika will say so.

"Yeah, we are. It's pretty awesome."

We join my others in the dining hall. My advisees, Laurel included, are waiting for me at a big round table. I spread a paper napkin across my lap and hold my fork aloft. "Bon appétite, *mes filles*."

"Bon appétite," everyone but Laurel echoes. Picking the shrimp from her bowl of pad thai, she noshes the soft flesh as if it's saltwater taffy. With a tinge of sadness, I note her flat affect. Though surrounded by her friends, it's as though she inhabits a planet of her own. *I miss you*, I beam to the top of her curly head.

A message buzzes my phone: Truman Parker. Wiping a finger on my napkin, I poke it open. *Hello, beautiful,* he's typed.
Pop in to see me before your one o'clock class? Imagining a kiss
or two behind the conference room door before the start of my
long afternoon, I flick the onions from my potato. I type, "As
you wish, my love," and hit send.

Sutton studies the lovestruck curl of my lips. "Ma-dame,"
she says with a creamy smile, "Monsieur Parker, I presume?"

I turn doe-wide eyes on her. *"Qu'elle?"* My eyes dart to
nearby tables. "What makes you think that?"

Penn gives me a sidelong look and wiggles her eyebrows.
She says in the voice of Pepé Le Pew, *"Tu ne peux pas cacher
l'amour"* ("You can't hide love").

I can't help but grin at the saucy talk.

"I knew you'd get together," Sutton says dreamily.

"It's just so romantic, reuniting with your first love," Penn
adds. "Someone should write the story." The other girls dig into
their lunches, laughing.

"Are you going to move into that beautiful old house downtown?" Madison asks, around a mouthful of salad.

A wisp of fear lifts my head. "What? No! I'd never leave my
home. And how do you know where he lives?"

Victoria shrugs. "Everyone knows."

Laurel segregates the pad thai in her bowl into mounds of bean
sprouts, noodles, and radishes and assiduously avoids my eyes.

Hollins wipes her mouth. "Why should she leave her house?
A woman doesn't have to move in with a man. Monsieur Parker
could move in with Madame."

"No one is moving in with anyone anytime soon," I say
prissily.

"Some couples keep separate residences," Emily insists.
"In France, most married couples keep separate bedrooms. For
sleeping, that is," she adds with narrowed eyes.

"*Mon dieu*, Emily!" I say. But being the object of such talk is a fizzy libation. The girls laugh and hoot Emily down. All but Laurel, who's building little cairns out of radishes and cubes of tofu on the plateau of her bowl.

At half past twelve, I step from the artificial chill, babble, and the odor of taco meat and bruised bananas and into the midday sun. The April sky is as beautiful as that of a new world's.

Shaking off my concern about Laurel for the moment, I think of Truman waiting for me. I quicken my pace, believing I could two-step to the admin building.

But when I open the conference room door, he starts in his chair and looks up as though I've caught him doing something illegal.

"What?" I say.

"Close the door and come look at this."

I push the door to and lean over the table, where he sits holding a burgundy copy of the 1949 *Willa Cather Carillon*, the yearbook named for the now-derelict bell tower. "Your mother's senior year?" Beneath the pristine copy of the '49 *Carillon* are volumes from previous years and a couple of musty college magazines.

My eyes move between the book and his muddled expression. "I'm still racking my brain," he says, "about what she's been up to. I couldn't find anything about her involvement with the school online, beyond the obvious."

I know what you mean. My cheeks grow warm at the thought of the investigations I had done. But Truman's on a roll and doesn't notice.

"So, on a hunch, I go to the library and ask to see the locked-up archival volumes. I thought the librarian was going to make me sign these out in blood." Truman opens the '49 to a photograph from the WCC spring formal. "Look what I found." Though she's little more than a smile beneath a tiara, I recognize Eleanor Parker. The words on the banner crossing her torso are obscured by a spray of roses in her arms. Standing next to her is a young man whose grainy head is topped with a crown. I bend closer. "Read the caption," Truman says.

"Queen Eleanor Trask Randall and her king, Beauregard Duffy, of George Wythe College." I do a double take at the king. "The chairman?" I ask, loud enough to be heard in Richmond. I fast-pitch my voice to a ragged whisper. "They've known each other since college?"

Truman shakes his head. "I knew Duffy was a George Wythe graduate, but not the year, or that there was a connection between him and my mother."

"Well, why wouldn't they say they were old friends? I mean, that's just weird . . ."

Truman rises from his chair and gathers me into his arms. "I know. I'm clueless." Though our interlude has taken on a troubled tinge, I lock my hands behind his neck. "I'm going to keep looking through these for a while. I still don't get why Beau brought my mother in on a confidential finance meeting."

"Shhh," I murmur, "kiss me, True."

⟡

On May Day, the faculty gathers in the library just before a five o'clock meeting. I rush in, a bulging tote full of papers banging against my shins, frazzled by a skirmish with a copy machine. I'd finally surrendered, dashed "out of order" across a sheet of crimped paper, and slapped it to the front of the beast with a snag of Scotch tape. Taking a deep breath, I spot Lina in the loosely populated third row. Making my way to her, I regard the advancement director seated in the front row with a ripple of annoyance: she hasn't acknowledged my email regarding my ideas about alumnae giving.

A small cry from the hall beyond the side entrance drives

that concern from my mind. A grim-faced Truman appears in the doorway with Jillian, the admissions director. She presses her knuckles against her lips. What the heck? Transfixed, I watch Truman take her by an elbow and lead her into the room and to a chair. A librarian takes over, sits beside Jillian, and places an arm around her trembling shoulders.

My stomach drops with déjà vu to the devastating January meeting in which we'd learned the school was in financial straits.

Dumbly, I drop into the seat next to Lina, who is speaking into her phone, and return my eyes to Truman. He removes his suit coat and wipes his forehead with a shirtsleeve. Leaning against a column, he takes his phone from his pocket and begins stabbing at it with his thumbs.

My phone buzzes in my hand. He's texting me. *Where are you?* That's when I notice a trio of missed calls from him. Ripples of fear move along my limbs. I wave a trembling hand above my head. Truman looks out over the burgeoning assembly, raises his chin in recognition, and strides my way. The ripples swell into a wave of alarm as I catch sight of Susan. The shift she wears hangs on her like a bag. How much weight has she lost? I try to gauge her expression, but it's difficult to make out the line of demarcation between her face and the white linen. She takes a seat in the front row next to Beau. Lina has ended her call but sits wordlessly, her eyes on Susan.

Truman sits heavily in the chair on my other side and gives Lina a somber nod.

"I've been trying to call you," he says to me, his eyes pools of dreadful knowledge. His hair is as damp and curly as it had been this morning when he'd returned from his run, whisked back the shower curtain—making me squeal—and climbed in with me.

Now everything is different and everything is wrong.

Tears well in my eyes. "I know. I—"

Beau Duffy's voice cloaks the room. "Ladies and gentlemen." The chairman pauses as the hush of a snow day falls over the assembly. I crane my neck and spot Susan in the front row. The way her chin drops to her chest and remains there deafens me to Beau's initial remarks. But this sentence rivets me: "Despite our attempts to bolster programs, enrollment has dropped—since January—almost 24 percent."

There is a plate shift in the room.

The chairman continues. "Maintenance costs to keep these hundred-year-old buildings safe for students continue to increase. We are still burdened with a twenty-million-dollar debt owed primarily to bondholders."

Truman gives a little tremor of response before closing his eyes. Does he feel partly responsible for not being able to help us? The chairman goes on, relentless. "We face default and the possibility of an accelerated lump-sum payment of the entire amount." I backpedal my shoes at the floor as though at the edge of a cliff. "With insolvency inevitable, Susan and I feel the responsible course is to make an advance announcement to the community." The chambers of my heart seem to get confused and pump blood in the wrong direction. "After 135 years, we will close our doors . . . on August 29."

Gasps and sobs erupt throughout the room. Lina raises her hands to place them over her face. The chairman's next words register with me only dimly, as though he's speaking them from a great distance: "With the last day of classes on May 30, our current students will be able to transfer at the beginning of the new fall term. The time will also allow us to honor our financial obligations." A hum escapes Truman. Blearily, I turn to him. His head slightly cocked, he looks as fixedly at Beau as a hound on point. The chairman goes on, "As for our students, rest assured, Sawyer Hays and the chaplain are breaking the news to them in the chapel at this moment." *I should be with my students;* my blasted brain says to me as Beau speaks of documents and emails. The chairman adjourns the meeting and abruptly leaves the room. The space quakes with silence.

And then we are on our feet. Faculty and staff turn woodenly to one another. The despair in their faces reminds me of a Renaissance painting that had frightened me as a child, a teeming sea of lost souls. My thoughts as topsy-turvy as a pen of ferrets, I stagger toward the emergency exit and shove the metal bar. An alarm sounds, but it's no competition for the clamor that greets me on the other side of the door.

Though a line still trickles from the chapel, most of the Willa Cather student body has gathered on the quad. They form tear-drenched group hugs, their keening freighted with disbelief, outrage, and grief.

I can't stop to comfort them. I have nothing for Laurel, nor for Hollins, for Penn or Malika, nor for any of the others. If I stop now, a wound could open in the earth beneath my feet and I could drop into some abyss, where I might never stop falling. Lina and Truman call my name. I know they are upset too, but my anxiety makes all this harder for me to process. Home. I have to get home.

I cut across the grass behind the dining hall and trip over a sprinkler head. Righting myself, I plunge on, vaguely aware that I've lost a shoe. I limp past deserted buildings: engineering, history, biology. I cut across the end of Faculty Road, loose gravel tearing at my foot. Before catching sight of my home, I stop on the corner. I stand there, heart in mouth, feeling as though if I look at it, the place will have disappeared. Eyes down, I move along the street in the gathering dim, past the homes of my neighbors, their cars, their lives as they know them.

Some secrets are like fossils,
and the stone has become too heavy to turn over.
—Delphine de Vigan

CHAPTER
FOURTEEN

It's been three days since the fateful faculty meeting. I've lain in bed as though suffering some epic, eighteenth-century illness like one on Outlander. My tears spring from an endless reservoir. I've slept prodigiously, getting up only to take care of most of Voltaire's needs though few of my own. Today, the litter box and I both smell bad. The red blotch between my breasts is the product of sleeping with a fist pressed to the place my heart cleaved in two.

Though I'd bailed on my colleagues, Truman, and my students after the faculty meeting, I'd done so not of the old panic—which the antidepressant has kept in check—but of grief. And last-ditch hope, as when one learns of a death but can't believe it's true until a silent ambulance crunches away from the scene. At last, I had stood before my home, dark and empty of life save for Voltaire who—at that time of day—should have been a contented crescent atop the dryer. I'd known it could no longer harbor me, that all too soon I'd be set adrift.

When my throbbing foot awakens me—and sends me limping for water and ibuprofen—I open emails and texts.

From Lina:

Let me know you're okay.
How are you today? Carmen spent the night at the paper.
Truman is worried about you.

I've responded to these with the least emotional emoticon, the yellow thumbs-up. This is monstrously unfair to my friend, who has to be grieving too. I will call her. Soon.

When I'd missed my appointment with Dr. Chu yesterday, she had called me herself and left me a voicemail. But Dr. Chu and a shopping spree behind the counter of the pharmacy couldn't fuse my flayed heart together.

There have been a handful of missed calls from Truman, two plaintive texts:

Georgie, just let me know you're okay. Please.
Lina said you're okay, but please call me.

And yesterday, a voicemail: *Georgie. Are you there? Will try you again soon. I know you're hurting, sweetheart. I love you.* And this morning when the five o'clock birds had begun their chorus: *You're not the only one who's hurting. I need your comfort.*

While I am sure Truman is gravely disappointed his efforts to rescue the school have been for naught, he came here committed to a single year. He bought the Victorian intending to flip it. He said he wanted to get to the heart of the place. But as yet, he's made only perfunctory plans to remodel. He could pack up his books, drive the stake of a for-sale sign into the lawn tomorrow, probably break even on his investment. He could climb into his Range Rover and return to Atlanta. He could move on to another consulting job, though he's said he's realized how lonely the itinerant life had been.

He's made no commitment to me. Though I believe him when he says he loves me.

I believe we are meant to be together.

Yet where would that be?

I try to squeeze past the enormity of the loss of my job and having to move from my home, to see if something waits for me on the other side, but I keep getting stuck.

After I've listened to Truman's voicemail again, I gather Voltaire—who moved into my house as little more than a mewling tuft—into my arms. I inform him of practical matters. The emails I've received from the board have been extensive. They are paying faculty until the last day of June, the staff until May 30. I cannot allow my mind to go to Mrs. King yet, or I will lie here until my smell alerts the neighbors. There will be no severance pay. Though I have no home equity, I've had free room and board and free dining hall meals for more than two decades. Because of these perks, I've managed to carton an ostrich-sized nest egg.

I cradle my cat and thumb through my voicemails again. I replay Dr. Chu's. She says she will see me anytime regardless of her schedule. Along with the doctor, the whole town—if not the whole region—undoubtedly knows the college is closing. If my mother gets wind, she will be frantic. I have to call my family and Lacey. But not yet.

One call to Dr. Chu and twenty minutes later, I'm shuffling through her office door in my pajamas, not giving two hoots about what anyone might think. The doctor takes me in from head to toe and gently smiles. That's when I notice that my bedroom slippers are on the wrong feet.

❧

As I'm stepping from the shower, my phone chimes from atop the vanity. "Madame Bricker?" a husky little voice from an unfamiliar number says.

Malika? I was expecting Truman to return the call I'd placed to him from the coupe on the way home from the doctor's office. "Malika?" I say, wrapping myself in a toweling robe. "Are you okay?" How could she be?

"I'm okay." Her voice splinters. "It's Laurel I'm calling about."
My heart tugs at the baste-stitch job Dr. Chu had given it.
"What about Laurel?"

"I'm with her . . . at the hospital. Foxfield Memorial."

Oh my Lord. "What happened, Malika?"

"Oh, Madame. We think she tried to kill herself." Gob-
smacked, I drop to the toilet lid. Why would Laurel do this?
Malika begins to sob. My jaws secrete the saliva of nausea into
my mouth. The school news is bad, but Laurel has so much
going for her. Wearily, I wonder if I should get up and open
the toilet lid. "We got together in Hollins and Madison's room
last night. We've been so upset about the school closing." I
breathe around the nausea, my mind taking a peek back to the
heart-wrenching scene on the quadrangle after the devastating
announcement. Malika's voice seems to be coming from inside
a throw pillow. "We got some seniors to buy us some booze.
Laurel hadn't seemed to take the news . . . well, any harder than
the rest of us. We all got . . . trashed."

Before, booze in the dorms would have sent my back bris-
tling, but what does it matter now? Malika goes on, "Laurel had
been to see Trask."

My blasted mind rebels. "Trask?"

"Her boyfriend." Laurel never mentioned her boyfriend to
me. Trask.

I grip my cell hard enough to crack the bumper case.
"Malika, what's his last name?"

"Parker. Trask Parker. He plays baseball for George Wythe.
They've been together since freshmen year."

"What happened, Malika? Did they break up?"

"She wouldn't talk about it. She . . . there was a bottle of Jack
Daniel's left over. I saw Laurel stick it under her bed." My nausea
surges. "This morning I couldn't wake her up!" Malika chokes
around her sobs. "She's . . . we're in a room now. Thirty-five

twelve, I think. Oh, Madame," she wails, "the doctor told me they pumped her stomach. It must have been horrible." Oh, my Laurel. Malika cries softly. Oh, my girls.

"Do you know if the hospital got in touch with her aunt?" I'm appalled at the thought of the elderly woman I'd met at freshman orientation receiving such anguishing news.

"They did. I heard the nurse tell her that she . . . consumed a near-lethal amount of alcohol. But, Madame . . . can you come?"

I storm my bedroom, snatching fresh clothes from drawers and hangers. For my Laurel, for Malika? "Hang on. I'll be right there."

⚭

As I enter Laurel's hospital room, Malika leaps from a chair in the corner. Wrapping her in a hug, I close my eyes—for the brief moment that her coconut-oil conditioner replaces the spooky metal-and-disinfectant-tinged air—and summon strength. I raise my eyes to the bed. My stomach clenches. Laurel lies impossibly small. The side rails have been pulled up as though she's an infant who might roll out. I hold Malika at arm's length and search her eyes. "You know you probably saved her life, don't you?"

Malika swallows, casts a glance at the bed, and nods. "I'm just glad . . . well . . ."

"I know. You're a wonderful friend, Malika." I hug her again. "No one could have known she would . . . do this."

"I know. I'm just . . . exhausted, Madame."

"Why don't you call one of the other girls to come and pick you up and go rest awhile. I'll stay with Laurel."

Malika lets out a breath that seems to have come from her toes. "Madison and Victoria were here earlier. But I'll call Hollins," she says. "Thank you so much." She loops her crossbody bag over her head, squares it across her torso, and, with a last, crestfallen glance at her roommate, steps from the room.

I stand over the bed. Laurel twitches in her sleep. She scratches at the white tape—stark against her dark right hand—that holds an intravenous tube in place, and the half-empty plastic bag swings on its pole. I touch her wrist to still her movement and aimlessly wonder why, in 2018, when they have multicultural everything else—crayons, markers, Band-Aids—they still use white tape in a hospital. Patiently, I watch her sleep, knowing that when she wakes, she will once again face whatever prompted her to try to take her own life.

Why had Laurel not asked for help? Knowing her as I do, I'm betting she believed the weight of her despair would burden others. And people say suicide is a selfish act.

I'd told Dr. Chu I felt ashamed of the way I'd shut out the people who love me after learning the college would close. But she'd said it had been an act of self-preservation. I watch liquid ooze along the tube and into Laurel's hand. How is it that some of us live for years with mental health issues, while others self-destruct? Weighing the private emotions of another is an impossible task. But, be it a life of panic and fear or an act as swiftly profound as suicide, mental anguish has no root in selfishness. And by the same coin, others are not to blame. Even if I'd known the degree of Laurel's despair, she still might have tried to end her life.

Her untethered hand flutters. It slides to her chest, slips from the blanket, and makes its way to her throat. She moans. I tuck the blanket back around her strong tawny arm and remember the banner with her image on the quadrangle. *Find Your Fierce.* My fierce girl, like an injured baby rabbit someone has tucked into a shoebox with soft swaddling. I close my eyes and shake my head. I'd admired her strength. Who could have guessed that she'd be the one to crumble? Laurel—like me—must withdraw when she wants to hide her fear.

But there will be no more hiding.

This morning, Dr. Chu stated something that, if I were the sort to tattoo myself, I would have inscribed on my palm: fear will no longer hijack my life. As it is, I will write it on Post-it squares and press them to my mirror, my refrigerator, the dash of my car, my computer.

I will fight for myself.

I will help Laurel fight for herself.

We will fight for each other.

"Madame?" her voice startles me. She clutches her throat as though it runs with lava.

I smooth her curls back from her forehead. "I'm here, Laurel."

With a *thunk* of the big metal door latch, a nurse glides into the room. "How are we doing?" he says officiously, his eyes scanning Laurel's vital signs on a monitor.

I give Laurel a tender smile. "She's awake."

The nurse pours a cup of water from the plastic pitcher. "Will you drink some water for me, hon?" he says, bending the straw to Laurel's mouth. She fits her cracked lips around it. "Not too much, now." He moves the cup away. "How are you feeling?"

She gives a little croak. "Like shit."

He gives her a smile. "You're going to be just fine." When he's finished his tasks, he pats her foot beneath the blanket. "The doctor will be in soon."

When we're alone again, Laurel's coffee-bean eyes brighten with tears. "I'm so ashamed for you to see me like this."

"You have *nothing* to be ashamed of, darling."

Tears slip from the corners of her eyes and into her unadorned ears. That's just it. I've always been your darling. But now you probably think I'm a fool, a stupid kid. I'm so sorry I've shut you out."

"You are my darling. Nothing will ever change that. I love you."

"I love you too." She closes her eyes. "Does my Auntie Mahalia know I'm here?"

"The doctor called her. Yes."

She buries her face in the crook of her arm and begins to weep. "I'm so embarrassed."

How does one soul speak to another in this situation? I decide to speak from my heart. "Would you like me to call your auntie? And let her know you're okay?"

Laurel nods against her arm and hitches the neck of her blue-print hospital gown to wipe her face. "Would you?" she asks, her face brimming with expectancy.

"Of course, I will." I locate a box of tissues on the broad windowsill and hand three of them off to Laurel.

Dabbing at her eyes, she looks at the door before returning her gaze to mine. "Madame, terrible things have happened."

I swallow another swoop of nausea. Should I allow her to talk, or should I wait for the doctor? Where is he or she? There are so many words in the world, and I can say them in two languages, yet I have none for this moment. I move to pull the chair up to the bed, take a seat, and rest a forearm on the bedrail. Laurel's eyes penetrate mine, and I'm surprised at the strength in her voice. "My boyfriend Trask is Truman Parker's son."

Where is the damned doctor? What if I say the wrong thing? "Well, I knew his sons went to George Wythe."

Fresh tears flood her eyes. "I was afraid Mr. Parker might be like his mother." Her eyes blaze then, as though anger has replaced regret. "Like Trask's horrible troll of a grandmother. She hates me because I'm biracial." Wordlessly, I stare at her. No wonder Laurel hadn't wanted any part of Truman or me once she knew we were together. I gulp and nod like a bobble-head in place of blathering. "I'm sorry, Madame."

I cast a longing glance at the door and choose my words as

though composing a treatise. "Don't be sorry. And you can trust me that Truman is a good man."

Laurel moans and fits her hand around her neck again. "My throat is killing." I reach for the cup of water, my hand trembling at her choice of word, and lower it over the rail. She takes a few deep pulls on the straw and then dismisses it with a shake of her head. She takes a deep breath. "Mr. Parker was nice to me . . . the one time we met. But then he wasn't around much. The boys haven't seen him in a while." *The consulting work.* I beam understanding with my eyes. "I was at their apartment in Mountainsburg yesterday morning."

She must have cut classes again. I imagine her rolling into an apartment parking lot in her little bumper-stickered car.

"We were hanging out. Talking. Bingeing Netflix, when Grand El—that's what the guys call her—phones Asher." *Asher.* "Madame, Trask and I are engaged."

"You're engaged?"

She straightens the fingers of her untethered left hand and examines it. "He didn't give me a ring, but we're planning to get married next summer, as soon as we graduate." A moan escapes her. She cries quietly for a space of time. I feed tissues into her hand, my chest ratcheting tighter with her every sob. At last, she speaks again, her eyes puffed and slitted. "I went to Atlanta with him to a party. . . in January. A big-deal anniversary party for his grandparents." *Eleanor and Conrad.* "Trask bought me a really pretty velvet dress to wear," Laurel goes on. "He introduced me as his girlfriend. There were, like, hundreds of people there, and I didn't get a chance to talk to them. We figured I'd get to know them . . . you know, another time, and we'd announce our engagement. But a week later, I get this letter in the mail." *Tell me it wasn't written on fine lavender notepaper, I beg her with my eyes.* "From his grandmother." Laurel makes a hard ball of the tissue in her fist. "She started out all nice, thanking me for coming to the party. Then . . ." A single tear coasts her right cheek. "She said that it was," Laurel lifts her hands and makes air quotes, "the family expectation that Trask marry a girl from a background like his own, a girl who is prepared to manage his social obligations and one who is better suited to his way of life. She said the matter should stay between the two of us." She looks miserable. "I didn't tell Trask! I was too ashamed. I wondered if she was right."

An aide clanks into the room with a tray and offers Laurel some cherry Jell-O, giving me a chance to process all that Laurel has said. No wonder she's been so upset. Failing in her work. So ready to give up on the school.

Laurel tells the aide she'll try some Jell-O, then watches her leave. She takes a deep breath and goes on. "Yesterday, when their grandmother called Asher—and I could tell who it was—I started to shake. So, I got up to go to the bathroom. Asher said, 'Hang on, Grand El, Trask's here, I'm going to put you on speaker.' I closed the bathroom door, took my time in there, hoping they would be off the phone when I came out. But when I did, I could tell Trask was talking about me. I stood in the hall, and, well, eavesdropped." Mucus oozes from her nose to her top lip, and I'm reminded how young she is. *What the hell has Eleanor Parker done to this lovely, bright child?* Laurel's damaged throat makes her whisper barely audible. I lean closer, my chest pressed against the cold rail. "She said that I am a half-breed, nobody from nothing."

I want to crawl under the bed. The words are hard enough to hear, let alone believe. Truman's parents had blackmailed him into marrying the "right sort of girl"; would they do the same to Trask? I want to kill Eleanor, to make a garrote out of her antique pearls and yank until her neck snaps.

Laurel stares dry-eyed at the ceiling. "Somehow, I managed to walk back in there. Trask was standing at the window by then, talking into the phone, his shoulders all bunched up. I told Asher I wasn't feeling well and that I'd call later. I slunk out with my tail between my legs and turned off my phone. I love Trask more than anything in the world, but I'll leave him if it means alienating him from his family."

This good, unselfish girl. "I'm sure he loves you too. And for exactly who you are," I say with all the fervency I can manage.

"In the emergency room, they thought I tried to kill myself. I didn't. I swear!" Her howl has mass. Adrenaline hurtles along my limbs. "I got trashed last night. We—a bunch of us did. But I couldn't make Trask's grandmother's words stop replaying in my head. When everybody went to bed, I just wanted to pass out. To stop *knowing*. So I drank a bunch more. The next thing I knew, people in scrubs were holding me down on a metal thing, ramming something hard down my throat." She grapples for my hand, and her lips form a hard line.

A heated mix of tears—of gratitude that Laurel hadn't meant to take her life and of chagrin at her misery—coast my own cheeks.

At last, the door opens, and a young doctor—his hair moussed up in front like an overgrown Kewpie doll—strides into the room. Too overcome to give him a where-the-hell-have-you-been look, I give Laurel's hand a squeeze and back away. The doctor greets Laurel and begins to examine her. I muster a smile and a reassuring wink for Laurel and slip quietly into the hall.

I lean against a cinder block wall, snatching at my thoughts as they begin to wheel. The terrible secret Laurel kept! If she had told Trask, maybe this wouldn't have happened to her. *You of all people know what keeping secrets can do, Georgie.* Gasping, I press my palms against the wall. No. I won't go down that trail.

Truman. He must be told about Laurel and about what his mother said. Has Trask talked to his father? If not, the awful task is mine. I despise being caught up in this thing. What on earth do I say? Do I serve up the brutal truth, quoting Laurel? Though Truman knows his mother is no saint, her hideous words will be hard for her son to hear. I dig my nails into my palms.

An elevator pings. A slight young man rounds the corner. Though his shorts are rumpled, his plaid shirt misbuttoned, the hitch of his shoulders is high. Aviator sunglasses hang from a black Croakie around his neck. Thunderstruck, I gape at him as he closes the short distance between us. His eyes zip to the number on the big door. The young man's shaggy hair is a singular strawberry blond, like the best apricot jam. Halting before Laurel's door, he runs his fingers through his hair, his mouth working. I breach the intense tunnel of his vision, saying, "Trask?"

The young man starts. His telltale blue eyes dart to mine. Though a truncated version of his father, Trask Parker peers at me out of Truman's young face. Tears sting my nose. "Yes, ma'am?" he says.

"I'm Georgie Bricker, Laurel's advisor from the college." His eyes bloom wide. He looks back at Laurel's door and pockets his hands as though restraining himself from forcing it open.

"Laurel. Is she . . . ?"

"The doctor's examining her now. She . . . she's going to be just fine." I am hoping my small smile doesn't look as false as it feels.

Trask rocks back on the heels of his sandals and exhales a sigh that ruffles my sleeve. He scrubs at his eyes with his palms. "Thank God." After a moment of ringing silence, he looks at me again. "Laurel's told me all about you, Madame Bricker." His tone and expression are the neutral pH between base and acid. "And I know about you and Dad."

Maybe I shouldn't have approached him. I search the young man's eyes.

Laurel's door unlatches and we both flinch.

The doctor's profile appears in a slice of open door. "Rest well tonight, Miss Cross," he's saying to Laurel. "And we'll see about getting you out of here tomorrow."

The husk of Laurel's voice floats behind him as he steps into the hall. "Thank you."

Trask rushes past the doctor.

He disappears from sight as though all along, he's been a figment of my imagination.

Knowing what must be done
does away with fear.
—Rosa Parks

CHAPTER
FIFTEEN

Though blessedly empty and private, the family lounge down
the hall retains a miasma of chewing gum, bad coffee,
and stinky sandwiches. With a fresh onslaught of nausea, I dry
heave over a trash can filled with the detritus of others who have
waited and worried. Dr. Chu says anxiety can afflict your body in
myriad ways, but this nausea is new, "And un-ac-ceptable," I say
aloud between deep breaths.

I center myself—breathing as Dr. Chu instructed—preparing for the three calls I have to make. The first to Truman. I
climb into one of the recliners in a bank of them provided for
those who wait overnight. At the thought of someone's greasy
hair on the headrest, his Cheetos fingers on the arms, a new
queasiness coils in my throat.

Breathing, breathing. I one-punch Truman's number from
my short list of favorites. True. If he hasn't talked to Trask and
doesn't know the truth about Eleanor, I will be the bearer of
pain.

He picks up on the second ring. "Georgie. Finally. I'm so
glad you called."

"Hi, sweetheart," I say quietly.

"I'm at the house. Where are you? Can you come over?"

"I'm at the hospital. I'm okay," I rush to add, "I mean, it's not me."

His sweet voice grows urgent. "Who?"

"It's Laurel . . . my favorite student. She . . . they thought she tried to commit suicide."

"Oh, my God."

"But she didn't. She was . . . terribly upset about the school closing, and something . . . else. She drank more than a fifth of liquor. To silence terrible words someone said about her."

Truman's voice climbs. "Georgie. What's Laurel's last name?"

"It's Cross, True. Laurel Cross. Do you know who that is?" I add softly.

Truman draws a shuddery breath. "Oh, no. I mean yes. Trask's girlfriend? They're still seeing each other?"

I want to weep that this man and his son know each other so little, when they could love each other so well. "Yes, True. He asked her to marry him. They plan to marry next summer."

Truman takes a wet sniff and then another. "And she's okay?"

I choose my words carefully. "She's okay physically, Truman."

"I have to see Trask, talk with him." He chokes back a sob. "I haven't talked to them in weeks. Why the hell haven't I been the one to reach out?" Footfalls, the snick of cabinets and slide of drawers, lets me know he's rummaging around, putting things up or taking things out, making ready to leave the house.

Loath to add to his regret, I turn my face into the fake leather of the recliner and ride another wave of nausea before speaking. "Truman, it was your mother . . . whose words hurt Laurel."

"What . . . do you mean?"

He should be here. We should be together for a conversation like this. But he doesn't know Laurel; he doesn't belong here. I look out the fishbowl windows of the waiting room, at the deserted halls. I have to tell him now. "Where are you?"

"In my bedroom."

"You need to sit down."

Swishes and thumps tell me he's pushing things off his bed. Well acquainted with the sounds the sleigh bed makes, the next *plumph* and *squill* means he's dropped to the mattress. If only I were with him, holding him tight, when I say what I have to say.

I close my eyes but then pop them wide. I'd made the mistake of imagining Eleanor's face as she said those hideous things when Laurel had first repeated them to me. I won't do it again. I fix my stare on a vending machine filled with things no one in a place that's supposed to heal people should eat. I rid myself of the serrating words: "Eleanor said to your sons on speakerphone that Laurel is a half-breed, nobody from nothing."

Truman is quiet for so long, I check my phone to make sure the call hasn't dropped, that he hasn't heard a thing I've said and I'll have to call him back, say it all again. But his voice reprises in a terrible coda: "By God, my mother—my parents— almost ruined my life. She won't ruin Trask's. Or Laurel's." For once, I'm glad I can't see his face, knowing it must be as contorted as he sounds. And then he begins to sob.

I say through tears of my own, "True. Trask is here now." From the recliner, I've kept an eye on Laurel's door.

"He is?" Truman says wetly.

"I've met him. He's lovely. He's . . . you."

The sleigh bed squeaks as though it is relieved of his weight. "I'll—"

"No, don't. Don't come here. Don't do it that way. Trask's been in Laurel's room for an hour now. The doctor was in before. He mentioned releasing her tomorrow."

"I have to talk to my son, Georgie."

I scoot to the edge of the chair. "I know. Of course. But let me see how they're doing first."

"But Trask. Those poor kids . . . this is my fault."

"It is not your fault. It is no one's fault. But your mother . . ."

"I will deal with my mother; you can be damned certain of that." Footsteps tell me he paces the wide-planked old floor. I picture his chin like an outcropping of rock, the twist of his hands.

"True. Let me see how they're doing. I promise to call you back within the hour."

"Will you tell Trask . . . that I want to see him?"

"Of course, darling. Why don't I ask him to let me feed him dinner? I'll ask him if it's okay if you come."

Truman heaves a sigh. "I thank God for you, Georgie. I mean, I do every day, but you are just . . . an extraordinary woman. Have I told you that enough? How brilliantly lucky I am to have you back in my life?"

His words slip around me, like his arms, embracing me and taking me from this place for a moment. "We're both brilliantly lucky, True. I love you."

After we've said goodbye, I take a deep breath and manage to peek around the huge reeking pile of the mess we're in. On the other side is a seamless love story.

My phone buzzes with an email notification and reminds me of the second call I must make. To Laurel's aunt.

I have an idea for Laurel. I just need to okay it with Susan.

Susan. That's a fourth call. I dread bothering the president. She was so terribly thin and shattered at the ill-fated meeting. Has she managed to reclaim her equanimity? Email directives for closing out a typical school year have whooshed into my faculty inbox with regularity, along with reminders to maintain focus on our students and their needs. For Susan, the commerce of helping secure transfers for the underclassmen must be like assembling the Eiffel Tower from pick-up sticks.

I slip the number I'd copied down for Mahalia Cross from my pocket and add it to the contacts on my phone, conscious that in doing so, I've made her part of my life. Grateful that I'm still alone in the waiting room, I place the call, and the woman answers on the first ring.

"Hello?" she says, her tone beautifully cultured.

"Mrs. Cross? This is Georgie Bricker, Laurel's advisor from Willa Cather College."

"Laurel's advisor. Yes, Ms. Bricker?" The anxious rush of words is as rickety as an old camp chair.

I hurry to assure her. "I wanted you to know that Laurel is doing just fine. The doctor says she can go home tomorrow."

"Praise Jesus."

"I would love to arrange transportation for you to come and see her."

"I'm afraid I don't travel anymore, Ms. Bricker. I broke my hip in December, you see."

"I'm so sorry. And call me Georgie, won't you?"

"I will, dear, if you'll call me Mahalia."

"Mahalia, you know that while Laurel needs rest, with the timing of the school closing, she is going to need to catch up on her classwork and prepare to transfer to another college. I can help her do that."

"We talked last week about a transfer. As you know, La-la was only able to attend Willa Cather because of the lacrosse scholarship." *La-la.* "Without scholarship, I can only manage to send her to public college. And in-state, here in Maryland. I know that's not what she wants. But the love between Laurel and Trask is true, Ms. . . . . Georgie. They are very young and can stand a year apart." I smile at the way she loves and understands her niece.

"Of course. I understand. But maybe there's another way. In

the meantime, would you allow me to take Laurel into my home to rest for a few days?"

"You love my child, don't you?"

My tired eyes well. "Mahalia, I never had a child of my own. I do love her. And you can trust me to take good care of her."

"Thank you, my dear."

"You are entirely welcome. I am here at the hospital now. And Trask is here as well. How about I have Laurel call you later?"

I end the call with a renewed feeling of accomplishment and hope. I need to check on Laurel. And Trask. I slide from the recliner and slide my feet into my espadrilles. An elevator pings and reveals Hollins, Sutton, Emily, and—unbelievably— behind a beaucoup bouquet, our president herself. I hurry out to greet them and let them know Trask is in with Laurel. "Let me just check on her," I say and tap on the door.

When I get no response, I lift my chin with an encouraging smile for the others and step softly into the room. My throat throbs at the scene on the bed. The guardrails lowered, Laurel lies in Trask's freckled arms. Eyes locked, they talk with quiet intensity, their heads and their feet aligned like meticulously trimmed timber. Dark and fair, they remind me of Meghan Markle and Prince Harry. Trask must have inherited his grandmother's fine-boned stature, or perhaps his mother's. Hopefully, the seeds of their temperaments found no purchase in the soil of this boy's heart.

Abruptly Trask sees me, raises his head, and pushes himself to sit, casting his legs over the edge of the bed. Laurel startles and reaches for him but catches sight of me and smiles.

I smile at them both and pick my heart up off the floor where it's tumbled. "How are you doing?"

Trask looks at Laurel. She dips her chin and looks at him— her eyes so full of love I am embarrassed—and then back at me. "I'm better now," she says softly.

I approach the bed, touch her blanketed foot. "When you are released tomorrow, would you like to come and stay at my house for a few days?" I'm taking a gamble here without running the idea by Susan first, though she is right outside, and I plan to corner her before I leave. I see no reason she would object, especially now that I have Mahalia's permission. "I'd like that," Laurel responds.

I smile. "Moi, aussi. Trask, would you like to come rest awhile at my house before you head back?"

"I mean, I don't want to leave Laurel." Wincing, he pulls a toothbrush from his back pocket. "I planned to stay." A shy grin plays across my lips; he's so like his father.

"How about I give you my address and you come when you're ready? I'd love to make dinner for you. Your father will be there." He looks at me. "He would like to see you."

Trask's blue gaze shifts toward the window, and he seems to let that sink in for a moment. "Can Asher come?"

Can Asher come? The words are poetry. I burst into tears of shell-shocked relief, humbled by love: Trask's for Laurel and Trask's for his brother. I am counting on Trask's love for his father.

"Madame?" Laurel murmurs from the bed.

Embarrassed, I snatch a tissue from the box and mop my face. "I'm fine! Just so happy that you're okay." I smile at Trask. "And that Trask is here. And yes, Asher can come." I bend to plant a kiss on Laurel's forehead. "*And* that you're going to let me pamper you for a few days."

Straightening myself, I remember the others waiting outside. "Some friends are here, and Susan Joshi! With a florist shop in her arms. May I send them in?"

Laurel's eyes flit to Trask's. He shifts feet and nods shyly. She smiles and straightens her gown. "Yes."

"You rest well. I'll be back for you in the morning."

I tread lightly with this young man of whom I know so little and want to know so much. I give him my address and start to provide directions, but he pulls out his phone and stops me with a polite smile.

"I can just put it into Waze."

I grin. "I have no idea what that is. So, I'm going to the market. You and your brother just come over whenever you like."

Laurel's eyes hold me a moment. "Thank you, Madame Bricker."

I swallow and then blow her a quick kiss.

I head through the parking lot, absorbing the sunlight like a cold-blooded creature. What do college men like to eat? I'm thinking spaghetti Bolognese, a big salad, and lots of buttery garlic bread—comfort food. Oh no, I should have asked if they are vegetarian or vegan.

I check the time on my phone. Truman had a meeting at three o'clock. I slide into the coupe, wincing at the heat of the leather beneath my thighs, power the engine, and stab at the AC button. I compose a quick text: *My love, both your boys may be coming for dinner.* I pause, fresh tears blurring my eyes, as I imagine his reaction. I consider the time, add enough for shopping and getting myself cleaned up, and add, *Come at five? The boys aren't vegetarian, are they?* Before sending, I add a trio of red heart emoticons. Hopefully, Truman will get back with me while I'm still at the market.

By the time I've backed out of my parking spot, I have a reply: three smiley faces with hearts for eyes, followed by *THANK YOU. I ADORE YOU. OMNIVORES. T.*

I chuckle at the thought of him thumbing this message beneath the edge of a conference table, and my heart swells again. I'm going to do some "big cooking," as my mother and I call it, enough for the boys to take some home for another meal. I wish Laurel could be with us, but I am glad two of the other girls are staying with her until ten o'clock, and then she'll be monitored by nurses for another night. Her vulnerability has stirred in me an almost-maternal feeling, one I thought I'd never experience. And in a small way, I'm feeling it for Truman's boys.

I owe my own mother a call.

She picks up on the second ring. "How are you, darling?" At the sweet tone of her voice, my nose stings with tears. I tell her all the news about the potential college closure while she listens in silence. Then I rush in to reassure her.

"I'm more positive and less anxious since I've been seeing Dr. Chu, despite trying to figure out what to do with my life."

"I know you're facing a huge challenge. But I also know that you will rise to it."

"Something else has happened." As I tell her about Laurel and then about Trask, she listens with little clucks of understanding. "Mom, I'm bringing Laurel to stay with me for a few days, until she's strong again."

"That's lovely. You will be so good for her."

"And Trask and Truman are coming for dinner tonight. And oh, Mom," I say with renewed incredulity, "maybe Asher too."

"Asher," she says as though it's been a long time since she's tasted the name. "God bless Truman for honoring your father. I don't want to intrude, especially with all you have going on, but I would love to see him again. And meet his boys," she says softly.

"I know. We'll arrange a visit somehow. I miss you, Mom." I swallow back the thought of the mess of the college and going back to my office, tending to the things I've left undone. "So tonight, I'm making a big pot of your quick-cooking spaghetti Bolognese."

"The boys should like that."

"I think so, and I'm hungry . . . for the first time in days. I think the medicine Dr. Chu gave me makes me nauseated. The ick hits me and then leaves as fast as it comes."

My mother is quiet for a long moment. "How long now since you've had a period?"

"I don't know . . . probably six months?" Making the turn into the market parking lot, I count back. "Seven, actually. You think it's hormonal?"

"Have you and Truman been . . . using birth control?" Swerving, I clip an errant shopping cart with my bumper and watch in horror until it snags on a high spot on the pavement and rolls to a stop before ramming a Porsche. I clutch the wheel, my blood turning to aspic in my veins. "I . . . I can't be pregnant, Mama. I'm too old."

"It's happened before."

I meticulously align the coupe in a parking place and ease the gearshift into park. "Yeah, like in the Bible!" I'm undone: first to be talking to my mother about having sex with Truman, and second at the thought of our lovemaking producing something besides satisfaction. Yet, at the same time, I feel a fathoms-deep tickle at the thought of a baby who's Truman and me. How would he feel about another child? And Trask and Asher? Would they be horrified? *Stop it, Georgie. This cannot be.* I grab for my shopping bags in the back seat. "I'm at the market, Mom."

My mother's voice takes on a stern edge. "Pick up a test, Daughter. A geriatric pregnancy can be dangerous." This surreal statement from my seventy-one-year-old mother makes me dizzy. Geriatric pregnancy. Is that what it's called? Oh, my Lord.

I end the conversation, promising to buy a test and to call her tomorrow, and I walk loose-kneed into the chill of the market.

At the bakery section, the singular sugar-and-butter bouquet of cupcakes meets my nose, and my gaze lingers. I recall the slumber party. The news of the college debt had unmoored my students, but at least they'd been afloat in the same cove. But now, it's Laurel that's entered untested waters. My thoughts turn to her. I wonder if I should pick up a few of the Loverboys. But it will take more than cupcakes this time to heal her emotions.

A tray of petit fours topped with blue and pink sugared booties makes my stomach lurch. Dear God, I cannot be pregnant. I smooth my hand down my tunic and poochy belly. Pregnant. I've never spoken that word to myself about myself. In college, when all the girls got the pill from the university health center, I followed suit and dutifully took it. For years. It's odd that neither Lacey nor I had children, though she relishes her role as Auntie Lacey to her sister Karen and brother-in-law Tom's five daughters. I try to remember what Lina said about how it felt to be pregnant with her son, how long it took until she felt morning sickness or the quickening.

I turn down the health-and-wellness aisle, cutting my eyes to the left and right and carting ibuprofen and vitamin C gummies, but stop short of the "sexual health" section, as furtive as a teenager buying a first condom. Pretending to study a box of protein bars, I find the most expensive brand of pregnancy test. As a woman and two children round the corner, I snare it. I bury it beneath bags of salad greens and accelerate to the relative safety of the bladder-control section.

I collect two pounds of pasta and cans of tomatoes, conjuring the smell of the yummy Bolognese sauce, without a blip of nausea. A virus is all I've had. Or a new manifestation of distress brought on by the school news and Laurel's hospitalization. As Lacey would say, Breathe and take a test, babe, and then move on. But never let Truman know.

I'll probably tell Lacey and Lina I've had a scare and then let my mother know I'm okay. I'll put it behind me.

Back in the coupe, I aim for home. Despite the ground sirloin, bacon, and ice cream in my back seat, I pull onto the hilltop shoulder just before the turnoff to the college. This perfect bird's-eye view of the campus that has been my home stops my breath and heart. In the slanting afternoon sun, it's an enchanted green isle, the rising sun-bleached steeples and towers like the turrets of a great castle, the winding roads like soft gray rivers. In twenty-five years, its beauty is undiminished. For a moment, I simply sit there, feeling a peculiar peace and stillness stealing over me and soothing my worries. I sit with my hands on the wheel, thinking of all the young women who arrived here first with trunks, then with smart hard Samsonite cases, then with boxes and monogrammed duffle bags full of hopes and dreams.

It isn't too late. I will not accept that there isn't a last-ditch way to save the school.

The alumnae are the answer. I've known it since the first time I called Elizabeth Pattison for help. I huff a little scoff at myself for once thinking that rescuing Willa Cather seemed an extreme notion.

My worst fears came to fruition.

Yet I'm still here.

Laurel's still here.

I check my side mirror and ease back onto the road, my mind sliding along possibility. Tomorrow. When I have made Laurel breakfast and settled her in, I will call Mrs. King. We'll put our heads together. As far as I know, the resources Elizabeth Pattison and her classmates provided for the study abroad program are still there. The women rallied behind the school once. If I know them, they will do it again.

At once, my course is mapped out like a runway lit for a night plane: a rally.

I'll organize a rally for alumnae.

It's not over till the old-maid French teacher with a pregnancy test at the bottom of her grocery bag sings.

Where there is great love,
there are always miracles.
—Willa Cather

CHAPTER
SIXTEEN

Hooking my foot around the kitchen door, I pull it shut. "Voltaire!" I call, hefting the grocery bags onto the counter. "We're having company, lots of company!"

A quadruple-point thump brings the cat down from his perch atop the dryer. He struts around the corner. "And look, handsome," I say, waggling a bag, "organic salmon treats." A bribe may be in order when Truman's sons arrive.

Trask seems a quiet and thoughtful boy, though we've met only briefly and under unpleasant circumstances. Asher, I know next to nothing about. "But that's about to change!" I say to Voltaire as I stuff the cold groceries into the refrigerator. I text Truman. *I might be in the shower when you get here. Let yourself in. G.*

Upstairs, I peel off my clothes and stand before the bathroom mirror, surveying my profile. Is my stomach bigger? The veins under the skin of my breasts are more prominent, more purple than blue. Is that a sign of pregnancy or just the May heat, to which I'm not yet accustomed? My heart picks up: the pregnancy test is still in the bags on the kitchen counter!

I rush down the stairs and peek out the kitchen door. Its

yellow blinker on, Truman's Range Rover is poised to turn into my drive. I snatch up a half-empty bag and root through it for the boxes. A packet of spaghetti falls to the floor and busts, pasta lengths strewing like barn straw across the tile. Truman's car noses into the drive. Stepping around the spaghetti, I ransack the second bag and come up with the narrow box. At the *thunk* of car door, I look wildly for a place to hide it. I open the sugar canister and stuff the box inside. Truman is at the kitchen doorstep, and that's when I notice that he has Trask with him.

And that I am naked.

"Knock-knock," Truman calls. Thankful for the old lace panel my mother made for the window in the door, I clutch my bobbling breasts and dash up the stairs. Eve banished from Eden.

"Georgie? You okay?" Truman calls up the stairwell.

"Yes! Just getting into the shower. I'll be right down."

Trask Parker in my house. His mother would probably be horrified. Anne Emerson had stalled on the divorce court date again last month. The nagging notion that she and Eleanor are in cahoots capers through my mind again. But I have too much to think about today to present a bouquet to that concern.

Breathing, breathing. I put on a lilac sleeveless dress and sandals. The television booms to life in the living room. At the sound of a sharp crack and roar of crowd, I grin. A father and son watching baseball: a most ordinary thing, yet remarkable. Truman longs to be close to his boys, to know them as adults. From my educational studies of how the sexes learn, I remember that while girls tend to sit face-to-face and feel compelled to fill silence with conversation, males are the opposite. They tend to sit side by side, engaged in their own occupations and talking only when something needs to be said. Boys enjoy just being together. I imagine Truman and Trask side by side on the sofa. As the low tones of occasional talk drift up the stairs, I'm hoping they're a good sign.

I give my hair a perfunctory blow-dry and twist it into its French knot. Though Truman prefers my hair down, it's better up for cooking—no one should end up with a hair wrapped around a tonsil. We haven't seen each other in days. I'll take my hair down for him later. Slowly, twisting it around my fingers. With a silky grin, I poke small silver fleur-de-lis stud earrings into my lobes.

"Georgie?"

Truman mounts the stairs to my bedroom. He's taken off his coat and tie and is wearing my favorite shirt, the French blue one that can never compete with his eyes.

He is the finest thing I've ever clapped eyes on.

"You look as beautiful as I've ever seen you," he says from the doorway, scanning me from head to toe.

I swallow a lump of emotion and glance beyond him to the stairs. "Trask?"

He waves a dismissive hand. "He's on the phone with Laurel. Sweetheart. Without you, I've felt like Prometheus. Chained to a rock. A volt of vultures feasting on my entrails."

I giggle. "Ouch. That bad, huh?"

"Worse." Taking me into his arms, he buries his face in my neck. "I've missed you so much."

I whisper into his ear, "The French say it better: *tu me manques*."

His lips tug into a lazy smile. "And that is?"

I translate, "You are missing from me; I miss the way I'm am when I'm with you."

"I like that." He puts his chin atop my head for a moment. "The second day of your . . . seclusion—"

"True, I'm sorry—"

He lays a soft finger across my lips. "No, don't be . . . it's what you needed to do. But that morning, I found one of your hair thingies—a bobby pin—in my bed. I carried the damned thing around with me in my shirt pocket all day."

I feel a primal love for him. I lift my lips. His kiss is lovely and long.

"Hey, Dad?" Trask calls up the stairs. "Asher's here."

I leap away from Truman, heart thudding in my throat. Asher.

Truman blows out a breath and smooths a hand over the front of his pants. "Good," he calls, "be right down!" He points a sideways finger at his face and forms a sappy puppy-dog grin.

"You go first. I'll be there faster than a casserole to a widower's doorstep. Hurry up; I'm starting to talk like my mother."

Truman chuckles and then starts down the stairs. "By the way," he says, turning. "What happened in the kitchen, the pasta all over the floor?"

My stomach flips. I turn to the mirror and pretend to straighten my updo. "Voltaire. That rascal. Has he been jumping to the kitchen counter again?"

Truman directs a funny half-smile into the mirror. "See you in a minute."

I smile after him, my heart full.

I trail my fingers across my abdomen. A trace of hope lifts as with the smoke from a pipe dream. A peachy cherub to hold. Maybe a little girl to twine her arms around Truman's neck. A sweetly dimpled hand to hold an ice cream cone.

I lean close to the mirror and examine the wrinkles around my eyes.

A pipe dream; that's all it is. I'll take the test and be done with it.

Back downstairs, he has cleaned up the mess on the floor. Though much of the one package of pasta is broken, it appears to have been rinsed off and placed on a double thickness of paper toweling on the counter. I stand there for a couple of beats listening to the smack and thump of the baseball game. I lift my nose. The boys seem to have marked their territory in my home: a masculine tang supplants the fresh basil on the counter—the acrid quality of Trask's worry, the tinge of Asher's wariness. I round the corner to the hall.

Truman is seated on the sofa. He takes sight of me and gets to his feet. "Here's Georgie."

Asher Parker unfolds his well-over-six-foot frame from one of my armchairs. He stares at me as though assessing me for specialness. Does he know he is named for my father? Why hadn't I asked Truman?

"Asher?" I say with a smile. I incline my hand, marveling at the difference in the twins' stature and coloring.

"This is Asher," Truman says, as though he just created him and found him a masterpiece.

Asher steps forward and tosses his shoulder-length dark hair back from his face. "Hello." His island-sized hand gives mine a pump. "It's nice to meet you." Truman's head turns from Asher to me and back again as though watching a game of tennis.

"Welcome. It's great to meet you too. I'm so glad you've joined us."

"Thank you for having us. You have a really nice house."

Trask has also attempted to rise. "I've been pinned by middleweight cat."

"Voltaire!" I say.

"No, no, he's all good," Trask says, "I love animals." Voltaire raises his throat for scratching and lets out a trill as Trask obliges.

"Please have a seat, fellas. Are you hungry?"

"I could eat," the boys say in tandem, before turning their attention to the game.

I grin and look from them to Truman, expecting a reaction, but no one seems to find the occurrence unusual. Twins. "Well, good. While the spaghetti sauce is cooking, I have hummus and spinach dip. I'll just be a minute. Excuse me."

Truman follows me into the kitchen. I pull an apron over my head and the dips from the refrigerator. "They're great," I whisper, "and Asher's so big!" And then louder, so the boys won't think we're talking about them, "Thanks for washing off the pasta."

He grins. "Trask did that."

"Thanks, Trask!" I call down the hall. "You've earned your supper."

"No problem," he calls.

I smile and pull out the tray I used for the snacks at the sleepover. "Will you put this stuff out for me?"

"Glad to."

"Would the guys like iced tea or bottled water?"

"Probably water." Truman assembles the snacks while I chop onions and garlic, celery and carrots, and start them browning.

"What teams are they watching?"

"Atlanta and San Francisco, the Braves and Giants."

"C'mon, ump!" Trask shouts. It's funny that his voice is deeper than his brother's.

Asher sounds outraged. "He was safe."

Trask pitches his voice low. "Shi-it, man. Two outs."

I giggle, select my Donald Fagan playlist from my phone, and turn on my Bose on low. "Which team are they pulling for?"

"We're Braves' fans," he says quietly and then carries the tray to the living room.

"We suck so bad," Trask says from the living room. I smother a giggle.

Truman comes back grinning. "God, I've missed them. It's been a long time since the three of us have been together." He leans against the counter as I stir the beef into the pot. "When they were kids, we went to the ballpark all the time." He shrugs. "Course my old man had box seats."

I grab a dish towel and swat at him. "Get in there and watch the game with them."

He looks at me as though I've just offered to buy the team for him, kisses me soundly, and is off like a shot.

I add tomato products and wine to the sauce and set it to simmer, then wash the vegetables for the salad, thinking of my brother, Ron, and how he worshipped our father. What a wonderful grandfather my father would have been. Wistfulness and regret fill my chest, but thanks to Dr. Chu's medicine, the emotions don't gather into a pummeling storm.

I gaze out the window at my garden. Tomorrow I bring Laurel home. If it's nice, she can sit out there on the chaise. Maybe she'd like to plant tomatoes and herbs with me. *Stop it tout de suite, Georgie Girl; she's coming here to rest, not to live with you. Besides, she's transferring to school probably in Maryland.* Sorrow tugs at my heart.

"All right, let's go, Newcomb," Truman says from the living room.

I whisk olive oil and balsamic vinegar together for dressing and check on the sauce.

I go into the living room wondering if I should call and check on Laurel, but I don't want to wake her if she's sleeping. Truman's back on the sofa. I perch on the arm, crossing my legs at the ankles. The boys are sitting in the big chairs, Asher with one leg thrown over the arm. He jiggles a baguette-length running shoe to the *stomp-stomp-clap* made by the stadium crowd. I love that he seems comfortable in my home. Truman and Trask have affected identical postures: leaning forward, their elbows on their knees, they rub their palms slowly together. I smile and softly sigh. In profile, Trask with his strawberry blond hair is a clone of his father at sixteen.

Truman sits back. "How you doing, sweetheart?"

"Good, another few minutes on the sauce. I need to go stir it."

In the kitchen, I tend to my pot. Trask wanders in.

"Hi," I say brightly. *Don't try too hard, Georgie. Just be yourself.*

179

"Where can I wash my hands?"

I tell him where the powder room is and then gather silver-ware, imagining him in there where the towels are pink and the seat is always down. I hear the gasp of the toilet and run of the sink.

Trask comes out, drying his palms on his tan shorts, the kind with loops and a little pocket on the leg for his phone. "May I help you in here?"

I ask him if he wants to put the bread in the hot oven while I toss the salad things together, and he does.

Finally, the four of us sit down to plates of spaghetti in the dining room. Truman offers up a quick blessing of thanks for the meal and for Laurel's recovery.

Trask starts the salad around. I wonder if he and the others are picturing Laurel in the hospital bed. "I told her I'd call her at eight," he says, locating the clock above the cabinets. It's half past seven. "It's really nice of you to have her come here, Ms. Bricker, where it's . . . quiet."

"Oh, you are so welcome," I say, taking the salad bowl. "It will be my pleasure. And you can call me Georgie." He glances at me, his brow furrowing slightly. "Or Madame," I add swiftly, "as Laurel does."

He smiles at his plate and gives a little shrug.

We dig into the meal. The boys' table manners are so impec-cable, I check my fork to be sure I'm holding it the right way.

"It's delicious," the boys say again at precisely the same moment. Asher helps himself to two more slices of the baguette.

"I love your Bolognese sauce," Truman adds, pointing to his plate with the tines of his fork.

"Thanks." I look at the boys. "There's plenty more, fellas. I'd hoped to send you home with leftovers."

"That would be great," Trask says. Asher nods, his mouth full of bread.

"Are you driving back tonight?" I ask them.

"I am," Asher says. "I have a thing in the morning."

Trask regards his father. "Can I stay the night with you, Dad, so I can check on Laurel in the morning?"

Truman's eyes pop like flashbulbs. "Of course," he says, and he gives me a secret smile of triumph. We eat for a space of time in a clinking silence, and then he sits back. "Guys, I want to talk to you about something. I've booked a flight to Atlanta."

Atlanta? This is news to me. Then a lonely yellow warning light flashes through my head.

Asher raises his dark brows and gives a little yeah-so-what-another-business-trip shrug.

Truman directs his next words to Trask with a brief glance at me. "I'm going to see your grandmother."

Clearly and roundly, Trask's blue eyes fasten on his father's face. "Well, hey. Give Grand El a message for me. Tell her I said she can go to hell."

Truman and I freeze and fall silent. I'm proud of Truman for not mitigating his mother's behavior by correcting Trask for talking like that about his grandmother.

Truman takes a deep pull on his glass and sets it down. He wipes his mouth with his napkin. "I'm going to see her in person. Because I'm going to tell her that if she wants to stay in your lives or in mine, she owes you and Laurel a formal apology."

Asher's brown eyes widen.

Trask's narrow. His words sprawl and flail around the room: "She's a fucking racist." His eyes flit to mine. "Sorry."

I give a little tremor of a nod but remain silent. With all that's happened, I'm not fool enough to believe the whole evening would be an episode of *The Waltons*.

Asher looks at his father. "Are you going to see Mom?"

Trask's gaze flips to me for a moment. I cross my legs beneath the table and breath shallowly as though I can make my presence unintelligible.

Truman closes his eyes a moment and gives his head a little shake. "No. I'm not sure if she's in town."

Trask swears under his breath and pushes his plate back. "Those two are thick as thieves. I wouldn't be surprised if Mom put Grand El up to it." I swallow a gasp. Trask glares at his father, and I'm surprised at the vehemence of his tone. "Mom's family won't run our lives. She's not going to tell us who we can love or who we can marry."

Truman's throat works, from either grief, shame, or embarrassment—or perhaps all three.

My heart silently wails.

"We don't want Grand El's money," Asher says.

From the kitchen, my phone rings. I stand on wobbling legs, grateful for the opportunity to slip away. "Excuse me?"

It's Laurel. "Hi, darling," I say quietly, and I duck into the laundry room off the kitchen, where Voltaire reclines atop the dryer again. "How are you feeling?" I say, with one ear on the dining room, where talk still rises and falls. It's a quarter past eight.

"Better. The doctor says I'll be released around ten. I can text you."

"Of course. That will be perfect."

"Thank you. Is Trask there?"

"He . . . he is. We're just finishing dinner. We sure missed you though," I say, adding a chipper note to my voice.

Trask appears. "That Laurel?" I nod and give him a tremulous smile.

"Tell her I'll call her right back, please?"

"I heard that," Laurel says creamily.

"I'll see you at ten. You call me if you need anything tonight, no matter the time."

"D'accord. Bonsoir, Madame." She's lapsed back into French with me. I'll take that as a good sign.

"Bonsoir."

Truman and Asher appear in the kitchen with armloads of dirty dishes and a whirlwind of apologies for the dinner table distress. But I'm grateful they felt at ease enough to have such an important conversation in my presence.

"No worries, please." Truman's pale cheeks rise. Knowing Asher has to get on the road, I bustle around looking for disposable containers. "Here, Asher, let me just fill these for you to take with you."

"I appreciate that, Ms. Bricker."

Trask addresses me the way Laurel does. "Madame, thanks so much for everything." He steps outside, already punching at his phone, and leans against the Range Rover.

I fill a paper shopping bag and hand it off to Asher.

Truman and I follow him out to the drive. He heads out to a topless old Jeep parked on the street. Truman calls after him, "Goodbye Son, I love you."

Asher doesn't break his stride but slowly raises his hand in the air and forms the I-love-you sign. A small sob escapes Truman. I slip my hand into his, and together we watch the Jeep turn the corner. I imagine Asher's long hair whipping in the wind on the darkened road.

Truman casts me a bleary smile. We walk past Trask, who is smiling at something Laurel's saying, and back into the kitchen. "I'm so sorry, baby," he says. His blue eyes are dark and pouched. I move into his arms. He tightens them around me. I feel the click of his throat, and a hot tear slides into the part in my hair. "I hate that you had to witness all that. But you were amazing."

"They shared their true feelings," I say against his shirtfront. "They love you." I look up into his face. "Truman Parker, you are a good father." He closes his eyes. I give him a little shake.

"Look at that young man out there talking to his girl." He does. "Look how well you taught him to love."

He seems to consider this. "I hope I played some part in that." He kisses me softly. "You should have been their mother."

"But then they wouldn't be who they are, would they?"

He shudders against me and wipes his eyes with the back of his hand. "I love you."

"I know. Now get out of here and get some sleep."

At the door, he turns a last time, nods, and takes a deep breath. I move to flip the dead bolt and kill the light. I grope my way along the counters like a blind woman, past the dirty dishes, and close my hands over the sugar canister.

When the Range Rover roars to life, I withdraw the box that will determine the rest of mine.

*Avoiding danger is no safer in the long run
than outright exposure. The fearful are
caught as often as the bold.*
—Helen Keller

CHAPTER
SEVENTEEN

I sit up in bed--as though God himself has called my name--and lean against the headboard, my heart pounding. The antide-pressant! If I'm pregnant, have chemicals already skirled into the baby's bloodstream and altered its formation? I scrabble from beneath the covers, inadvertently shoving Voltaire to the floor, where he lands on his feet and then gives me a snarly-lipped, once-a-year hiss.

Heart in throat, I snare my phone and head to the bath-room. The pregnancy-test box is carefully aligned atop the page of instructions I'd pulled out and read twice last night. I open it and follow the directions. Dipping the magic wand into the bath cup of warm urine, I count to five in French. Withdrawing it, I set it on a fold of tissue as though it is a soap bubble. I pro-gram the timer on my phone. Three minutes: time enough to boil a kettle, launch a kite, find Waldo.

Checking my texts, I find one from Truman at 5:47 a.m., before his flight to Atlanta. I prod the icon with a pinky, as though I might inadvertently activate a vis-à-vis feature and give him a peek at what I'm up to. *Sweetheart, thanks for last night. I can't tell you what it meant. T and I had a talk about the divorce. Will fill you in. Remind me to tell you about Beau Duffy. Love, T.*

Beau Duffy? The board chairman's name springs like a leak in the pipeline of my focus. Patching it with a muttered, "Not now," I close the message and check the timer.

Nine seconds. Holding the plastic wand, I fix my eyes on the results window. One line equals not pregnant; two lines equals pregnant.

For a breathless moment, hot tears blur twin lines into one.

I blink and they separate, hot pink and pulsing.

I spring to my feet, outraged. "What? Why now, Lord? When my life is a mess!"

I tear open my robe and gape at my belly in the mirror.

My heart plops into my stomach and sends up bursts and sparkles and fizzes of light.

I laugh aloud, wonderstruck and giddy.

I press my hands to the spot where a tiny trace of life nestles deep. I whisper, "What took you so long, my little darling?" I sit on the side of the tub, rocking back and forth for a long time, tears streaming my face. "You are real. You are true." Truman. How he loves his boys. He wishes I had been their mother. "You will be so loved, *mon bébé*. Just wait until your father knows you have come."

I spring to my feet again. Wait! Wait! Can I really carry a baby at my age? Will my worries pass on to it, or will it inherit Truman's equability? I grapple to close my robe and phone and dial a number to be used only in case of emergency. I cradle my belly. "Don't worry, *mon ange*. I will leap galaxies like stepping stones to protect you."

"Dr. Chu? It's Georgie Bricker."

"Yes, Ms. Bricker. What's going on?"

The tears reprise and my words come out all quavery. "I'm pregnant."

The squeak of her desk chair, whisk of papers, and rattle of her pencil cup give me a measure of reassurance. "How far along are you?"

I pick up the plastic wand with the two quarter-inch, earth-shattering lines. Do the lines fade away or remain? "I . . . I don't know. I just took the test. I'm scared, Dr. Chu. Can the antidepressant I take hurt the baby? Could it have already?"

"Many women continue to take their medications during pregnancy without problems."

"What are the risks of carrying a baby at my age?"

"Is that what you want to do?"

Yesterday I'd wanted to rescue Willa Cather, wanted Laurel to be strong again, wanted things to be as they were before, only with Truman at my side. Yet something extraordinary has happened.

Truman and I created life from love.

I'd assumed my eggs were past their expiration date. Yet somehow, a survivor had made itself lovely and soft and sweetly penetrable. A survivor like me.

"Yes, I want the baby," I finally answer.

Dr. Chu raps at her keyboard. "Continue your medication. Make an appointment with an OB right away. I'll see you Friday for your regular appointment. Madame, try not to worry. We'll talk it through."

I look at the two pink lines. How can *I* be positive things will work out?

⚭

Nothing was penetrating the carapace I'd fashioned for myself— for my heart and my head—before stepping into Collier Hall. I can't breathe a peep about the baby until I've talked to Truman. Mrs. King has made coffee and offers to bring me a cup, but the robust aroma brings a queasy roll to my stomach and reminds me of the OB appointment I've already booked for next Tuesday. "I've had too much this morning already, but thanks."

My secretary studies me. Averting my gaze, I sit and regard a new stack of correspondence on my desk. If I meet her eyes, she'll have it out of me before I could say "No icky sherbet punch at the baby shower." I stride to my desk. I sift through the college closing documents in black and white. "You didn't have to make me hard copies of all this." It had been less scary viewing them from my laptop screen.

"I thought you might like me to file them."

"Of course, I'm sorry." I find myself stroking my abdomen and sit on my fingers. "Listen, I have another idea. Remember how Elizabeth Pattison's class was so eager to help us?"

Mrs. King sits down and primly folds her hands in her lap, her shorthand for "Okay, if you're not going to tell me what's really going on, go ahead, I'm listening."

I push myself to my feet and pace from my desk to the window and back. "I want to organize a rally for the alums. I assume they are up in arms about the closing."

She lifts an eyebrow. "Haven't you seen the Facebook page?"

"I . . . no, I've been preoccupied." I have a tiny person growing inside me. "I didn't know you were on Facebook."

She lifts her chin. "I'm all about Facebook. I have seventy-nine friends."

Though I purse my lips like a drawstring bag, my cheeks rise.

"The Willa Cather College page has exploded with outrage from the alums. It's been quite exciting," she says.

"Well, okay! I knew they'd want to rescue us! There have to be other ways they can help. I bet some would even come and volunteer their time."

Her eyes widen and gleam. "Will this be like the March on Washington? I'd like being part of something radical before I die."

I laugh. "Yeah, actually, it could be." I look out at the quad-rangle. "I'm imagining something big." Like me, waddling around the quad with a megaphone. I toss her a notepad and a pen. "Let's start with this. Set up a meeting with my advisees. Find out who the junior-class marketing majors are. And the graphic design majors. Invite all of them. Let's do it Monday afternoon." Mrs. King scribbles furiously.

I pull out my laptop, plug it in, bring it chiming to life. "How soon can you get me a list of the alumni class presidents for the last . . . say, forty years?"

Pooching out her lips, she turns her wrist over to peer at her Timex, then smugly holds up two fingers. "*Deux heures.*"

I grin at her and grab my binder. "You work on that; I'll be back in a flash." Before I can do anything, I have to talk with Susan, get her approval. I root in my tracks in the hallway. I forgot to ask her permission about bringing Laurel home.

Five minutes later, I stride inside the admin building feeling as conspicuous as though I'm wearing one of those cheesy tops emblazoned with "BABY" and a down arrow. Thank God Tru-man's on his way to Atlanta. The last place I want to tell him about our baby is in the conference room. He has to face his mother now. Eleanor. She would be horrified that Truman had fathered a child with someone like me, a woman of no social standing. I shake my head briskly. No. I can't think about her now, or I'll lose my mind. I have to talk to Susan about the rally and then collect Laurel from the hospital.

Susan is in her office, the door opened wide. She's bent over her desk, the fingers of one hand supporting her forehead.

She looks up. "Come in, Georgie." She removes her reading glasses, and for a moment her face is as vacuous as the back of a spoon. "Will you have a seat? I'm afraid I've been . . . out of touch with my faculty."

Tears sting my throat. We cannot let my beloved college

close without a fight. I reach for her hand across the desk, give it a squeeze. "I have one last card up my sleeve, the ace of hearts."

I lay out my idea for the rally. Susan sits back. She seems to ruminate on my words as though they are a six-course meal.

"What have we got to lose?" she finally says. And then our gazes lock. The look that passes between us seems to assert, *Willa Cather College, everything.* Her face brushes with animation. "I believe I know what this place means to you," she says slowly. Then her eyes slip from mine.

"It's okay," I say, recapturing her eyes. "I know . . . you must have picked up on my illness . . . that I didn't have the flu that day in my office, but a panic attack." I pull a smile. "I'm getting help now."

She sits straight and adjusts the scarf at her throat. "I can see that, Madame Bricker. I won't stand in your way. I think this rally . . . is yours to do. You have my blessing." My eyes grow bright with tears. "And, Georgie, if I haven't told you in a while, you are a marvelous teacher, a nurturer. Laurel and all your students are blessed to have you."

I say the two words I can manage without bawling. "Thank you."

❦

Back in the office—fresh from my conversation with Susan where I'd secured permission to bring Laurel home with me— Mrs. King has the alumni list I'd requested. As well, she's sent the email to the students I mentioned. Fourteen affirmative replies to the meeting request have already sailed in. The baby and I give her a big hug. The baby. For a second, I almost blurt my news. But the clock over my secretary's head says it's eight minutes until ten, and I'm due at the hospital to pick up Laurel. I leave the office in Mrs. King's deft hands.

❧

I thank the hospital attendant who's pushed Laurel under the portico in a wheelchair and open the passenger-side door. As we drive away, Laurel cranes her neck to look back and flares a nostril. "I thought the dude was going to pick me up and put me in the car and buckle me in."

I grin at her. That's my girl. The rebel.

"A freaking wheelchair." She fishes her bag for aviator sunglasses and puts them on. "I got your email."

"My email?"

"About the student meeting Monday. What's up?"

My heart lifts. Laurel's back to business; she must be okay. A text pings my phone. Truman. Stopping at a traffic light, I poke it open. *On the ground in Atlanta. Say a prayer for me. I love you. T.*

I look at Laurel. She gives me the wide-eyed and deliberate nod of someone encouraging the feebleminded. "First," I say to her, "I want to make sure you know what's going on with Trask's family."

She rips off the sunglasses and stares at me. "What now?"

That's when I notice that smudges make crescents beneath her big dark eyes. She hasn't slept well in the hospital. She's still fragile. *Tread carefully, Georgie.* "Truman has made a trip to Atlanta."

"He really went? Trask told me what he said."

Good. At least I don't have to give her the gory details of the conversation. I indicate my phone with a flip of my hand. "He's there now."

Laurel pulls her hair up and pins it against the headrest without comment. She is quiet until we've reached my home. "Your house is so pretty, Madame. It's like I get to stay in a fancy B and B."

My chest warms. I'm so glad Susan granted me permission to have Laurel stay here. "Well you pretend that it is and relax."

I make sandwiches, and we sit to eat our lunch at the kitchen table. Voltaire appears to twine Laurel's legs. "Aww, he remembers me."

I hide my smile behind a glass of iced tea. "Of course, he does."

After lunch, I tell her to veg out in the living room in front of the TV. She chooses the same chair as Trask had chosen, as though she's sussed out his scent. I slide a tufted hassock under her feet and hand her an afghan from the back of the sofa. She sets up camp with her laptop, phone, and charging cords.

"I'll be in the kitchen. If you need one thing, you call me."

"I am really fine. Just tired. Thank you so much, Madame."

"You are so welcome, darling."

Thank goodness I'd cancelled my classes for a few days and posted online assignments. I set up my laptop in the kitchen and am astonished when fifty-one emails pack my inbox. Distractedly wading through them, a reminder about picking up faculty caps and gowns for graduation on Sunday waves its arms at me. How in the world has graduation fallen from my radar? The forgetfulness during pregnancy that women talk about must be real. "Momnesia," they call it. I smile, give the baby a pat, and return to my mail.

Later, I look in on Laurel. She's deeply asleep in the chair, her mouth slack. Voltaire, wedged at her side, opens one eye. *The Princess Bride* flickers on the screen. I smile at her choice of comfort movie and then pull the afghan up to cover her torso and arms. Will I be a good mother after spending most of my adult life alone, wrapped up in and tending to my own concerns? Have I unwittingly cultivated self-centeredness? Susan called me a nurturer. I have nurtured my students. But I've not walked the floor with them on restless nights, made their Easter dresses, dabbed their chicken pox with calamine lotion, nor wiped their bottoms. Am I capable of these things? Am I too old?

I return to the kitchen table, longing to hear my mother's voice, to seek her counsel. But it's Truman I have to tell about the baby first. What will Mom think? Will she worry? Glancing at the calendar, I feel a pang that I haven't seen her since her visit nearly eleven months ago.

My heart capsizes. My life has been satisfying enough to me, but if we rescue the school, what kind of life will it be for a child, confined to a college campus and the small enclave of Foxfield? This microcosm of a life might satisfy a child for a time. But how would she feel growing up with a mother who couldn't take her to see the Statue of Liberty, a sequoia, an ocean? Would she come to resent me?

I pull my notepad from my bag and add this to my list of concerns for Dr. Chu as though it will clear it from my mind. Maybe this baby will be a blessing in more ways than one. Maybe her life will force me to finally expand my own. Before the baby is born, I will find my fierce. For both of us.

☙✞❧

Truman's been away longer than either of us counted on. I've lived for his nightly calls. Now my phone lights along with my heart. "Hello, darling."

He sighs deeply. "Georgie. It has been a week."

"I know. Are you home?"

"Actually, no. I'm at the InterContinental Buckhead. I've decided to stay the weekend."

My voice rings high and shrill, "The weekend?" I won't be able to tell him about the baby tomorrow?

"I spent three hours with my mother today, and I'm exhausted. And I really need some time in my office while I'm here." Ice cubes tinkle in a glass and make me wish for a stiff drink of my own. "Anne Emerson is in town; I'm going to try to see her."

The thought of Truman with his wife drives all else from my mind. "I didn't think of that," I say stupidly.

"No, neither did I, but mother told me she's in town. If I can persuade my mother to make peace with the boys, I figure I can take on Anne Emerson, persuade her to sign the divorce papers."

Foreboding pokes my belly with a sharp toe. What if she won't let him go?

I rub the spot that radiates low in my abdomen. "Do it. Whatever it takes."

⚘

The graduation-Sunday morning sky is lusterless and hatched with rain. Lina and I process along the loggia from the administration building to the chapel with the rest of the faculty, raindrops leaping white on the driveway. The faculty fills only three rows now that more young instructors have left "to pursue other opportunities"; we could fit on a single school bus. I shift in my seat, pulling at the light wool academic gown that clings to me like a dank shower curtain. The forward ranks of seniors, their mortar boards bobby-pinned in place, turn grim faces to the valedictorian as she begins her speech. Distracted for the moment from the whirling mind blend of my condition and the thought of Truman with Anne Emerson, I am struck. This could be the last class ever to graduate from Willa Cather College. My eyes tear along with the valedictorian's. She speaks of the extraordinary education she and her classmates were afforded, of traditions, of happy memories. A flurry of gulps and sobs whisks through the assemblage, giving the ceremony a funereal texture. I stare out the tall windows at the gusts of rain tumbling the treetops.

When the ceremony concludes, I follow the recessional, my eyes glued to Lina's back. Outside, I duck from line. The rain has let up. I scurry toward Collier Hall, skipping the graduation reception for the first time in twenty-five years. I prepare for the student meeting as if it's a session of the French National Assembly.

I'm banking on it to reverse the course of history.

◈

After classes on Monday afternoon, I stride to the conference room down the hall from my office in Collins. Mrs. King is setting out cookies she has made herself and bottles of chilled water. We exchange a hug for luck. The girls begin filling the room, plugging in their laptops. I introduce myself to the marketing and design majors I've not met and thank them for their belief in the school, their willingness to help. All of my advisees show up, including Laurel, who's gotten a ride from Malika. The chairs along the big table fill. A handful of students sit on the floor, their backs against the wall, their gazes raised.

I nod at Mrs. King, who dims the lights and, with a flourishing finger, powers up the presentation I've created, projecting it onto the SMART board. The first page—her inspiration and contribution—is a black-and-white photograph of the National Mall from the 1963 March on Washington, the obelisk reflected in the rectangular pool surrounded by a pixelated legion of passionate Americans. I survey the girls as they study the photograph, some with crinkled brows, others breaking into grins. After a moment, I say, "We are going to fill this campus to bursting with alumnae, parents, friends of the school." I signal Mrs. King to move to the next page, the title of the presentation, RESCUING WILLA CATHER. "Ladies, we are going to rescue Willa Cather. I need task force groups."

"Hell yeah," someone seated at the table says, and I can't

help but grin. "First, we need someone to spearhead the creation of a website specifically for the rally. This will be information central. And we'll need a donate button. This is where you graphic design students come in. I'll pay for the domain name myself."

"I'll do it," two of the girls say at once.

"Thank you. Mrs. King, please take both their names."

We proceed through the pages of the presentation, the leaders and task groups forming.

The meeting concluded, I have something I can sink my teeth into.

❦

"Can I meet you at your house when you get here?" I say to Truman on the phone the next afternoon. "I have . . . news."

"Man, me too. There's a lot to catch up on. My flight's due into Mountainsburg at 7:40. Meet you there about nine?"

When the lights of the Range Rover arc across the Victorian, I am sitting on the front steps in my lilac dress, my hair freshly shampooed and flowing softly about my shoulders. The night is close, the wisteria climbing the end of the porch, cloying. I stand as Truman approaches, my heart pounding with excitement and terror.

"You're a sight for sore eyes," he says with a pinched smile. Even in the dim, I can see that his eyes are shadowed, his mouth lined. Maybe I should wait until he is rested to tell him. He sets his brief case and small black duffle down on the steps and takes me into his arms. His rumpled clothing smells of stale air and battle fatigue. "Hold me tight, baby. Never let me go," he says.

After a moment, I pull away and smile shyly. Does the news show on my face? Can he read its headline? I can wait no longer. "Sit with me?"

He surveys the steps. "Here?"

"Yes, here."

We sit, and he eyes me curiously. "What is it, sweetheart?"

"True. I'm going to have a baby."

He blinks hard, swallows. His gaze drops to my stomach then leaps to my face. An incredulous smile spreads his lips wide. "A baby?"

"Yes."

He takes a bit of his bottom lip between his teeth, shakes his head. "We. Made. A baby?"

"We did."

"At our age?"

I laugh with the sheerest joy I've ever known. "Apparently it's called a geriatric pregnancy."

"Geriatric my ass." He gets to his feet. "Let me take a quick shower, and I'll show you geriatric."

My grin is all over the place. "I can't stay."

"You can't stay? You drop news like this on me, and you can't stay?"

I get to my feet. "Laurel's at my house."

He reaches around me and cups my bottom, pulling me to him, and murmurs into my neck. "She's a big girl."

My breath is coming fast in my throat. "True. I'm not sure it's safe to make love. I go to the doctor tomorrow."

He looks at me again, and his eyes fill with tears. "Can I go with?"

"Of course."

"Do you think . . . do you think it's a girl?"

"I feel like it's a girl."

He scrubs his forehead against mine. "Oh, love, it would be like having you as a girl again."

We kiss and kiss, declaring our love for each other and our baby.

He puts me in my car and then pulls me out again, caressing my face and belly, kissing me and kissing me until I'm knock-kneed and dizzy.

It is everything we've never known we wanted.

Living with fear stops us taking risks,
but if you don't go out on the branch,
you're never going to get the best fruit.
—Sarah Parish

CHAPTER EIGHTEEN

I have the most vivid and distinct dream. A high sun stings the fair skin of my shoulders. I slowly lift a red plastic bucket from a packed haul of sand to reveal a crumbly-turreted castle.

Ronnie claps with undiluted, two-year-old delight. "Do more!" he cries.

"First we make windows," I say, showing my little brother how to poke holes along the sides with an index finger, "so the king and queen will have light inside."

Ronnie makes windows, a triangle of pink tongue protruding from one corner of his mouth. Our parents stand holding hands in the shallows, the surf breaking against their thighs, our mother gasping as the sea splashes the tender skin between the two pieces of her bathing suit. Our father spouting something about the ocean from Shakespeare's *The Tempest*; our mother laughing and splashing him with a toe of ocean.

Sleepy, Ronnie crawls into my lap. "Don't rub your eyes with sandy hands," I tell him. In my arms he suddenly morphs into a newborn. Strawberry hair gilds the top of his head. The pattern of Truman's freckles wash his tiny nose and cheeks. His face glows with a celestial light.

My mother emerges from the sea. She reaches for the baby, her long dark hair dripping and making nickel-then dime-sized craters in the sand. "Time to put him down for his nap."

"No. Don't take the baby. Just let me keep it a little longer."

❦

I awake in the semidarkness of a hospital room but lie in stillness, every breath shallow. For every breath is without the baby. Every heartbeat. Every twitch. Every part of my lips. I don't dare cough or sneeze, or she might leave me entirely, and I am not ready for her to go. Was it the girl I'd thought, or the boy in the dream? Though she'd been with me mere weeks, her soul was the truest thing about me.

In the rind of my periphery, two shadowy figures slump in chairs. They talk quietly. I cannot hear what they are saying over the rampant racing of my heart. My mind ebbs in and out with the tide. *Where did Mama take the baby?* My nostrils quiver at the tang of artificial lime. *Has Mrs. King made sherbet punch after all?* I drift.

❦

I jerk awake. Sunlight falls in stripes across the hospital bed, the first I've slept in in my life. I move my hand, wincing at the memory of the needle thrust up the flesh of its skin. Though that was but a small tweak of pain, it is one of the starburst memories popping through the blackness of unremembrance. The bandage is the same white that Laurel's was when she was here. Is it from the same roll? I turn my head to the rolling tray table, the water cup and pitcher, a little bowl of green Jell-O.

"Georgie?" my mother says, rising from a chair and dropping a magazine into its seat. Her hair is pixie cut and threaded with gray.

I rise weakly to my elbows. "Mom, you came?" A scrabble of seagulls seems to tear at my lower belly.

"I'm here, darling, she says, brushing my hair from my brow. "Mrs. King was just here too."

Mrs. King! Oh, no, oh, no! I didn't want to tell her I was pregnant before I told Truman. I hope her feelings aren't hurt. I reach for my mother's soft, age-spotted hand, tears seeping from the corners of my eyes. "I can't believe you're here."

"Truman called yesterday. When you were in surgery. I took the next plane." *Truman.* He was so happy about the baby.

"How is he? Where is he?"

"I sent him home to get some rest. That sweet man hasn't slept in two days."

"Oh, Mama," I say, tears oozing into my ears. "I never knew I wanted a baby."

She closes her eyes and nods her understanding. I writhe, breathing into an ache. "This one was special. I won't have another."

"That's not something you have to think about now."

"How could I be a good mother? I couldn't keep this one safe."

"I never told you," she softly says, "but I had two miscarriages between you and Ronnie."

My sweet mother suffered the loss of two babies and then my father? I try to turn to her, roll onto my side, but the pain gnashes me. "Oh, Mama. I'm sorry. It's so awful." *Is it more awful than watching your father drown before your eyes? Watching his head go under for the last time?* Clutching her hand, I batten my eyes against the vision.

"It *is* awful," she says, punctuating each word with a little pump of my hand. "You grieve. In your own time, in your own way. And one day you wake up, and it's better."

I lie quietly for a moment, savoring my mother's presence. "I love you, Mom."

"I love you too. And your brother—I talked to him last night—sends his love." She looks up at a clatter of conversation in the hall. "You have such good friends. Lina was here last night. And your president, Susan," she says as though referring to the POTUS. "The flowers are from the school. Aren't they lovely?"

I roll my head on the papery pillow to regard an extravagant bouquet on the windowsill: masses of white peonies, pink roses, trailing ivy. Pink roses. *Was it a girl?*

Mom rambles on. "Lina carried a huge pan of lasagna to your house. And salad. And tiramisu." *Lina.* I know she is preparing to go and spend some time with her son and daughter-in-law in Portland, Maine.

"And that Laurel," Mom gushes, "she's a doll."

Mom met Laurel. *Laurel.* Another bubble of memory breaks the surface: pain searing my belly like a brand. The spate of lifeblood on the kitchen floor; I can smell the brine and tin of it. Laurel sitting me in a chair, her dark eyes forests of fear, then taking the stairs two at a time. Bringing towels and stuffing them between my legs. Calling campus emergency and Truman from my cell. Revolving red lights in my driveway. Being lifted onto a gurney. Was it Monday night? Pain presses low. Coldness spreads through my chest, and I shiver. I wish someone would bind me to a rotisserie, spin me round and round, and for Voltaire to curl into my side.

"Voltaire. Is Laurel taking care of him?"

Pulling an extra blanket from the foot of the bed over me, she smiles. "You better know it."

A rotund nurse waddles in with a small paper cup that I hope contains pain pills. "Here you are, Ms. Bricker, can you sit up for me?"

"Why am I in such pain?" I ask her after swallowing two enormous tablets.

She casts a quizzical glance at my mother and adjusts my pillow, her arms reeking of drugstore perfume. My mother nods once as if giving the nurse permission to tell me. "Your miscarriage was incomplete, Ms. Bricker. Dr. Katz found remaining . . . tissue in your uterus. That's why he performed the D&C."

Tissue. I cradle my belly and begin to weep. Not tissue; a baby. My baby hadn't wanted to part from me either.

"Dr. Katz will be in to talk with you this evening when he comes for rounds. You get your rest now." She smiles grimly at my mother and waddles out, closing the door behind her. My mother talks to me of her husband Barrett's work on a new sea-facing screened porch for their home. Her voice is a swaddling of cotton batting.

The pain medicine comes on then and makes two of her.

I close my sandpapered eyes.

I think she tells me I would have been a good mother.

I drift again. To a place where a thousand babies rock in an array of cradles beneath a glowing crescent moon.

◈

When I wake again, the beige blinds are drawn and opaque. My hand is untethered.

Truman, who is freshly shaven and smells of leaves and love, leans over the bed rail. He peers into my face. "Sweetheart? How do you feel?"

I swallow, my mouth muzzy and, I'm sure, foul. "Better, I think. May I have some water?"

He whisks a plastic cup from the rolling tray table and inclines the straw to my lips. "I think it's Sprite." I sip until the straw makes a rude slurp and ask for more. "Are you hungry?" he asks after ringing the nurse for another cup.

"Not for lime Jell-O."

He huffs a short laugh through his nose. "Lina sent you a

piece of lasagna," he says, tilting his head toward a foil-wrapped plate on the broad windowsill. "It's delicious."

Have Truman and my mother and Laurel been eating together? Like family? A spurt of satisfaction at the image traces my veins.

"I'm not ready to eat just yet. How's Laurel? Is she okay?"

He nods. "I think she's good. She went back to classes today."

"That's good." Will she leave me then? Will I be back to living alone?

"She was so strong for you."

Tears smart my lids. "Yes. She was."

A silence unfolds between Truman and me.

Will we talk about the baby?

"Is it okay if I sit down?" he asks. "I'll be careful."

I nod, gulping back tears at the thought of the conversation we have to have. He sits on the edge of the bed and takes my chilled hands. His hands are not much warmer. He ducks his head, his throat working. "Georgie," he says and then clears his throat. He looks at me and starts again, "I'm so sorry about the baby. What you've been through. If I could take the pain for you, I would."

My eyes fill. "Oh, darling. I know you're hurting too."

His eyes mirror mine. "I feel useless."

"Just love me," I say, through sobs. "As long as you love me, I can get through anything."

He lifts my hands and kisses them, wetting them with tears of his own. "I do love you. That will never change, whether we have a baby or not." The sea blue of his eyes pours into mine. "I want us ro be married. Forever."

My heart stops. I've dreamed of this moment since we were kids, and then again when we were reunited. But is this a sympathy or guilt proposal?

I inventory his eyes and see that it is not.

Marry my first love, the boy of my dreams who returned to me a man?

"I'm all yours, Georgie. Anne Emerson signed the papers." He gives a backhand wave. "She's been involved with someone for months—some rich playboy—and couldn't be bothered to fulfill her obligations."

"You are? She did? I can't believe it."

"I'm free."

He's been divorced mere hours yet wants to rush into a marriage with me. He says he's ready, but how can he be? He's reacting this way because I've lost the baby. His face says the gesture didn't spring from pity, but maybe he thinks a marriage proposal will make up for my loss. He is free, but I am not. How can I bind his heart to mine, love him for better or for worse the rest of his life as he deserves, when fear still tethers me? Fear is the opposite of love. Yet I want to lavish unfettered love on him—give him my whole heart.

"I'm not ready, True."

The muscles of his face sag almost imperceptibly, before he offers me a small smile. "Of course, you're not," he says, his eyes sweeping my body. "I'm sorry I hit you with that. Let's focus on getting you home. And healed."

"Don't be sorry." *I love you so. Don't forget that you wanted to marry me.*

He sighs and surveys the medical equipment for a moment. "Life is fragile, isn't it?"

Fatigue, simple and clear, sweeps me. I close my eyes. "Yes."

If there were no girls like them in the world,
there would be no poetry.
—Willa Cather

CHAPTER
NINETEEN

L aurel and I sit reading in my garden, a hidden world brimming with life. A vivid butterfly, a purple hairstreak, flits about the riot of orange blanket flowers. Clematis snakes up a trellis, reminding me it's survived another winter to burst forth again with sweet, star-like flowers. I pray that Willa Cather will reopen and return to its former glory and that I will help tend it along with my perennials next spring. My eyes fall on a toad—almost in-frognito—in the shade of a weathered cement pot. It hops close to the coffee mug Laurel has set on the stones beside her chaise. "You have a visitor," I say to her.

She looks up from her textbook, follows my eyes to the toad, and gives a startled cry. "Gross, I hate frogs!" she says, scooping up the mug and angling her body away.

I grin. "They eat bugs."

Returning to *Economics of Discrimination*, she mutters, "Surely there's a better organic pest control."

Laurel came into my home to heal, yet it is she who is healing me. The hummingbird-flit of her attention warms me to my toes. She vacuums cat hair from my rugs. Her bedroom is a mess—clothes on the floor, her bed unmade. She forgets to hang up her towels, leaves toothpaste in the sink. She pesters me about sulfates in my shampoo, hydrogenated oil in my creamer. About recycling and reusing. She leaves dishes of half-eaten ice cream in the living room. She doesn't care if the house is immaculate; she just wants something interesting to do and a place to sprawl. She tells me about her childhood in Baltimore, living with an aunt instead of two parents. She washed a pickle jar and keeps it filled with flowers from the garden for my bedside table. She told me how she met Trask and about the kind of wedding they wanted to have. She says she hasn't made up her mind about marrying into his family, and I find it oddly comforting that though we're in very different stages of life, we're in the same boat. She brings me fancy coffees from the café, though I know she has little spending money. She makes me hoot with laughter at a time I thought I might never laugh again.

When my mother had returned to South Carolina last week, Laurel—thrilled to get her hands on the wheel of my coupe—had driven me to Dr. Chu's office for my appointment. She'd parked out front to drop me off, but I'd stuck my head back through the window. "Now, no rawhiding it in my coupe," I'd warned her. "And keep the radio low so you can hear emergency vehicles."

She had grinned, running her hands along the smooth leather of the wheel. "Okay, okay."

"And no texting!"

"Anything else, Madame?" she'd said, pretending to take notes in the air.

Once in Dr. Chu's office, the psychiatrist had ever-brilliantly summed up my contretemps, my conflict: "All at once, you've lost both your opportunities for nurturing: your child and your students."

Yet there is Laurel.

Now in the garden, I smile at the lopsided knot she's made of her hair.

She's becoming like a daughter to me, just when I need one most.

She turns a page and absently scratches at a bug bite on her ankle. It has been two weeks since I lost the baby. I'm still pressing mini-pads to my panties to soak up trickles of brown blood. I'm assured the residual bleeding will soon resolve, leaving my body as it was before. Before she was there. Though my emotional stings aren't visible, they prickle at me. When they itch, I scratch them and they open again. But each day they seem to itch a little less.

Last week, Lina and Mrs. King came to visit with incomprehensible news. The graphic design students delivered on the website and donate button. Within forty-eight hours, the campaign netted 1.8 million dollars in pledges to "the cause" (as Mrs. King has taken to calling it, as though Virginia is still at war with the Yankees).

The rally is set for June 23. Social media is stoking the campaign for donations from alumnae and FOW: Friends of Willa. Though most of the faculty have applied for or secured positions at other colleges, Lina says hope traces their features again. Of course, Susan would allow anyone to stay on if they changed their minds; without instructors we couldn't reopen.

Most of the underclassmen, who for a time moved about campus like bewildered soldiers dragging wounded limbs, have responded to the rally cry with bravado. I'd asked Laurel if she would serve as the student liaison for the campaign. She'd grinned and said, "Hundo p, Madame," which I figured meant I could count on her to give her all.

Months ago, I remember thinking of her as the one to lead the senior class next year, and if we pull this thing off, she may do so in ways I never expected.

Now, she looks at me. "I have an idea," she says. "WCC needs a badass mascot. I mean, how long have we been The Belles? Most of us are not even Southern, and we're, none of us, the simpering type."

I snort a laugh. "True that. I love it, and I'm sure the other students will. I'll run it by the president."

"We could have a contest to come up with a good mascot."

"Tag. As student liaison, you're in charge of that."

She gives me a thumbs-up.

Not only is my physical strength returning, but I'm absorbing Laurel's fierce by osmosis, as though it seeps through the air-conditioning vent in my room while I sleep. She is teaching me about courage; I am teaching her to appreciate seventies folk rock and to cook without using a microwave.

And then there is my *parfit gentil* knight. Truman has turned up every evening with *petit* bouquets, chocolate-dipped strawberries, and, twice, big gooey pizzas from Huck's. Days he spends in the conference room—fueled by coffee and single-mindedness—scratching up the tired old earth of school finances and burying himself in trying to discover where it all went wrong. This afternoon, he is coming by and wants to talk about Beau Duffy, a conversation we've been putting off since before I had the miscarriage.

Laurel closes her book, stretches her arms wide, and casts her long legs over one side of the chaise. "I'm supposed to meet Sutton and Penn to do some yoga." She gives me a slantwise look. "You know, yoga would be really good for you."

"Dr. Chu suggested that actually. Maybe you can show me the positions."

She grins and strikes a pose—which even I recognize as one of the warriors—and holds it for a moment. "I can totally do that. Need anything before I go?"

"I'm good. Really good today. Truman's coming over . . ." I

peer through my readers at the tiny clock at the top of my laptop screen. "In a couple of hours."

She cocks a saucy eyebrow. "You know everyone's loving this romance. You guys are one true pair."

"They are?" The coffee in my stomach sloshes. "Do people know . . . about the . . . our . . . baby?" Secluded here and still as fragile as dandelion fluff, I hadn't thought of that.

She looks down. "Yeah. Even with all the rally stuff going down, the word's gotten around."

My heart takes a jog; I feel as though I've taken a spin around campus buck naked.

Laurel's eyes zip to mine again. "It wasn't me who told." She looks into the middle distance for a moment. "Believe me, I know how rumors can spread after what happened to me."

"I understand."

"We all want you to be happy; that's why we're rooting for the romance. Remember how cool we thought it was when you told us about Truman at the slumber party, how he was your first love?"

"I do. But I told you girls that story because I wanted you to believe in Truman's sincerity."

"Yeah. He's a really good man. Trask loves him." She surveys the stone wall my brother, Ron, helped me build. "I just wish he could have . . . done more."

"Don't count him out yet," I say, carefully, anticipating the news he's bringing me today.

Laurel surveys me on the chaise. "When the girls heard about your miscarriage, they were so sad. They wanted to make cards, write you notes, but they felt awkward and didn't know if it would be, you know, appropriate."

"You tell them I'd appreciate any sweet notes I can get. And that I can't wait to see them next week."

"Oh, I forgot to tell you, we're going to start making signs for the rally."

"Signs?"

"Well, yeah. You know, to hold up."

"Well. I hadn't thought that far yet."

"Is that okay?"

"As long as they're positive. Text me pictures."

She gives me a big thumbs-up. "Will do."

"Well, au revoir then."

She gives me a little hug, her scent as fresh as a spray of water from the hose. "Au revoir."

I watch her go, remembering what she said about everyone knowing about the miscarriage. I imagine knots of them whispering about me in stairwells, in the dining hall, on the tennis courts. Since I've been taking the medicine and seeing Dr. Chu, something has been nibbling away at the edges of my anxiety. Many of my old insecurities seem to be losing their power. Do I really care what people say or think? Susan supports me; my friends love me. That's all that should matter.

Let them talk. I lie back, intending to take a ten-minute catnap. The day heats. I drowse to the rasp of cicadas.

Truman's hand on my shoulder is like a warm pouring of sand. "Sleeping Beauty, I presume?"

"Mmm," I murmur, "kiss me awake then."

The prince takes of his jacket and tie and complies until my lips tingle.

Then he flops onto Laurel's chaise.

"It's hot out here," I say. "Don't you want to go inside and have some iced tea?"

A pair of cardinals chirr and ruffle in the maple tree. Truman looks out over the garden and sighs. I notice the strain around his eyes. "It's so nice out here after being in the confer-ence room all day."

"Oh, of course. We'll stay."

His face relaxes. "How about I scoot the umbrella over here; would that work?"

"That would be great," I say, getting up. "Actually, I have to go pee. I'll bring the iced tea when I come back. Lemon?"

"Please," he says, pooching his lips out to me in an air kiss and digging his laptop out of his bag.

"Be right back."

I return with two glasses and find the tired sleuth—still more Mark Harmon than Peter Falk—in the shade, making notes on a pad. I'm glad Laurel's not around to overhear our conversation.

"How do you say 'this is war' in French?"

"C'est la guerre."

His eyes light on my lips and move slowly up to my eyes. "You know it turns me on when you speak French. One day, I was in Collins and passed your classroom. I heard you speaking French and got a boner."

"True!" I gasp, a blush heating my cheeks. "You did not!"

"I did. I had to duck into the men's room."

I press my glass to a cheek, delighted. "Don't we have busi-ness to discuss? You're going to get *me* aroused, and we can't do it until after I go back to the doctor."

"Right." I watch his face grow grim. He shifts to sit on the side of his chaise, his feet on the stones.

I follow his lead. We sit in the shade of the umbrella, our knees almost touching. "I'm about to wage war on the chief financial officer. Sawyer Hays has been responsible for the development department. And it's a hot, throbbing mess. Cur-rently, we have no access to donor records—"

"I know! I looked for them myself a while back." Actually, when I was looking for a history of Eleanor's giving.

"There's more, and it's all no-brainer stuff. It's like no one's been flying the command ship for two years."

"But someone was. Sawyer Hays."

He nods gravely and sips at his tea before setting it down. "There are so many irregularities: leadership stipends and compensation without documentation to back them up. Remember when I found out that Duffy and my mother knew each other in college?" He draws his long hands into fists along his thighs. "When I was in Atlanta two weeks ago, I realized I was Duffy's bait to get my mother involved. I believe the bastard's been embezzling. And he's been hoping to use his old friend's money to help cover his tracks." *Eleanor's an accessory to all this?* "Mother doesn't know what Duffy's done," he says, one step ahead of my thoughts. "Believe me; she was just after an ego boost. She was probably hoping they would name a building for her."

"How does Sawyer Hays fit into all of this?"

Truman scrubs his forehead back and forth. "That's what I'm still investigating. But I think Beau Duffy is Sawyer's pawn.

Our trusted, good-guy chairman. *Chou de dieu.*

Remember the day Beau announced that the school would close, and I had gotten word before the meeting? I knew what was coming, so I watched him closely."

"Beau was robotic, delivering that profound news—devoid of emotion—when he's usually so personable."

A regular guy. A pediatrician. I would have probably taken our baby to see him.

Loss prods my heart.

Truman picks up his glass and takes a deep swallow. "I watched the way he shifted from one foot to the other, crossed his arms and leaned back on his heels. He was distancing himself from the assembly."

I squeeze my wedge of lemon into my glass and try to remember Beau's demeanor, but the memory's as murky as the tea.

"Before the meeting," he continues, "I saw him go into the men's room off the library. Remember I kept trying to call you and getting your voicemail? I never saw him come out. I went in there to splash my face, and he was still in there in a stall. I recognized his shoes. The thing was, there was no smell—if you know what I mean—so what was he doing in there? Hiding?"

My mind swims with indignation. "Are you going to confront him?"

"First, I'm going to look into the irregularities I'm seeing with these leadership stipends. Get into the minutes from board meetings. Then I'm going to pay our president a visit."

Dread prickles at the back of my neck. "When?"

"As soon as I have something concrete. Before your rally."

I take his hand. "Our rally. I couldn't do any of this without your love and support."

"Yes, you could," he says, his eyes darkening. "You've had the power to be a badass all along, Georgie; you just didn't know it."

Tears sting my nose. "Badass. I've heard that term twice today."

Truman is quiet for a moment but then turns his blue eyes loose on me the way he had that night in the hospital, when he'd asked me to marry him. "We're great together, sweetheart. You know we'd be forever."

I've waited so long to be with him; why rush now? "True. I—"

"Yoo-hoo, anybody home?" Mrs. King calls from inside the house. "I've brought news!"

⚬⟡⚬

Truman stands and greets my secretary as she comes grinning down the brick steps to the garden, wearing Big Bird–yellow oven mitts on her hands. "I hope I'm not interrupting."

"No, you're fine." I smile at the mitts and get to my feet. "What are you up to?"

She removes the mitts and stuffs them under one arm. "I brought a chicken pot pie for your dinner. Beaucoup carrots. It's on the stove."

"Thank you so much! But you have to stop feeding me comfort food, or I'll be as big as Humpback Rock," I say, gesturing toward the mountains.

She laughs. "I do have some great news. The electronic rally invitation went out at four o'clock yesterday after you and Susan approved the proof."

"Great! What was the total number?"

"Including FOW and members of the community, over two thousand were sent. But what I came to tell you is that the invitation task force just reported over three hundred affirmative responses, some from as far away as Alaska and New Zealand!"

I open my mouth and then close it.

She goes on, her eyes as bright as a squirrel's. "In fewer than twenty-four hours! There will be more to come. Remember the baseball field movie with that cute Kevin Costner? 'If you build it, they will come'?"

My old nemesis, panic, tries to make camp in my head. "But how are we going to feed all those people?"

"Well, we'll figure it out. The girls will help."

Suddenly, I feel the way I had when I'd taken on the study abroad initiative without considering all of the complexities. "Will we need portable toilets and a first aid station? What if it rains?" My mind ticks to film footage of the great field at Yasgur's Farm. Hippies covered in mud. Woodstock at Willa Cather. I sway on my feet.

"Sit down, honey," Mrs. King says, and Truman takes my arm and eases me back onto the chaise. The two exchange concerned glances.

"Listen, Georgie," he says, "you guys have weeks to iron out the details. It will all work out."

"I hope you're right. I never dreamed we'd have so many people. Can we really handle an event of this magnitude?"

A chorus of female voices seems to come from the street in front of my house and grows louder. A small parade of students bearing signs—made of poster board and wooden paint stirrers for handles—spills into the garden. In the lead, Malika peeks around her sign. "This is a drill," she says with a grin.

The sign asserts in red letters, "Where there's a Willa, there's a way."

❦

The next day, I venture out to my office for the first time since the miscarriage. Will people fall silent as I pass? Avoid me? Look at me with pity? Lengthening my stride, I decide to blow off the lingering panicky thought as paranoia. I smile, thinking of how far I've come, and greet the art history professor seated on a bench outside her building. "Beautiful morning, *n'est pas?*"

"It truly is, Georgie. Have a good day."

Mrs. King stands outside my office door, her hands astride her broad hips. "Look who's here."

"Oops, *excuse moi*, Madame," Malika says, scooting from her seat on the carpeted floor of my office and clearing a path to my desk for me. "Welcome back."

Emily and Morgan sit against the wall, balancing their laptops on their legs, and appear to be transferring data from paper bundles onto spreadsheets. "We're working on rally stuff, but if the conference room is free now, we can move in there," Morgan says.

"No, no, stay where you are." My students want to be near me. My students are taking charge. Tears of gratitude and pride clog my throat.

"Madame, you have to see the T-shirts the graphic arts girls designed; they look amazing," Morgan says. "Our colors aqua

216

and red, so cute! Event-staff shirts are all aqua; students, red; guests, both colors. I'll send you a picture."

"Wait, wait, who's paying for these T-shirts?"

Morgan's brow furrows as if the answer is obvious. "The attendees are," she says. "There's an option on the registration form to order one. Ten bucks! But we found a print shop in Mountainsburg to do them for us for five," she adds with a foxy wink.

"Okay, you guys are seriously good. I can't believe it. What else have I missed?"

Emily smiles. "I'm actually writing up a progress report for you right now."

I swallow back tears. "Good. I can't wait to see what you've accomplished." I hoist my bag onto my desk and begin unpacking it.

"Coffee?" my secretary asks me.

And just like that, I'm back.

ᔆᕽᓭ

That night, I sit on my kitchen stool, directing Laurel in making a citrus-kale salad. Mrs. King's eyes-to-the-skies-good chicken pie is heating in the oven, and its aroma whets my appetite. Though it takes her some time, Laurel peels grapefruits and oranges with a sharp knife. "Great job," I tell her. "That's hard to do, without leaving pith behind."

She regards the pulpy globes. "Well, look at them go," she says, pleased.

I sip from my glass of pinot gris as she measures orange juice, champagne vinegar, Dijon mustard that Madame Beaulieu sends me from Paris every Christmas, and other ingredients for the dressing into a small bowl. "Now, when you add the olive oil, you'll want to whisk it in.

She gives me a smart-ass look and mimics the hand motion I've made. "Whisk."

I grin. "There's a little wire whisk in the drawer to your right."

I sip my wine, swinging my foot to Laurel's choice of music—a Baltimore band, Beach House—and watch the economy of her movements. She's a natural. I imagine her cooking for Trask, or the two of them cooking together in a kitchen of their own.

"How's Trask?"

She turns, her face aglow. "He's great." She picks up the roll of goat cheese and begins to crumble it as the recipe directs. She sneaks a bite before adding it to the bowl. "I've been meaning to ask you . . . if you'd mind if I spent Friday and Saturday nights in Mountainsburg."

I regard the back of her WCC tank top. "You don't have to ask my permission to do that."

"No, I know. It's just . . . I don't know how much longer I'll be . . . staying with you."

I set my glass on the counter. "Oh, Laurel. You know what? You have taken such good care of me and been a wonderful comfort, wonderful company, but you're not responsible for me. You can leave anytime you like."

She turns on the faucet and looks out the window at the garden while she washes the cheese from her hands. She takes up the dish towel and turns to me. "I love it here. With you. But I have something to tell you. It's actually fabulous news if it happens. Rumor has it that George Wythe College has approached Willa Cather about a merger."

A merger? My breath leaves me. Why have I heard nothing about this?

"Trask says everyone at GW is talking about it. We could take online classes or go to either campus. If it happens, I could live with Trask and Asher for senior year, and I'd still be close to you. It would be so perfect."

ELIZABETH SUMNER WAFLER

My mind rushes headlong, but my words come slowly. "But our schools were built on the ideals of single-sex education. A merger would destroy everything we're about."

Laurel worries the hem of the dish towel with her fingers. She meets my eyes. "But it would rescue Willa Cather."

Rescue Willa Cather. Yes, it would do that. But it would be like throwing a lifeline to a mermaid. Pulling her ashore so she could make prosthetic legs in a factory.

"Do you know who the head of GW has been talking with here about this merger?" *Beau Duffy? Sawyer Hays? Not Susan.*

She notes my twisting hands. "No. I have no idea. I'm so sorry if I upset you, Madame."

I slide from the stool and move to put my arm around her. "No, darling. You're fine. Don't think another thing of it. Go spend those nights in Mountainsburg. And tell Trask I said hello." *Truman will spend those nights with me.* I smile and pour another glass of wine. "How's that salad looking?" I want to move beyond this conversation, so Laurel won't feel like she's done anything wrong. I never want her to hesitate in telling me something, like this news.

After dinner, when Laurel's gone to her room, I take a long soak in my tub, thinking of all she has said. While I would love to keep her in a college nearby, there's no way I would support a merger. If the college survived but lost sight of its mission, I would leave here. *And just where would you go, Madame? And how?* I yank the drain plug out with a toe.

Tomorrow, I will get to the bottom of this merger rumor. That's all it is, a rumor.

As the water recedes from my rounded reef of belly, a rip current of sadness threatens to overpower me. Truman hasn't mentioned the baby lately, though sometimes I see a shadow cross his face, while I dream of her often. Tonight, instead of fighting the current, I swim alongside the shore of my sadness

219

until the waters have sluiced away. The chill urges me to reach for a towel.

I lotion my body, climb into bed, and check my email. The report Emily mentioned has arrived. I poke it open and skim through it. The grateful tears I'd quashed earlier stream my face. As of this afternoon, the task forces have:

- Designed and activated a Facebook campaign page.
- Received $400,050 in donations.
- Received $2.3M in the form of pledges.
- Designed e-vites for rally; sent 2,027.
- Received 386 affirmative replies.
- Started a database of donors.

I wipe my face and blow my nose. We don't need mergers to rescue Willa Cather. We just need the people who love us, who believe in us and our mission. A small thud at my window startles me from my thoughts. "Oh, no, Voltaire. I hope that wasn't a bird."

Like a medieval prince, reclining on his throne, my cat gives one lazy flick of his tail and goes back to grooming a paw.

I'm padding to the window when a second thud comes. "What on earth?" I pull back the curtain and peer out. My coupe gleams white in the gloom. But just behind it, I make out a figure. I raise the window, swipe at a spider's silk. "Truman?"

A flash of hand: he's saluted me. "Georgie Girl."

My heart grows wings. I pitch my voice low. "What are you doing down there?"

His grin flashes in the dim. "I wanted to see you."

"Meet you at the kitchen door."

I grin at his boyish behavior all the way downstairs. Tossing pebbles at my window. What's next? A ukulele serenade?

Drawing my robe around my gown, I let him in and place a finger to my lips. "Laurel's in her room, but her light's still on."

Truman's sexy in his gray Emory T-shirt and washed-out jeans. Though he's gorgeous in a suit and tie, I love it when he's comfortable. He reaches for me, his boyishness disappearing.

"Wait. Let's go upstairs," I whisper.

We start up, the stairs creaking wildly in spots they never creak. "You smell good."

Truman hasn't spent the night since Laurel's been with me. "Shh," I say, feeling like a sixties' college girl smuggling a boy into her dorm room.

Inside, I twist the lock on the door. He gathers me into his arms. Voltaire plunges to the floor and retreats under the bed. "I love you," Truman whispers into my ear. He kisses my mouth and works his way down my neck. He slides a finger under a strap on my shoulder.

A glutton for his touch, my lids drop to half-mast. "You know we can't have intercourse till I see the doctor again."

He dips his chin and looks up at me in the way that turns me inside out. "I do." He whispers against my mouth. "But we can still make love." He takes my hand and leads me to the bed. "Tell me how to love you, baby."

My breath hitching in my throat, I glance at the door lock. I turn off my lamp and power on the Bose.

Fleetwood Mac's "Warm Ways" floats up as Truman and I drift down.

The fears are paper tigers.
—Amelia Earhart

CHAPTER
TWENTY

Fifteen days until the rally.

Fifteen minutes until I need to leave for the meeting I'm attending as faculty liaison with Susan, Truman, and Beau Duffy. As Truman said, Duffy's doo-doo is about to hit the fan. As if dressing for a memorial service, I pull out my good gray suit. But the love-languid pounds I've gained won't allow the skirt to zip. If I had to suffer a miscarriage, couldn't I at least have lost weight?

The baby. According to the week-by-week online pregnancy tracker, the baby would have been the size of a peach pit now. The old sadness forms a glacier around my heart. I toss the suit into the back corner of the closet, where other size twelves wait to be bagged and donated to the women's shelter. The magazines say if you haven't worn something in two years, you should give it away. I sigh and pull on a navy wrap dress with spandex. There should be a grief tracker for women who miscarry: by week one, your grief will be the size of an African elephant, by week four, the size of a Volkswagen . . . I'll never forget my baby, but I don't want sadness hanging in my heart like unworn clothing two years from now. Slipping into gray pumps, I make a mental note to discuss it with Dr. Chu.

I start down the stairs. *Two years.* Will I marry Truman by then? Where will we live? Would it be too late to try for another baby? Would I even want to try? Voltaire tears past me into the kitchen, in hopes I'll give him a salmon treat from the little red tin on the counter on my way out the door. I do.

I haven't darkened the door of the administration building or conference room in weeks. Coffee, vetiver, and woody-almond reams of paper meet my nose: Truman. At the end of the table, he lifts his face and distractedly greets me before returning to his laptop. I bend to plant a kiss on his cheek, hug him briefly around his shoulders. "Where would you like me to sit?"

As Susan clips into the room in red pumps and a camel-colored suit, I straighten and assume a businesslike posture. But her demeanor today is more lioness than camel. "Truman and I will sit next to each other on one side of the table," she crisply says, "and Dr. Duffy across from us."

I do a double take at her the way one would at a spot on a wall to make sure it's not a spider. Dr. Duffy? I've never heard Susan or anyone refer to the chairman as anything but Beau.

Behind his reading glasses, Truman's eyes darken. "Certainly," he says. He rises, buttons his suit coat, and relocates his things to a place along the side of the table. I can't help but admire the cut of his suit, the broad shoulders that I like to nuzzle and knead with my hands.

Taking a seat to his right, Susan fixes me with her gaze. "Georgie, will you please take notes for us, transcribing the discourse?"

"Yes. Of course." This crucial conversation then, one that could destroy a man's career, will be mine to record. I open my laptop with wobbly hands and power it up.

"Good morning," Beau Duffy says, a moment later, striding into the room with a friendly smile. I imagine him in his white doctor's coat, presenting a purple lollipop to a child.

"Good morning, Dr. Duffy," Susan says evenly, as Truman and I say, "Good morning," in tandem.

Beau stops short. He looks about him the way one does when he's unsure of the terrain. He sets a leather folder and a paper coffee cup with the logo from Antonia's Café on the table. He rubs his palms slowly together. "Where would you like me?"

Susan inclines a hand to the seat opposite her and Truman and replies, "There, please." She glances at me. "Madame Bricker is here to take notes as faculty liaison to Truman's committee." I squirm under Beau's gaze. Susan turns to me and tilts her head to the door as if to say: Will you please close that? Truman slides a list of bullet-pointed notes onto the table in front of himself.

I rise to close the door. In the hall, two instructors carrying boxes pass by, their eyes zipping to the conference table through the slice of open door as it closes. I take my seat again, nervousness prickling my arms. I create a new document in Word and save it as "Committee Meeting/Beau Duffy" and add the date and time. Truman precisely aligns the pages in front of him with the inlaid wood border of the table. He clears his throat and fixes Beau with his blue eyes.

The chairman settles his forearms along the armrests and lifts his chin.

Truman begins. "As you know, part of what I came to Willa Cather to do was to complete an independent audit of the finances." Truman holds Beau's eyes until the man looks at his cup and picks it up, fumbling it slightly. I watch a bubble of coffee break at the hole in the lid, and my mouth tugs down at the mess it could have made on the table. Truman glances at me. I start, remembering I'm supposed to take notes, and hastily type what he's said.

Truman studies Beau and waits for a space of time. The moment is as tense as the string of an archer's bow. I am amazed at Truman's cool, his skillful examination of the chairman. I imagine him, elegant and powerful in Atlanta's Buckhead conference rooms. His next words ring out, "Beau, I have found irregularities."

I record the terse statement. Susan uncrosses her legs and scoots her chair closer to the table. "Please tell us what you have found, Truman," her eyes never leaving the chairman. Sweat beads begin to glimmer on Beau's brow. He swings his head to look at Susan and back at Truman. He straightens his tie.

"There are leadership stipends and compensation without backup documentation," Truman says, as patient as a prospector. Beau raises his coffee cup, takes a sip, and holds the cup in front of his mouth, rubbing the rim back and forth across his lips. "Further, documents have been falsified." Beau opens his leather folder as though those documents could be found inside. His brow sweat trickles down the side of his face closest to me; a drop plops onto the table. I look at Truman over my laptop to see if he noticed. Abruptly, I remember a meeting between Truman and me—that must have been in February—when the chairman had popped in. I recall the way he had surveyed us, the way his blue collar had been dark with perspiration. Was he nervous then about what Truman would find?

Truman looks at Beau and then pointedly at the tiny puddle on the table before adding to his statement, "Executive board meeting minutes were filed for meetings that never actually occurred."

Beau's cup shakes alarmingly. "Now, wait just a damned minute," he says, setting it down again. His coat sleeve smears the sweat puddle across the table. "The committee secretary was out . . . on maternity leave for quite a while." He raises his palms. "Perhaps those minutes are incomplete because they were hastily taken by . . . a substitute. I can . . ." His words die on his lips. He licks them and looks at Susan. I return to my keyboard.

Susan coolly says, "I have looked into the meetings Mr. Parker cited, Dr. Duffy. Nine meetings. Nine meetings that neither I nor any board member attended. And in which the only items recorded in the minutes were the approval of leadership stipends."

Beau leans back in his chair. He runs a neat hand over his white hair. He looks at Susan. His lips part. "Perhaps Mr. Parker has the dates mixed up. I'm sure I can clear this up. In all honesty—"

Susan interrupts. "Interesting choice of words, Dr. Duffy." She slowly taps the palm side of a chunky gold ring I've never seen on the edge of the table. *Tap tap tap.* On its face is a gold lion's head. Beau seems riveted by the ring until my fingers tap my keyboard again. He shoots me a dagger of a look as if all of this is somehow my fault. I swallow a gasp.

Truman consults his notes again. He slips off his readers and regards Beau. "In April, you made the faculty aware of the twenty . . . million . . . dollar . . . budget deficit . . ." He takes an agonizing pause. "You reported you had been forced to draw from unrestricted funds to meet operating expenses."

I type the last statements, remembering that day, when Beau had stood in the library in front of the faculty. How cool and collected he'd been then, in his immaculate suit and tie. As though I've projected the image on a screen above my head, Beau sits taller. "Yes. That is correct," he says matter-of-factly. "It takes a great deal of money to run this school, maintain the physical campus. You know that." He seems to gain some inner momentum, an arrogant expert witness.

But the chairman is the defendant in this "trial." And Truman's next words underscore the fact. "I believe an official investigation will prove that many of these expenditures were allocated not to benefit the school, but for your personal benefit." I flinch and type the ominous words, then peek at Beau over the laptop. A rough red blush rises from his snowy collar to his hairline. He casts a look at the door and pushes his feet against the floor, easing his chair back. He crosses his legs at the knee.

"There's more," Truman says presently. "For the past five years, a sixty-thousand-dollar per annum faculty salary was allocated but not connected with any member of the faculty." He seems to let that sink in. Beau crosses his arms over his chest. "Dr. Duffy, we believe that salary was created for you." I draw my shoulders in, as though awaiting thunder after an epic bolt of lightning splits the sky.

Susan, the lioness with the ring to prove it, goes for his throat. "What is it, Dr. Duffy, gambling debts?" She pauses, her words resounding. "Malpractice premiums too high for a country doctor to enjoy a jet-set lifestyle?" I marvel at her prosaic delivery of the barbed words. A country doctor: a label that could apply to a stranger. And suddenly that's exactly what he is. I stare at him as if to recall some familiar expression. I can't believe I've sipped cocktails in his lovely Georgian home on Park Drive, chatted with and exchanged recipes with his pretty wife, Jill, tutored his eldest daughter in French, eaten fish tacos with our fingers with him in the dining hall. Beau worked among us, shoring up the scaffolding of our programs, while, all the time, callously tearing them apart. I shake my head slightly, forgetting for a moment to record Susan's words. I bend over the keyboard again like a spider furiously wrapping silk.

Beau glares at me. I start and drag my gaze sideways. Does he hate me because I'm the one making the terrible words real?

The chairman angles his torso toward Susan, as though she might be his last hope. He places his palms on the table as if to hold the whole mess down, to keep it from rising and leaving the room, making its way into the town. "Susan, we've been friends for many years. You know me." His voice cracks with audible panic. Susan gazes mildly at him. Waits for him to fill the ringing silence. We thought we knew the man, but as the Bible says, only God can know a man's heart.

Truman's next words tumble onto the table, bounce against the opposite wall. "Who's behind you in this, Beau?" My hands skitter on the keyboard. Beau shifts, puts his elbows on the table. He drops his chin to his knuckles and rubs it across them. The rasp of his beard is like the scurry of little rat feet. Have his whiskers popped along with his sweat in the time we've been in this room? Truman continues, his tone precise and even, "The next call I make will be to the college attorneys, who I'm sure will be in contact with the FBI immediately."

Beau's head flies up. He leaps to his feet, the legs of his chair making a loud *scr-unnk* on the floor. My heart strikes a trot.

Susan again casually taps the back of the ring against the edge of the table. *Rap rap rap.* "Make it easier on yourself, Dr. Duffy. If you tell the truth about your involvement, perhaps a federal grand jury will be more lenient in your indictment."

The striking of my computer keys ring out like pellets from a gun. Heart pounding, I sneak another glance at Beau. He stares at Susan, and the blood seems to leak from his face. At a flurry of chatter in the hall, he looks at the door. His eyes seem to scan the squares of floor tile between his chair and the exit. He picks up his cup, tries to drink from it, and lowers it to the table with a hollow clunk. His eyes scan the periphery of the room and stop on a trash can behind me. He crumples the cup and lets it fly. I flinch violently as it narrowly misses my arm.

Truman rises from his chair with a menacing frown. I expect him to draw a sword. Four feet of table separate the men. Truman makes a don't-fuck-with-me face. Beau regards him, and, for a beat, defiance lights his eyes, before trepidation snuffs it out.

Susan seems to try another tact. "Gentlemen, will you please take a seat?" They do; Truman immediately, Beau after glancing at the door once more as though considering flight. "Beau, you have a sterling reputation in this community as a doctor and friend, a colleague. Was it Sawyer Hays?" she asks softly. "Did he put you up to this, Beau?"

The chairman's mouth opens. Mine does too. My fingers freeze to the keyboard. I glance at Truman. Did he figure this out? Sawyer Hays. Painstakingly, I type Susan's question and await Beau's reply. He studies his soft-looking physician's hands, his manicured nails. He toys with a gold cuff link. Finally, he speaks, his voice coming out hoarse and wrong. I type his measured reply. Three damning letters. Y-e-s.

For the next hour, Truman asks Beau questions about debits and credits and approvals and meetings that either did or didn't take place. I do my best to capture the conversation word for word, but the financial parts often elude me. The parts I do understand all seem to implicate Sawyer Hays.

Finally, Truman gathers the various sheets of paper they'd examined into a pile and slides them back into a folder. "I appreciate your cooperation, Beau."

"Thank you, Dr. Duffy," Susan replies, her tone textured with pity and regret. "I suggest that you go home now. And get your house in order. Prepare your family." I imagine the police coming for him. Raising the handsome brass knocker—a lion's head—on the door and giving it a smart tap.

Beau gets to his feet again. His hands shake on the back of his chair as he pushes it in. He walks to the door. He turns back once and surveys us, his face a death mask.

After he has closed the door, the three of us sit numbly. The stench of the chairman's desperation presses in on me. I have to get out of this room.

Susan sits back. Tears fill her eyes. She rubs wet fingers from the inside corners to the outside, leaving crescents of mascara. She huffs a punch-drunk laugh. "And I though higher education was a civilized business. Can we take a break for a few minutes? Meet in my office in, say, fifteen minutes? There are details to discuss." She stands, a lioness.

Truman and I follow her into the empty hallway. She goes into her office and closes the door. Through the textured glass, her shoulders, her dark head appear to press against it for a moment and then fade from sight as she moves toward her desk. My heart aches for our president. Truman and I take a seat on a bench padded with aqua vinyl. The hall smells faintly of lemon polish and like the insides of my grandmother's old chest of drawers. He lays his head against the wall, his hands on his knees, and lets go a long breath. With most of the administrative staff gone for the summer—or just plain gone, I realize grimly—the hall fairly screeches with silence. I picture the building, the campus beyond as a fairy-tale kingdom under an evil curse: weeds and vines growing to choke and bring rot and decay, untended buildings crumbling to dust, serpents slithering through broken windows. Shuddering, I lay my head on Truman's shoulder for a moment. He takes my hand. We turn to look at each other and simultaneously shake our heads, as though reliving the meeting.

A single question fills my head.

"True, how did you know that Beau didn't act alone?"

A transient smile traces his tired face. "*Law & Order.*"

Never worry about bad press; all that matters
is that they spell your name right.
—Kate Hudson

CHAPTER
TWENTY-ONE

T en days until the rally.

A mind-skewing six hundred fifty-five people—women and men—have registered to attend the rally, most of them purchasing "Where There's a Willa, There's a Way" T-shirts, netting for the campaign an extra few thousand for expenses.

Most days, local news crews roll onto campus in their flashy, multi-antennaed vans, seeking interviews with students and faculty. Like well-mannered vultures, they watch and wait. Laurel and the remaining students treat them as royal guests, trotting out to them endless cups of coffee from Antonia's in paper cups. Getting the word out to the world is paramount. Most evenings, we make the local news with human-interest stories. The last, an interview with a freshman who dreamed of attending Willa Cather half her life, only to have her hopes dashed as against rock.

Hollins and her committee assiduously account for every penny that goes out, every penny that comes in. The task force leaders report to her as though each expense is a military maneuver. Donations from the WCC community to date are $1.5 million dollars in cash donations, $19.5 million in pledges:

twenty-one million dollars! And the rally is still to come. I am humbled by the swell of giving that I hope will crest and tumble in on the shore of our big day.

My students have prepared doggedly for the event. Pounding the pavement of the town and hitting up the merchants for donations has garnered—as Laurel oh so charmingly said—a "buttload" of support. (She gets a charge out of my mock-shocked expressions.) When the town of Foxfield got wind of the staggering number of people we expected, they came through in novel ways. Huck Hampton threw down the gauntlet for the other business owners with a pledge of one hundred pizzas. Carmen DiMora reported in *The Foxfield Journal* that Burger Bob's owner had good-naturedly answered his poker buddy Huck with, "I'll see your hun'erd pizzas and raise you a hun'erd wieners and a hun'erd patties. With buns." Not to be outdone, the owner of Casa Taco promised one hundred bean burritos. The Women's Club of Foxfield will cart in pans of brownies, homemade cookies. Grohlier's Foods has donated bottled water, potato chips, and condiments, and Carter's Market, where I shop, granola bars and bananas. I'm counting on the food and drink to be as supernaturally prolific as the loaves and fishes in the Bible, feeding everyone with leftovers to spare. And that rain won't prevent the crowd from eating lunch on the athletic fields.

We've set no rain date. The women of Willa Cather College aren't the melting type. Laurel reports hundreds of votes for a new mascot so far, including Eagles, Red Raiders, Turkeys—which I fervently hope is a joke—Empresses, Warriors, and Rattlers. Nevertheless, I check my weather app obsessively and pray for a nice day.

The people of the town of Foxfield, who understand that a thriving college stimulates their economy, maintains their infrastructure and streets, and provides intellectual and cultural opportunities—art, music, theater—come through, offering their guest rooms and garage apartments to alums for the week-end. The owners of the Sleeping Beauty Motel have reserved every one of their thirty-two air-conditioned units for alumnae, free of charge.

They have hired the maintenance and groundskeepers that were laid off from the college and put them to work in their homes, businesses, and yards.

The city has already set up a string of blue portable toilets downwind from the lacrosse field. The hospital has promised first aid supplies, and two female doctors, alumnae of WCC, have volunteered to run a first aid tent.

The faculty team and student task force leaders have down-loaded and practiced using a walkie-talkie app so that we can locate and communicate with one another quickly.

Satisfied we've covered every base, I spend a few hours in my office every day, updating files of students who may or may not return, researching successful study abroad programs, and sometimes staring out the window. Yesterday, I created a week's worth of lesson plans, insurance for the reopening I believe will happen.

Mrs. King shows up every morning. With Lina away, and our skeleton crew of foreign-language instructors taking vacation days, often my secretary and I are the only ones in the building. She waters and prunes our plants, cleans—even the scummy microwave—and organizes the break room, brings me my mail. Most of my summer mail is offers to extend my membership in professional organizations. I place the envelopes unopened in two stacks on my desk: If We Reopen, If We Don't. Mrs. King wholeheartedly believes that the rally will harvest enough attention and additional funds for us to reopen. "We'll just have smaller departments until we can get back on our feet," she says. "It will all work out," she promises and pats my shoulder. I tease her about wearing a granny dress, a hard hat, and combat boots to the rally, and she grins, "That's not a bad idea. I could put my picture on Facebook. It could be my profile pic!"

I think back to the meeting with Truman and Susan, when they confronted Beau Duffy, and what we've learned about Sawyer Hays's involvement from the police. As Truman had suspected from his investigations, the mastermind behind the scheme to embezzle from our sleepy little college was our chief financial officer all along. Sawyer Hays had played us like a kite. We may have plunged and flared, but he had held the string and, for a time, had handed it off to Beau Duffy.

After a call from one of our attorneys, the police quietly arrested Beau at his home. Carmen DiMora's *Foxfield Journal* headline read, "Enlightenment by Embezzlement." Lina—still in Portland—requested that her husband not run photographs of the chairman in handcuffs but of his smiling headshot from last year's *Carillon*. And Carmen, who played tennis with Beau, followed her heed.

News cameras from the Richmond affiliate of Fox News materialized to swarm the town square and the periphery of the campus. Students and faculty received an email from Susan, politely requesting they not speak of the matter to reporters. That evening, Sawyer Hays—who had never bothered cultivating friendships with any of us—was arrested at his sumptuous Foxfield home. Carmen featured the story the next morning, only this time the picture that landed on every driveway in town bore the CFO's scowling mug shots.

Susan summarily fired the two men from Willa Cather College. A team of attorneys—WCC alums—have offered to serve as legal counsel for the brewing civil suits. Along with three other devoted faculty members, Susan has asked Lina and me to serve on a search committee to help fill the positions vacated by Sawyer and Beau if we reopen, though who would take on jobs like these that are anything but a sure bet? Susan has asked Truman if he would consider staying on for the fall term as interim CFO. Mulishly, I push away thoughts of him leaving Foxfield. He doesn't comment on whether he's considering Susan's offer. And I don't ask. But sometimes when he looks at me, I feel like he's thinking about our future. And though he's been as lovely and attentive as ever, sometimes when we talk about the college, there is a skittish quality to his gaze.

Has he decided what he wants to do? Is he keeping it from me?

ᘛᘚ

Four days until the rally.

Tuesday night before the Saturday rally, Truman and I take the Rover into town to Huck's. "I can't thank you enough for what you are doing for the rally," I say to Huck, once we've placed our orders over the laminate counter.

"No problem," he says, handing Truman a number on a stob for our table. "Hey, business from the college keeps mah bread buttered," he laughs, "er maybe that should be 'keeps mah crust covered,' er somethin'."

We laugh with him and take the small round table by the window, away from a table of eight loud summer tourists in hiking clothes. I think of the panic attack I'd had here all those months ago—when Huck had thought I needed an inhaler—and abruptly, I feel free.

Peter Frampton's "Baby, I Love Your Way" thumps from the speakers. I smile and reach across the table to finger a longish lock of True's silver hair. The memory of the first time my mother allowed me to have him over for dinner at our faculty apartment glows in my mind. How shaggy his red-gold hair had been. How his presence had seemed to fill the kitchen, had made it warmer and cozier. "Remember how my father was always telling you to get a haircut?"

He laughs and sips his beer. "I do. He'd probably say that

235

now." His face grows thoughtful. "It's so great that you can think of him again without the old grief. You've come a long way." We lock eyes. Grief. He gives his head a shake and squeezes my hand. "I'm sorry. I know you are still grieving the . . . baby."

I pull my hand back. "Aren't you?"

He brings his brows together. "Yes. Sure. But I hurt more for you than for myself. I never dreamed of having another child. I mean, until you told me you were pregnant, and, well, I still have the boys."

I wipe the condensation from my wine glass with a paper napkin. This is the most Truman has said about the baby since the night we talked about it in the hospital. I'm glad he's shared his feelings. That he's not hiding them. "I know."

Huck comes between us with our order. "A Popeye Pizza for Madame with extra spinach, an' a basic Margherita topped with shaved country ham, arugula, lemon vinaigrette, and aged Parmesan for the monsieur," he says, pronouncing the word like "mon-sewer." I smother a grin and thank him. "Another round?"

"Yes, please," Truman and I say at the same time. We moan over the aroma of pork and garlic and sharp cheese for a moment before digging in. Overhead, the Eagles strum "Lyin' Eyes." We smile at each other and bob our heads, chewing bites of hot pizza.

Huck returns with the drinks, pours what's left of my first glass into the second. He sets the extra glasses on the vacant table behind him. "Hey, is it true there might be a merger between Willa Cather an' George Wythe up at Mountainsburg?"

An ember of irritation reignites in my chest.

I put my mouth in park, my brain in neutral.

I take a gulp of wine.

Huck sticks his hands in the back pockets of his faded jeans and shifts from one foot to the other. "I mean, that's the rumor."

Truman drags a wedge of pizza from the pan to his plate,

the cheese stretching long. His eyes skip short of mine before answering Huck. "Can't comment on that, Huck," he says politely and lays his fork at the edge of his plate. *As the song says, you can't hide your lyin' eyes.*

"Fair enough," Huck concedes, and he moves off to chat up a small table of locals in the back. Truman picks up his pizza and takes a bite.

I put my brain in park, my mouth in drive. "Truman Parker, what do you know about this merger rumor?" Is this what he's been keeping from me?

He reads my tone, my eyes, and drops the slice to his plate, pitches his voice low. "Georgie. Mike Mason is an old friend from Columbia. He contacted me with the idea. I don't know how the hell word got around."

"How could you? When you know the value of single-sex education. When you're a successful product of it yourself." I glare at him. "As are your sons!" I add, punctuating the four words with bitchy jabs of my finger at the red-and-white-checked tablecloth and making the levels of our glasses jump. Though I'd known about the rumor since Laurel mentioned it, I hadn't dreamed that Truman had been involved.

Truman shifts his legs and bangs his knee on the metal table, swears under his breath. The tourists at the big table look at us as though we're the most interesting feature they've seen all day. Truman leans forward as if to encapsulate us, his elbows on the table. "It was just a discourse, Georgie. Another idea for saving the college. There have been a several successful mergers between colleges, including Pembroke and Brown, and Radcliffe and Harvard."

My eyes fill. I feel like he's betrayed my trust. Again.

The people at the table for eight howl with laughter at something the big gloop wearing his baseball cap backward is saying. They get up to leave and troop by us, untwisting red-and-white peppermints from plastic or working toothpicks around their mouths—a practice my mother and I consider an egregious breach of etiquette, in her words, common and ordinary—their eyes bouncing between Truman and me as they file through the door.

"Georgie," he says, ignoring the tourists, "can we talk about this later?"

"No!" I glance at Huck and a young woman working behind the counter and lower my voice. "I feel like you've betrayed my trust again."

Truman holds a slice of his pizza aloft. "Georgie . . ."

"Remember when you kept the truth about your divorce, or non-divorce, from me?"

He motions to Huck and makes a check mark in the air. "And I apologized profusely. I thought we were past all that." Huck brings the check and Truman hands him a credit card.

I slug back the rest of my wine. "So did I," I say when Huck moves away, and I wipe my mouth with the back of my hand. My public display of anger has made me common and ordinary.

Truman drives me home. My heart feels cauterized, seared by hot iron. Neither of us speak until we reach my driveway. I need to process my feelings before letting go of my anger. "I just think that you should have shared that with me, knowing how I would feel about it. I had to hear of it from Laurel!"

"What?"

"Yes, she mentioned it."

"So, you knew, too, and didn't mention it to me."

Suddenly, I feel like one of God's own fools. My mouth twists. "Touché."

Solemnly, he dips his chin and inclines a crooked pinky finger to me.

I grasp it with one of my own. "Pinky swear," I say. "No more secrets."

"Not a one, *mon ami*."

༻༺

Three days before the rally.

I awake from a disorienting dream in which Lacey and I were thirteen and messing around with a toy Magic 8 Ball she'd received for her birthday. The dream Lacey—in cut-off blue jean shorts and a tank top—held the ball between her palms and said, "Now remember to ask it only yes-or-no questions."

I grinned and asked in the floaty voice of a medium, "Magic 8 Ball, how did I do on the math test? Wait, that's not a yes-or-no question!" I try again. "Did I do well on the math test?" Lacey nods and turns the ball slowly over in her hands, her short nails bubblegum pink. The triangle containing the message rises into view. Outlook good. "Yay!" I say, making a mock swipe of relief across my brow.

"My turn," Lacey says, handing me the ball. "Magic 8 Ball, does Truman Parker like Georgie Bricker?"

I purse my lips over a grin, my eyes wide. I rotate the ball and hold my breath as the answer surfaces. You may rely on it. I collapse in rapture on the carpet between Lacey and Karen's twin beds, planting smooches all over the clunky black ball.

"You know good and well he likes you, G.," Lacey retorts. "He's held your hand twice." She wrestles the ball from me. And then her face ages before my eyes. "Magic 8 Ball," she says, in her clipped adult New York voice, "will Georgie rescue Willa Cather?"

The ball turns in her manicured hands.

Cannot predict now.

༻༺

Two days before the rally.

I receive a text from Susan:

Truman and I are meeting with the college attorneys today.
Will you meet with the student campaign committee a final

time to make sure all is in place for the rally? What are we forgetting? Thanks, Susan.

I reply to Susan:

Yes, happy to. I'll use the new walkie-talkie app to ask them for a time. I'll let you know how the meeting goes. GB.

Laurel replies to my request and tells me the girls are meeting at the boathouse at two o'clock to lie in the June sun. They are due a long afternoon to relax. I tell Laurel I will meet with them there around four.

At noon, I meet Lina, back from her trip to Portland just in time for the rally and full of news about her daughter-in-law, who's expecting. She tells me about the anticipated grandbaby boy and covers my hand on the table with hers. Her eyes ask me: Is it okay to talk about this?

I find a supportive smile and a loving response. "I love hearing about your grandbaby. Don't worry about me for one second." I listen to my friend with only a soupçon of sorrow—of ultrasound details and of bite-size baby clothes with alligator appliqués.

At one o'clock, Lina and I meet Bob from Bob's Burgers behind the dining hall and help him unload boxes of hotdogs and hamburger patties and load them into the big refrigerator inside, echoey from the summer clean-out. I imagine the kitchen full to bursting again with food and chatter in the fall. Let it be.

At half past one, I receive an email from Truman: *G, I'm back from the meeting. I mentioned the call I received from Mike Mason about a merger with GW to Susan. She not only agrees that it would adversely affect the integrity of both school's missions but believes foremost that an organization should acquire another only if it brings new value not present in the acquiring organization, not to save it. Our attorneys agreed. You can take this worry off your plate. Love, T.*

My chest fills with ease and gratitude for this most generous of men. The man who understands me and loves me as only he can. *True-ly.* A text from Mrs. King sets the phone a-chime in my hand: *Our spa appt. booked for tomorrow afternoon. Thank you for giving me this treat. I can't wait!*

To relax tomorrow under practiced hands, hot stones, and lavender oil.

But first, I think, checking the time and breaking into a grin, I have a few minutes to pay a quick visit to the admin building.

๑Ｙ๑

One day before the rally.

An aesthetician smooths and exfoliates my feet and legs with a citrus sugar scrub, rinses them with a spray nozzle, and then wraps them in hot towels. Tomorrow, I will march on these feet to rescue Willa Cather.

"Yikes, stripes!" Mrs. King cries, writhing in the pedicure chair next to mine as though in the throes of a convulsion. "This is some treat," she gasps.

I let go a spate of giggles. "I'd forgotten you were so ticklish."

Her pedicurist stops his scraping and holds the implement of torture, which resembles a cheese grater, aloft. He grasps her heel in his free hand. "I just need to get under your big toes, and I'm done."

"Okay, okay. Just give me a bullet to bite on." She takes a deep breath, clutches the bottle of OPI Tickle My France-y pink polish she has chosen for her toenails, and braces for the final grating.

I hoot with laughter and return to my phone as the aesthetician begins to file my toenails. I'm so glad I thought to do this for Mrs. King. Her presence, so cheerful, humorous, and distinguished, blesses all I do. She's amazingly supportive and faithful, not only to me but to the college, going over and above what anyone could have expected to aid the rescue effort. I smile at her again before settling into the next wave of the massage chair's kneading.

I cradle my cell and reread the text I received from Truman this morning.

G, Let me grill a steak for us at my house tonight. And stay with me. I need you, body and soul. Come at eight? All my love, T.

Laurel, in a flurry of texts to her friends, has already left to spend the day and night with Trask in Mountainsburg. She and the boys will drive back to Foxfield in the morning for the rally. Laurel and Hollins and I will meet at my house at eight o'clock for a last-minute huddle. I appraise my softened feet and think of the night again. Truman and I haven't made love fully since the miscarriage. But I've gotten the green light from the doctor, and tonight's the night.

Mrs. King leans over the *Cosmopolitan* magazine spread across her lap to peer at one foot. "I think the polish on my pinkie toe has a bubble in it."

The aesthetician grimaces. "I'll get that on the second coat."

I grin at my secretary. "I don't know why you're so worried about your toes looking perfect. The combat boots will cover them anyway."

She swats me with the magazine. "Just so you know, the store was out of my size."

⚘

I step out of the coupe in strappy sandals and the raspberry-colored wrap dress I bought at The Bus Stop boutique this afternoon. The Victorian's mansard roof and scalloped gables hulk dark against a twilit sky adrift with pink-spun clouds.

The windows of the house are dark and silent, the only light that from the lamppost at the front walk. A note taped to it flutters easily in a warm breeze: *Follow the candles around to the back.*

Anticipation fills my veins. I turn and catch sight of what appear to be brown paper lunch bags filled with candles, illuminating a curved brick path to the backyard. When did he have time to do all this? Nearing the old wrought iron gate, I hear music, the song "Beginnings" from Truman's playlist by the band Chicago. He looks up and catches sight of me.

"Bonsoir, Monsieur Parker," I silkily say.

He steps from behind a new green egg-shaped barbecue grill set on a small paving of brick and surveys me head to polished toe. "Bonsoir, Madame." He's wearing my favorite of his casual shirts, a short-sleeved navy-and-white gingham-checked Polo, and khaki shorts. The hair along his arms and legs—and I know his chest beneath the shirt—is reddish and softly curled. My exhalations are wobbly. "Damn, woman, you look fine," he says huskily, "new dress?"

I nod. He takes me in his arms, kisses me deeply, and pivots me in a little dip. The top of my head feels ready to pop off, spilling the mush he's making of my brain. But a question remains. "When in the world did you do all this?" I ask, inclining my head to the brickwork, the grill, the luminaries.

He laughs. "I've been working my ass off the last few evenings, scraping out dirt. I'd ordered the brick from Richmond, and Asher and a couple of his buddies helped me lay the path yesterday. I'm going to finish a patio for us."

My head reels again. A patio for us? Has he decided to keep the house, stay in Foxfield? Does he expect I'll move in here? Will he ask me to marry him again?

The playlist segues into "Colour My World." He's timed the music perfectly. He leads me in a slow dance on the small patch of patio that is complete and like a tiny dance floor ringed with paper-bag lanterns.

"Oh, True," I say, leaning my head back to look up into his night-navy eyes, "You remembered."

"Of course, I did," he says, smiling down at me. "A guy doesn't forget his first slow dance with a pretty girl."

I lay my face against his shoulder, inhaling his leafy essence, his solid dearness. Insects tick and chirp. We sway together as the flute solo floats into the trees.

After filet mignon, twice-baked potatoes, and broccoli salad—"from Carter's Market, I'm no cook, but I can grill a steak"—at his candlelit kitchen table, Truman tops up our glasses with a dry summer rosé, and we sit back in our chairs.

"I loved dancing with you tonight. But when did you learn how? I mean, you were so bad at it."

He leans his head back and huffs with a laugh, "I was." He grows serious, toying with the stem of his glass. "I guess too many charity balls with Anne Emerson."

The picture of Anne Emerson I've imagined too often in my head comes for me. She's reedlike and elegant in a strapless column of silk, her thin shoulders shimmering. Why did I have to ask? Now he's probably picturing her too. But my mind won't let it alone. I take a sip of wine. "Truman, I have to ask. Do you miss that . . . life at all? I mean, do you miss having a glamorous woman . . . like her?"

He sighs and sets his glass on the table. "I guess it's natural for you to be curious about Anne Emerson. She is the mother of my children. But she's a selfish, repressed woman, thoughtless and cold. In bed and out."

I gulp and shove away the picture my brain's trying to form of the two of them in bed. Nodding, I concentrate on his blue eyes.

"As I told you the first night we were together, what I love most about you is your warmth, your loving nature. When you're not with me in the mornings, I wake up wanting to feel your soft hands on me, your breasts against my chest, your welcoming curves."

I'm like butter tossed into a cast-iron skillet, foamy and roiling inside. "True."

"Georgie, I want to make plans with you. I want you to be free. The fortress you've built for yourself here in Foxfield is beautiful. It is. But it doesn't make a full life. I love to travel. And I want to do it with you, to see the things you've never seen through your green eyes. I want to sit at a Parisienne café with you."

I sit, sipping my wine, caught between want and self-reproach. I've always thought of Truman sharing my life. But he has a life too, and he wants to share it with me. He takes my hand and tries with all of his good being to give me his safety and optimism. "Your anxiety has lessened so much. If the school reopens—and I believe it will—and your career is secure again . . . would you let me take you away?"

Does he mean for a trip, or *away* away, like to live in another place? I'm going to pretend it's the former. I think of all the places I haven't been, a world vast and lost to me.

But an image of the two of us snuggling in adjacent airplane seats—sipping champagne and excitedly planning an itinerary—appears, grows textured, authentic, and edged with brightness. "I want to be able to go away with you, True."

"Maybe after the rally, we could drive over to the Outer Banks. It would be a start."

I stare into the candle flame and recall the dream I had about being on the beach with my family when I was in the hospital, how Ronnie had become the baby I'd lost. I haven't seen the ocean since I was twelve. I'd love to lie on the beach next to Truman, to swim in the sea with him. Dr. Chu, she could help me prepare. "Maybe," I say with a smile, pulling the door to on the subject. "But tonight, I want you to make love to me."

Upstairs, in the shower, the warm water that's plastered his hair into silver whorls beats over my back. He caresses me. I look up at him. "I'm a little nervous."

He kisses me, taking my bottom lip between his teeth the way that makes me woozy. I open my eyes. He surveys my face. "I love you, Georgie. You know I'd never hurt you . . . I'll be easy. We'll take it slow."

A space of time later, the sleigh bed is a planet where only the two of us can breathe. I dive into his eyes and imagine a warm blue splash enveloping me.

We take it easy. We take it slow.

Rapture rolls over me like a vapor.

It's in that moment that I realize this: no matter what happens with the school—whether we reopen, whether we padlock the gates—I'll do whatever I have to do to share this man's life.

Words have power. TV has power.
My pen has power.
—Shonda Rhimes

CHAPTER
TWENTY-TWO

Five hours until the rally.

Hollins, who has never taken a class earlier than nine o'clock—so she wouldn't have to roll out of bed before eight forty-five—texts me at 6:00 a.m. with an update on the fundraising campaign: $2.1M in donations, $22.5M in pledges.

I close the text and cartwheel out of bed. "*Chou de dieu!*" I cry, waking Truman from his sleep. "Twenty-five freaking million dollars!"

He gives me a sleepy grin. "Where there's a Georgie Girl, there's a way."

He's so adorable, I hop back into bed for quick good luck snuggle.

When I arrive at home to meet Laurel and Hollins, Laurel's little car is already in the driveway. Opening the kitchen door, coffee meets my nose. She and Hollins sit at the table with their laptops, two of my mismatched coffee mugs, and a grease-spotted bag of donut holes. "Bonjour, Madame," they say, scooting things over to make room for me.

"Bonjour, *mes filles!*" I give each of them a little hug around their shoulders and then pour myself a mug.

Laurel gives me her saucy-eyed look. "Welcome home. Did you have an inspiring night?"

I respond with a trace of a woman-to-woman smile. "As a matter of fact, I'm quite inspired about the day."

Voltaire trots in, his nose in the air. I scoop him up and scrub the pink Laurel's brought to my cheeks into his coat.

"I fed the prince when I got here," she says.

"Merci," I say, sitting down with the cat in my lap.

Hollins updates me on how they're preparing to accept donations at the event. Yesterday, they set up tables on the quad, where she and Victoria and Emily, along with the treasurer of the board—whom I had no idea they had solicited to help but who graciously accepted—will sit a half hour before the rally and then for several hours after lunch and the march, as long as guests linger. "I have the Square readers in my car; we'll be able to accept any credit card."

I pop a donut hole into my mouth and chew it, marveling at this technology.

Laurel says, "And we borrowed cash boxes from the athletic boosters, for people who bring cash." Tears sting my lids at their competence, at their unswerving belief in a successful rally. It comes to me what I will say when it's my turn to speak on the soundstage, and I file it into my mental bank. "When will Dr. Joshi announce whether or not we'll reopen?" she asks, her eyes guarded. "I mean, how much do we have to raise today?"

I, along with faculty and staff, had received an email from Susan last night. "Well, as I'm sure you're aware, we can't reopen based on pledges that may or may not be honored in the long run. I think it's about the cash at this point. Since you guys are keeping a running total with your insanely brilliant system," I say, waggling my head as though mind-boggled on the word brilliant. "Dr. Joshi and the board may be able to let us know something as early as tomorrow." I put a shoring-up hand on Hollins shoulder and rise.

"Oh, there's a surprise for you at the quad," Laurel says.

"A surprise? I don't know if I can take it."

The girls exchange smiles. "I think you'll like this one," Laurel says.

Upstairs, getting dressed a few minutes later, I tie a red bandanna around my neck to go with the aqua T-shirt. I open my jewelry box, looking for a talisman, an icon to take into battle with me. My cross pendant? I consider the Breathe bracelet Lacey gave me, take it up and run my thumb over the silver. This I haven't worn in a long time or felt the need for. Lacey. I wish she could be here with me today. I work the cuff onto my wrist, deciding she will be, at least in spirit.

Twenty minutes later, I'm striding toward the quad in sneakers, a red hat, and a denim skirt with pockets—yay pockets!—for my phone, folded speech note, and keys. I scan the cloud-scudded sky, but none appear to be storm makers. Though the sun won't have a starring role in this show, at least the air should be cooler than in recent days. The campus looks refreshed, all spiffed up. Alumnae from the classes of '98 and '08—who could well have held fancy parties to celebrate their reunions—instead came to campus days early to plant flowers, to dust and vacuum and wash windows.

I smile as laughter and excited squeals float from the lacrosse field. Scanning the people gathered there, I estimate one hundred aqua and red T-shirts. The ranks of charcoal grills townspeople have donated to cook hotdogs and burgers stand ready on the sidelines. The shabby old St. Mary's College lacrosse-team bus is parked in the drive. I'm grateful those girls—sisters in women's education—have come to support the rally and play an exhibition game after the march with our team.

My heart skips a beat at the flashy news vans lining the drive to the quadrangle. The Associated Press, NBC, CNN, and Fox News! As I draw closer, I shoot Truman a text: *Where are you?*

I trot the steps, excitement building in my chest.

He replies: *On the platform. I see you. Red hat.*

I spot his waving arm, his silver hair and broad shoulders in a red T-shirt.

I stop short, allowing a string of students carrying boxes of T-shirts to pass, and text him back: *I see you too, and I'm crazy about you.*

Crazy about you, he replies. *No matter how this turns out, I'm proud of you.*

I pick my way across the quadrangle, teeming with students, who've turned the pedestrian gathering place into an alien landscape of sight and sound. The platform Truman's sons and their friends helped the girls cobble together is impressive: scaffolded sides and a lattice roof with a tarp rolled at the back in case of rain. Truman's climbed up on the scaffolding, where Asher and Trask seem to be connecting wiring for honking black stereo speakers. I watch Trask laughing and happily realize how much the boys and Truman have bonded in the last month. That's already a tick in the box of our success.

I turn to help students who are lining up big open boxes of T-shirts according to size. My walkie-talkie app burrs. "Madame Bricker, are you on the quad?" It's Laurel. "Did you see your surprise?"

I grin and speak into my phone, "Down by the platform. Not yet."

"Look over by the library," she says. On the library porch, the signs the students have made—dozens of them—wait against the balustrade.

"The signs? They look fabulous."

"No. Look up."

My stomach somersaults.

A new marketing banner has been added to the ones that have hung since the start of winter term. It's me. My faculty photo with three words below: This Is Fierce.

Laurel and the rest of my advisees show up, swooping and surrounding me, cheering, hugging, and jostling me until my hat flies off.

Malika hands it to me. "None of this," she says, "would be possible without you, Madame."

I swallow around a lump of emotion in my throat. "No. Though you've touched me deeply, it's all you, *mes filles*, my girls. I'm so proud of you."

A tiny reporter scurries our way, a cameraman shouldering a huge-eyed camera ambling in her wake. "I'm Katie Kallen with CNN," she says, looking round at us and smiling toothily at me. "How many people are you expecting for today's rally?" I smile, look at Laurel, and step back. I turn away, silently passing her the torch.

"Okay, give 'em a try," Trask shouts down from the scaffolding.

Asher, at the back of the platform, powers the music: The Rolling Stones' "Start Me Up" blasts from the speakers. People turn and cheer. The music promptly dies. Shaking their heads, the guys mount the scaffolding again. Three hours till the rally: we have to have sound.

My phone vibrates. I pull it from my pocket again: a call from Genevieve Beaulieu. How sweet of her to call and wish me well today! I move toward a copse of trees beyond the quad and accept the call. "Bonjour, Madame!"

"Bonjour, Georgette! Your big day," she says in French. I love that she still calls me Georgette after all these years—as no one else does—and remember how she'd first done so in French class, when I'd been ashamed of having a boyish name.

I respond in kind, "Yes, we're almost ready. The students have done an amazing job. I'm overwhelmed, really." A new group approaches the quad, and my mouth makes another exaggerated O of astonished joy as I wave at former students. "So many people are here early."

"Have you room for two more?" Genevieve asks.

"*Pardonnez-moi?*"

"After many delays, I have arrived at a charming little *aéroport* in Mountainsburg," she replies in French. And I've brought you a surprise."

My pulse picks up. "You're here in Virginia?"

Madame chuckles. "I couldn't allow such an important event to happen without being here to witness it firsthand, to support you. After all, I'm counting on getting back to work on our study abroad endeavor when your college reopens."

"Genevieve, how wonderful! I can't believe it." It's fifty miles or so to Mountainsburg. Does she know how to rent transportation?

"Un moment, Georgette," Madame says. She holds a muffled conversation with someone and returns to the line. "They have no automobiles."

Alumnae attending the rally must have rented all the cars. I consult the time—and turn back to the platform, my thoughts churning. If someone left right away, they could be back in plenty of time for the start of the rally. "Madame, I'll send someone for you right away." But who?

"Of course, you are busy with preparations."

Madame has no idea that I don't leave town. My gut rolls with regret. "Let me call you back in five minutes," I say. Laurel and crew are still speaking with the reporter. Truman, Trask, Asher, and one of their buddies from George Wythe are up on the scaffolding. Mrs. King, in a red T-shirt and cropped white pants, her hands on her hips, is apparently attempting to supervise, though she knows as much about wiring as I do about algebraic geometry.

Truman wrestles one of the big speakers and lowers it to the platform, Asher the other. "Truman," I call, my heart pounding. "Genevieve Beaulieu is here from Paris."

"You're kidding." He trots down the crude steps of the platform, smiling distractedly, his T-shirt darkened with sweat. He looks around. "Where is she?"

"Well . . . she's at the airport in Mountainsburg."

From the scaffolding, Asher shouts, "Dude, we're going to need fourteen-gauge wire."

"I'll go get it," Trask swiftly replies. He calls to Truman, "Dad, who in town will have speaker wire?"

"Hold up; I'll ride with you," Truman answers him.

"But there are no rental . . ." My voice—a bleat suffused with shame—dies on the vine. The twins hop from the platform as though they've choreographed the move.

Truman holds up a finger to them: one minute. The boys glance from their father to me, their eyes questioning.

The day seems to wait.

It was Genevieve Beaulieu who taught me to believe in my academic talents. It was she who inspired me to become a French teacher. Who taught me the alchemy of inspiring students. How to nurture them and to spur them on.

This is my moment, my call to the throne.

Beyond Truman, the new banner with my picture catches my eye.

This is fierce.

The library doors swing open. Leading a crew of cackling alumnae, Susan strides across the porch and down the steps. The words she said when she'd given me permission to hold the rally buttress my thoughts: I believe this rally is yours to do.

This errand, too, is mine to do.

I incline my phone to a nonplussed Trask, my trembling making it waggle like a fresh-caught trout in my grasp. "Monsieur Parker. Will you show me how to get that Waze thing you told me about? I'm driving to Mountainsburg."

Truman's blue eyes pop and study mine. *Are you sure?* they ask.

I swallow and give him a hard nod.

"I'll be damned," he murmurs.

Asher sticks out a palm for the phone. "Actually, Trask and Dad are about to go into town for speaker wire, but I can show you how to download the app." Truman gives him a soft elbow, and the two exchange a look. Asher looks at me. "How 'bout I ride with you instead?"

Hysterical laughter bubbles in my throat and threatens to have its way with me. *Chou de dieu!* I'm driving a boy named after my father to collect my first French teacher whom I haven't seen since Richard Nixon was president. Whee! Where there's a will, there's a Waze! I sputter a cough and dig my keys from my pocket.

Asher peers at me. "Wait. Unless you're planning to strap the French lady to the roof, the three of us won't fit into that coupe of yours."

Truman, who looks as though he's been awarded the Presidential Medal of Freedom, inclines his keys to me and quips in his best Italian *Godfather* accent, "Leave the coupe; take the Rover."

❦

I drive through the gates of campus, my hands already fuggy on the wheel of the Range Rover, wishing I had had time to swing by Dr. Chu's for a tête-à-tête. I glance up at Asher in the passenger seat. Even in the Rover, he seems to fill the space, his hair brushing the ceiling.

"How tall are you, by the way?"

He smiles. "Six three. I take after my mother's side of the family; Trask takes after Dad's. People are surprised when they find out we're twins."

"Hmm." I knew Anne Emerson was tall! I wonder if Asher's features resemble his mother's, if she's dark of hair and eye. "Do you look like your mother?" I ask, daring to hope he might show me a picture of her on his phone.

"Yeah." The gust of his breath smells faintly of wintergreen; I hope mine doesn't stink of fear. My tongue is the texture of concrete. I wish I'd thought to grab one of the million bottles of water iced down for the rally before I left.

A mechanical voice blurts from my phone, and I jump as if at a five-alarm fire: "In one thousand feet, turn left onto Mountainsburg Road." I drag my left hand from the wheel and put on the blinker. Ahead of us now, the blue cloud-hung mountains form a cinematographic backdrop for the journey. We pass the car dealership, who ordered the coupe for me ten years ago, and the Sleeping Beauty Motel, its parking lot filled with cars and women. I flip the AC on high and grip the wheel as I would the arms of an oral-surgery chair. I close my eyes for a second and then peer into the rearview mirror at the Foxfield city-limit sign.

Asher rubs at his upper arms. "Are you, um, cool enough now?" he politely asks.

My voice comes out like one of the Chipmunk's: "Yes, sorry." I peel my clammy right hand from the wheel long enough to punch down the temperature.

In my periphery, Asher studies me.

The first time I'm alone with Truman's son, and it's in this situation. If anxiety gets the best of me, he will be my witness. How humiliating it will be if I have to pull over and ask him to take the wheel! *Courage, Georgie Girl, courage,* I say to myself in French. We pass a big antique store—the brick painted bright pink, with ladder-back kitchen chairs, blue pots spilling flowering vines, and an old mint-green baby buggy out front—on the right. The baby. "Oh, a new shop," I chirp.

"Callahan's?" I feel his eyes again. "That's been there since I've been driving this route. At least three years. They used to keep soda in vintage bottles on ice inside. Trask liked to stop and get one sometimes."

He thinks I'm looney. "Continue west for fifty-one miles." The laughter fills my throat again. Fifty-one miles!

The God-sweet boy—man—looks at me. "You don't get away much, do you?" Though his eyes are dark, they are kind like his father's and brother's. I compose a reply.

"No, but I'm starting to again. It's . . . good . . . to get away, isn't it?"

"It is." He looks out the window. "We were supposed to go hiking this weekend—Trask and me and some buddies—down around Charlottesville, but then Dad told us about the rally."

"Oh. Sorry about that."

He shrugs his broad shoulders, brushing his arm against mine. "S'okay. We're going next weekend. It worked out."

I realize my hands have relaxed on the wheel. "I'm glad." I smile at him. "And I'm grateful you guys came to support the school. It means a lot to me. And to your father."

Asher's phone pings; he looks at it. I wonder how he feels about Truman and me as a couple. What are we exactly? Boyfriend and girlfriend, as we were when his cheeks were as smooth as mine and I wore Baby Soft cologne? Lovers? "Lovers" sounds trashy, I decide. And common.

"No problem, Georgie." Asher stretches his legs and checks his phone.

He's called me by name! My heart zigzags with joy, and I almost run off the road. "Sor-ry," I sing out. "Pothole." I want to know everything about him. "Do you have a girlfriend?"

He tells me about a girl—a student at WCC—he saw for two years and about a new girl, who he's seen three times. I imagine most girls find this big soul-eyed guy appealing. I tell him I knew of his former girl, a sustainability major. He asks me if I'd always known I wanted to teach French. I tell him the story of my first French class with Genevieve and how I'd won the coveted award at the end of the year, sharing it with Jeffrey Butts, who deserved it way more than I.

The Waze voice intones, "In one thousand feet, turn right onto Airport Road."

I look at Asher, astonished. Awash with accomplishment, the steady, singing old riff of my fear extinguishes and drowns. My head meets the headrest as though afterburners propel me ahead. Through the windshield, the tiny airport looks like the Palace of Versailles.

I've done it. I am fifty miles from home.

I glance at Truman's odometer for confirmation. At once, I'm Sally Ride, Amelia Earhart, Sacagawea.

The Waze confirms this: "You have reached your destination."

Asher gives me a knowing smile and quotes Dr. Seuss: "Kid, you'll move mountains."

⚙

"There she is!" I say to Asher as I pull the Rover to the curb in front of the tiny terminal and slam it into park. Few passengers linger on the pavement, pacing and speaking into their phones or typing into them, probably trying to figure out how to get transportation. Genevieve, in a white sweater, navy pants, and white sneakers, spots me behind the wheel of the Rover, smiles, and waves, bringing a black wheeled bag to a halt beside a column.

I undo my seat belt and open my door, calling around it, "Genevieve!"

Asher thumbs at his phone. "Let me finish this text to Dad to let him know we made it, and I'll help with the bags." Truman. He'll be so happy for me.

Madame Beaulieu calls, "Georgette!"

Asher grins. "Georgette, huh?" he says, and he lopes around to open the back of the Rover.

I meet my mentor in a tearful embrace and we hold each other at arm's length. Her long hair has gone white with the years, and she's tied it back with a Hermès scarf. Though rose lipstick is her only makeup, her complexion bears the patina of oft-polished silver plate, and her cheeks are cherub rosy with happiness. I remember her wardrobe of fuchsia and emerald and scarlet dresses and the flashy cosmetic palette she wore to teach French, before learning she was pregnant. I say to her in French, "It's been too long, my friend."

Though she's traveled for countless hours, her eyes sparkle with a vim that belies her age. "*Mais oui.*" She turns and calls to a tall young woman on the other side of the column in black sunglasses, a black hoodie, Army-green cargo pants, and pink running shoes, thumbs zinging across the keyboard of a phone. "Marie-Victoire!"

The young woman looks up and smiles. She lowers an enormous backpack to the pavement, her zip-front hoodie gaping open to reveal David Bowie's face from his Ziggy Stardust days on her T-shirt. She moves to Genevieve's side. Genevieve puts a proud arm around her. "Georgie Bricker, may I present my granddaughter, Marie-Victoire Beaulieu?"

Marie-Victoire slides her sunglasses up into her fringy blonde bob and extends a cool beringed hand. "It's nice to meet you, Madame," she says in flawless English. "*Grand-mère* has told me a lot about you."

"Oh, Marie-Victoire, how lovely to meet you." Tears sting my nose. I look at Genevieve. "This is the daughter of the baby you were expecting when you taught me?"

She flutes a laugh. "*Oui*, that baby is my son Don."

Remembering Truman's son, I turn to look for him. He's standing with one foot on the curb next to the Rover, his dark eyes big and dazed and fixed on Marie-Victoire, his phone apparently forgotten in one hand, his Ray-Bans dangling from a fingertip of the other. I look at Genevieve's granddaughter and see her allure as through his eyes: the quickness of her movements, the smallness of her hands and feet, the curves of her hips, the sherry color of her eyes: a surprise in her blond fairness. "Asher," I say. He drags his gaze to me and grins sheepishly. "Come and meet Genevieve Beaulieu and her granddaughter. Marie-Victoire."

Genevieve greets Asher; then he and Marie-Victoire exchange a greeting and handshake. Their eyes touch for a long beat and bounce back to Genevieve and me. Asher fidgets with his long hair, neatens his ponytail.

"Marie-Victoire and I will meet her parents in DC next week. She has been accepted at my alma mater, Georgetown University, and will begin fall term as a sophomore." At this last bit of information, Asher's eyes turn into friction spinners, bright sparks shooting from them. I grin. "Asher, you grabbing the bags?"

One corner of Marie-Victoire's lips curl. She shoulders her backpack and hauls her own duffle around to the back of the Rover. Asher nods at Madame Beaulieu and picks up her bag, meeting Marie-Victoire at the rear and helping her situate the bags.

Madame regards Asher's long legs. "I believe I'll sit with my granddaughter in the back seat. And if you don't mind, Georgette, I could use a little toes-up before we arrive in Foxfield."

"Bien sûr, Madame, please make yourself comfortable," I say, wishing I had a pillow for her.

We climb into the Rover. Marie-Victoire leans over the rear seat and tugs one of those travel neck pillows from her backpack. "Here, *Grand-mère*," she says, slipping it behind Genevieve's head.

"Do you want to use Waze?" Asher asks.

I smile at him. "I've got this." I pull into the light flow of traffic with aplomb.

He shoots me a grin and lays his head back against the seat.

By the time I've pulled back onto Mountainsburg Road, the sun has peeped through the haze and both women are asleep. At a snort from Marie-Victoire, Asher grins and pulls his earbuds from his pocket, screws them in his ears. I wonder what music the lovely young woman has inspired.

The dashboard clock reads 9:20 a.m.

One hour and ten minutes until the rally.

Nervous energy traces my limbs. I hit the accelerator. I hope Truman and the guys have worked out the issues with the sound. I should have texted him. Filled with a new sense of power and picturing a mass of aqua and red T-shirts and myself behind a working microphone, I mentally rehearse the short speech I'll make as rally coordinator after the president kicks us off.

I have driven to Mountainsburg, a task that six months ago would have been like scaling an alp.

I can do anything now, save a college, take a trip with the man I love.

I will tell Truman I can go with him to the beach. I'll call Dr. Chu for her counsel. I might even order a bathing suit for the first time since college. Maybe a two-piece. Maybe one of those tankinis.

By the time I've passed the antique store again, the women are stirring. I smile at Asher, his knees lofty and jiggling to a beat only he can hear. At some point he's lowered his sun visor. His eyes in the vanity mirror are dreamy and trained on the young woman in the back seat. Marie-Victoire, minus her hoodie, stretches and murmurs something to her grandmother.

I grin and poke Asher in the thigh. He starts and rips out his earbuds. Reading my amused expression, he flips up the visor. "Asher," I say after a moment, "I want to thank you for being here for me today, in more ways than you know."

He nods and rearranges his long legs. "Not a problem, Georgette."

*If the first woman God ever made was strong
enough to turn the world upside down all alone,
these together ought to be able to turn it back
and get it right side up again.*
—Sojourner Truth

CHAPTER
TWENTY-THREE

Twenty-one minutes until we kick off the rally.

I corner into a faculty-only parking place and spring from the Rover, leaving Marie-Victoire and Asher to see that Madame Beaulieu gets safely to the quad. "Bonne chance, Georgette," she calls behind me. My heart surges as Tom Petty's "I Won't Back Down" thunders from the speakers. Yay, guys!

I shoulder through the crowd that has swelled to Kentucky Derby proportions in the last hours. Local and national news crews, situated like strategically placed pieces on a chessboard, work the swarm. Hollins and her team are working down two lines of people with wallets at the ready. Mrs. King and others are still handing out wristbands from the package of one thousand they ordered. "Mrs. King!" I call to her. "I'm back. What can I do?"

She gives me a hug so tight it takes what's left of my breath. "I am so proud of you, Madame. Of your courage. There's no stopping you now."

I smile into her eyes. "There's no stopping us."

Her eyes slide sideways. "Can you handle another surprise?"

A blast of adrenaline sends my legs trembling. What now?

Mrs. King turns and points to where Truman's head rises above a group of others near the steps of the platform. Truman shifts to attend to something Trask is asking him from the platform and reveals Lacey Mattson as glossy and stylish as a racehorse.

I break into a gallop. "La-ceeee!"

Lacey and I hug, then clutch each other's hands, bouncing up and down. "Hey, you know this gal?" Truman asks me, laughing at our exuberance.

"Oh, my God, I can't believe you came," I say to Lacey. "Can you stay with me?"

"I sure hope so," she says, and she scans the quad. "There can't be a closet left in this hamlet."

"Stay close, Lace," I say, kissing her cheek, as Susan, Elizabeth Pattison, and Laurel approach to take the stage.

I fill my lungs and reach for Truman's hand. "Aren't you coming up?"

He shakes his head. "I'm just a roadie—you know, one of those hot, ripped ones. This, my love, is yours to do."

Mine to do, mine to do. The words fill my head like helium as I rise to the stage.

❦

Susan takes the microphone, just as—perfectly orchestrated by Trask—the last beats of Aretha Franklin's anthem "Respect" concludes. The assembly applauds the president and falls silent at her first words. "In 1845 Virginia, timid seven-year-old Louisa Winchester's mother handed her a clean pail. She told her to head down by the creek and fill the pail with pie berries. When Louisa returned home hours later—her bonnet hanging down her back, her bare feet muddy to the ankles, her pinafore wet and torn and smelling of the creek—the pail was filled not with berries but with frogs. That day, Louisa had made her first friend, intrepid eight-year-old Willa Cather." Susan smiles and nods at appreciative murmurs from the crowd. "A year later, Louisa was stricken with tuberculosis and sent to a sanitarium. Willa's family moved to the plains of Nebraska, where she began writing a series of adventure stories for girls and sending them in the form of letters to her friend Louisa. Those spunky little stories sustained Louisa through a sixteen-year confinement. When twenty-eight-year-old Louisa used her inheritance to found a women's college in 1869, she attributed her bold spirit to her faithful and inspiring friend Willa Cather. For 149 years, the women of Willa Cather College have been filling their pails with frogs: photographing and painting them; calculating their average speed and velocity; dissecting them; and leaping like them in dance studios and on playing fields." Susan collects her notes from the podium and waits for a beat, surveying the assembly. "Please. Don't let us croak now."

Women turn to each other in delighted astonishment and erupt into roaring cheers and raucous applause.

Chou de dieu! I have to follow that? But I love that Susan chose an alternative sort of speech and neatly sidestepped any mention of our CFO and board chairman's corruption. I adjust the knot in my bandanna and take the podium. "Ladies and gentlemen, thank you so much for being here to support us today." Abruptly, the saucer-eyed news cameras trained on me blot out everything else, the T-shirts, the hats and faces. My limbs turn to wood, my lips to stone. The cameras bore. My face blazes in competition with my bandanna.

Then, below the podium, a face, taller than the rest, comes into focus. Asher. He nods slowly. He furrows his brow in a way that all at once gives my butt a swift kick and reminds me of how far I've come.

I finger the notes in my pocket but leave them be. My lips part. "Who has come the farthest?" My fierce makes me rise on my toes. "C'mon, shout it out!"

"Auckland, New Zealand!" a thirty-something-year-old in a baseball cap yells.

"Maine!"

"London!" a well-heeled older alum yells.

"Richmond!" a middle-aged couple's kids cry.

My laugh through the microphone sends a big poof resounding across the quad. "Well, let's hear it for Richmond!" I pause until the laughter dies away. My eyes sweep the others on the platform, the students at the front of the assembly. "I represent a small band of students, who arrived as girls on this beautiful campus to sample what Willa Cather College had to offer. They drank deeply of our mission and stand here today, incredible women. Though I was tasked with spearheading and supervising them in planning and executing this rally," I smile at Laurel on my right, "it is they who have taught me about leadership. These women have developed cooperation, collaboration, and management skills they will take with them into the world. They have ignited a torch to pass to our youngest students," I add, looking pointedly at a band of freshmen to the left of the stage, "lighting their paths, whether they leave here tomorrow or three years from now."

The freshmen jump up and down, yelling and chanting, "Where there's a Willa, there's a way! Let us stay! Let us stay!" The crowd responds with applause.

I smile and aim my next words at a group of older alums standing near the dining hall steps, their arms linked. "I suspect the tug-of-war emotions these young women have experienced—as the school they love has been wrenched from their hands—has bonded them in a singular sisterhood, one as fixed as the sun." The older women lead the group in hardy clapping and cheering. I seek and touch, one by one with my gaze, the sisters who've lit my path: Lacey. Mrs. King. Lina. Madame Beaulieu. Susan.

At once, I scrap what I'd planned to say in conclusion. I turn to look at my Laurel, who, at least in my book, has fulfilled the prediction I made, earning her place as leader of next year's senior class. I reach for her hand, and all she's been through—a devastating hurt, a near-death experience and hospitalization, and the battle to save the school—moves between us like current. As the applause peters away, I end my remarks with these: "Let them stay. Let them st—"

A pale oval with coiffured hair and red lipstick—smack in the center of the crowd—snags my eyes. A face I haven't seen in months: Eleanor Parker's. My mind slips its tracks and scuds along the earth. The people pick up the chant: "Let them stay. Let them stay."

How had I been fool enough to forget that Truman's mother was an alumna and to believe she wouldn't show up? Though from a distance of at least twenty yards, her gaze prowls my face and body, makes silly and wrong my long ponytail and red hat, the denim skirt I thought was so cute. I step back from the podium, wishing I could disappear.

᙭

Laurel gives me a hug around the shoulders and whispers, "That was awesome, Madame, you got them fired up." The board treasurer—whom Susan has named the interim chairman—addresses the crowd, pointing out the donations table in a "nudge, nudge, wink-wink" fashion and drawing enthusiastic laughter and applause. As the hopeful odor of burning charcoal drifts onto the platform, he reminds them that the next two hours are set aside for visiting with old friends and for campus tours (led by sophomore volunteers) and for lunch.

Though hyperconscious of Eleanor somewhere in the assembly, I trot down the steps behind Laurel, ticking off the first speeches from my mental list and turning my attention to the afternoon. Following the lunch break, Laurel, alumna Elizabeth Pattison, and her fourteen-year-old daughter, Isabelle—representing the present, past, and future of Willa Cather—will kick off the march.

Morgan and Sutton weave full tilt through the group, and Morgan reaches out to clutch my arm. "Madame. We just counted the leftover wristbands. Two hundred and one," Sutton pauses, breathless. "Seven hundred ninety-nine people have shown up!"

I let that sink in a moment and do the math, tears glazing my eyes. Seven hundred ninety-nine wrists to clutch as they pull us from dangerous waters equals 1,598 arms—of all sizes, colors, and textures—to link together and wrap around Willa Cather.

I glance at the donation tables, where two more lines have formed. An older woman in a tennis skirt and diamonds rolls her eyes at a talkative man taking a long time to pay and taps a fancy platinum credit card against her lips. Anticipation flutter-kicks through my midsection. Credit cards are as good as cash. I restrain myself from taking a stroll behind the tables—to see if I can get a look at the running total on Hollins's laptop—by thinking of Eleanor.

From beneath the brim of my hat, I scan the dispersing crowd for her taffy hair and aqua cotton blouse I recognized from the cover of the Talbots catalog. If Truman has talked with his mother since his trip to Atlanta, he hasn't mentioned it to me. Is she contrite about the way she treated Laurel and her grandsons? Has she apologized to them? Could she be here to make amends? What if there's a confrontation? I have to find Truman.

I check in with Susan and then start down the grassy slope toward the fields, where I agreed to meet up with him and my friends for lunch, stopping every few yards to exchange greetings and hugs with former students.

Clouds slip from the face of the sun; it glares and turns my hat and T-shirt into insulation material. Wishing I had my sunglasses, I survey the field for Truman. He's nowhere in sight, but Lina and Carmen, Lacey, Mrs. King, and Madame Beaulieu are gathered for lunch on bright quilts spread in the shade of a sprawling sycamore. I smile: of course, Mrs. King has scouted the best shade and thought to bring quilts. The grass is freshly mowed. The Foxfield High football team had come out this week, opening the groundskeepers' sheds for the first time in weeks. They'd hauled out the riding mowers, the string trimmers and edgers, sharpened the blades, and attacked the neglected grounds with the ferocity with which they mow down their rivals.

I stop at Mrs. King's quilt and toss my hat onto it. Everyone compliments me on my speech as I untie my bandanna and mop at my wet face and neck. I offer to bring Genevieve and Mrs. King plates, and they accept with thanks.

Lacey excuses herself from conversation with Lina. "I'll go with you."

Beside Lacey's New York–casual skinny jeans, black pointed-toe flats, chic bun, and oversized sunglasses, I feel like a frump. A runner of sweat slips down my back and into my bottom cleavage.

But my oldest friend locks her arm in mine. "You look incredible, G. Ten years younger than when I saw you last year. Love has made you softer, lovelier."

Six months ago, I would have auto-deflected such a compliment, but now that much of the pain and disappointment and the flaws in my life have diminished, I thank her. "Oh, thanks,

Lace. I'm so glad you came! Let's have a sleepover and talk and drink wine and stay up late."

"I'm ready. It's so great to be face-to-face."

"Maybe one of these days," I say, coyly, "I'll show up in New York."

She stops before the flaming charcoal grills and lifts her sunglasses to stare at me. "Georgie Bricker, what are you telling me?"

I grin smugly, my shoulders rising as I think of the morning's drive to the airport. "I have a lot to tell you." A line has formed behind us. It crowds close. Lacey eyes me as we pick up paper plates and napkins. "What?" I say, huffing a laugh.

"You're different. And in a very good way." Yes, I am.

"Hotdogs, ladies?" a man named Pete from town asks, waving away flies with a spatula.

Lacey and I wait for hotdogs, and I pick up foil-wrapped burgers for the ladies. "By the way, babe," she says, "what's the plan for tonight? Can I take you guys to dinner? You and Truman?"

"That would be wonderful." I glance up the hillside where aqua- and red-clad figures trickle down. But none of them are Truman. Is he with his mother? "The ever-elegant Eleanor showed up."

"You're kidding. I mean, I know she's an alum, but . . ." I'd filled Lacey in on the Laurel-Eleanor Affair weeks ago.

"I kid you not. She's here. He must be with her now." Squirting a thick line of mustard from a plastic bottle the length of my hotdog, I tell Lacey about my heart-plunge panic on the podium, when I'd caught sight of Eleanor. I take a double handful of chips and three brownies to share with the ladies. "I don't know if Eleanor's staying or what. If she's not, I'm sure True would love to have dinner."

Lacey licks mustard from her thumb. "True," she says dreamily. "You guys are still adorable."

I scan the slope again. "I wish his adorable ass would hurry up."

Lacey hoots a laugh as we move along the tree line again. Cicadas harangue in the oaks. We pass Elizabeth Pattison, eating with her family and Susan and another family in pop-up camp chairs. I stop to welcome her. She praises me for the speech and for the rally turnout and introduces Lacey and me to her husband and daughter. My respect for Elizabeth grows when I see that Isabelle is Asian, an adopted child.

"Are you ready for your speech, Isabelle?" I ask the pretty child. "I'm excited to hear it."

She smiles, and her expression reminds me so much of her mother when she was a student. "I am. I'm just a little nervous."

"Isabelle wrote her own speech," Elizabeth says proudly. "By the way, have you seen Eleanor Parker yet?"

My professional composure drops out from under me. "El . . . uh . . . no, not yet."

Elizabeth's eyes sparkle with something I can't read. "Well, you two enjoy your hotdogs before they get cold," she says and nods at Lacey. "We'll catch up later." What *about* Eleanor? What could sweet Elizabeth have in common with her?

Back at our quilt, I hand Genevieve her lunch and remember Marie-Victoire. "Where's that beautiful granddaughter of yours?"

Genevieve smiles and flips a palm toward a spot on the grassy field. "Voilà."

Marie-Victoire's white-blond head, between Laurel and Malika's dark ones, commands my eye. Morgan and Sutton and Penn sit with them, eating and laughing and tilting back bottles of water, their legs stretched out on the grass. I send my worries of Truman's mother to time-out. Leave it to my kind girls to seek out the newcomer and make her welcome. I grin, watching them intent on something Marie-Victoire is saying. If I know

---

them, they are thrilled to be talking with a girl from France and are probably pumping her for information. At the edge of this group of queen bees, Trask and Asher sit munching on burgers, clearly content in the honey flow of their laughter.

A hand comes down on the crown of my head and slides down to tug at my ponytail. "Here's Truman," Lacey says. Apprehension flutters in my stomach among bites of hotdog. I look up at him.

"Hello, ladies," he says easily.

Mrs. King swats a fly. "Did you get something to eat, Truman?"

"I'm going now." He surveys our quartet. "What does anybody need?" he asks.

"We may need more brownies," Mrs. King replies with a who's-with-me wiggle of her brows.

I put on my hat, get to my feet, and join Truman. We weave our way through the expanding crowd. Though my cheeks are already sore from greeting old friends, I give a radiant smile to everyone I pass. We have the number of people we needed; now we just need the cash. I hook a pinky finger with Truman's, and he looks down at me. There's a crease on his forehead that wasn't there this morning, but he's his usual thoughtful self. "How are you, sweetheart?" he asks. "Your speech was terrific."

My heart warms; he's thinking of me when he may have had a confrontation with his mother. "Thanks, baby. Are you okay? Where were you?"

His pinky finger tugs back on mine, stopping us short of the line that's formed at the tables. He looks toward the hill. "My mother's here."

"I know," I say quietly. "I saw her." I try to read his eyes.

"She and a friend came to support the rally, and she wants to try to patch things up with the boys. She asked if we can all meet her after the match, at four. Laurel too."

"Wow." I look back to where the young people sprawl on the grass. "Do you think they will?"

"I hope so." He looks at me. "I want you there too."

"Me?"

"It's a family thing," he says, his eyes the blue lure of the sea. "You belong with us."

◈

The halfway mark of the rally. Raphael Saadiq's "Keep Marchin" pumps from the speakers. The girls dance down from the library porch with the signs they made and hand them out to participants who didn't make or bring their own. Many of the placards read, "Where There's a Willa, There's a Way," like our T-shirts, but other clever ones catch my eye: "I Am Girl-cotting This Closing"; "What Would Willa Do?"; and my favorite, "Willa Cather Women Don't Wear Pink Hats; We Wear All the Hats." I wait for the speeches to begin—bouncing on my toes to the music, my heart racing with hope—next to Truman and my friends while monitoring the buzz at the donation tables. Someone from the ground behind the platform calls, "Dudes, bring out that last cooler of water bottles," and from there, in a tarp shadow so deep my eyes almost skim over them, stand Laurel and Trask locked in an embrace so intense that I gulp and touch my breastbone. Trask seems to speak into Laurel's ear. Last-minute words of inspiration, love? God bless them.

My fingers come away damp from where I've touched my T-shirt. Am I sweating that badly? Rubbing them together, I look down. *Merde*, it's mustard! A long swath of it paints a yellow exclamation point after the word "Willa." I wipe my fingers on the dark denim of my skirt. I have to face Truman's mother like this? My chagrin makes giddiness bubble up inside me: *Pardon me, Eleanor, would you have any Grey Poupon?*

To our right, Elizabeth Pattison parts the sea of people like the prow of a ship, Isabelle striding in her mother's wake in cork-soled platform heels. I tear myself away from the mustard stain to look at Laurel and make sure she catches sight of them. She does, and she turns from Trask to join them at the steps.

Keep on marchin'.

Forgetting my appearance, I take a deep breath.

For both of us.

⁂

Elizabeth moves to the microphone first. "I'm Elizabeth Pattison from the class of '98, and I represent the past of Willa Cather College. This morning, our president, Susan Joshi, charmed us with a story of friendship between two little girls and how that friendship inspired Louisa Winchester to found a college for women." Elizabeth pauses as the people cheer. "When we visit the past, we gain perspective. And perspective gives us a sense of what truly matters. We must recall, in the heat of the moment, what is most important. Without perspective, it is easier to do what is easy rather than what is right. Perspective provides vision for awareness, strategy, and choices. Ladies and gentlemen, if you'll pardon the rhetoric, Willa Cather College matters." She pauses while the crowd erupts in cheers. "It matters to every woman who ever stepped onto this campus, rich in traditions celebrated since our founding. Traditions that promoted empowerment and sisterhood. I've loved seeing the sisterhood demonstrated here today. My alum sisters in Atlanta and I have honored and maintained the support system we built at Willa Cather. This morning, I've heard stories of women in their twenties and women in their eighties meeting for the first time and bonding." The crowd completes a circuit of light applause.

I turn my head to scan the swarm. Most people stand, eyes on the platform, their signs under their arms or propped against them; many hold their hands together in an attitude of prayer.

"Closing Willa Cather is the easy thing to do; it is not the right thing to do." The assembly hoots and cheers. "Our French teacher, Georgie Bricker"—my heart jerks hard at the mention of my name—"and the young women who put this rescue campaign together have done all the right things." Scrambled from top to bottom with emotion, I manage to bring my hands together along with the crowd, my eyes never leaving Elizabeth's face.

"Awareness," she reiterates. "This media coverage . . ."—a chorus of whoo-whoos resounds for the media—". . . is bringing awareness to our situation and to that of other small women's liberal arts colleges on the endangered list. Strategy. These young women have employed phenomenal strategy, creating a website for their mission, already raising a large sum of money, and bringing women and men from across the globe here today. I think Louisa and Willa would be pleased." Chants of "Where there's a Willa, there's a way" echo. "Choice. You have a choice. Don't do the easy thing today by assuming that someone will donate in your stead or that someone else's donation is more important. Each gift will help insure the present and future of this venerable institution." She collects her notes. Her eyes flash. "Help us rescue Willa Cather College."

Laurel steps forward and nods to the chanting crowd, forming the I-love-you sign in the air above her head. "I'm Laurel Cross, a rising senior of the class of 2019. I represent the present of Willa Cather College." A chorus of "Let them stay" rings.

I begin a silent blubbering as the image of Laurel lying in a hospital bed only last month comes to mind. Tears coast my cheeks, plopping on my shirt. Truman puts his arm around me and hugs my face to his chest for a moment. "The present," Laurel says, her voice steady and strong, "is our current reality, where we stand in the moment. From this vantage point, we see how our ways of thinking and behaving impact not just our own

274

lives, but the lives of others." She pauses and seems to stall for a moment, her lips a bitter line. She casts a narrow-eyed stare around the quad. "Unfortunately, there were those among us whose behavior was the bale that broke the back of those who went before us." Murmurs turn to angry rumblings. Lina and I exchange uh-oh glances. Laurel has alluded to the embezzlement, though we all agreed we would not. I seek out Susan's profile, but she stands impassive. Laurel continues, "But they will answer for their actions. And we. Will. Not. Allow this . . . setback . . . to be the end of us." The crowd roars until my ears ring. "As leaders, we must know where we stand, where our vulnerabilities lie if we are to form realistic plans and make lasting changes." Laurel looks down at her notes and grins up at the crowd. "The women of Willa Cather College are badasses."

The crowd shouts its approval. A woman behind me screams and bonks the back of my head as she raises a sign. Shielding my head with an arm, I look up at its bobbing message: "Belles are badasses." The mascot. "We have to do something about our mascot," I say to Lina out of the corner of my mouth.

She nods a wide-eyed I know as Laurel continues, "Among students at WCC, feminism is a regular topic. We are fortunate to attend a women's college where we are given the encouragement, the advice, and the support we need to succeed as gate-crashers and leaders. To take this college into the future, to look forward at all times, and to identify who we want to be, we must be brave and seek change while still honoring the traditions that make us who we are. Help us rescue Willa Cather College."

Laurel scoops her notes from the podium and turns to Isabelle. As the two exchange high fives to applause and cheers, the quad quakes beneath my feet.

Isabelle places her notes on the podium with both hands. She looks up at the mic, grins back at much-taller Laurel, and tugs it down, adjusting it to the level of her chin. "I am Isabelle Lofton," she says, "the class of 2026, and I represent the future of Willa Cather College." Women break out in yeahs and yays, woot-woots. Like a pro, Isabelle waits until the chants subside, then looks at her mother. "My mother is the best storyteller. She raised me on stories about her years at WCC: the places she liked to study; her favorite tree to climb and write in her secret journal; about canoeing and swimming at the lake; about parties with the boys from George Wythe at the boathouse, strung with Chinese lanterns, while dreaming of being a designer." Her dark eyes sparkle in the light of the cameras. "I am going to be an architect."

Lacey turns and grins at me. I know she's tickled as I am at the way Isabelle has said "I am going to be."

"Most architects are men," Isabelle goes on. "The women that are architects are mostly Caucasian. WCC will help me change that. At a girl's college, I won't be the only girl in a class of mostly boys. It's cool that the class presidents are all girls, the student council members are all girls, the actors in the plays are all girls, the sports stars are all girls. I've dreamed about coming to Willa Cather, like my mom, since I was ten and came here with her for a reunion." She folds her notes and pauses. She surveys us, and her chest rises. "Help us rescue Willa Cather College; I want to climb that tree." Hoots and chants explode, a whistler making me cover my ears.

When Elizabeth, Isabelle, and Laurel have stepped from the platform, a bugle cuts through the ruffling crowd. We turn as one to its source at the end of the quad nearest the fields. Laurel and the girls didn't mention anything about a bugle call. But it's completely brilliant. I shield my eyes and stand on my toes to see who's playing the horn. The instrumental music teacher who had left us!

I grin as she plays "First Call," as is done to signal the start

of a horse race, followed by "Reveille," the call to awaken soldiers. I clutch Lina's and Lacey's arms, my heart bebopping in
my chest.

It's the call to march.

☙❧

After the exhilaration and heart-tumult of the hour march for
the news cameras, I don't know if I have it in me to go meet
with Truman's mother. But his fingers locked in mine—as he
half tows me across the quad—reminds me he needs me. On
the way to the chapel—the most unlikely of places to meet
a she-devil—I see Susan and the interim CFO mounting the
steps of the admin building. I imagine them staggering beneath
the weight of quarry rocks. I'm grateful I am not the one responsible for making the decision about reopening.

"Dad, hold up," Asher calls from behind us. We turn, Truman letting go of my clammy hand and putting a palm to the
small of my sweat-soaked lower back. It's the dynamic trio, as
I've taken to calling them: Asher, Trask, and Laurel. Laurel's in
the middle, holding both of their hands. The three appear to
be competing for the title of most hopeful expression. Laurel's
lacrosse uniform is dark at the pits with sweat, her curly hair out
of her eyes and twisted atop her head.

"Thank you," Truman says to them simply. He wraps them
in a group hug before we go inside. Wordless with fatigue, I give
them a bleary smile.

Inside the still, dim, and cool chapel, I blink at the late sun
shining around the crossbeams of the window over the altar.
The architect had designed the window to give the worship-
per a view of the outside world through the perspective of the
cross. Grace; that's what's brought us here together. Our footsteps echo in the empty space that smells of polished old wood,
leather Bibles, and hymnals. Eleanor is seated in the first pew

but rises as we start down the slate aisle: Truman, Asher, Trask, Laurel, me. Eleanor regards our approach in silence, her figure slight beneath the cross. And in that moment, it's pity I feel for her. What woman would want to create a rift in her own family? To see her wounds in her child's and grandchildren's eyes? Truman once told me that she loved her grandsons, had been special to them as they were growing up. I'm banking on that still being true. Despite the mustard on my shirt that seems to iridesce in the dim, I take off my hat, fluff my hair with my fingers, and give her a tight smile.

Eleanor holds her purse before her, fidgets with the handles. "Thank you all for coming," she says, her vowels softly rounded. "Will you sit?"

"Hello, Grand El," the boys say in unison. They file into the second row with Truman. Eleanor sits again and turns sideways on the pew to face them. I stumble into the third pew with Laurel at my heels. We take a seat behind the guys.

Eleanor looks down. The snap of her metal purse clasp echoes in the room. "Boys," she says, addressing Trask and Asher, and I remember that she's already talked with Truman. The back of his neck above his T-shirt radiates with sunburn. It will smart later.

Eleanor continues, "I am so very sorry that I have hurt you." She cranes her neck around Truman, seeking to include Laurel in her cool blue gaze. "Laurel," she says, her voice coming out wobbly.

I reach for Laurel's hand, but she gets to her feet.

She moves into the aisle, her feet resolute, her carriage regal.

She steps forward, putting a hand on Trask's shoulder as she passes him and takes a seat in the front row. She turns to face his grandmother.

My mouth contorts in a howl that wants to throw itself from my throat at her lioness heart, her composure. The guys shift in their seats. Laurel's face is mild as she regards Eleanor. Eleanor looks down, and I'm gratified to see her mouth and small chin working. Truman turns to look at me, motioning with his head for me to come and sit beside him. I rise, my eyes bolt-stuck to his mother. She looks back at the boys and breaks the silence. "I have been wrong . . . on many levels. I don't want . . . to lose you. And Laurel," she says, looking levelly at her, "I'd like to get to know you. I hear you are a very fine young woman." Tears roll Trask's and Laurel's cheeks. Truman trembles against me, and a sob escapes him. I put my arm around him. Eleanor continues, "Asher, Trask and Laurel, Georgie,"—I flinch when she says my name—"will you forgive me? And allow me to try to make it up to you?" She shuffles something in her lap and holds aloft a stack of lavender envelopes. She fans them like a hand of cards. Mesmerized, I count five.

Asher holds up a big palm. "Grand El. We don't want your money."

"No," she says, and presses the envelopes to her chest. "These are apology letters, one for each of you." I read the one on top, written in careful, beautiful script: Laurel. One by one, she extends the envelopes with a trembling hand. "I hope you will read them later," she says. The kids hold them between their fingers. Does Truman get one? What are the fourth and fifth? "Georgie," she says, reading the fourth envelope and making my heart hammer. She passes the two remaining envelopes to Asher to pass to me. "One of them is for you and the other for your campaign." For my campaign? A bowling ball trundles through my midsection. I take the envelopes and run a finger across my name. It touches me that she had taken the time to pen my name as beautifully as she had Laurel's.

"Thank you," I say, meeting her eyes.

"Will you open the campaign envelope now? The check is not a personal one, but one drawn on a special account." A *special account?* "Led by Elizabeth Pattison, the Atlanta-area Willa Cather alumnae hosted a fundraiser, a gala," she colors slightly, "at my country club." She regards Laurel, who I realize may or may not be welcomed at that club.

I slide my thumbnail along the flap.

To me, fearless is living in spite of those things
that scare you to death.
—Taylor Swift

CHAPTER
TWENTY-FOUR

After a wine-soaked dinner at the Red Fox Inn, Truman and Lacey and I sit in my garden in our pajamas. Madame Beaulieu, who had pronounced her bowl of mussels bathed in white wine, butter, and garlic *délicieux*, has long since said her bonsoirs and gone to bed. The boys and Laurel and Marie-Victoire had gone to Huck's for pizza with friends and then to who knows where. Marie-Victoire and Asher couldn't peel their eyes from each other by the time we left the rally. I wonder if she will return to sleep at my house tonight.

From the space between the tallest pines, an ambitious three-quarter moon provides our only light. Its work is almost done, yet it shines on toward wholeness.

I breathe a sigh of satisfaction: we did for the college today all that was humanly possible. And my Jericho-battle moment had come. On the road to Mountainsburg, the walls of my prison had at last tumbled. Trumpets of freedom and possibility still ring in my ears. We wait for word from Susan about the college, hoping it will come tonight. My cell lays—fully charged, the ringer on—on a little table next to my chaise. Regardless of the outcome, I too will shine on.

I peer at Lacey. Her profile reminds me of an old-fashioned silhouette. The shape of her nose, lips, and chin is so much the same as when we were kids, only slightly downturned by gravity. I grin in the darkness, happy she is here.

The night cools. The cicadas tone their droning. I draw the skirt of my cotton gown over my tented legs and lie back, surveying the star-tufted navy sky. Truman shifts in his chaise, crosses his legs. I recall the night we went stargazing. The night gleams in my memory because he had told me he loved me; he had said it first. But today, I became part of his family. What would Eleanor think if she knew I'd once carried his child? That he had asked me to marry him?

Laurel and I have been drifting along in the same craft, reluctant to marry the men we love. Perhaps after she and Trask have had time to process Eleanor's apologies, they will resume their wedding plans. I roll my head to look at Truman, lying back on his chaise, his arms crossed behind his head, his hair silvered by moonlight. And True and me?

Lacey takes the last sip of a foot-tall bottle of Smartwater. She sits up. "Who's ready for a glass of wine?"

"Me, me," I say, my hand in the air. I close one eye and trace a swath of stars with my palm.

"Sure," Truman says, his smile as lazy as mine feels.

"Hey, Lacey-boo," I call after her, "will you bring me an afghan from the living room? And one for yourself? Truman?"

"I'll get them," True says, getting up. "I need to use the bathroom anyway."

When they've gone inside, I grin up at the moon and its light fills me. The two people I love best in the world are together in my home. I'll not allow too much time to pass before I see Lacey again. I will go to New York. Before I'm fifty. Maybe for my fiftieth birthday. I will drive there myself. Maybe I will fly on an airplane for the first time in my life.

Lacey and Truman return, and he lays one of the afghans over me. "Oh, thanks, love," I say, snuggling into its smell: Voltaire and fabric softener.

Lacey's opened the wine inside and pours three glasses. "To Willa Cather," she says, inclining her glass to ours. "May she live long and prosper."

"Here, here," Truman and I say.

We are quiet for a time. Then talk of the past inevitably begins, the way it does when old friends get together.

Lacey asks Truman what he knows about Findley Leach. But they have long since lost touch. We laugh about Findley's size-fourteen feet and what a good dancer he was despite them. We talk about Miss Foxie Frame and how wise she was, and I say I should write to her. Truman recalls the time my little brother streaked around Hampton Circle, wearing only a cowboy hat and holsters. We laugh about our friend Walter Goforth and his ever-improving stories, the one about the stray dog he named Dammit. "*Come, Dammit!*" he'd said, making us hoot. "*Dammit, you're a fine dog!*"

Lacey goes on about how her sister Karen tried to grow weed in a pot on their bedroom windowsill. She's topping up our wine glasses when my phone chimes. Sitting upright, I flail. The bottle clanks against the lip of the glass, hard enough to break it. The three of us look at each other.

If it's a night owl telemarketer, I will scream.

The light from my phone flares. Susan Joshi. My heart gives a great lurch. I stand, the afghan puddling at my feet.

"Georgie," the president says, and in the timbre of those two syllables, I know.

My eyes lock with Truman's.

I grin, baring my teeth. "Yes, Susan. How . . . are you?"

"I'm good. I'm really good. I'm sending a blast email out in the morning, but I wanted you to be the first to know. We reopen August 25."

I drop back to the chaise, undone. Tears—will they be the last of the day?—slipping from beneath my lids. "Oh, Susan, thank you, thank you."

"Madame Bricker, thank you. The rally was yours to do, and you pulled it off."

"Susan, may I put you on speaker? Truman's here."

She sniffs, and I can hear a smile in her voice. "Yes, go ahead. Hello, Truman."

"Susan. Thank you. I'm stunned."

"The check your mother brought—the twenty million dollars generated by the Buckhead Atlanta gala—made the difference in our being able to reopen. It will go directly to our endowment."

Truman shakes his head and smiles tightly.

Both of us had been marrow-shocked at the amount when we'd seen it in the chapel.

But that Eleanor Parker would be the one to make the wish I'd made on my birthday come true? It was mind-skewing.

It was *extraordinary*.

"How much did the rally raise, Susan?" I ask, standing again and filling my diaphragm.

"Including the Atlanta donation, 28 million in cash; 11.1 million in pledges."

"Mother-of-pearl," Lacey mouths, her eyes enormous.

I rock back on my heels. "I can't believe it. How will we ever write all those thank-you notes?"

Susan laughs. "The students, of course; they need to relearn the fine art of cursive." Her voice tightens. "Georgie and Truman, take a vacation, I mean now. You've earned it. I can't . . . thank you both enough."

Overcome, we murmur, "You're welcome."

"If I don't go to bed now," she says, "I'll be joining the ranks of dead presidents."

"Good night, Susan," Truman and I reply as one.

I press "end," my head filling with beginnings.

I'm tossing my cell aside when it comes to life again. I tighten my hold on its slippery sides. *What else tonight?* My friends' phones are sounding off too—Lacey's with a chime like mine, Truman's with his power ping. I look at the screen: another Amber Alert. In my periphery, the others glance at their screens and go back to celebrating Susan's call.

Ten-year-old girl kidnapped by suspected pedophile . . .

I flinch as though water's been flicked in my face.

The alert has lifted a drop cloth from the worst memory of all. The memory I've kept so deeply buried I could only glimpse its edges. Its shadow leaps and looms on the garden wall behind Truman.

"What's wrong, baby?" he says, as though from a great distance.

My heart hammers as pictures of a long-ago night move like the pages of a flip-book. Panting, I leap to my feet. My fingers forget to how to grip my wine stem, and the glass plummets, shattering against the bricks.

Gaping at me, Truman and Lacey rise by degrees.

I clutch my throat. "It's . . . the alert."

Lacey goes for her phone. Truman guides me to the back steps.

Lacey catches up with us. "Truman," she says, her stage whisper wounded. She plants her cell in front of his face.

His throat moves. The two exchange a knowing look.

I grip my knees and draw them to my chest. The name I haven't allowed to drop to my tongue in more than three decades spews like projectile vomit. "Cal Wright."

Lacey closes her eyes.

"He's . . . dead and gone, Georgie," Truman says.

Lacey's voice is hushed and meant for Truman. "She hasn't talked about what happened that night, not the whole of it."

"She has to," he says, the blue of his eyes darkening.

"Don't talk about me like I'm not here!" I hiss at the two people who were there when my father chased Cal Wright into the Laurel River.

"Oh, babe, I'm so sorry," Lacey says gently. They lower themselves to the step below me, the three of us forming an intimate triangle and closing off the sounds of the night.

"Tell it, Georgie," True says. "Let it go. Now," he says with some sharpness.

I'm transported to the long-ago night our group of friends sneaked out to the ball fields at Browning to try the marijuana Lacey found in her sister's dresser drawer. Unwilling to risk jeopardizing his scholarship, our friend Larry, the first African American student to be admitted to the school, won't join us, but he's agreed to act as our lookout. Larry shouts a warning just in time for us to witness Cal Wright slipping from the equipment shed where he'd hidden after disposing of Clover's body.

My mind moves on. Lacey and I are back in the safety of her twin beds. She pleads with me not to tell my parents that we snuck out and get us all in trouble. And then it's the next day. We're slogging the fields with the search party, the sulfur from the storm fouling the air, the rain pelting our slickers.

Truman's adult arms come around me and tighten. I shiver, despite their warmth, as fragmented images keep coming.

I tell my father the truth at last. He turns toward the river where Cal Wright had fled. His beloved voice shouts to my friends and me, *Go back! Go home!* But we chase after him. Through the slanting storm, he wades into the river, yelling Cal's name. At the blast of a gunshot, Cal collapses with the force of his self-inflicted wound. My father pinwheels. He struggles to free a rock-lodged foot. He drops below the swiftly moving water. As I watch in terror, his anguished face surfaces twice before the waters close over his head for the last time.

Now, in the high-pitched timbre of the child I was, I say to Lacey, "I had to tell the truth about where we'd been that night, what we saw, or Larry would have been framed for the murder."

"Yes. You did," she says through tears.

My thoughts ricochet like bats trapped inside a box. "But we knew all those things about Cal. That closet full of magazines. *Kiddie* porn, Lacey! And how he patted your bottom when he walked you home from babysitting. And we kept it secret. By the time we told my father we thought Cal had taken Clover, it was too late. But if we *hadn't* told him, my father might have stayed with the searchers instead of chasing after him. Maybe he would have lived. Cal murdered Clover," I bleat. "But he may as well have murdered my father too. Except for that one was *my* fault!"

Truman puts a hand over his face, massages his eyes.

"Georgie," Lacey says after a moment, "you can't beat yourself up for surviving."

Truman reaches for me again. "You were just a kid."

"Why did it have to happen?" I wail. I cry into his shirt as though I've invented tears.

His chest rises and sharply falls. After a space of minutes, he puts me away from him, makes me look into his eyes. They are so full of understanding and sorrow I can't hold them. I look at Lacey.

She gives me a tremulous smile. "I don't know why your father had to die. I think we won't know why terrible things happen until we get to heaven. But he was proud of you, G., and he would have been *so proud* of all you've accomplished." Truman holds me close again. I feel the click of his throat, the nod he gives Lacey over my head.

My breath loses its ragged edge. I'm safe. I lift my head and give my two dearest ones a smile. Presently, a rogue shower pelts the garden bricks. The three of us turn and watch as it sweeps the bottom steps. Tacitly, we get up and go into the house.

I've moved through treacherous water and come out dripping love on the other side.

Whatever our souls are made of,
his and mine are the same.
—Emily Brontë

CHAPTER
TWENTY-FIVE

The boom of the surf propels me to the sea. I shuffle along a sand-strewn path in flip-flops. I stop short of the tall flight of weathered steps, bordered by scrubby wax myrtle and yaupon, that lead from the road to the dune line. I adjust my grip on a cooler in one hand and the rope handles of a whale-print tote in the other.

"You got it? You okay?" Truman says, catching up with me, his white grin sexy below the black Ray-Bans. In plaid swim trunks and his faded gray Columbia T-shirt, he's burdened with two beach chaises and an enormous blue umbrella.

"Got it; you okay?"

He hoists the umbrella higher on his shoulder. "Yep. Just keep moving." My heart soaring along with the gulls, I make my way to the top. Setting my bag down, I shut my eyes tight, abruptly afraid I'll be overwhelmed by the enormity of the horizon. Truman reaches the top and nudges my behind with his knee. "Let's go, woman."

Heart a-pounding, I open my eyes and gaze at the heaving Atlantic, blue and green and breaking in a white and ruffled skirt along a golden beach. "Oh, True, it's so beautiful!"

"It's the perfect day," he says, trundling past me toward an empty spot of beach.

I've ticked another box for the extraordinary: washing up on a beach with Truman Parker. In my driveway, I'd handed a house key to Malika, who'd agreed to come in twice a day to look after Voltaire, and jumped into the passenger seat of the Range Rover. I'd navigated eight hours of drive time for us. It had taken three hours longer because I'd asked if I could set my new driving app to stay off the hectic highways. Truman had pursed his lips in consideration before he had agreed. "Lewis, I *am* your Clark."

We'd taken it easy. We'd taken it slow.

And we'd discovered exotic vistas—full of history and intrigue—before rolling at last into the charming town of Duck, part of the windswept and dune-straddled chain of barrier islands off the coast of North Carolina.

Now, battling swoops of salt-brined wind, Truman augers the umbrella into the sand. We set up camp. I break out the sandwiches I'd prepared in the Barbie Dream House–sized kitchen of our funky periwinkle-shingled cottage. Fresh sour dough bread and sun-warm tomatoes we'd bought at a farm stand, the tomatoes thickly-sliced and with lots of mayo and salt and pepper. We spray the tops of our feet with sunscreen and lazily lie watching the surf, our fingers entwined.

I smile, marveling at how relaxed I am, when my thoughts return to the rally and all that happened afterward. Before heading back to New York, Lacey and I had our slumber party, and she'd helped me shop for swimsuits and beach clothes. Trask, Asher, and Laurel had driven Eleanor to the airport in Mountainsburg for her return to Atlanta. Then Laurel and Trask had left for a getaway of their own, hopping a train to visit Laurel's Aunt Mahalia in Baltimore. Laurel mentioned taking a first look at wedding dresses while in the city. The two have set a wedding date for the day after she graduates from Willa Cather College next May. After saying

goodbye to Marie-Victoire the morning she and Madame Beaulieu left to meet her parents in DC, a lovestruck Asher shoved off
in his Jeep for I guess the equivalent of a cold shower: a hiking trip
with his buddies. I can't wait to see what develops between those
two. Meanwhile, Truman began work again on the Victorian,
installing shelves in the front room/library, sanding and painting
and measuring for new leaded windows to replace the old ones—
as cracked and opaque as lake ice. "It's going to be spectacular,"
Lacey had said when I'd taken her by for a tour.

Now, he skins out of his T-shirt and asks, "Want to read
awhile?"

I wiggle my brows at his chest. "Sure."

He grins. "'Cause I need to check on the Braves game."

I pull my paperback and his phone from my tote and hand
it to him. "Ready for your beer?"

He surveys the sky. "Happy hour at the beach is what? Three
fifteen?"

"Works for me." I dig into the cooler and pull two cans from
their ice bath. I flick his torso with the chill water from my fingers before handing him his can. "Cheers!"

"I'll get you back for that," he says with an evil leer.

Truman immerses himself in the baseball game and I in a
great old John Fowles novel until the shadows of our chaises
have lengthened, and he gets up to resituate the umbrella. A
young couple strolls from behind us on the beach, a baby girl in
a pink floppy hat with an elastic band around her chin astride
the woman's bikini-clad hip. I toy with the tassels on the hem
of my cover-up and watch the man and woman as they take the
toddler's hands and, smiling at each other, walk her to the edge
of the sea. The child crows and does a little dance as the water
leaps against her chubby legs. "Whooo!" her parents cry.

Truman looks up at them and crosses an ankle over his knee.
"That's so damned cute," he says.

My heart lists. If he marries me, he will miss his chance to have another child—maybe a daughter—forever. As attractive, smart, and romantic as he is, a younger woman would jump at the chance to marry him, grow his babies inside her. I uncap my water bottle and take a long sip, my heart plunging as I think of him with another woman, a size six with an MBA.

"Uh-oh," the father of the baby calls above the roar of the surf. "Someone's taken another poopie. I'll get it," he says, sweeping up the child and leaving the woman to wade out into the water.

Truman raises his chin and huffs a little laugh. "I sure don't miss those days," he says, bobbing his bare foot. "There's a lot to be said for adult children." He grins. "How about Trask and Laurel setting a date . . ." he goes on, happy and oblivious to the fact that he's just made my life.

I turn to face him. "I know! I'm so happy for them."

He looks out to sea, where a shrimp boat churns past. "Next May will be here before we know it."

A silence opens between us. Though my job is secure, I wonder if Truman's thinking as I am of the unfinished Portrait of Us: marriage, his career, one home. Since he'd made it clear he wants me to travel with him, I've made two successful trips.

I have the freedom to say yes when he asks me to marry him again.

He's told Susan he will stay on at WCC to help the interim CFO restructure the budget, but only until we reopen. Though he is capable, Truman never wanted to be a CFO.

Sometimes when that line appears between his eyes, I sense a seditious stirring in him. I suppose he could stay in Foxfield and do something else, working remotely. Many people work from home these days. But if he takes another consulting position, he would have to go. I imagine myself—as an undulating sea creature in the secret depths of the ocean—wavering between the two polestars of my life: Willa Cather College and Truman. As for sharing a home, I've grown fond of the Victorian. But how can I leave the home that has sheltered me for more than two decades?

Truman sighs and breaks the silence. He reaches to tug at a tassel on my sleeve. "When are you going to take that thing off?"

"Now!" I rip off my hat, leap to my feet, and skin out of the cover-up. I trot toward the water and plunge out into the waves in my new red tankini: teenage again, without bobbling breasts and big thighs. I turn, wiping the water from my face just as Truman comes galumphing toward me, sending up great sprays of sea. Together, we ride the waves out until the water reaches our shoulders.

He fingers the neck of the tankini. "I like." Bobbing in the surf, we cling to each other, kissing and kissing. Breathless, I move my fingers along the tender skin of his freckled arms, his firm triceps.

My lips stretch into a grin against his mouth. "How 'bout we head back for a nap?"

෴

Truman has made a reservation at AQUA on the waterfront, and we arrive in time to have a cocktail. A waft of the special—scallops, citrus, and thyme—meets my nose and awakens my hunger. We take seats on stools at the copper-topped bar, Basia's "If Not Now Then When" playing low. Though I've spotted a sauvignon blanc on the menu, Truman holds up two fingers to the bartender. "Champagne, please. Two." As a woman across the bar checks him out, I lay a proprietary hand on the sleeve of the navy linen jacket he's wearing over a crisp white shirt.

"A special occasion," the bartender coyly says, setting two flutes on the bar and giving us the eye.

"Yes," Truman says, lowering his chin at me and giving me his sexiest sideways smile.

My heart pounds.

The bartender indicates a narrow deck beyond open French doors. "Sunset's soon. Should be corker."

"Let's check it out," Truman says, picking up his glass.

On wobbling legs, I follow him onto the deck. He looks down at me, takes my hand. Side by side, we gaze at the slipping sphere of sun. The colors of the water mirror the sky—fanning from gold to tangerine to neon blue and indigo—and backlight the dark seagrass at the edge of the water. We take a sip of champagne.

"Delicious; thank you," I say.

Truman sets his glass on the weathered gray railing. He dips a hand into his coat pocket and withdraws a tiny black box. My heart gives a gazelle-like leap. I close my eyes, my hands frozen around my champagne stem. I open them, and he is down on one knee, the sun washing him in golden light, his eyes the blue of the sky above the dunes. He opens the box. I look from a brilliant pear-shaped solitaire to his face.

"This time, I hope I'm doing this right," he says. "I loved you when you were fifteen. I love the beautiful, vibrant woman you are now." He swallows and surveys my eyes. "Our path may be uncertain, but I want to take it with you. Elizabeth George Bricker, will you marry me?"

I set my glass on the railing, my soul lighting and glowing with the last rays of sun. I extend my left hand, expecting the light to shoot from my fingers. "Yes, Truman Charles Parker. I will marry you."

He gets to his feet and slips the ring on my finger. It's a perfect fit, and I'm wondering who had a hand in making sure it did—Lina? Laurel?—as the restaurant beyond the doors erupts into polite applause.

That night, beneath a wholly finished moon in the periwinkle cottage, we sleep enclosed in each other, two seeds in a single pod.

Be generous with yourself;
don't stop short of splendid things.
—Louisa May Alcott

CHAPTER
TWENTY-SIX

At our favorite table in Antonia's, Lina reads to me from the July Fourth issue of *The Foxfield Journal* I'd missed while at the beach, ". . . the CFO and chairman were each indicted by a grand jury for embezzling more than ten million dollars from the college. The alleged fraud scheme included unauthorized compensation, reimbursement for personal expenses, and fraudulent charitable contributions, as well as money laundering . . ." She shakes her head and folds the paper, drops it to the table. "*È pazzesco,*" she says, Italian for "It's crazy."

Cradling my ceramic cup, I sip my latte. "Sì."

Lina lifts her chin, brightening. "Let me see that fabulous ring again before you go."

Susan has asked me to meet with her in her office, so I have to go. Extending a hand as graceful as Kate Middleton's or Meghan Markle's, I glow under Lina's lavish approval.

Leaving her to linger over her crossword puzzle, I walk to the administration building. Gazing at the hazy sky, the hazier mountains, I realize the days are getting shorter. Six weeks until we reopen. Truman has begun working with the interim CFO. I stick my head through the open conference room door and find him there alone for the moment. His eyes are bolted to his laptop. "Hiya, handsome," I whisper.

He starts and whips off his readers. "Well, hel-lo, beach buddy," he says, closing the lid of his laptop.

"Don't let me interrupt your work. I'm about to meet with Susan and just wanted to say hi."

He gives me a snappy salute, and, grinning, I move on to tap at Susan's door. "Susan?"

"Come in, Georgie," she calls. Her office, always precise, looks as though a poltergeist has taken a whirling frolic through it. "Excuse my mess," she says happily, and she drops another stack of files to the floor beside her desk. "I'm inviting instructors back and playing tug-of-war with admissions directors—from near and far—to bring our students back."

I smile. "If I can help you with that, let me know." Wondering for the hundredth time how many of my French students will return, I take a seat across from her desk, and a wisp of Truman's vetiver shaving cream meets my nose. Was he in this chair earlier?

"I really think it's all going to work out. Enrollment has spiked 30 percent already."

"That's fabulous." I open my notebook and pull out a pen, and the magnificent ring on my left hand takes me by surprise again. Though I've worn it a week, it still gives me a shout-out at the most unexpected times.

Susan smiles. "Georgie, I have two things I want to talk with you about. First, we are moving ahead with the study abroad program. We have the funding in place. I know you've coordinated with Genevieve electronically, but the administration of Ecole Viardot has requested that you come to Paris, meet the mentors and students, get a full read on things from that end." The pen trembles in my hand. Travel to Paris? An eight-hour trip to North Carolina was one thing, but Paris? Susan flips a page on her desk calendar, pokes at weeks with the point of a pencil. Yet, I've come so far. I said I would travel to New York to see Lacey. I've said I will travel with Truman. "I need you to go before we reopen," Susan continues, tapping the pencil on the calendar. Paris. I've always dreamed of going. I could stay with Genevieve. Susan looks up at me, her eyes kind but single-minded. "Will you go?"

A flutter of butterflies unfurl themselves in my belly, stretch, and make strong their damp and delicate wings. "I will. It's mine to do."

She gives me a brilliant smile. "You'll need a passport, you know."

I jot it down in my notebook: *Get a passport.* As though it's *Pick up a bag of cat litter.*

I'm mentally strolling the Champs-Élysées when Susan goes on. "Secondly, I am creating a new position: dean of students, something the college has sorely needed."

"Oh. I mean, yes. I agree."

"With your experience and proven leadership, I would like to offer you the position."

The words drop from my brain to my tongue: "Me? But I'm a teacher."

Susan leans forward on her elbows. "Boosting enrollment is paramount as we reopen. We need to attract more international students. With your experience in . . . almost single-handedly," she waves a hand, "creating a study abroad program and getting it funded, you could coordinate services for international and transfer students, as well as supervise campus programs."

I sit staring at her dumbly. I'm wrapping my head around making a trip to Paris, and now she wants me to make a colossal career change? My thoughts form a twister, smoky and churning, picking up momentum as it collects her next words: "Georgie, since the rally, you have proven your ability to lead outside the classroom. You're a marvelous teacher, but I'd like to see you grow beyond what you've done for so many years. I'd like to see you take on a new challenge." My students. How could I abandon them? My rising seniors? Susan takes on a personal tone and continues, "These young women adore you. You are a born nurturer. You'd be great at handling and developing new policies regarding student life, program development, and orientation for incoming students. And you'd be a terrific liaison between student organizations and administrators."

I'd still be working with students. The winds of the twister slacken. "I am stunned. I am . . . flattered."

Susan hands me a copy of the job description she's outlined for the new position. I take it with a trembling hand, scan it, and wonder if this is a fait accompli as far as the president is concerned.

But she asks me, "Will you think about it and get back to me in a week?"

A week? A week ago, I'd lain on the beach with Truman. The twister collects the debris of my old panic and sends it pelting through me. I clutch my notebook and scoot to the edge of my seat. I take a deep breath. "If I decline the new position, do I . . . still have a job?"

She gives me a gentle smile. "Of course, you do."

I stand. "Thank you for your confidence in me. I will get back with you soon."

Susan smiles. "Georgie, before you go, do you have news you'd like to share?" News? She holds up her left hand and waggles the fingers.

I look at my ring, and a cool breeze of joy takes some of the twister's turbulence. I smile, slightly embarrassed at the opulence of the diamond. "I'm engaged."

"It's a beautiful ring. Congratulations to you and Truman. I wish you every happiness."

I tread from the building and toward my classroom as from point A to point B along a ray. On the quad, Truman is talking with the admissions director. He catches sight of me and excuses himself, trots to catch up with me. The director enters the library, leaving us alone on the quad. "Georgie, got a second? I have news."

News. I give him a distracted smile. "I'm just headed to . . . spend some time in my classroom." Irritation flares behind my eyes, making my head ache. I need to be alone. Though I've always lived alone, since Truman and I have been together, I've not felt crowded by his presence—or Laurel's, for that matter— but I feel crowded now. I have to process this job offer, decide how I feel about it, *before* I can discuss it with anyone else. "I really need some me-time," I tell him.

His blue eyes dim, and the line pleats his forehead again. "You okay?"

"I am, I promise." I squeeze his arm.

"Well, sure. Of course," he says.

Is his news what had riveted him to his laptop earlier? It better not be bad news; I can't take it. I sigh inwardly. "Walk with me as far as Collins and tell me your news?"

We turn down a path bordered by pink phlox planted by alumnae. "I've accepted a job," he says.

My heart plummets and roots me in my tracks. "You what?"

"I applied for it before we left for the beach."

I stare at him as though he has grown flippers, a tale with flukes.

He smiles at my expression. "I think you'll be happy for me." He pockets his hands, suddenly shy. "I'm going to teach English."

"Teach English?" My heart hovers above his words. His schoolboy dream, the one his parents had squelched and extinguished. "Oh, True, your old dream. Where?"

"At a fine women's college."

My mind holds its breath and tries to peek at his next words, the way a child would peek around a door on Christmas morning to make sure Santa had come. "Willa Cather?" I whisper.

"Willa Cather. An instructor from the department isn't returning. Susan gave me a contract today."

A great tide of exultation buoys my heart.

I launch myself at him like a paintball. Reeling and laughing, he holds me. "Georgie, it's real," he says into my hair. "I'm staying."

I put him away from me. "I am . . . so proud of you. You're making your soul happy. You'll make a lovely teacher."

"I . . . can't wait. I'm going to teach the freshman and sophomores. You have to show me how to write lesson plans." He rushes on, "I'm such a schmuck; I'm imagining us spending evenings by the fireplace—when I get it working, that is—grading papers." I try to picture the cozy scene in the Victorian, but my mind shifts the setting to the rug in front of my own fireplace.

I can't tell him now about Susan's offer, steal his thunder.

Truman's phone trills, saving me. "It's Asher," he says, looking at the screen. "I need to take this."

"Call me later," I say. Blowing him a kiss, I skim down the steps that will take me to my building.

On my floor in Collins, I turn the satiny old brass knob on my classroom door, enter, and stand surveying the space that is mine. Untouched for weeks, the surfaces are fleecy with dust. Cobwebs string like tired old clotheslines between the windows and the SMART board, the tall bookcase and file cabinet. I move to open a window where desiccated bugs are trapped in more webbing on the sills, wishing I'd brought my dusting supplies. But with the school reopening and staff rehired, the custodians will be back.

A breeze tinged with inchoate fall fills my nose, teases at my hair. I take a seat in my rump-sprung director's chair and regard the ranks of desks. I picture the legion of young women who have sat in them and hear their voices floating and joining with mine in frank discussion and laughter. My eyes follow the spines of books on the shelves. The same curriculum, the same routine for twenty-five years. At once, the job has grown as stagnant and dusty as the classroom, as used as my dinged-up metal desk.

A realization sweeps me like wildfire.

I can leave this.

I can move on, tackle a new challenge.

I'm no longer the woman who lived in a prison of her own fears, who panicked and flinched and flailed at every memory, every change. I can build a better self on the ruins of the old one.

I'd thought I was meant to be a French teacher, but maybe I'll make an even better dean of students. When I call Genevieve to tell her I am coming to Paris, she will be proud of me. Tomorrow, I will accept Susan's offer and sign a new contract. But with a couple of stipulations. The first, that I am allowed to teach a single section of French for one final year, my seniors: Laurel's class. I hope the new French teacher won't mind sharing her classroom with me for a few hours a week. The second stipulation may take a bit more finesse; I'll put my mind to it.

Darkness is falling outside. I rise and close the window, turn out the light. My lips forming a fond smile, I take a last look back and gently close the door.

⚛

Recent sessions with Dr. Chu have helped resolve my feelings of lifelong guilt and shame over the deaths of Clover Kane and my father. At my appointment today, and before I can build my new life with Truman, I want to discuss with her leaving my home and moving into the Victorian. Not only will I be leaving my place of comfort, but I'll be giving up the autonomy of having everything the way I want it, without having to consider input from anyone other than my fur baby.

When I'm seated on the purple slipper chair with a cup of tea, I slip off my shoes and prop my feet up on the hassock next to hers. I begin by telling her the latest news: After Truman and I are married in the chapel at WCC next week, he will accompany me to Paris. I'll take care of my business, and we will have our honeymoon.

"Madame," Dr. Chu says, her dark eyes gleaming, "I'm so happy for you." Her lab coat parts, revealing a small mound of belly.

I gape at her. "Dr. Chu, you're going to have a baby!"

Her eyes slip from mine.

"No, don't," I say, drawing her eyes. "It's my turn to be happy for you. You'll make a wonderful mother." We smile at each other and sip our tea for a moment.

"Tell me why you are here, other than to show off that ice rink on your finger."

I sigh. "Truman and I have been living like nomads between my house and his. I feel it's disconcerting for Voltaire. I'm doing well with planning for Paris and taking on the new job. But I'm still grappling with leaving my home. Why can't I just let it go and move in with him? The president hasn't said, but I assume the new French teacher will need my place."

Dr. Chu pours more tea for both of us from her little blue pot. She props her feet up again and regards me over the fragile rim of her cup. "When your father died, you were forced to leave the only home you'd ever known. You lost the support of your friends and neighbors to whom you were very attached. After that, your grandmother's home wasn't a happy or nurturing place for you. And then your college dorm and apartment experiences were temporal. When you moved into your town house here, you were home for the first time since you were a child. You put down a taproot." She eyes me. "Then you made your home a beautiful prison."

My teeth clack against the rim of the china cup. "I did!"

"But you're free now. You'll need to be patient with yourself as you adjust to a new life. Give yourself time to adjust to the house you'll be sharing with Truman. It's a great old place. Make it your forever home, yours and Truman's."

But I've been on my own—just Voltaire and me—for so many years. Do I have a clue of how to do "together" with a man? Tears roll down my cheeks and onto my chin. At last, an image comes: True and me reclining on the rug from my living room, in the front room of the Victorian. Voltaire licking his paws. A wintergreeny birch fire snapping in the fireplace. My Herend collection mingling with his wooden figures from Africa atop the mantle.

I smile. "We'll fill it with love."

∘✛∘

All that was closed to True and me has reopened.

He will be my husband. Like in the game of chess, I will be his queen, placed next to him, yet on a space of my own color. A powerful piece, the queen can move any number of spaces in any direction she chooses. The game is not over when she is lost. When I feel lost, or have a setback, I am strong enough to find my way back.

Truman and I will support each other's independent flourishing.

It is proof that the extraordinary happens.

A shimmering new life beckons.

If your actions create a legacy that inspires
others to dream more, learn more, do more,
and become more, then you are an excellent leader.
—Dolly Parton

CHAPTER
TWENTY-SEVEN

M y secretary sets a vase of yellow roses on my desk.
"Mrs. King, you *are* my queen." The second part of the
deal I made with the president was that I be allowed to take my
secretary with me to the new job.

Mrs. King surveys the flowers, my new office in the administration building. "They do look lovely with the wall color, don't
they?"

Shifting my laptop and new academic-year calendar, I
make room for the vase. "They do! Thanks so much." I grin at
the mascot emblazoned on the calendar—a snarling lioness—
before unloading the next item from a cardboard moving box, a
framed photograph taken at our wedding: True and me, the boys
and Laurel. A family.

Before his classes at George Wythe had begun, Asher
devoted an afternoon to putting a fresh coat of apricot paint on
the walls for me.

Sometimes I look at him—tilting my head or squinting my
eyes—to try and make him resemble my father. But he doesn't.
He's Asher Parker. My father would have loved him.

I dig into the box again, unearthing the pencil cup I brought back from Ecole Viardot. And the antique paperweight I bought in Strasbourg, when I'd taken a solo day trip into Germany by train. The day a grizzled chef astride a pink bicycle stopped to present me with a bouquet of fresh parsley. Extraordinary.

A new bell, installed in the old tower in honor of the class of 2019, begins its bonging. Pausing, I look out the window and through the leaves of the sugar maples, toward Collins. Tomorrow, I meet with my French IV students. The new French teacher's name is Sam, and she is twenty-six. She and the new Mandarin teacher move into my empty town house next week. Lina and I are taking them a meal.

"Heads up, chickie," Mrs. King whispers, looking into the hallway. "Your first appointment just arrived."

I get to my feet, a big smile stretching my lips. "Please send her in."

A young freshman, who missed the second flight of her journey from Beijing to Richmond—and subsequently orientation—steps through the door, her small chin a-tremble. I remember reading in her file that her Chinese name means persistence. I aim to remind her of that.

I move around the desk and take her hand. "Qing Shan? Welcome to Willa Cather College. We're delighted you're here. I'm Dean Bricker."

ACKNOWLEDGMENTS

I owe thanks to the boss women of SWP: to Brooke Warner for her incredible vision for authors; to Shannon Green for being an expert, patient, and supportive project manager; and to Barrett Briske for her eagle-eyed editing. I also owe a debt of gratitude to the cover and layout teams for producing such a beautiful quality book.

I value talented writer and book coach Sheila Athens for helping me hone the novel that landed me a literary agent. Many thanks to Pamela Harty of the Knight Agency for loving the story, for telling me how many times it made her cry, and for believing in me. Though she was unable to find the right home for the manuscript, I am grateful for her effort and encouragement. I thank my formatter Julie Klein for her superior skill and for her patience with all my questions. I appreciate all the terrific ideas and feedback from writer Elizabeth Bass Parman, who served as a critique partner. And last but not least, big hugs to my faithful and attentive beta readers Lina Dimora and Lynne Niva.

To my husband Porter, thank you for encouraging and helping me every step of the way. And to my daughter Olivia, who praised me for "putting my art out there." I love you both beyond measure.

AUTHOR'S NOTE

Thank you so much for being a part of this journey with Georgie, Truman, Laurel, and the rest of my beloved cast. I hope the story will inspire and resonate with you and that you will tell your friends about it. When it comes to an author's success, it really is *all about you*, the reader. Will you consider posting a brief review for the novel on the book-cataloging website of your choice?

I'd also love to hear from you via my website: www.elizabethsumnerwafler.com. Book clubbers can find a list of questions for discussion about A *Cleft in the World* there.

Follow me on Instagram: @elizabeth_sumner_wafler

All the best,
Elizabeth

ABOUT THE AUTHOR

Photo credit: Porter Wafer

The author of four novels—with another on the way—Elizabeth writes evocative women's fiction and romance. She can be found working at her blue desk, at a farmer's market, poking through an indie bookstore (with a luscious latte in hand), gardening, or enjoying a pretty cocktail on her porch. She resides with her husband in Greenville, South Carolina.

SELECTED TITLES FROM SHE WRITES PRESS

She Writes Press is an independent publishing
company founded to serve women writers everywhere.
Visit us at www.shewritespress.com.

After Happily Ever After by Leslie A. Rasmussen. $16.95, 978-1-64742-014-7. Maggie Dolin, forty-five years old, isn't dealing with getting older as well as she would like. But with her daughter about to leave for college, her husband acting increasingly distant, and her father—always her rock—deteriorating both physically and mentally, who can blame her?

Bring the Rain by JoAnn Franklin. $16.95, 978-1-63152-507-0. When sixty-three-year-old psychology professor Dart Sommers discovers that the one thing she has always been able to count on—her brain—is failing her, she struggles to accept the diagnosis, and to let love enter her life.

The Greek Persuasion by Kimberly K. Robeson. $16.95, 978-1-63152-565-0. During a summer in Greece, Greek American professor Thair Mylopoulos-Wright begins writing about her mother and grandmother's early-life experiences—an exercise that starts her on a quest for wholeness, and ultimately inspires her to forge a path for herself that goes beyond the traditional.

The Fourteenth of September by Rita Dragonette. $16.95, 978-1-63152-453-0. In 1969, as mounting tensions over the Vietnam War are dividing America, a young woman in college on an Army scholarship risks future and family to go undercover in the anti-war counterculture when she begins to doubt her convictions—and is ultimately forced to make a life-altering choice as fateful as that of any Lottery draftee.

All the Right Mistakes by Laura Jamison. $16.95, 978-1-63152-709-8. When the most successful of five women who have been friends since college publishes an advice book detailing the key life "mistakes" of the others—opting out, ramping off, giving half effort, and forgetting your fertility—they spend their fortieth year considering their lives against the backdrop of their outspoken friend's cruel words.

The Other New Girl by LB Gschwandtner. $16.95, 978-1-63152-306-9. In a fresh take on the prep school lit genre, sassy sophomore Susannah Greenwood enters Quaker prep Foxhall School—and soon finds herself in an impossible situation when "the other new girl," an outcast whom she has befriended, mysteriously disappears.